BERKLEY TITLES BY VIRGINIA KANTRA

Home Before Midnight
Close Up
Meg & Jo
Beth & Amy
The Fairytale Life of Dorothy Gale

THE CHILDREN OF THE SEA NOVELS

Sea Witch
Sea Fever
Sea Lord
Immortal Sea
Forgotten Sea

THE DARE ISLAND NOVELS

Carolina Home
Carolina Girl
Carolina Man
Carolina Blues
Carolina Dreaming
Carolina Heart

NOVELLAS

Midsummer Night's Magic

ANTHOLOGIES

Over the Moon
(with MaryJanice Davidson and Angela Knight)
Shifter
(with Alyssa Day, Angela Knight, Nalini Singh, and Meljean Brook)
Burning Up
(with Angela Knight and Nalini Singh)
Tied with a Bow
(with Kimberly Frost, Lora Leigh, and Eileen Wilks)
Ask Me Why
(with Marie Force, Shirley Jump, and Jodi Thomas)

PRAISE FOR

BETH & AMY

"Kantra (*Meg & Jo*) continues her delightful twenty-first-century retelling of *Little Women*. . . . Kantra's compulsively readable update will attract a whole new group of readers, as well as satisfy Alcott devotees." —*Publishers Weekly*

"A delightful surprise. . . . This was Meg, Jo, Beth, and Amy on the page. And in *Beth & Amy*, Kantra did what no one has been able to do before, not even Alcott—she made me like Amy." —*Star Tribune*

"Under the pen of veteran novelist Virginia Kantra, a sequel to the sequel of *Little Women* is as timely and important today as was the original in 1868." —MountainTimes.com

"A pitch-perfect retelling of *Little Women*. . . . It completely captures the personalities of the March girls and their friends and family, while bringing them convincingly into the modern era. I loved it." —Smart Bitches Trashy Books

THE
FAIRYTALE LIFE
OF
DOROTHY GALE

VIRGINIA KANTRA

BERKLEY
NEW YORK

BERKLEY
An imprint of Penguin Random House LLC
penguinrandomhouse.com

Copyright © 2023 by Virginia Kantra
Readers Guide copyright © 2023 by Virginia Kantra
Penguin Random House supports copyright. Copyright fuels creativity, encourages diverse voices,
promotes free speech, and creates a vibrant culture. Thank you for buying an authorized edition
of this book and for complying with copyright laws by not reproducing, scanning, or distributing
any part of it in any form without permission. You are supporting writers and allowing
Penguin Random House to continue to publish books for every reader.

BERKLEY and the BERKLEY & B colophon are registered trademarks of
Penguin Random House LLC.

Library of Congress Cataloging-in-Publication Data

Names: Kantra, Virginia, author.
Title: The fairytale life of Dorothy Gale / Virginia Kantra.
Description: First edition. | New York: Berkley, 2023.
Identifiers: LCCN 2023005361 (print) | LCCN 2023005362 (ebook) |
ISBN 9780593547717 (trade paperback) |
ISBN 9780593547724 (ebook) Subjects: LCGFT: Novels.
Classification: LCC PS3561.A518 F35 2023 (print) | LCC PS3561.A518 (ebook) |
DDC 813/.54—dc23/eng/20230206
LC record available at https://lccn.loc.gov/2023005361
LC ebook record available at https://lccn.loc.gov/2023005362

First Edition: December 2023

Printed in the United States of America
1st Printing

Book design by George Towne

This book is dedicated to Michael.
Thank you for being my Tim. And also my Sam.
But mostly Tim.

"*The Wonderful Wizard of Oz* was written solely to please children of today. It aspires to being a modernized fairy tale, in which the wonderment and joy are retained and the heartaches and nightmares are left out."

—L. FRANK BAUM, FROM THE INTRODUCTION
TO *The Wonderful Wizard of Oz*, 1900

"Witches can be right."

—STEPHEN SONDHEIM, *Into the Woods*

ONE

Our mother was Judy Gale. The artist. Every time she left us behind with a friend or a nanny or (when friends and nannies couldn't be found) bundled us off to Kansas, I'd tell my sister we were off on an adventure. Like the Pevensies fleeing wartime London or Harry taking the train to Hogwarts. Sometimes we were princesses in exile or orphans escaping cruel relatives. I dropped the orphans bit after our mother died. But lots of stories I told my little sister still began that way, with children on a trip into the magical unknown.

There was nothing magic about the English department office at Trinity College Dublin. The metal frame chairs and cinderblock walls were straight from my high school media center. The familiar smells of toner and floor cleaner overlaid the whiff of graduate student desperation in the air. Except for the glimpse of Georgian architecture through the windows and the bust of Yeats on a filing cabinet, I could almost be back in Kansas.

But this was Ireland, land of poets and fairies, witches and warriors, Jonathan Swift and Derek Mahon. I was finally moving on. Getting somewhere. Leaving my old self behind.

And maybe I was still telling myself stories to make me feel better.

I smiled hopefully at the gatekeeper behind the desk. A round woman, a cardigan draping her plump shoulders, green-framed glasses on a silver chain around her neck. "Hi. I'm here to see Dr. Eastwick?"

Her glasses flashed at me. "Sorry?"

"I have an appointment. Ten o'clock." My flight from Newark had been delayed. I'd taken a cab straight from the Dublin airport so I wouldn't be late.

"You're American."

"Yes."

She tapped her keyboard. "Name?"

My heart raced. I cleared my throat. "Dorothy Gale."

After my maternal grandmother. Dodo and Toto, Toni dubbed us when she was small. I'd never minded my old-fashioned name. It was unique, right? Mine. Nothing to be ashamed of. Until this past year, when Destiny Gayle, the titular character of a novel by critically acclaimed author Grayson Kettering, spent thirty-two weeks at the top of the *New York Times* and Amazon bestseller lists. It wasn't just the similarity in our names. Destiny dressed like me, in vintage skirts and thrift shop sweaters. ("*Her wardrobe reflected her mind*," the novel's hero said on page 32, "*only gently used, full of secondhand ideas and castoff morality*.") Plus, anyone who read his bio knew Grayson Kettering was an adjunct faculty member at the University of Kansas. And anyone who did a little digging— the features writer at *New York* magazine, say, or a book reviewer at the *Washington Post* or the host of *Entertainment Tonight*—could discover he had a two-year relationship with a graduate student there who bore a strong resemblance to brown-haired, cow-eyed Destiny.

Casting had recently started on *Destiny Gayle*, the movie. Fortified by a box of tissues and a cup of tea, I'd watched the *ET* interview from the couch in my aunt's living room.

"Was she the real-life inspiration for your character?" the host had asked Gray.

On television, Gray looked exactly like his author photo, silver threading his thick hair, the top two buttons of his shirt undone. The camera and the interviewer had loved him. An ache stabbed my chest.

I leaned forward to catch his reply.

"A case of art imitating life?" His dark, deep-set eyes twinkled. "I suppose the comparison is inevitable, if somewhat reductive. You might as well say, life imitates art."

"What about the relationship Destiny has with her professor?" the host asked.

My hand twitched, sloshing hot tea on my Winnie-the-Pooh pajamas.

"A professor at the college," Gray corrected. "Technically, she's not enrolled in any of his classes. He has no real power over her. She exerts her power—her will, her desires—over him."

I listened, stunned. The host raised an expertly threaded eyebrow. "Are you saying their relationship is appropriate?"

"It's certainly unwise," Gray admitted ruefully. Of course he had to say that *now*. Before, he said I was his soul mate. He told me . . . Well. Not that he loved me. Not in so many words. But he said he couldn't imagine his life without me.

"But let's not strip young Destiny of her agency," he told the interviewer. "She pursues an older man, her mentor, as willfully and aggressively as he imagines he is pursuing her." He looked into the camera with disarming directness. "You could argue that he is the one being exploited in the relationship. It's not until he's free of her stifling domesticity that he can truly express himself."

"You *jerk*," I yelled at my aunt's TV. Not that anyone heard me. Not the interviewer. Not my thesis advisor at KU. Certainly not Gray. Aside from that one horrible scene in his office, I'd never been able to tell him . . . to tell him . . . Anyway, I blamed myself. Gray had never coerced me into anything. I *loved* him. Everything he'd done, I'd let him do. Everything he'd written . . . Well, it must be partly true, right? He was Grayson Kettering, one of the modern masters of autobiographical fiction.

Aunt Em paused on her way into the kitchen. "Turn that off. Nobody cares about that garbage."

My heart burned. I rubbed at the damp spot spreading on Pooh's face. "Only four million viewers and the entire English department."

"Nobody that matters," Em amended. Which pretty much summed up her opinion of my entire postgraduate education. Her eyes narrowed in what might have been concern. "You should call the bookstore about that job. You can't sit around drinking tea in your pajamas forever."

"At least I'm not guzzling wine under a bridge."

My aunt looked disapproving. Basically, her default expression. "You need to get out more. Go somewhere. Do something."

Out of her house, she meant. Not out of the country.

But here I was.

H ere you are," the department officer said, consulting her computer screen. "Dorothy Gale, ten o'clock. You're to see Dr. Norton over in the writing center."

"I don't understand. My appointment is with Dr. Eastwick. I have an email."

"Dr. Eastwick cannot meet with anyone anymore. She's dead."

The blood rushed in my ears. Obviously, my hearing was affected. Still adjusting to changes in the cabin pressure or jet lag or her Irish accent or something. "I'm sorry?"

"Don't be. It's not like you killed her. Very sudden, it was."

The room whirled. My stomach dropped. It had to be a joke. A hoax. I'd never met Dr. Eastwick. I had emailed her without any real hope that she would actually reply. But she had answered all my questions. She'd encouraged me to apply. She couldn't be . . .

"Dead?"

"Monday. Not that she'll be missed, God rest her soul."

Another joke?

I tightened my grip on my suitcase. The administrative officer was still talking, something about needing to meet with Dr. Norton to discuss my registration. "She'll be in her office until one. The Oscar Wilde house. 21 Westland Row," she said. "You know the way?"

I didn't, of course. I'd only seen pictures online. I nodded.

"The writing center. Right at the edge of campus. Go in through the Hamilton building. Front concourse, ground floor. There's a sign." She looked at me doubtfully, as if questioning my ability to read. "Or the security guard can help you."

I thanked her.

I paused on the steps outside, squinting. After Kansas and the airport, everything was bewilderingly bright and green. Fat white seagulls dotted the emerald lawn like sheep. Students with backpacks strolled the walks. A tour group stopped to take pictures of the library.

Some of my best memories were of libraries. Sitting on the carpet of the Brooklyn Public Library with Toni snuggled on my lap for toddler time. Hiding in the stacks in a gray-shingled cottage in Connecticut. Begging a ride in my uncle's truck to the squat brick drive-through that housed the library in Council Grove, Kansas. By the time I was fifteen, I had seven different library cards. While our mother traveled the world, creating art installations we saw only in photographs, my sister, Toni, and I shuttled from our New York apartment to the pullout couches of friends-of-friends to the tiny back bedroom of Uncle Henry's farmhouse. Books became my friends. The library was my magic kingdom, my refuge, my escape. As long as I could find the library, I was home.

I started walking.

One step at a time, I told myself. Just because my faculty contact was dead didn't mean I was doomed. Staff changes happened, right? Professors retired or went on sabbatical. Instructors failed to get tenure and moved on to other institutions or new careers. Graduate students dropped out and found jobs. Or were publicly humiliated in their former lover's bestselling novel and fled across the Atlantic rather than ever face him again.

Okay, maybe that was just me.

"If you'd come to me before . . ." My advisor at KU had looked down at his desk, not meeting my eyes. *"But after two years . . ."*

Two years when Gray and I had been a couple. Two years of begging for extensions, of blowing off meetings with my advisor to discuss my progress (or lack of progress) on my thesis.

"You don't need him. You can talk to me," Gray had said.

I took a deep breath. Blew it out. I could deal with this. It was a bump in the road, not the end of the world.

I'd applied to Trinity in a desperate bid to prove—to Gray, to the world, to myself—that I was not the literary vampire, the creative succubus, he'd portrayed in his novel. I hadn't expected I'd actually be accepted. I'd never dreamed I would actually come, leaving my sister behind.

But my tuition was paid. I'd had to show a receipt at the airport, along with my passport and a bank statement proving I could support myself for the next year. Which I could, even though Toni was starting college now, too. Whatever else our mother had or hadn't done for her daughters, she'd taken care of us financially. The licensing fees from photographs of her art—plus a hefty life insurance policy—were her legacy to us.

I couldn't turn back now.

The campus spread around me, windows and arches and towers of stone. It was like stumbling onto the grounds of Pemberley or into a fairy tale. Beyond the abstract sculpture thingy was a square with green on both sides. Trees. Buildings. No signs. No security guard, either.

I wandered through a gate onto a street looking for . . . What had the administrative officer said? Westland? Westmoreland? Dubliners brushed by, everyone around me moving at speed and with purpose while I trudged along, not quite sure where I was going.

Story of my life, really.

My rollaway bumped rhythmically behind me over the stones. Glancing automatically to my left, I stepped off the sidewalk and into the path of a bus. Tram. *Shit.*

Metal squealed. Hot wind gusted on my cheek. I jerked back, tripping over the curb, breaking the wheel on my suitcase.

I stood shaking on the sidewalk as the passengers debarked.

"You all right, dear?"

"Yeah. I . . ." A yellow caution sign across the road swam in my vision: FÉACH GACH TREO. LOOK BOTH WAYS. I pulled myself together. "Yeah, thank you. I'm fine."

To prove it, I walked another block.

A bridge spanned the river ahead. I dragged my bag toward it, drawn by the sun sparkling on the water. *The weary traveler left the path, following the dancing light over the water, and was lost forever in the mists as the will-o'-the-wisp disappeared in a burst of goblin laughter* . . .

I shook my head to clear it. The woman at the desk said the writing center was at the edge of campus. I just had to keep walking.

But when I reached the other side, it was clear I'd gone too far. The street was lined with shops—a hair salon, a dry cleaners, a kebab house advertising pizzas and falafel. On the corner, between a metal shutter scrawled with graffiti and a sign for lottery tickets, was a blue-painted storefront with a neon OPEN sign. CLERY'S NEWSAGENTS.

I went in to ask directions.

The bell jangled cheerfully as I opened the door. The broken wheel of my bag scraped the tile floor. Embarrassed, I picked it up.

The inside was a jumble of cheap plastic toys and bright candy wrappers, shelves crowded with packaged convenience foods, crates of fresh produce and buckets of flowers with prices scrawled on handwritten signs. Newspapers with foreign headlines were displayed by the register. A tall steel rolling shelf, stacked with loaves of bread, occupied one corner near the front of the shop.

"What can I get you?" asked the man behind the counter, closing his book.

I couldn't read the title. I jerked my gaze back to his face.

He quirked an eyebrow. "Coffee?"

I swallowed, suddenly parched with longing. "Do you have tea?"

"You're in Ireland," he said. "You can always have tea. Or Guinness or whiskey."

He was tall and skinny, dressed in black jeans and a rumpled gray T-shirt, his hair tied back from a narrow face. His long jaw was covered in stubble, like an incognito movie star or a dissolute poet after a three-day binge.

"Tea would be great. Chai? To go," I said.

"Masala chai?" He had a lovely voice, a lilt running over the deeper tones like water over rocks. *He was a songwriter. Single, of course. He performed at night in indie clubs, taking inspiration from the strangers he encountered at his day job, and he wrote a song based on me that became a hit on both sides of the Atlantic and Gray heard it and . . .*

Okay, so being someone else's muse hadn't worked out so well for me.

"Excuse me?"

"Spiced tea," he said patiently. "Do you want milk?"

"Yeah. Um. Maybe a little sugar?" I set down my bag to pay, counting out the unfamiliar currency before curling my hands gratefully around the fragrant cup. "Thank you."

"You're American."

"I guess the accent gives me away," I said ruefully.

Humor creased his face. "That, and the boots."

"What? Oh." I glanced down at my cowboy boots, a going-away present from Toni. "I suppose those would be a clue."

"And the suitcase."

The suitcase. I sighed. I wasn't eager to drag my busted bag through the unfamiliar streets of Dublin with a hot to-go cup in one hand. I had time—didn't I?—to sit down with a cup of tea before I went to see Dr. Norton.

My stomach rumbled, reminding me I hadn't eaten since breakfast on the plane. I glanced at the rack of baked goods. "Could I have a biscuit, too, please?"

"What kind?"

"Oh . . ." I wavered. "Anything."

He set a pack of some unfamiliar brand of cookies on the counter.

"No, I meant . . ." I flapped my hand at the shelves. "One of those."

The smile deepened around his eyes, making him look older. Closer to my age, twenty-six. "Baked fresh this morning. Toasted?"

"Please. Thank you."

I sat at one of two tiny tables jammed by the window to drink my tea. A woman wearing a hijab bought a bun for her toddler and a bunch of flowers. A young man purchased a lottery ticket and a drink from the refrigerator case by the entrance.

I took a sip of chai and almost spewed it over the table. The milk hadn't cooled it at all, and it was much spicier than the tea bags back home. I gulped like a frog, scorching my throat. Got up to hold open the door for the woman with the toddler. As they passed, the baby peeped at me from her stroller. She looked like Toni at that age, all big dark eyes and silky hair.

I wondered how my little sister was doing without me. She hadn't seemed very excited when I'd taken her to KU's freshman orientation. But then, she'd already seen the campus a hundred times, visiting me. Once her classes actually started, she'd have a great time. Making friends came easily to Toni. Everyone liked her. Or if they didn't, she didn't care. Unlike me.

I arranged my bun, studded with tiny raisins, and to-go cup on the cramped tabletop. I'd deleted my Twitter account. I never went on Facebook or posted on Insta anymore. But I framed the shot in the window and sent it to Toni so she'd see it when she woke up. **Thinking of you.**

Almost immediately, three dots appeared. **Ooh, breakfast!**

The knot in my chest eased. **What are you doing up?** It was five in the morning in Kansas.

Missing you came the prompt reply.

Tears stung my eyes. We had been apart before. But never with an ocean between us.

It's only twelve months, I reminded her. A one-year program, to make up for the four years I'd lost. *Wasted.* Maybe I can come home for Christmas.

TONI: How's it going?

My flight was delayed and I almost got run over by a bus and lost my way and broke the wheel on my suitcase. Also, the teacher who told me to apply here is dead.

No.

Great, I typed. Telling her a story to make us both feel better. Call you tonight?

We exchanged emojis—thumbs-up, hearts, smiles, kisses. I ate my toast. Drank my tea. It had cooled enough for me to taste individual spices, cinnamon and cloves, and . . . Well. Spices. A man in a flat cap picked up one of the newspapers by the register and sat at the other table to read.

The poet behind the counter raised an eyebrow. "You thinking to buy that paper, Tom?"

The man huffed. "Why should I pay for the news when I can read it for free online?"

"I'll stop ordering it in, then."

The man grumbled, paid, and left, the newspaper folded under his arm. I took another cautious sip of tea. An elderly woman shuffled to the register, her string bag bulging with cans.

"Any bread today, Sheila?" asked the poet guy as he rang her up.

She looked longingly at the shelves behind him before her mouth firmed in a hard line. "As if I'd pay those prices for a loaf."

"It's fresh baked this morning."

She sniffed. "It's robbery, that's what it is. When your da ran the shop, you had proper bread at proper prices."

He shook his head, smiling. "You're a hard woman, Sheila. We might have cheaper in the back. Fee!" he called. "Got any bread in the kitchen from yesterday?"

A girl with short blue hair and floured arms emerged from the depths of the shop. "Bread from yesterday? Are you kidding me?"

"Sheila here was wanting a loaf on discount. See what you can find, okay?"

He held her gaze. Despite their difference in height—he was very tall, she was short—there was something similar about their faces. Same blue-green eyes, same long nose, same dramatic eyebrows. Was she his sister? I wondered. His boss? His girlfriend?

"Right," she said grudgingly. "I'll just have a look, then."

Returning, she slapped a loaf on the counter. It looked to me exactly like the loaves on the shelves behind her.

"I'm only taking it to keep you lot from throwing it away," the older woman said as she counted out her money.

The blue-haired girl rolled her eyes.

"We appreciate your business," the guy behind the register said.

The bells over the door jangled as she left.

The girl—Fee—folded her arms across her floured apron. "What is your head stuffed with, straw? There's no point in me baking to sell if you're going to give it away."

He shrugged. "Good neighbors make good customers. We take care of them, they take care of us."

"The neighborhood is changing. We need to change with it."

I listened, fascinated by their little drama. *"You'll be the ruin of us," she cried, clutching her baby to her breast. "If we cannot pay the rent, we'll be forced to emigrate to America."*

The poet—who was quite hot, actually—caught me staring. One eyebrow flicked up.

Flushing, I gathered up my cup and napkin to throw them away. "Thank you for the tea. And the toast."

"No bother."

"I, um, guess you get a lot of tourists in here."

"More than last year," he said.

During the pandemic, he meant. "And students," I offered.

Something subtle shuttered in his face. "Some."

Obviously, he had better things to do than make conversation with a dorky American grad student. "Do you know the way to the writing center? On . . ." What was it? "West Something Road?"

"The Oscar Wilde house. Westland Row. Turn left across the bridge, then follow the road past campus. Right on Townsend, left on Pearse." I nodded, still pretending I knew where I was going. But apparently I didn't fool him, because he added, "It's not far. About fifteen minutes' walk."

"Thank you." I lifted my bag to avoid scraping the broken wheel across the floor.

"I can call you a taxi," he said.

"If it's not too much trouble . . ."

"No trouble. My uncle Gerry's a cabbie."

"Oh. Well . . ." A headline scrolled through my tired brain. *Abducted Woman's Body Pulled from River, Still Wearing Cowboy Boots.*

The eyebrow quirked again. "He won't take advantage, if that's what you're thinking."

My face was hot. "I wasn't thinking that at all." I didn't even *like* true crime stories.

"Or he can drop you at your hotel. Get rid of that bag."

"Thanks, but I can't check in until three. Anyway, I have to get to an appointment." I shifted my weight, clutching the handle of my suitcase, oddly reluctant to be on my way. "Wish me luck?"

"'Luck is believing you're lucky.'"

"I like that. An old Irish saying?"

"American. Tennessee Williams."

I blinked.

He smiled. "Have a nice day."

TWO

The bells rattled against the door. Sam watched through the window as the pretty American smiled at his uncle Gerry, pushing her rope of hair over one shoulder, hefting her bag in the other hand.

"Don't stand there with a pole up your arse," his sister Fiadh said. "Go after her, why don't you."

The hell of it was, Sam wanted to. He pictured it, taking her suitcase from her and loading it into the boot, sliding into the back of the cab beside her. He would hold her hand—this was his fantasy, after all—as they crossed the river to where the other half lived, to the university where he'd never truly belonged.

He blinked, dispelling the vision. Outside, the taxi pulled away from the curb. "Too late," he said. *Nine years too late*, if he let himself go there, which he mostly did not. It was the girl, her privilege or the way she'd set off so hopefully without a clue where she was going.

Fiadh crossed her arms. "And whose fault is that?"

Nobody's fault. It was the way things were. "I can't leave the shop. I'm working," he said.

"I'm here."

"In the back."

After Fiadh got her certificate in baking and pastry, Sam figured she'd be off, to London, maybe. But then the Covid happened, and she'd settled into her old room above the shop, selling her bread from behind the counter. For the past year, she'd been pushing Sam to invest in a new mixer, a new oven, to expand the business.

"So ask Mam," Fiadh said. "Or Grace."

Sam shook his head. The responsibility of the shop was on him. Always on him, since their father died. "Mam is busy. And Grace is too young."

"Sixteen. Older than you were when you started working the register."

He'd never minded, really, sweeping the floors and stocking the shelves with their father. He'd thought then it was only temporary, a way to help out, to earn some spending money until he could go to uni. "She should be studying."

Grace was starting sixth year, taking all higher levels. She needed to do well. He went over her English essays, even helped her study for her Leaving Certificate in maths, but it had been too long. His brain was too full of daily takings and cash deposits, calculating taxes and inventory, to make the switch easily to functions and graphs.

Fiadh tilted her head, regarding him. "You're a sad, lonely gom. You need a girl."

"I have girls," Sam protested.

"For a night. Three, tops."

Because he took care not to go home with partners who were looking for more. He winked, hoping to distract her. "I get no complaints."

Fiadh snorted. "Because you only shag alley cats."

"Like the girls you date are any better."

"Everything all right?" their mother asked.

Janette had always had an uncanny ability to catch her children at their worst.

"Grand," Sam said.

Fiadh made a face. "I was just telling Sam he needs to settle down."

"I'm only twenty-eight," Sam said.

"I was twenty-one when I married your father," Janette said.

And forty-one when he died, leaving her with five mouths to feed and a shop to run and no money for burial expenses.

Sam smiled. "You were one of the lucky ones," he said, but he didn't believe it.

"There was a girl in the shop," Fiadh said. "An American. Very pretty."

Janette looked at Sam. "And?"

His family's love surrounded him, warm and suffocating. Like wading through a haystack, it was.

"He called her a taxi," Fiadh said.

"Uncle Gerry. He was glad for the fare," Sam said.

And Sam . . . He was glad to do it. Taking care of his family. That's what he did, that's who he was now. That's all he could be.

THREE

'm sorry we're meeting like this," Glenda Norton said.

Her long, thin white hands were folded on top of the nineteenth-century desk in front of her. Behind her, sunlight streamed through the tall, narrow window of the house where Oscar Wilde once lived, sliding lovingly over a photo of two little girls on the glass-fronted bookcase and illuminating her hair to gold—Eileen in *A Portrait of the Artist as a Young Man*, the gilt-edged Madonna in every art book triptych ever, the Blessed Damozel leaning down from heaven. She was everything I wanted to be: beautiful, smart, composed. Sure of herself and the power she wielded. I wanted her to adopt me or at least to tell me what to do.

"Yeah," I said. "I'm really sorry about Dr. Eastwick."

"Yes. Poor Morrigan. Tragic. Unfortunately, her death leaves us in a bit of a quandary."

I waited, my heart thrumming.

Dr. Norton sighed. "I had hoped to speak with you before you arrived." If her voice weren't so sweet, she would have sounded almost cross.

"I know orientation doesn't start for a couple of weeks. I just . . ." *Needed to get away.* "Was really excited to come. I've never been to Ireland before." Or out of the country. Unlike our mother, who was always off draping fabric on volcanoes or twisting rope across ravines, creating the massive art installations that made her famous. "I wanted to get settled."

"You didn't reply to my email," Dr. Norton said with gentle reproach.

Heat swept my face. *Guilty.* It was one thing to drop off social media. But I'd also been avoiding my inbox. My old account, dgale@ku.edu, had been flooded with emails from prying reporters and creepy fans, strangers searching for the fictional Destiny Gayle. I deleted them unread. Mostly unread. My new Trinity account had felt like a fresh start. A new identity. A chance to be someone else—or maybe to be my old self again. But I still flinched at opening email from unknown senders.

"I must have missed it," I said.

Dr. Norton hummed. "You were at the University of Kansas for . . ." She consulted her open MacBook. "Four years?"

In a three-year program. I cleared my throat. "The first two years were mostly coursework. I also taught English composition."

Dr. Norton templed her long white fingers. "We welcome writers at all stages of life. And your grades are very, very impressive. Well done, you. But there was some concern about your transferring programs at this point in your academic career. Some of the staff questioned whether you had the necessary, ah, commitment to succeed."

I sat up straighter. "One of the things that attracted me to Trinity was that it's a one-year program," I said. "*One and done,*" I'd said to Toni as I left her at her freshman dorm. "I'm eager to finish my dissertation and move on to the next stage of my life."

Which wasn't a lie, exactly. I didn't have a clue what I wanted to do after graduation. But one step at a time, right? And simply coming here had been a giant leap into the unknown.

Another hum. "Morrigan was a vocal advocate for your admission. But now that she's no longer with us . . ." Dr. Norton trailed off delicately.

I wasn't welcome anymore.

I swallowed a familiar lump of anxiety, a relic of all those years of getting dumped on my mother's friends. Sooner or later, the Leslies and Cecilys, that nice gay couple in Connecticut, uncles Jeff and Brad, would decide they'd had enough. I didn't blame them. I got good at making myself small and useful, at fitting myself and Toni into the margins of their lives.

Change the subject. Keep her talking.

"What happened to Dr. Eastwick?" I asked.

"It was very sad."

I waited. Maybe she'd been stabbed in the back by a jealous colleague. Poisoned by a disgruntled graduate student.

Dr. Norton sighed. "She attempted to pass a mobile housing unit on the motorway when the lorry driver swerved. Morrigan was killed by the, ah, falling house. She died instantly."

"Oh my God. I'm so sorry."

Dr. Norton bent a look at me, stern and beautiful as an angel at the gates of paradise. "Generally speaking, if you were a doctoral candidate and your supervisor suddenly became unavailable, we'd do our best to assign you to another member of staff. But given that you're barely in the program . . . Well. It's a question of finding an appropriate match."

"I can work under anybody," I said. An image surfaced—me under Gray—the memory sweaty and shocking in this cool, pale, golden room. "I could work with you."

"I'm afraid that's not possible," Dr. Norton said gently. "My administrative duties unfortunately preclude my doing as much personal instruction as I would like. And, of course, I have responsibilities outside the school as well."

The two little blond girls smiled at me smugly from their silver frame.

"I understand," I said numbly.

"We have several members of staff who work on the creative writing side of things who might be able to advise you. Dr. Ward is the obvious choice, but . . . We'll need to set up a meeting. Where are you staying?"

"The Clontarf." A real Norman castle. My treat to myself on my first visit to Ireland. I suppressed a little bounce of excitement.

Dr. Norton smiled faintly. "I hear it's very popular with tourists."

"It's only for two nights," I said. "I'm applying for on-campus housing."

"You'll find, if you stay, that very few postgraduate students are housed on campus. But you can certainly explore the off-campus options for international students at the Student Union's service."

The lump returned. *If* I stay? "I'll do that."

"I will, of course, do my very best to resolve this before orientation. You'll want to check your email," she added with a touch of astringency—a slice of lemon in a cup of Earl Grey.

"I will," I promised.

"At Trinity, we want every student to succeed. In the meantime, you should visit the library. Acquaint yourself with the center." Another smile touched her lips. "Think of us as your temporary home."

I beamed. "Thank you."

It took me another minute to realize I had been dismissed. And I had no idea where to go from here, except forward. Because going home, going back, wasn't an option.

t turned out my hotel room wasn't in the actual castle. The building itself had been completely reconstructed in the 1830s, and the wings, which housed the guest rooms, were even more modern than that.

But still. There was a giant stone fireplace in the lobby and suits of armor in the hall and a stag's head over the reception desk. "*Very popular with tourists,*" Dr. Norton had said. Maybe I was wrong to be impressed? But I was. Everything was so different from Kansas. Different and lonely.

I curled on the tufted window seat, munching airplane pretzels and checking my inbox. Both my inboxes. Nothing. Yet.

Two years ago, there would have been an email from Gray. Several emails. No dick pics, no texts, from the author of *Unabridged*. He'd courted me for months with long, intimate, flattering letters praising my "old soul and fresh, unspoiled mind" (that was my favorite, I printed out that one), so different from the other students'.

I scrolled down, ignoring the prying requests from reporters inviting me to tell my side of the story. The creepers who wanted sex with the girl who slept with Grayson Kettering. The crazies who wanted to reenact scenes from the novel. (That scene with the horned mask? Especially popular, and we'd never even done that. At least, he hadn't done it with me.) Then there were the Grayson Kettering fans who wanted me dead because I—that is, Destiny—was a heartless vampire who had sucked the soul of their literary hero. Sometimes the letter writers wanted both: the sex and my death. Usually in that order, although they weren't always clear.

Finally I found the original email from Glenda Norton asking me to contact the school at my earliest convenience (too late for that!) as Dr. Eastwick was "unfortunately no longer with us." *Unfortunate.* Like it was just my bad luck.

Worse luck for her. Poor Dr. Eastwick. I searched online for her obituary. There it was, a few column inches in the campus paper. The administrative officer's voice came back to me. *"Not that she'll be missed, God rest her soul."*

When my mother died, her friends back East didn't come to her funeral service in Kansas. But her obituary was in *ARTnews* and the *New York Times*. "Fearless." *"A force of nature,"* they said, quoting various gallery owners. I kept the clippings in the box under my bed along with Toni's first tooth and my first stories.

I wondered what my obituary would say. Would it talk about my writing? Or would it read like Gray's reviews? *Dorothy Gale, the inspiration for Grayson Kettering's corn-fed seductress Destiny Gayle, has died.*

I shuddered.

"You need to stop imagining things," Gray had said when I'd asked him once if he ever wrote emails to other female students.

Forget about Gray.

Except . . . There was his name, at the top of my search history. I clicked. His face filled the screen, that familiar smile exposing his teeth, curling one corner of his mouth.

My chest ached. I clicked again, compulsively. *Destiny Gayle*—the paperback edition—had dropped to #9 on the Amazon charts. Another click. Dakota Fanning was reported to be in talks to star in *Destiny Gayle*, the movie. A photo of the actress accompanied the announcement. She was perfect, small and blond with blue eyes. It was like finding out Tinker Bell had been cast to play the part of the blue fairy in *Sleeping Beauty*, the bouncy one, what was her name? Merryweather, that was it.

The pretzels congealed in my throat. I needed some real food. Or a cup of tea and my sister. But I was not calling Toni in—my mind fumbled with the time change—the middle of the school day. She might be in class. She was just starting her freshman year. Growing up. Moving on. We were both moving on. I needed to set a good example.

Although if this were Toni's first night in Ireland, she wouldn't be alone in her hotel room eating leftover snacks from the plane. My gaze fell on the minibar. A tiny green bottle of Jameson whiskey winked at me. What had Hot Poet said? *"You're in Ireland. You can always have tea. Or Guinness or whiskey."*

Somehow drinking alone in my hotel room was even worse than eating alone. I was trying to become a stronger, wiser, and more confident Dee. To take control of my own destiny. (Even the word—*destiny*—made me flinch). Shutting my laptop on Gray, I grabbed my purse and room key.

My new courage took me as far as the hotel bar.

"Will you be joining us for dinner this evening?" the black-clad server inquired.

"Yes, please."

"Table for one?"

I gripped my bag tighter. I wasn't really alone. I had a book with me, *Anne of Green Gables*, my emergency read for the plane. For most of my life, actually. Plucky, passionate, imaginative orphan Anne Shirley had been my best friend growing up.

The server cleared his throat. Waiting for me to answer.

"Um. One. Yeah. Thanks."

"Right this way."

This way led to a table in the corner. I ordered a whiskey—when in Ireland, right?—while I read the menu. But even the lovely descriptions (braised Wicklow lamb slow-cooked in a rich lamb broth with Chantenay carrots and pearl barley; homemade scones and parsley butter; *tarte aux pommes* with crème anglaise, *yum*) couldn't hold my attention for long.

Two tables over, an older couple sampled six different appetizers, the woman occasionally breaking off their conversation to take a picture of their food or speak into her phone. She was a restaurant critic, I decided, and he was . . . I squinted at his left hand. Her husband. Somebody's husband, anyway. Every now and then she would put something on his plate, and he'd chew stolidly before commenting.

Under the tall windows, a table of business types leaned forward over their plates, talking in low voices like they were plotting a hostile takeover. Or an assassination.

I took a sip of whiskey and choked. I grabbed my napkin, dabbing at my eyes, looking around at my fellow diners to see if anyone noticed.

A pair of honeymooners sat at the long oak bar. Okay, probably not honeymooners, not unless they'd just come from their wedding. He was in a slim, dark, conservative suit and tie. Nice-looking in a stuffed shirt sort of way, his square jaw clean-shaven, his eyes half-hidden behind steely spectacles. His . . . bride? Fiancée? I peeked. No ring. His girlfriend, then, perched on the green leather barstool beside him, her pose and her dress showing off her long, smooth, bare legs, a fall of sleek, shining hair tucked casually behind her ears. She looked like a sexy Kate Middleton. Pippa, maybe.

As I watched, she slipped off one skyscraper heel, stroking her toes up his ankle. He stiffened. Well. A lot of guys weren't comfortable showing affection in public. Gray . . . No. *Stop thinking about Gray.*

Maybe she wasn't the Suit's girlfriend yet. Maybe in ten or twenty years, they would tell the story of how they met to their children, adorable twins who had a dog and rabbits in a hutch at the bottom of the garden and maybe a pony. I smiled.

While I was naming their kids, her foot got stuck halfway up his calf, trapped by his pants leg. Abandoning the attempt, she put her hand on his knee. I admired her confidence. Although . . . He shifted his leg. Away. She laughed, undeterred, and said something that made a muscle bunch in his jaw.

None of my business, really. He was a grown man, right? She touched his arm, smiling. Flirting. Not rapey at all.

Now if he'd been the one touching her . . . I frowned.

His shoulders tensed under his suit jacket. If his spine got any more rigid, he'd turn to stone. She gestured, making a point. This time, her fingers landed high on his thigh. Wow. Okay. Or maybe not okay?

The first time I went to Gray's house, he'd invited the entire graduate student cohort over for cocktails. Eight of us, dazzled by the great man's reputation, competing self-consciously for his attention. I mean, he was *Grayson Kettering.* I was flattered when he asked me to stay after to help clean up. But unbidden, a memory surfaced of that first, unexpected touch, his hand on my hip as I stood at the sink. His thumb, exploring under my sweater. The surprise, the thrill, the discomfort of it. I'd frozen with my hands in hot water. Speechless. Stuck.

Her hand drifted higher. A flush washed his neck, red against his starched white collar.

What would New Dee do? And almost before I'd stopped to think, I catapulted out of my seat and across the room as if I'd witnessed some drunken frat boy hitting on my little sister. "Hi, babe." I went in for a quick one, hug and release. No PDA, in case that was his issue. "Sorry I'm late."

Their faces turned to me wearing identical expressions of polite, blank surprise. I cringed inside. Oh God. I'd gotten it all wrong. She *was* his girlfriend. He liked her, or at least he didn't mind being touched by her. Why would he? She was gorgeous, and he was a guy.

And then he said, stiffly, "That's all right." A pause. "Darling." I beamed at him in relief.

The woman didn't budge from her barstool. "Who is this?"

"This. Yes." He looked at me. "This is . . ."

"Dee." I stuck out my hand. "Hi."

"You're American."

I smiled harder. "That's right."

"Laura Smith. Hello." She watched me closely, like I was supposed to recognize her name. Maybe she really was a friend of the Middletons. "Here on holiday?"

"Uh, no."

"Then . . . I'm sorry, how did you two meet?"

"I . . ." I glanced at my silent coconspirator. Useless. Although, to be fair, I had taken him by surprise. "I'm a graduate student at Trinity."

"How nice," Laura said politely. "Are you in the business school, then, with Tim?"

"Um. The creative writing program, actually."

"Oh, a writer. Would I have heard of you?"

"Probably not." *Not unless you're a Grayson Kettering fan.*

"Laura's visiting from the UK office," the Suit—Tim—said. "She's part of our AIFM management task force."

I nodded as if I had the faintest idea what he was talking about.

Laura touched his arm. "We should probably rejoin the rest of the team."

The team?

His glasses flashed as he glanced over her shoulder at the assassins' table. "You go on," he said. "I'll see you tomorrow."

"I'm looking forward to it. Darling." Her gaze rested lightly, assessingly, on me. "You want to be careful with this one," she told me. "He has no heart."

She moved away, all hips and balance, like a racehorse on stiletto heels.

"Well." I released my breath. "That was awkward."

"Quite."

"So, you and Laura . . . You're coworkers?"

"Yes."

"And I interrupted you."

"Yes." Another pause. "Why?"

"I . . ." I fingered the strap of my purse. There was no way I could explain the protective instinct that had propelled me across the bar. "You looked uncomfortable."

"And being an American, you felt you needed to ride to the rescue."

"Something like that. You're welcome," I added pointedly.

"Oh. Ah, thank you." He looked at me, a speculative gleam in his eyes. Or maybe that was his glasses. "May I buy you a drink?"

Did he think I was *hitting* on him? "I have a drink." I waved my hand. "Over there."

"Very good."

I glanced toward the assassins' table. Lovely Laura looked up from her conversation and smiled pleasantly. "Would . . . Would you like to join me for dinner?"

"Why?" he asked again.

Asshole. "Because everybody over there is watching us, and if you don't have dinner with me now, they're going to wonder why."

His lips compressed briefly, as if he were in pain. "Very well. If you're sure."

"I'm not asking you to pay."

"I thought you might be dining with someone else," he said stiffly.

"Oh. No. Only Anne Shirley."

"Excuse me?"

"I brought a book."

Did his mouth actually relax a fraction? "Never trust anyone who hasn't brought a book with them."

"Lemony Snicket!" I exclaimed, delighted.

He blinked. Right. He was not quoting one of my favorite children's authors. He'd probably never even read *A Series of Unfortunate Events*.

"If we're going to have dinner, I should probably know your name," I said. *In case I want to Google you later. Or file a police report.*

"Woodman. Tim."

"Like, Bond, James?"

"You're quite safe," he said, deadpan. "I left my license to kill at home."

I was almost sure he was joking. "Haha. I'm Dee."

"So you said." He paused expectantly.

Nuh-uh. Nope. No last name. I didn't want him Googling me. "My table's over here."

He followed, waiting as I slid into the banquette before taking the chair across from me. Old-fashioned manners. Aunt Em would have approved.

"Perhaps I can buy you a refill." He looked at my almost untouched drink. "Or something else. They do a very nice gin cocktail here."

Was *he* hitting on *me*? But no. There was no vibe. No threat. Nothing in his voice besides polite disinterest.

"Maybe a glass of white wine?" The apple juice of adult beverages, Gray called it. I might as well have asked for a sippy lid or a red plastic cup.

He signaled the server. "A glass of the Pouilly-Fumé, please. And a Sexton's."

The waiter disappeared with our order.

"So." I smiled brightly, determined to make the best of my impulsive invitation. "You're in the business school."

"Yes." Apparently good manners required he continue, because he added, "Second year. Mostly online."

"A nontraditional student."

"Very traditional, I assure you."

Another joke? Impossible to tell. "I meant . . . What is it you do, exactly?"

"I'm a regulatory consultant. And you're a writer."

I squirmed, embarrassed. "I haven't published anything yet." A short story in a literary magazine. Some fanfic online.

"But you write."

"Yes." One word. Oh God, I was starting to sound like him.

"I believe that qualifies you as a writer."

Which was quite possibly the nicest thing anybody had said to me in a while.

The server reappeared with our drinks. I gulped my wine, a warmth spreading in my cheeks that had nothing to do with the alcohol. "How long have you been a consultant?"

"Five years."

"You look older." I set down my glass hastily. "Not that you look old. Exactly. It's the suit." *Worse and worse.*

The waiter gave me a sympathetic look. "Ready to order?"

I smiled at him gratefully. "Yeah, thanks. What do you recommend?"

We had a nice chat about the menu before he left. I took another sip of wine, which did not taste like any drink I'd had at any graduate student party ever.

"Thirty," Tim Woodman said unexpectedly.

I swallowed. "Sorry?"

"My age. If that's what you were asking."

"I wasn't asking." I was totally asking. "I'm twenty-six."

"Returning to school, then."

"Um, no. I'm kind of a late starter. We moved around a lot as kids, and I had to repeat a grade." When our mother died and we moved in with Aunt Em and Uncle Henry. Not to mention the years I'd wasted when I should have been working on my master's thesis. All my energy and creativity had gone into nurturing Gray's writing, running his errands, doing his laundry, offering little meals as encouragement on the altar of his genius . . .

I reached for my wineglass. Tim Woodman regarded me across the table, eyes unreadable behind his silver-rimmed specs.

"Not that there's anything wrong with taking time off," I assured him. "My sister, Toni—she started at KU in August—anyway, she tried to talk me into letting her take a gap year after high school to 'see the world.'" I put air quotes around it. "Which I totally get. I mean, look at me. I'm in Ireland. But I thought it would help Toni to stay close to home, at least for her first year. We didn't have the most stable childhood."

He didn't say anything.

"So, what about you?" I prompted. "Did you see the world?"

"Parts of it."

"Which parts?"

"Kabul, mostly."

"Afghanistan? What, were you in the army?"

"Yes." I waited. He shifted his knife a quarter inch to the right. "I was with the British Quick Reaction Force."

Not seeing the world. Saving the world. I opened my mouth to blurt an apology. But what came out was, "You're British."

"I have dual citizenship." He cleared his throat. "It's very useful. Dublin is the new hub into the single market."

So we weren't going to talk about his military service.

Our server—his name was Conor, I found out—returned with food, locally sourced lamb chops and peas for me, turbot for Tim. Conor's parents ran a sheep farm in Galway.

"Real culchies," he said.

I didn't know the word. "We never had sheep," I confessed. "Only chickens. And pigs."

After he left, I became aware of Tim, wooden across the table. I winced. "Sorry."

"Why?"

"I didn't mean to be rude."

"I thought you were being polite."

To the waiter. "You didn't mind?"

Gray had never liked it when I chatted with the waitstaff. When I was with him, he wanted all my attention to himself.

"No." Another one-word answer. But, oddly, I believed him. Maybe sometimes one word was enough.

The food was really good.

"Thanks for having dinner with me," I said after I'd stuffed my face.

"Thank you for inviting me," Tim said politely.

"You wouldn't rather be plotting financial world domination at the assassins' table?" *Shit.* Had I said that out loud?

His spectacles glinted. "Our business is done for the day."

I glanced at the table by the window. "They're still talking."

"I believe they're planning Rob's stag weekend."

"You're not going?"

"My presence would only put a damper on things. Especially if strippers are involved."

I laughed. "I'd think Laura's presence would do that."

"Laura prefers to think of herself as one of the guys."

I drank more wine, enjoying the unfamiliar glow. "And you're not? One of the guys?"

"We can't be mates, no."

"No good in groups?" I asked sympathetically.

"I'm their boss."

"Oh."

Maybe he took pity on me then, because he said, "I'm also not particularly adept with other people."

"You're doing fine."

"I do better when I'm lubricated."

I managed not to choke. I was sure—almost sure—the double entendre was unintentional, never mind what I'd read about dry British humor.

He signaled across the room to Conor. "Buy you another?"

I stared rather regretfully at my now-empty wineglass. "I shouldn't. I have a meeting with one of my teachers tomorrow. I need a clear head."

He didn't argue. So he wasn't planning on getting me drunk and following me up to my room. Although maybe . . . Beneath his tailored jacket, his shoulders looked solid and broad. His hair was thick and dark.

I tore my gaze away. Okay, I had definitely had enough to drink.

"Another Sexton's, please," Tim said to Conor.

"And for you, miss?"

"Nothing, thanks." After he left, I said, "Laura said you had no heart. What kind of a thing is that to say to your boss?"

For a moment, I thought Tim wasn't going to answer. Why would he? It's not like I had some mysterious power over men that made them confide their deepest secrets to me.

"She has her reasons." He shook his head. "And I can't believe I just told you that."

"I did ask."

His mouth pressed into a firm line. "Still."

"Maybe you do have a heart," I suggested. "Maybe someone you love hurt you"—*the way Gray hurt me*—"maybe Laura hurt you, and now you need to protect your tender heart."

"You're quite the writer," Tim said coolly. "Do you do deep character analysis on everyone you meet?"

I blinked, more confused than offended. "Is it true?"

"I'm not a character in a book. Don't put me in one of your stories."

I winced. "I would never."

Because I knew what that felt like.

FOUR

The girl (*woman—Dee*, Tim corrected himself) walked away, her loose braid swinging above the curve of her backside. He felt a schoolboy urge to grab it and tug her back.

He could have asked for her number.

Or at least her last name.

Listening to her talk, watching her hands and her eyes as she tackled her food and the conversation with equal enthusiasm, he'd felt almost connected. Almost alive. Animated by a jolt of electricity like Frankenstein's monster.

The elevator doors closed behind her. *Going up.* For a moment something stirred in him, sharper than regret, deeper than lust. Something in the region of his heart.

He rubbed two fingers in the center of his chest, feeling the ridge of the scar under the fine cotton.

"Laura said you have no heart."

"She has her reasons."

"Bad luck, darling," Laura said behind him.

Tim straightened his shoulders, mentally steeling himself before he turned. He composed his face to its usual blank. *Nothing to see here. Move along.* "I don't know what you're talking about."

But Laura wasn't put off. She knew him too well. "The girl. Did she shoot you down? Or . . . No. You turned her down, didn't you?" She smiled wryly. "You're good at that."

"This is hardly an appropriate conversation for work," he said.

"It's after hours."

"Woodman and Wainwright promotes a culture of respect at all times." He sounded like a robot. He was a robot. Very rusty.

"Tell it to that lot," Laura said, nodding at the table under the window. "Right now they're going on about hiring lap dancers for Rob's stag weekend."

Tim sighed mentally. "I'll have a word with them."

"Don't you dare. Not on my account. It's not like they're getting in the way of me doing my job."

"It doesn't matter," Tim said. Although legally, of course, it did. "An organization reflects the values of its leadership."

"Relax. I'm not running to HR to file a grievance. You need to loosen up." She tilted her head. "Oh, wait. I forgot who I was talking to."

Heat crawled up the back of his neck. "Your boss. Was there anything else?"

"Yes. Your mother says hello." Laura took a step closer. She lowered her voice. "She misses you, you know."

He did know. His family was not given to displays of emotion. But he was her only child, born late in life after his parents had despaired of his mother ever carrying any pregnancy to term. When he was in hospital, Caroline had left her dogs in a neighbor's care so she could see him every day, sitting for endless hours by his bed, getting up needlessly now and then to adjust his blankets or the light. Sightlessly turning the pages of her magazine, her eyes full of terror.

He'd promised her no more risks. But there was a limit to what he was prepared to do, even for his mother.

"I'll call her," he said.

"Or you could come to London for a visit. Stay a few days." Laura reached up to smooth his lapel. "We all miss you."

He looked down at her pink nails against his dark suit coat and felt . . . absolutely nothing.

Quite a relief, that, actually.

FIVE

I definitely wasn't in Kansas anymore.

I used to dread being the new kid in school, trying to find the cafeteria or the girls' bathroom or someone to sit with at lunch. Even when I went to college, I'd struggled to find my place. To fit in. But I refused to let the strangeness of everything here crush my mood.

After three days, Glenda Norton had emailed with the name of the woman who had agreed to meet with me, whose guidance would shape the next year of my life. I squeezed my hands together. I couldn't wait to meet her.

I paced the writing center's common room, stopping in front of the notice board to read an announcement about some prize award in poetry. A poster for an upcoming guest lecture by American children's author Oscar Diggs. Note cards offering Rollerblades for sale and tutoring in Italian. There were housing ads, too, thumbtacked near the bottom. *Accommodation required. Seeking accommodation. Seeking single room to let. Three-bedroom house available to rent in Swords.* Not that I could afford a house. But I certainly couldn't afford to stay in the hotel much longer. The minibar charges were killing me. Maybe I could find a housemate?

I eyed the only other occupant of the room, a slim, dark girl reading on the couch. She had a gorgeous mane of glossy waves and black-fringed eyes. What if we became friends? Best friends. My first friend in Dublin. I imagined us going to pubs together or the library. *I know this great place to get a cup of tea,* I'd say after we emerged from a late night of studying, and we'd cross the bridge to Clery's Newsagents and Hot Poet would bring us toasted buns and linger at our table to listen to our deep, passionate, intellectual discussions about . . . about . . .

"Do you need help or something?" the girl asked.

Oh God, she'd caught me staring. My face heated. "Oh. No. I . . . I was just wondering what you were reading."

She turned the cover so I could see. *Selected Poems* by Derek Mahon.

"I *love* Derek Mahon," I said. "I read his poem 'Everything Is Going To Be All Right,' like, a thousand times."

She regarded me with amber-colored eyes. "You're new."

"I . . . Yeah?"

"American."

After three days wandering around Dublin, I'd realized that commenting on where you were from was a friendly conversation starter, like talking about the weather. I nodded.

"And you read poetry." She didn't sound very Irish. More like a Bollywood actress dropping in on the set of *Downton Abbey.*

I smiled. "Sometimes. We're not all uneducated. I'm Dee." No last name.

"Reeti."

"Nice to meet you, Reeti." I copied her pronunciation carefully. *Reet-tea.*

She returned the smile, exposing very white, slightly uneven teeth. "When did you start?"

"I haven't yet. I'm meeting with one of the faculty today. Dr. Ward?"

Assistant Professor Maeve Ward. I'd looked her up online, of course. Her debut novel had been longlisted for a Booker Prize nine years ago, and since then she'd had an impressive list of research papers published in peer-reviewed journals. I hadn't read any of them yet. But still. She was an award-winning author! She was willing to work with me!

The girl pulled a face. "Poor you."

The glow I'd felt since opening Glenda Norton's email this morning faded. "Why?"

"She's a witch."

A lump of unease rose in my throat. "Is she your advisor?"

"I took her senior sophister class last year. She's brilliant. Terrifying, actually." Reeti shuddered dramatically. "Scared me to death."

"Are you . . . are you in the writing program?"

"No, I used to be an English major."

"I hope you didn't switch because of Dr. Ward," I said, joking. Mostly joking.

"Ha. No. I love English. Might have gone on, honestly. But I graduated in June, and my parents want me to get a diploma in accounting, so . . ." She shrugged.

"My aunt would say that's very practical of you."

"Right." Reeti rolled her eyes. "Plus, I need a nice professional job so I can get a good professional husband."

A vision flashed of the guy in the bar, with his solid shoulders and charcoal suit and metal-rimmed glasses. Definitely professional husband material.

"I have a . . ." *Friend?* Not a friend. He didn't like me. He'd accused me of wanting to put him into a book. "I met someone in the business school," I said. "Tim Woodman?"

"Oh, Tim," she said. "He's in the executive program. Not really in my league."

I couldn't tell if she meant academically or as a potential marriage partner. "But you know each other."

"He lives downstairs from me." She tilted her head. "You should come hang out sometime. I'm a fair cook."

The glow was back, a warm tingle. I'd never made friends easily, shunned by the cool girls, ignored by the crush-worthy guys. And she'd just invited me to dinner! "I'd like that."

"Or we can go to Hugh Lane and get pissed."

"Pissed?" I repeated.

"Langers. Wasted. Drunk. You'll need it," she added, "after meeting with The Ward."

think we're done. I don't know why Glenda wants you here." Maeve Ward was tall and gaunt, her lipstick so dark a red as to appear almost black, her manner both terrifying and perfunctory. "But now that you are, we'll both have to make the best of it. You'll pick up the rest at orientation."

I knew the rules of being in a new place. Don't talk back to the teacher. Make your bed every day. Double-check that Toni has her lunch money/homework/permission slips. Be tidy, agreeable, and quiet, and maybe you can stay.

But.

"Don't you want to talk about my writing?"

"You have a three-hour workshop every week to discuss your work with other students. New work," Dr. Ward emphasized. "I'll be your instructor this term. I'd encourage you to use your time at Trinity to experiment with different forms. Different genres."

I swallowed my dismay. I didn't want to argue. I was an expert in argument avoidance, actually. "Dr. Eastwick said I'd already made a good start on my novel."

"The thesis you were working on at Kansas."

"It was part of my application portfolio." She was supposed to advise me. Mentor me. Hadn't she read it?

"But essentially the same work you were doing before. I'd question whether that's where you want to focus your energies now."

"But I was accepted."

"Well, if all you aspire to is acceptance . . ." I winced. Maeve Ward leaned back in her chair. "Fine. Tell me about it."

I floundered, as usual, when asked to distill all my painstakingly written pages into an elevator pitch. "Well." I gulped. "It's sort of autobiographical."

Nothing about our mother dying, of course. Nothing about Gray, even though he'd encouraged me to set my story—a bleak American Gothic tale about a farmer's daughter who falls in love with a traveling magician in the 1930s Dust Bowl days—in the world I knew. Consequently, there was a lot of scenery, flat gray Kansas farmland blasted by high winds and choking storms.

"First novels always are."

"Excuse me?"

"Writers in their twenties invariably feel their lives are more interesting than they really are. Like memoirists in their eighties."

"Dr. Eastwick said I showed individuality of approach in theme and content." I'd memorized the compliment.

"It's possible," Maeve Ward said in a voice that suggested she didn't believe it for a minute. "It takes a very special writer to tap immediately into their own authentic voice."

I sat up straighter, willing her to like me. Wanting her to see me as one of the special ones. "That's why I'm here," I said. "To find my voice." To become New Dee.

"Is it?"

"Yes. All I need is a fresh start."

"A clean slate? Or . . ." She swiveled her chair, facing away from me. "A chance to run away?"

She plucked something from the shelves behind her. My stomach twisted. Even before she turned, I knew.

She placed the book flat on the desk between us. The bright graphic cover stared up at me. *Destiny Gayle, a Novel*, by Grayson Kettering.

told you you'd need a drink by the time The Ward was through with you," Reeti said. "How bad was it?"

The pub was packed with people off from work or out to dinner, the air thick with the smell of grease and beer. The cheerful noise of music and conversation wrapped our table in a bubble of privacy.

"Bad." I took a sip of Guinness. The chosen drink of Ireland puckered my mouth. Like I'd made a mistake in ordering it. In being here at all. "She had his book. Grayson Kettering's. She showed it to me."

"What book?"

"*Destiny Gayle*."

"So?"

Maybe I should pretend that everything was okay. That I was okay. I didn't want to watch the sympathy fade from Reeti's face, replaced by contempt. I wasn't running away, I told myself. I hadn't slunk off to my hotel room to lick my wounds and search the Internet for scraps about Gray's bestseller rank and upcoming movie. I was out for dinner in a real Irish pub, drinking a real

Irish Guinness. Trying new things. Making a new friend. *Take that, Dr. Ward.*

Except . . . *A clean slate.*

A fresh start.

Weren't friends supposed to tell each other things?

I swallowed. "That's my name. I'm Dee Gale."

Reeti's brow furrowed. "I don't understand. I mean, the name . . . That's a weird coincidence, sure. But Grayson Kettering . . . He's kind of a big deal, isn't he? I mean, it's not like he wrote a book about you."

"Actually . . ." I rubbed the wet ring from my glass on the tabletop. Forced myself to go on. The worst that could happen . . . It had already happened, right? What did I have to lose by being honest? Other than Reeti's respect. "He did. At least . . . He based her on me. His character, Destiny. We . . . We knew each other at the University of Kansas."

"Wow." Reeti sat back. "So you're, like, famous."

I grimaced into my glass, afraid to look at her. "Me and Hester Prynne."

She laughed. "It can't be that bad."

"Have you read it? The book?"

"Not yet."

"It's sort of a Pygmalion story." That's how Gray had described it whenever I asked him what he was working on. "*An engrossing—if occasionally sordid—exploration of creativity and obsession,*" according to the *Times* review. "About a young female graduate student who moves in with a professor in her writing program and basically ruins his life until he escapes her sexual thrall."

"Whoa." Her eyes narrowed. "Wait. You lived with him?"

I lowered my gaze. "Not me. Destiny. In the book." Gray had always been protective of his privacy. Careful about appearances.

Toni knew there was someone. She'd even met Gray when she

came to visit me on campus. Aunt Em suspected we were involved. But I'd never told anyone how serious we had been. I
had been.

"He gave me a key," I said.

So I could pick up his dry cleaning and drop off his groceries
and water his plants. And every time I'd let myself into his house,
I'd felt a little thrill that he trusted me in his space. Another bitter
swallow.

"Fucker."

I looked up, shocked and warmed by her immediate defense.

"He was your professor," she said. "You should have reported
him to your university."

"I wasn't in any of his classes." He'd been careful about that,
too, I realized. "Anyway, I loved him. We were together for two
years."

"Loved," Reeti repeated. "Past tense?"

"Y-y-yes." Anything else would be too pathetic.

And yet whatever I told Reeti or myself, there was a part of me
that still needed to get over him. At least in Ireland I wouldn't be
confronted by reminders of him everywhere. The sound of his
laugh down the hall from the office I shared with four other graduate students. The way he'd catch my eye across the table at de-
partmental meetings. His books on my shelf. His sweater in my
closet. A menu from his favorite takeout place at the back of my
kitchen drawer.

"So, did you tell The Ward?"

I dragged my attention back to Reeti. "She already knows. I
mean, obviously she read the book."

"*His* book. She only knows his side of the story."

I managed a smile. "Are you saying I should put Gray in a
book?"

Reeti nodded. "And then kill him."

The real Gray? Or the fictional one? "Or I could avoid Maeve Ward for the rest of the year."

"Bit difficult," Reeti said. "Seeing as you're in her class this term."

"Yeah."

"Right. Better get sloshed then." Reeti smiled and raised her glass. "Cheers."

Relief relaxed my face. I smiled back and took another sip of Guinness, and after the Scary Big Truth about Gray, the next admission was easy. "I don't really like beer," I confessed.

"I never tasted it until I moved to Dublin. I'm sick."

"I'm sorry," I said automatically.

She laughed. "No, British *Sikh*," she repeated, and this time I heard it, that little, almost silent breath at the end. "My grandparents emigrated from Punjab. My family generally avoids alcohol. My father serves it in his restaurants, though. And they don't mind that I drink with my friends."

Friends. The word warmed me more than beer.

"I'm really more of a tea drinker," I said.

"I love chai."

Something uncurled inside me like a smile, like comfort or hope. "I know a place we can get a cup of chai," I said.

T he bells over the door at Clery's Newsagents chimed a welcome as we went in.

The ponytailed poet was behind the counter, his three-day stubble now a beard. He smiled as he took our order, creases flashing in his long, thin face. "Boots! You're back. How's school?"

"Oh." I waved vaguely. Now was not the time to practice my new Honesty-Is-the-Best Friendship Policy. "Okay. I haven't really started yet. I register tomorrow."

He raised an eyebrow. "Good luck with that."

"'Luck is believing you're lucky,'" I quoted back at him, and felt ridiculously rewarded when he laughed.

"Do you come here often?" Reeti asked as we took our seats by the window.

"Just once. A few days ago."

She waggled her eyebrows. "And the hot boy behind the counter is already hitting on you."

My face heated. "Don't be silly. I don't even know his name."

"Sam," he said, setting two thick china mugs on the table.

I felt my blush deepen. "Dee. Dorothy, actually. My name. After my grandmother." I was babbling.

He smiled kindly. "Can I get you something to eat, Dee-Dorothy?"

"No, thank you. We just had dinner."

"Another time, then."

He was only offering to take my order, not suggesting a future date. But my insides melted anyway, warm and golden, like a pat of butter.

"Definitely hitting on you," Reeti said when Sam went back behind the counter. Out of earshot, I hoped.

I resisted the urge to crane around. "He's just being nice. It's part of his job. Like being a bartender."

"He offered you food. That's courtship feeding. Standard mating behavior."

"You asked me to dinner, and you're not hitting on me. Not that there's anything wrong with that," I added. "If you were, I mean."

Hey, I was an ally. My sister, Toni, had been out and proud since she was a junior in high school. Em hadn't said a word when the large pride flag appeared above Toni's bed, but I'd worried my little sister would be bullied in school. But Toni's faith in herself swept through doubts and criticism. That year she'd worn a rainbow dress and an enormous smile to prom, the coolest of her friend group.

"You are not my type. I like men. So we can only be friends." Reeti gave me another tooth-edged smile. "Alas."

"Friends sounds great," I said sincerely. I couldn't believe it. I was out on a Tuesday night with someone my own age, someone young and fun and pretty who wanted to be friends with me.

She picked up her mug. Sniffed. "Also, my parents would be disappointed if I brought home anyone who wasn't Sikh."

"I get it. I'm from Kansas. My family can be pretty conservative, too."

"My parents are very progressive, actually. Although my mother did freak out when I wanted to go away to school."

I thought of Toni. "She was probably worried about your safety."

"Oh yes. She keeps sending me links to articles about the dangers of women living alone."

"That sounds . . ."

"Scary?"

"Caring," I decided.

"Absolutely. My parents are very supportive. But protective. And they expect us to be who they want us to be. Sheena is a lawyer and Rajveer is to be a doctor and I am supposed to get my degree and work in my father's restaurants."

"You cook?"

"Only for my own family. But until I marry, I will work for him in the business office. It is a good job. Financial manager for the London region." A small shrug. "It's just not what I want to do."

"Which is?"

"Teach English."

"How do your parents feel about that?"

"We don't discuss it. My mother is very good at shutting down things she doesn't want to hear. And my father would listen and look at me and not say anything, which is worse."

"I don't understand. What's so bad about being an English teacher?"

"My parents don't object to *what* I want to teach. It's *where* I want to teach that they don't like. When I was in high school, my gurdwara did a camp at the big temple in Southall. There's a huge Punjabi community there. I got to tutor other young girls my age, girls who didn't have my opportunities." Her eyes shone. "Empowering women. It's been my dream ever since."

"And your parents don't approve?"

"They're afraid."

"Of what?"

Reeti shrugged. "Maybe that I'll become too conservative and marry some mama's boy and spend the rest of my life waiting on my husband's family. Or maybe I won't be conservative enough, and I'll piss off some patriarchal arsehole who basically thinks women shouldn't even learn to read, and I'll be attacked walking to the train."

"Does that worry you?"

"I'm not attracted to mama's boys. Or scared of arseholes, really. But I am terrified of disappointing my parents. I am a complete coward where they are concerned."

Her admission felt like a present, a piece of herself given in exchange for my earlier confession about Gray. Like she was trusting me with her truth, too. "Or you love them," I said.

"That, too. What about your parents? Are they happy you are studying in Ireland?"

Unbidden, a memory rose of the scene at the airport, Em's face and Henry's hug as they said good-bye. I took a sip of tea to wash down the lump in my throat. "My mother died when I was twelve. I never knew my father."

"I'm so sorry."

"It's okay. It wasn't like I was raised by wolves or sent to an orphanage or anything. My sister and I—I have a younger sister, Toni—we went to live with my aunt and uncle. My mother's brother."

"But still . . . You were only twelve. I bet that was an adjustment. For everybody."

I didn't talk about it. I didn't think about it—or our mother—very often.

"Yes." The word fell hard and sharp like an ax. An echo of Tim Woodman. To soften it, I smiled and added, "At least I never had to worry about disappointing them." *Because they never wanted me in the first place.* "As long as I did my chores, they pretty much left me alone."

Reeti shook her head. "Amazing."

"It's not that they didn't care," I said, driven to defend them. "But farm life isn't easy." Uncle Henry got up early every morning and was out until dusk—tilling, planting, harvesting in season—sun, work, and worry carving furrows in his face until he resembled the land he lived on. Aunt Em kept the books and the house, paid the bills, and fed us and the farmhands. I helped where I could, collecting eggs and cleaning the chicken coop, weeding the dusty vegetable patch by the house, picking flowers for the kitchen table where Toni and I did our homework. But nothing I did was enough. "By the time Toni and I got dumped on them, they'd given up on the whole idea of children."

"No, I meant . . . You're amazing. Here I am, with every advantage, complaining because I have two loving parents and a guaranteed future and I'm afraid to even tell them what I want. And you have no mother and a shit boyfriend who humiliates you in his stupid book, and you're still going after your dream. You're very brave."

"But I'm not. I have, like, zero confidence." Not in myself. Not in my judgment. Not even in my writing.

"And yet, here you are."

Her unexpected generosity stung tears to my eyes. "Here we are."

She raised her cup. We clinked. "You need to believe in yourself," she said.

I gave a watery chuckle. "I'd settle for Dr. Ward believing in me."

"The witch," Reeti said darkly into her mug. "You should change instructors."

I looked at her in sudden hope. Maybe she was right. Maybe all I needed was a different teacher. And a place to live that didn't charge for the minibar.

"I'll talk to Dr. Norton tomorrow," I said. "Maybe she'll let me switch sections or something."

But tonight . . . I settled into my chair. Tonight, I'd revealed something about myself to someone. And instead of being embarrassed or rejected, I felt . . . seen. Accepted. I curled my hands around the mug, warming myself on the thick china and an unfamiliar sense of freedom.

I snuck another peek at the poet behind the counter.

Tonight, "here" wasn't a bad place to be at all.

SIX

The apartment was a dud.

Reeti had warned me. "Sheriff Street?" she said when I showed her the card thumbtacked to the notice board. "You don't want to live there. That's a super dodgy neighborhood."

I smiled. "Let me guess. Your mother sent you a link with crime statistics."

"She didn't need to." Reeti's eyes were wide with worry. "You know, you could stay with me. At least for a few nights, until you find something else."

"Oh, I couldn't," I protested automatically.

"Of course you can. My parents bought a flat in Ballsbridge. Super safe area. It's a little far to walk, but there's a bus. And you'd have your own bedroom."

I stared at her, speechless with gratitude. *My own room?* At my cool new friend's place. I wanted to say yes. But I didn't want to strain our fledgling friendship, or maybe I didn't quite trust it yet. I didn't have much experience making friends, but moving in together after one night was never a good idea, right? Living with someone destroyed the magic in a relationship. That's what Gray said.

Besides, I wasn't like my mother, always taking advantage. I was putting the days in which I slept on the couches of friends-of-friends behind me. *A fresh start.*

"Thank you," I said, finding my voice. "I . . . Well, that's so nice of you. But I'll be fine. I should at least look at this place."

According to the map on my phone, the rental unit was fifteen minutes' walk beyond the newsagents, behind the Custom House, not far from the river.

After leaving Reeti, I turned right on New Wapping, past a large construction site. Daylight filtered through the gray clouds and narrow streets. It could have been picturesque, with the cobblestone walks and the Georgian buildings split into flats. Except for the wheeled bins overflowing with trash. And the graffiti message painted ten feet high on a long brick wall at the top of the street: GUARDS STAY OUT. RATS STAY OUT.

A woman pushed a baby buggy past a couple of old men chatting in front of an iron grate. A delivery rider buzzed by on a stripped-down motorbike. A group of teenage boys hung out on the corner. I crossed the street to avoid them.

The buzzer was broken for Number 2D. The rental guy— squat and tattooed, with bad teeth—met me in the foyer. I followed him up the stairs to a single room with a slanted ceiling. There was a dingy comforter over the sagging mattress, and a metal desk jammed under the window. I was used to making do, to finding the best in bad accommodations. But the shared bath down the hall was filthy, the lock on the bathroom door didn't work, and the rent was barely within my budget.

"I'll have to think it about it," I told the rental guy.

He grinned, exposing a missing incisor. "Better think fast. Prime place like this won't be around long."

When I came out, the older men were gone. The boys were still on the corner, nudging, talking. Somebody whistled. I tucked my head down and kept walking.

"Looking for something?" one of them called.

I shook my head. Increased my pace.

"I got a thing she can look at."

More whistles as they crossed the road toward me. My stomach sank. *Boys.* Just boys, I told myself, younger than Toni. I rounded my shoulders, closing my body in on itself, as if I could make myself invisible.

They fell in behind me. "Give us a smile, then."

"Where you from?"

No one else was on the street. My heart quickened, along with my footsteps. *Do not engage. Do not escalate.* Down an entire block.

"What's your hurry?"

"Thinks she's too good for us."

"Speak for yourself, faggot."

Another half block, past parked cars and trash bins. Past the empty construction lot. (Another headline for Reeti's mother: *Missing Girl's Body Found in Building Site.*) They were beside me now. In front of me. I hugged my sweater around me like protective armor and turned the corner, praying to see traffic. Pedestrians.

A boy with ears sticking out like a monkey's cut me off. "Fancy a lift?"

"You've got no car, mate."

"Oooh, ride me, then."

A burst of laughter. I averted my face, stepping off the curb to get around them, and almost stumbled.

"Watch yourself!" A hand grabbed my arm.

Another grabbed my butt. I jerked my elbow free. "Let go."

"Ah, here! You lot!" A shout from up ahead.

I looked in the direction of the voice, to where the blue

sign of Clery's Newsagents shone like a patch of sky on the gray block.

Sam stood on the sidewalk, eyebrows raised. "What's this, then?"

The boy who had touched me took a step back, holding up his hands like a kid caught raiding the cookie jar. "We was just slagging, Sam."

"She were alone," Monkey Ears said. "We didn't want her to get lost."

"*You* get lost." The blue-haired girl appeared behind Sam, arms crossed over her impressive bosom. "Fuckers."

There were catcalls and kissy sounds. "Love you, Fee."

"Fuck off, Danny Doyle. Before I tie your tiny dick in a knot."

Sam's gaze cut to the girl. "Get her a cup of tea."

I froze, feeling my tiny measure of control slipping away.

"You can wait inside," Fee said. "If you want."

I forced my feet to move, my legs to stop shaking. "Okay. Thank you."

"I want to talk to you lads," Sam said with quiet menace as I slipped by.

"Ooh, I'm so scared," a boy jeered.

"Or I can come round later and have a word with your mam," Sam said.

"Shit."

The girl touched my arm, kindly pretending not to notice when I flinched. "All right?"

I nodded, shamed and grateful, following her into the shop.

"Chai latte, is it?" she asked, moving behind the counter.

I nodded. "Um. Please." I was reaching for my wallet to pay when Sam came in.

He shook his head. "On the house."

"Don't be too nice to me," I warned. "I'll cry."

"Look, they're obnoxious little shits, but they won't bother you again."

"Unless they're high," the girl said, setting down the thick white mug. "Or pissed."

"What were you doing anyway?" Sam asked me.

"Looking at apartments."

The girl rounded on him. "What does it matter what she was doing? Don't blame the victim."

He looked taken aback. "I wasn't. But you're an outsider," he said to me. "That makes you a target. Best to ignore them and move on."

I nodded. That's what I'd always done, what I saw other women do, accepting the catcalls, come-ons, and lurking threats as the cost of being a woman—the crime of being female in public.

"Hard to ignore," Fee said. "When they're following you around, making comments on your body like you're a fecking statue in the park. Entitled pricks. They only run off at the mouth because they think they can get away with it."

Sam frowned. "They don't bother *you*, do they?"

"They try. Pick on the gay girl, right? It's practically a sport to them."

"I'll talk to them."

"I don't need you to protect me, brother dear. I can take care of myself. And Gracie and Aoife, if it comes to that."

She sounded so much like Toni that I smiled. "I wish I were as brave as you."

"Don't be brave," Sam said. "Be smart."

I picked up my mug and sat at my little table, waiting for my heart rate to slow. It was oddly soothing, watching Sam sell things from behind the register—Tayto Crisps and a liter carton of milk to a young woman in black tights, a Cadbury bar and a copy of the

Irish Times to an older gentleman, everything the same and subtly not-the-same as a convenience store in Kansas.

"You're here a lot," I said when there was a break in the line and he'd picked up his book again.

He looked up and winked. "Could say the same of you."

I buried my blush in my mug, breathing in the milky sweetness and familiar scent of spices. "Because I like it here."

"Ta."

He didn't say he liked it, I noticed. "It seems like a nice place to work."

Fee snorted.

"It's all right," Sam said.

"Except the boss is thick as a plank," Fee added.

"The boss?" I looked from her to Sam. "This is your place," I realized. "Clery's Newsagents. You're . . ."

He nodded. "Sam Clery."

"Fiadh Clery." It sounded so pretty. *FEE-uh*.

"Dee Gale."

I bit my lip as soon as the words were out. But what was the harm, really, in sharing my name? I was glad to be more than an anonymous crime statistic, an unidentified victim in one of Reeti's mother's stories. It felt good to be seen, to be recognized as a regular—the American girl in cowboy boots. Like I was reclaiming a little piece of myself or constructing a new identity.

Besides, there was no reason why Sam should associate me with the fictional Destiny Gayle. Just because he could quote Tennessee Williams didn't mean he read Grayson Kettering.

But Dr. Ward did. She was probably showing Gray's book around the faculty room right now.

The tea in my stomach turned to acid.

"Sure you're all right?" Sam asked. "Need anything else?"

A new instructor.

I banished whatever expression he'd seen on my face. Smiled. "I'm good, thanks."

Or I would be, as soon as I met with Dr. Norton.

don't quite understand." Glenda Norton's perfect brow pleated slightly. "Do you have a problem working with Dr. Ward?"

I winced. "Not a problem." I didn't want this wonderful woman to see me as a student with a problem. A problem student. Any kind of problem. "It's only . . . I just wondered if it would be possible for me to change classes."

"I'm afraid not. The writing workshop is a required module."

"Right. Of course. But if I could maybe transfer to a different section . . . Another teacher . . ."

She blinked in pretty confusion. "There is no other teacher. Not since Dr. Eastwick . . ." *Died. Killed by a falling house.* "Became unavailable."

"I just don't think we're a good fit," I said humbly.

"That's unfortunate." Glenda sighed. "You're not the only one to express reservations. Maeve was concerned you might have . . ." She trailed off delicately.

"Have . . . ?"

"Difficulties with, ah, faculty supervision." She gave me an apologetic look. "Because of your experience in your previous program."

Gray. She meant Gray. My pulse throbbed in my ears. Obviously, my secret was out. "But he wasn't . . . I didn't have any problems with my faculty advisor at KU."

"No?"

"No." *Not really.*

During our last meeting in his office, Barry, my advisor, had been regretful. And deeply uncomfortable. After two years of me blowing him off, I hadn't really expected anything more. *"An allegation of sexual misconduct could ruin Gray's reputation. It might even destroy his career,"* my advisor had said. *"Is that what you want?"*

Of course I'd said no.

I'd still been reeling from that last horrible, tearful confrontation with Gray. The problem (that word again!) was that Gray had made it painfully clear that I'd already lost everything I'd ever wanted—his love, his approval, his respect. Based on his novel, I didn't deserve them. I didn't deserve him. A meeting with my advisor wasn't going to fix that.

"I can't discourage you from filing a complaint. Naturally, the university disapproves of any relationship where there's a professional power differential," Barry had said. He leaned forward as if to pat my hand and then drew back, clearly thinking better of initiating physical contact with a student. *"But you've admitted the relationship was consensual. As long as Gray was never in a position to evaluate your work . . ."*

"It's not my *work I'm upset about,"* I'd said. Two *years* when I should have been writing my thesis, wasted. *"It's his.* Destiny Gayle."

Barry had dropped his gaze, straightening a folder on his desk. *"Unfortunately, whatever fictional liberties Gray may have taken with you— that is, with your character—er, with Destiny—are not within the scope of the faculty committee to address."*

"I'm happy to hear it," Glenda said, jerking me back to the present. She smiled, obviously pleased to have dispensed with the problem (aka, me). "Then, if that's all . . ."

Wait. What? "What about Dr. Ward?"

Her smile froze slightly. "We have a limited number of faculty at the writing center. All of our students take one writing module with each of our two workshop instructors. So even if I accommodated your request, you would still have Maeve as an instructor next term. I am very grateful to her for her willingness to step in for Dr. Eastwick at the last minute. As, I imagine, you must be."

"But she doesn't like me."

"Oh, my dear. She doesn't need to like you to supervise your work." Glenda glanced at her phone, clearly ready to move on.

I knotted my hands together in my lap. Reeti said I was brave. Sam thought I was smart. It was stupid to keep ignoring the big Gray elephant in the room. Stupid and cowardly. "Right. The thing is, I think she's judging me on the basis of Gray's book."

Glenda sighed. "You're referring to Kettering's novel."

I nodded.

"I'm certain your instructors and examiners will consider your work entirely on its own merits. If, when the time comes to start work formally on your dissertation, you find one of them a better 'fit,' as you say, I'd encourage you to apply to them. In the meantime, Maeve is highly qualified. She's quite capable of evaluating you apart from anything Kettering may have written."

Have you read it? I was desperate to ask. But my courage didn't extend that far.

Besides, Glenda was already gathering up her things, reaching for her phone, opening a drawer to retrieve her bag, every movement signaling that this conversation was over. "So, now that's settled, you'll have to excuse me. I need to pick up the girls from school. If there's nothing else . . . ?"

"Just . . . My housing? I went to the Student Union, like you said, but—"

Her phone buzzed. "Of course, of course. You might consider getting a roommate." She glanced from the phone to me, her expression clearly saying, *Go away now, please.* "Excuse me. I have to take this."

"Okay. Sure." I stood, reluctantly. "Thank you for your . . ."

"Hello? Yes, Richard, I got your email. I'm afraid now isn't a good . . ." Another confused look—*Why are you still here?*—before she turned her back on me. "Oh dear. I really can't," I heard her say as I lingered in the doorway. "I have to pick up . . . Yes. Yes, of course, I understand. All right. Five minutes."

She ended the call. "Shit."

"I could get them," I heard myself say.

"Excuse me?"

I took a step forward. "Your daughters? I could pick them up from school." I wanted to make myself useful. I wanted her to like me.

Her blue eyes rested on me thoughtfully. "I suppose you're quite trustworthy."

"Totally," I promised. "I used to watch my sister all the time."

"If it were anyone but Richard . . . And you *are* in the program."

I held my breath. *I was in the program.*

"Yes. All right." She smiled suddenly, making us allies. "Some of my colleagues still behave as if a penis is a prerequisite for serious scholarship. As a mother, I simply can't appear to ask for special treatment."

I smiled back, honored by her confiding in me. Trusting me. "I'm happy to help."

"Sophie has football practice."

"I can take her. As long as it's not too far." I didn't have a car. Maybe I could call a cab?

"There's a bus. Quite simple. Lily knows the way. But the school won't release Sophie to her sister unless I make prior arrangements."

I nodded sympathetically. "I get it. I used to have the same problem with Toni. My sister." By the time I was nine, I had become an expert at forging our mother's signature on release forms and permission slips. A fact I did not share. But I asked, "Is there some kind of form or—"

"I need to call the school."

"I can wait."

But she was already speaking into her phone, one finger raised in the universal gesture for *Don't interrupt.* "Glenda Norton. I need to authorize an emergency pickup. Yes, for today." She opened a drawer and withdrew a sheet of paper. "You'll have to take this with you," she said to me.

She trusted me! "Sure."

She bent over her desk, pen poised. "Dee, you said?"

I gaped. Didn't she know my name? "Um. It's Dorothy, actually. Dorothy Gale." I spelled it for her, just in case. "G-a-l-e."

She wrote it down, scrawling her signature with a flourish. "There. You'll need to show ID at the office."

I listened as she gave bus routes and directions, grateful to have specific marching orders.

She handed me the form. "Lily and Sophie. If they ask, our safe word is 'hairbrush.'"

"Hairbrush." I committed it to memory.

"Give me your phone number." I entered it into her phone. "My husband will pick up the girls after practice. You'll stay until he gets there."

"No problem," I assured her.

I was used to accommodating someone else's schedule—those friends-of-friends, Aunt Em, or Gray. Helping out. Fitting in. *Not a problem*, that was me.

"So helpful," she murmured.

I beamed, feeling as though I were finally getting somewhere with her.

And if it felt a lot like someplace I'd been before . . . Well, that wasn't a problem, either.

SEVEN

"C an you watch the register for a couple hours?" Sam asked Fiadh.

His sister widened her eyes in exaggerated shock. "You're leaving the shop?"

"I am, yeah."

"What's the occasion?"

"I thought I'd take a look in at Aoife's practice."

"Since when are you interested in our sister playing football? It's not like you can give her pointers."

Sam grinned, acknowledging the hit. He'd always been rubbish at sports. "I just want to see how she's getting on."

Aoife played youth football at the community center after school. Their brother, Jack, did, too, on alternating days. Young people needed activities to keep them out of mischief, their mother, Janette, said. But after today, Sam wasn't so sure. The park was safe enough during the day. Practice was supervised, the teams coached by off-duty police or reformed thugs or well-meaning volunteers from the other side of the river. But . . .

"Ah Jesus," Fiadh said, her eyes narrowing. "This is about those fecking boys, isn't it? You're doing that man-of-the-family shit again. Keeping an eye on the womenfolk."

He shrugged, not denying it. The memory of Dee's white face as she sat in his shop, her fingers curled around her mug, hadn't left him all day. "*I can take care of myself,*" Fee had boasted. But Aoife was only eleven. It was stupid, backward, sexist—but if the neighbor boys were messing with his sisters, Sam had to know.

"You know our Gracie goes with her to practice," Fiadh said.

"All the more reason to check in." Sixteen-year-old Grace was the smart one in the family now, gentle and studious. What if something got in the way of her going to university? A rape. A baby. Sam couldn't stand it. "I don't want any of those boyos bothering her."

"What are you going to do if they are? Challenge them to a duel?"

"I thought I'd wag my dick at them."

She gave him a playful shove. "Sure, there's a sight would scare anyone off."

"Look, will you mind the register or not?"

"Fine." Fiadh waved him off. "Go. But when I told you to get out of the shop, I didn't mean for you to hang around the football pitch flexing and being manly."

He smiled. "I'll leave the flexing to you."

Other boys saw sports as a way out, an escape to a better life. Not Sam. Between school and the shop, there'd been no time for football, even if he'd wanted to play. Which he did not. He was a skinny, awkward kid—a reader like Grace, a dreamer like their mother, a teacher's pet. He'd survived by becoming a bit of a clown, speaking up in class as often to joke as to answer a question. He'd learned to downplay his grades, to keep his mouth shut about his exam results. He'd been almost as surprised as everyone else when he was accepted to Trinity.

Not so surprised when it all ended.

The field was divided in half for practice, with two different teams running drills on opposite sides.

Aoife was easy to spot, her ponytail flying like a flag behind her. Sam watched her run up and down the pitch, legs pumping, face scowling with fierce determination. She and Jack took after their father, strong and quick and confident.

Grace sat on a bench, reading.

And there on the sidelines, as if his thoughts had conjured her out of the damp air, was the girl—Dee, Dorothy Gale—clutching a water bottle, backpacks on the ground at her feet, like some football mum bringing her kids to practice.

A very young, pretty mum. In cowboy boots.

Watching her, Sam felt a tug of resentment. She was looking about her with big, wide eyes, like the world was this magical place and she was simply waiting for her adventure to begin. So hopeful, so eager, so . . . American.

And then he remembered her face when she came into his shop that morning and was ashamed.

He strolled over. "Which one's yours?"

"Oh." She jumped and then smiled. The curve of her lips was like a touch on his skin, light and intimate. "Hi. None of them. That is, those two. That's Sophie, playing"—she nodded toward one of Aoife's teammates—"and that's Lily, sitting on the Ping-Pong table, pretending she doesn't know us. I'm watching them until their father picks them up."

He smiled back. "So, you're a nanny now."

"Oh no. Their mother is one of my professors. I'm just helping out. Are you . . ." She glanced at the few adults on the sidelines. "Here with anyone?"

"My sister. Aoife." He jerked his chin toward her, driving toward the rusty goal. "And our Gracie, over there with her nose in a book."

"You have three sisters?"

"That's right, Aoife, Grace, and Fiadh. And a brother, Jack."

"It must be nice to come from a large family."

"Sure. Unless you need to use the toilet."

She laughed. "Sharing a bathroom is hard. Even with one sister."

There was a break in the action on the other side of the field. A boyo from the other side left his teammates and approached Grace. Sam gave him a slit-eyed look.

The boys' coach caught him glaring and came over, his legs like pale tree trunks under shorts, a whistle around his neck. He was Sam's height and a good two stones heavier, like he ate raw eggs for breakfast. A regular rugger bugger.

"Hello," he said. Not to Sam. To Dee.

"Hi." She greeted him with the same smile she'd given Sam. Maybe a little more guarded. "I didn't recognize you without your suit. I mean, your glasses." Her face turned pink.

"Contacts," he said briefly. He nodded to Sam.

"Oh, I'm sorry," Dee said, all flustered-like. "Tim Woodman, this is Sam Clery."

Tim put his hand out. "I know you." His accent was posh, his handshake firm and a bit stiff.

"Don't think so, mate," Sam said, nasal and quick.

"I recognize you. From Trinity dining hall."

Working behind a shop counter, you learned to remember faces, even if you forgot names. This one came back to Sam. He'd served him in the eating Commons, under the old portraits of privileged men of previous generations.

"You worked at Trinity?" Dee asked.

"He went to Trinity," Tim said. "Only students serve at dinner."

The financial aid students, dressed in black like waiters, to distinguish them from the dining Scholars.

Another year, and Sam could have been one of them. When the university scholarships were announced in April of his freshman year, Sam had stood in the square and heard the Provost call his name. His mam had been so proud. His da . . . Well. Martin Clery believed you learned more from the school of hard knocks than from any university. But to Sam, the recognition had been more than an honor, more than an acknowledgment of his hard work. It meant money: tuition paid, housing paid, a free meal in the dining hall every day. It meant freedom from guilt over his parents' sacrifice, over leaving the shop behind.

His da died six weeks later. June 19th. The day of the funeral, the shop was closed. Out of respect, Janette said. The day after, Sam opened it up. He hadn't left since.

"It was a long time ago," he said.

"It's good to see you again," Tim said politely. He did not ask what Sam was doing here or what he was up to now. He glanced over his shoulder at his team of young louts. "I should get back to them."

"I'm surprised you have time to coach," Dee said.

He moved his shoulders, apparently uncomfortable. "The firm sponsors the team. Community involvement. Excuse me." Another nod and he trotted off, like a good show pony.

Dee turned her deep-brown gaze on Sam. "What did you study at Trinity?"

It was his turn to squirm. "English," he admitted.

Her smile this time dazzled. It caught him right between the eyes. "Like me." Her phone buzzed. Her smile faded. "Sorry, I have to . . ." She dug in her bag, dropping the water bottle.

Sam listened shamelessly as he stooped to pick it up.

"Right here . . . Yeah, of course . . . No, I don't mind at all."

"That was my professor," Dee explained, tucking the phone away. "Her husband isn't coming. I have to take the girls home."

Sam raised his brows. "Bit of an ask, isn't it? On such short notice."

"I don't mind. I like to feel useful. Anyway, they shouldn't walk alone."

"Neither should you."

"I'll be all right. I'm significantly older than they are." She smiled bravely. "Anyway, it's only as far as the bus stop."

She was right. He was being stupid. It was broad daylight. His sisters took the bus home every day.

Frowning, he watched the boys milling about the other end of the field. "I'll walk with you."

"I don't want to be a bother."

"No bother." He winked. "It's on our way."

EIGHT

Glenda Norton lived in a narrow-fronted town house near St. Stephen's Green.

I stared up at the entrance, guarded by elegant iron railings and crowned with a fanlight, and wondered how it would feel to belong in a house like that. Also, I wondered what Mr. Professor Norton did for a living. Because having spent the better part of a week searching for someplace to live, I was pretty sure you couldn't afford that house on a teacher's salary.

Sophie ran lightly up the shallow stone steps. A princess, returning home.

The front door was painted bright blue with a yellow brass knob and knocker. I half expected a hobbit to answer the bell. Or a Minnipin. Or at least a butler.

But then Lily pulled a key on a lanyard from her book bag. As she fit it into the shiny lock, the door opened from the inside, and a figure stood framed in the light of the hall. Not a hobbit. Not even a butler, though he was every bit as intimidating. A tall man in tweeds, with a round, intelligent face and aristocratically gray-ing hair.

"Daddy!" Sophie said.

"Hello, munchkins." He patted both girls absently, smiling at me over their heads. "You must be the sitter."

"Yeah, hi." I hung back at the bottom of the steps, still clutch-ing Sophie's book bag. "I didn't know anyone would be home yet." "*Poor James has to work late,*" Glenda had said with a put-upon sigh. "*So if you wouldn't mind . . .*" And of course I didn't. Anything to earn her good opinion.

"James Norton. But where are my manners?" He stepped back from the open door. "Please, come in."

The hall was tiled in black-and-white marble. A big gilt mirror reflected back a humongous bouquet of actual flowers, lilies and stuff, like an arrangement from a hotel lobby or a very fancy wed-ding reception. I stopped dead on the exquisitely patterned rug, Aunt Em's voice in my head shouting, "*Wipe your feet.*" (Her stan-dard after-school greeting. As if every day would be the one time I forgot and tracked the muck of the barnyard onto her nice clean floor.)

"I suppose you girls should get started on your homework," James said.

Lily frowned. "But we just got home."

"Snack first, Daddy," Sophie said.

"Snack. Yes. Of course." He cleared his throat. "The thing is . . . Sharon has already left for the day. Maybe when Mummy gets home . . ."

"What time?" Lily demanded.

"But I'm hungry now," Sophie said, sounding like a much younger Toni. "When's dinner?"

"Ah, dinner. That's another domestic dilemma, isn't it?"

"I could get them something," I heard myself say.

"That's very kind of you. Why don't you girls show . . ."

"Dee," I said.

"Dee to the kitchen."

I followed the girls' smooth blond heads down the narrow hallway, feeling like a total interloper.

"Make yourself at home," James said behind me.

Right. Anything less like home would be hard to imagine. The kitchen was the size of a dragon's cave, with concrete countertops and modern light fixtures that looked like they belonged in an art museum. Or a dungeon.

I had a flash of memory—Aunt Em, sitting me down at the farmhouse table before she shooed me outside to start my chores. Apple slices and peanut butter almost every day, the same snack that she fed Toni, the same snack she gave us on all those visits before our mother died. No store-bought treats, no home-made cookies, nothing that could spoil our dinner from Aunt Em, no, ma'am. Still, there was something reassuring about the routine. About knowing what you were getting. About watching her bustle around the kitchen making dinner while I recovered from whatever had happened at school that day.

I took a deep breath and opened the fridge. *Apples.* Hooray. "Do you have any peanut butter?" Did Irish children eat peanut butter?

Sophie slid off her stool. "I'll get it."

"I'm fairly certain I know where the tea things are," James said. "If you'd like a cup."

"I don't want to intrude."

"Not at all. I could join you," he suggested.

"It's not . . ." I met his expectant gaze. *Oh.* "That is, would you like some tea?"

He smiled charmingly. "Tea sounds wonderful. Girls, do you want tea?"

"I want soda," Lily said.

I looked at James, who shrugged. "I'm having tea," I said brightly. "With milk and sugar. How does that sound?"

It sounded okay.

"This is very nice," James said when he and the girls were all seated at the island with tea and a plate of peeled apple slices. "We've been lost since our last au pair left. Our housekeeper does what she can, but she's not exactly stimulating company for the girls. However did Glenda find you?"

"Oh, she didn't . . . I mean, I'm not . . . I'm just helping out."

"Well, we're very grateful. Aren't we, girls?"

Sophie stuck an apple slice into her peanut butter.

Lily glanced from her father to me. "I guess."

"So, what is it that you do when you're not 'helping out,' Dee?" James asked.

"I'm a graduate student at Trinity. In the writing program."

He smiled slightly. "And now all is explained. How are you finding school?"

"I haven't started classes yet." Sophie had spilled her tea. I wiped it up. "I've mostly been looking for a place to live."

"Ah yes, the Dublin housing shortage. As global companies move in, it's definitely increased demand for rental properties. We need more construction in this city."

"I passed a construction site this morning."

"Obviously, there are cranes everywhere. The skyline is a disaster. But what's being built is offices, hotels, luxury apartments. Not a lot out there for your average renter. And the lack of planning for social housing has only made things worse."

"Don't get James started on the lack of urban planning. He's an architect." Glenda stood in the kitchen doorway. "You're home early," she said to her husband.

"Client decided to make it a Zoom meeting. And you're rather late. The girls and I missed you."

Her gaze skated over the kitchen island—four mugs, a plate, two little bowls smeared with peanut butter. "You look very cozy to me."

I felt suddenly awkward. "I should go."

"Don't rush off on Glenda's account. Dee here was telling me she's having trouble finding housing," James said.

Glenda sighed. "A perennial student problem, I'm afraid."

"I thought perhaps we might offer her a solution."

A look passed between them. "Girls, it's homework time," Glenda said.

Sophie slid obediently off her stool.

"I don't have any homework," Lily said.

"I thought you had a story due in English," Glenda said.

"Mom. Not until Monday."

"Which means you should get started now."

"I don't want to. It's boring. School is boring. I don't like any of my classes, except art."

Glenda's face froze. I felt a stab of sympathy for her. She was a senior female academic. Her daughter's contempt for school must feel like a personal rejection.

"You like to draw?" I asked.

"Yeah. So?" asked Lily.

It was really none of my business. I rinsed my tea mug in the sink. "I was just wondering . . . Would your teacher let you tell your story with pictures? Like a comic book."

"That would be cool."

"Get out the assignment and we'll see," Glenda said.

"It's in my room."

Glenda raised her eyebrows in gentle reproof.

"Fine," Lily grumbled, and stomped upstairs with her sister.

I cleared their snack bowls from the marble island.

"I don't see how drawing pictures helps develop her writing," James said.

I swallowed. "Well . . ."

"Comics require creating a story line, organizing and presenting ideas, and producing dialogue. All very pertinent skills." Glenda looked at me. "You're good with children."

I flushed at her praise. Okay, so she wasn't complimenting my writing or my out-of-the-box thinking. But her approval still made me feel good. "Toni—my sister?—she was sort of the same way." Disinterested in study, always drawing in the margins of her notebooks. "I used to find things for her to do." Keeping her busy. Keeping her happy. Keeping her quiet, so we didn't disturb whoever we were staying with.

I put my empty mug in the dishwasher along with the girls' bowls.

"You took care of her, you said."

I beamed. "That's right. Toni was only four when our mother—"

"Our previous au pair lived with the family," Glenda continued as if she hadn't heard. "We really had no choice. Someone had to be here full-time. James and I were both working from home during the pandemic, and with the girls learning online . . . Well, you can imagine."

I nodded sympathetically. Online learning had been tough for Toni, too.

"Obviously, now that Lily and Sophie are attending school in person, they don't require the same level of supervision. But the room is empty. And it occurs to me . . ."

Hope rose in my throat. I waited breathlessly. Was she offering to let me *live* with her?

"Perhaps you might consider helping out with the girls. Not at the same salary as our previous au pair, of course. It's not as if you would be taking care of the girls full-time. But you did say you need a place to stay."

"You want me to work for you?"

"I don't want you to feel any pressure. You're a student in the department. But there would obviously be . . . advantages to the arrangement. For both of us." She smiled. "You'd almost be like one of the family. Temporarily, of course."

I knew all about being a temporary member of a family. "I'd love to," I said.

don't get it," Reeti said. It was Sunday—my day off—and she had invited me for dinner. "You didn't want to stay with me. Why are you moving in with Dr. Norton?"

"She's paying me."

"Au pairs make shit."

I was making less than the previous au pair. "Every little bit helps."

I was lucky. Our mother's trust paid my tuition and left me a cushion to live on. But this trip to Dublin—and the extra two years I'd spent in the program at KU—had definitely made a dent in the fund.

"Anyway, it's only temporary," I said. "Until I find a place of my own."

Reeti stirred the pan simmering on the stove, chicken in a thick red sauce. It smelled delicious, spicy and unfamiliar. "Living with me would also be temporary. What's the difference?"

Was that a flash of hurt in her eyes? "I don't want to impose," I said. "You've already done so much for me."

"Like what?"

You're my friend. But that sounded pathetic. "You're making me dinner."

"You brought dessert."

"Because the girls and I baked cookies yesterday," I said.

"And flowers."

"They were so pretty I couldn't resist."

Reeti waved her dripping spoon at me. "My point is, we're friends. You don't need to pay me back for an invitation. Friends do things for one another. It is my pleasure to have you."

Her words curled warmly around my heart. *It is my pleasure to have you.* But the fear remained that I was somehow pushing myself on her, like an inconvenient child being dumped on a reluctant friend. Like a presumptuous girlfriend taking up drawer space, leaving a toothbrush and tampons at her lover's house. Could I really be welcome?

Impossible to ask.

"Thanks," I said instead. Napkins and place mats were stacked on the counter. I found forks and knives in a drawer and started to set the table. "That smells amazing. What is it?"

"Butter chicken." She drizzled a swirl of heavy cream over the red sauce.

A sound penetrated the apartment. Banging. Knocking. "Are you expecting more company?"

"No." Reeti lifted the lid of a saucepan filled with fluffy rice. "Just us."

"That's a lot of food for two people," I said.

She smiled ruefully. "Blame my parents. My mother always makes enough for langar—community meal—at temple. And my father cooks for a restaurant full of people, so . . ." She shrugged. "You can take leftovers home."

I thought of Glenda's modern kitchen, the half shelf that had been designated as mine in the refrigerator.

"Unless you eat all your meals with the family," Reeti added.

So far I'd made the girls lunch, twice. And last night, when their parents went out, I heated soup and fixed grilled cheese sandwiches for the three of us. Despite watching all six seasons of *Downton Abbey*, I wasn't exactly sure of my place in the Nortons' household. Was I a guest? Was I the help? Or was I something in between? "We don't really have a routine yet," I said. "But I'd love to have leftovers. Thanks."

Another thump from the hall outside.

"Did you hear that?"

Reeti sprinkled something green on the chicken dish. "It's just the neighbors."

Her building was divided into four large apartments set above the street, two upstairs and two down. "Are they okay?"

"Yes. Shit. No. I should check. The lady across the hall is ninety-one."

She banged the lid back on the pot, stalked through the apartment, and flung open the door. "What are you doing?"

A man's voice came up the stairs. "The banister is loose."

I stopped. That voice . . . Did I know that voice?

"Did you call maintenance?" Reeti asked.

"I did." Cool. Clipped. Passionless. *Tim Woodman.*

"And?" Reeti prompted.

I edged to the doorway. Reeti was leaning over the landing rail. Below her I could see the top of Tim's head, his thick, dark hair, and then his shoulders, filling out his dress shirt.

"Bernie tried installing a bracket, but there's too much distance between the wall and the railing. It's not secure. I made a standoff block to attach the bracket to the rim joist."

"I just love it when you talk carpenter," Reeti said. "I'm getting handyman fantasies."

His face was wooden.

"You did it for her, didn't you?" I said to Tim. "Your ninety-one-year-old neighbor."

"Mrs. Kinsella," Reeti said. "Aw, that's so sweet. Come up when you're done."

"I don't . . ." He hesitated, his gaze flickering to me. "Perhaps for a moment."

While Reeti dished up, I set another place at the table. Five minutes later, Tim knocked politely on the open door.

"Come in," Reeti called.

He stopped on the threshold, his gaze traveling over the table. One hand rubbed absently at his chest. "You're having dinner."

"*We* are having dinner. Consider it thanks for fixing the banister."

"I don't need to be rewarded for taking a simple safety precaution," he said stiffly.

"It's okay," I assured him. "Reeti doesn't believe in payback. But she does believe in friends doing nice things for one another."

"We hardly know each other."

"And we won't as long as you have that giant stick up your arse," Reeti said.

His breath gusted out, a huff of . . . amusement? Annoyance?

I smothered a grin. "Please stay. I promise I won't put you in a book."

"It would be a very boring story if you did," he said dryly.

I wasn't so sure. There were layers to this guy.

"Sit," Reeti commanded.

"I need to wash my hands first," he said.

She made an elaborate gesture toward the kitchen. "Be my guest."

He washed his hands at the sink, drying them on a dish towel before rolling down his shirtsleeves. He had nice forearms, I noticed as he buttoned his cuffs.

"How long have you been neighbors?" I asked after we sat down. Smoothing things over. I was good at that.

"A year," Tim said.

"Where did you live before?" Reeti asked.

He hesitated. "London, mostly." No mention of his time in Afghanistan.

"I've been here five years." She scrunched her nose. "My parents wanted me to live near the gurdwara. Plus, they thought a flat would be a good investment."

"They're right," Tim said. "About the investment, at least. There's a limited supply of housing in Dublin and continued growth, especially in the technology and financial sectors."

"James says most of the new construction is offices and luxury apartments," I offered.

"'James'?" Reeti echoed.

"Glenda Norton's husband."

"Hm."

"Who is Glenda Norton?" Tim asked.

"A professor at Trinity. She invited me to stay with her while I look for an apartment. I'm watching her kids."

"The little blond girl at football practice."

"Sophie, yes. And her sister, Lily. They're very nice, and the house is gorgeous. It's like living with the Banks family."

"Who?" Reeti asked.

"*Mary Poppins*?"

"Blown in on the east wind," Tim murmured.

"That's the one with the neglectful mother and the shit dad, yeah?" Reeti said. "I heard there was a problem with the last au pair. I'd watch out if I were you. The last thing you need is some other fucker bothering you."

I swallowed hard, conscious of Tim across the table, a heat rising in my cheeks that had nothing to do with the spice levels in the chicken. "It's not like that. At all." I was valued. I was needed. An integral part of the family. Temporarily.

"Don't let them take advantage," Reeti said.

"I won't. I'm not. Glenda made it clear that once classes start, my first priority has to be school. I'm really lucky to be working for her."

"Because of the room."

"Because of the room and because she's, like, an ally in the department now," I said earnestly. Which I needed, since my writing instructor didn't like me.

"Just be careful around the husband. Or you'll not only be out of the house, you could be out of the program. Sucks, but there it is." Her voice was sympathetic. "The girl always gets blamed."

My throat went dry. *The girl always gets blamed.*

"I wouldn't think being an au pair would leave you much time to study," Tim said.

I took a gulp of water. "You work and go to school."

"That's different." He ate neatly, knife in the right hand, fork in the left, tines down. "I have set hours."

"And no social life," Reeti said.

A faint flush stained his cheekbones.

"Tim coaches soccer," I said. "Football, I mean."

"Good for you. Where?" Reeti asked.

"We sponsor a team on the north side."

"Reeti wants to teach English to at-risk girls in Southall," I said, relieved at the turn in the conversation.

"I thought you were in the business school," Tim said to her.

"I am. I'm going to work for my father after I get my diploma. Baljeet Singh, the chef."

"Your father is Bobby Singh? I've eaten at his restaurant in London."

"Daddy-ji's very talented. I'm super proud of him. But I don't want to be his accountant."

Tim rubbed two fingers absently against his sternum. "I understand parental pressure. But you can work for your father and still volunteer. Our company partners with several nonprofits. Community service is good business practice."

She gave him a feline grin. "Saving the world for investment bankers?"

He picked up his knife again. "If people with money don't improve society, who will?"

"You do more than give money," I said.

"It's important to set an example," he said stiffly. "Studies have shown that integrating volunteer programs with corporate giving improves employee satisfaction and retention, which ultimately saves the company money."

"So, you volunteer to improve your bottom line," Reeti said.

"My personal feelings aren't relevant." He set his knife and fork parallel in the center of his empty plate. "I'm not a very sentimental man," he said almost apologetically.

"*When someone tells you who they are, believe them,*" Oprah said. Or maybe that was Maya Angelou. Or was it, when someone *shows* you who they are?

Because the heartless suit spouting corporate speak was not the Tim Woodman who coached football and repaired banisters for little old ladies.

"What are you doing?" Reeti asked.

I looked down at the stacked plates in my hands. "Clearing the table."

"Sit down. Talk."

"I don't mind," I said honestly. "I like being useful."

"Dee, you don't have to be useful to be liked. Not here, anyway."

I blinked at her. "I can talk and load the dishwasher at the same time."

Tim stood and carried his plate through to the kitchen. "Actually, multitasking has been shown to decrease productivity."

"Only in men," Reeti said. "Women do it all the time."

Which is how the three of us ended up in the kitchen, doing dishes and chatting about not much of anything at all. That warm feeling around my heart was back. It took me a minute to recognize it.

Happiness.

NINE

had three classes a week. Leaving me with plenty of time, as Glenda said, to look after the girls and explore the city.

I'd never been to Orlando, but Dublin was what I'd pictured Wizarding World to be, quaint shops and strange things to eat and drink. Flowers everywhere, spilling from stalls and planters, crowding tiny gardens, springing from chimney pots and cracks in the cobblestones. And tourists, and music floating out of unexpected places, and the old library, like Hogwarts, dreaming at the center of it all.

At night, on my evenings off, I went out with Reeti to pubs or hung out in her flat, watching cooking shows on television. Sometimes we crossed the bridge, dropping in on Sam for tea and a chat. During the day, while Lily and Sophie were in school, I poked along the market stalls, buying vintage sweaters to ward off the chill, searching the bookstores for authors Sam had recommended. Dublin was everything I'd hoped for or imagined.

And then there were the seven hours a week I spent in class.

With sixteen students—total—in the writing program, there was no place to hide. Even in this diverse group of writers, I didn't fit in. It was my accent. Or my boots. Or the fact that I was sleeping with one of the professors.

I winced. Not that I was sleeping with Glenda, except literally. I was rooming in her house, taking care of her children. But working as her nanny definitely put me in an awkward position, somewhere both above and below my classmates on the social scale.

They were all so smart. I listened to them volunteer their opinions in class, these cool girls and earnest boys, so confident of their talent, their causes, and their clothes, and felt like a total impostor.

I spent hours in the library, reading the assigned texts and catching up on the hundred or so years of Irish literature that had not been part of my education until now. I read alone in my room at night and in the common room before class, hoping, fearing someone would talk to me. Constantly expecting someone to say, *Dee Gale? Any relation to Destiny Gayle?* and then laugh, and it wouldn't be a joke.

"Adjusting to a new school is always hard," I told Toni at the end of September. I was leaving the writing center through the seldom-used front door, bag on one shoulder, phone in my other hand. "You remember."

Or maybe not. She was only four, an active, happy kid, when we went to live with Uncle Henry and Aunt Em for good.

"Hard for you, maybe," Toni said. "I would love to go to a different school."

When our mother went away, it became my job to watch over Toni, to comb her hair and zip her coat and hold her hand crossing the street. After Mom died, I carried on the way I thought she would want me to, teaching my little sister to tie her shoes, putting a dollar under her pillow when she lost a tooth. But now I had exactly fourteen minutes to meet Lily and Sophie before school let out. I hurried to the corner. "It's natural to be homesick."

"I'm not homesick. I hate it here."

"Give it time," I said. "Once you get involved—"

"It's been *six weeks*." She made it sound like an eternity.

"How are things going with your roommate? Madison?"

"Fine. We don't really hang out together. Her boyfriend is here, so she's either at his place or I'm sleeping in the lounge."

I hummed sympathetically. "But you have other friends."

"You're kidding, right?" I could hear her eye roll through the phone. "Half my graduating class is here. It's like I never left high school."

"You'll meet new people, too," I said. "Maybe if you signed up for some clubs . . ."

"Dodo, you're not listening to me."

Guilty. "Sorry, honey. I have to pick up Sophie for soccer practice."

"It's like you care about them more than you care about me."

The guilt intensified. "You know that's not true. I'm in a hurry, that's all. My workshop ran late."

The three-hour workshop, where students read and gave feedback on one another's work. We'd been divided into two groups of eight, so everyone could contribute, which gave me even less chance to hide. The other students, most of them, didn't seem to mind. As if exposing their fears and neuroses and that time they got felt up in the Louvre trying to buy a postcard was just good story material. I was shamed by their courage. Intimidated by their writing, as colorful and contemporary as graffiti.

So far, I hadn't offered much—a poem, an opening paragraph, the most constructive critiques I could devise. But next week was my turn to share something longer. "*Something new*," Dr. Ward had said, with a significant look in my direction.

I'd stayed back after class to speak with her.

Her face got the pinched look she usually wore when she saw me. "Was there something else?"

"I was just wondering . . ." If Gray were right. What if—my throat closed—I didn't actually have anything to say? *"A parasite, feeding on an older man's celebrity and creativity,"* the reviewer in *The Atlantic* said. No fresh ideas, no groundbreaking story, no voice. I cleared my throat. "Do they know?" I asked instead.

"Does who know what?"

"Do the other students know? About . . ." Me. *"Destiny Gayle?"*

She cocked her head. "Since Kettering's book is not on the required reading list, I have no idea. You would have to ask them."

As if.

And maybe, after all, I was okay postponing any discussion of my lack of creativity. I needed to pick up the girls from school. I was already late.

"Sorry I bothered you," Toni said in an injured voice.

"You're never a bother. I love you."

"Love you, too."

"I'll call you tonight," I promised.

I'd read every student parent guide online, trying to help Toni with her transition. *Constantly talking and texting with your freshman may only make matters worse,* they all said. *Don't be too available.* Fine for Uncle Henry, who had always treated his growing nieces with careful, distant affection. Fine for Aunt Em, who was never demonstrative.

But my little sister needed me.

A tourist stood stock-still in the middle of the sidewalk, staring at her phone. I dodged around her.

"Excuse me," she said plaintively. "Can you tell me how to get to the Book of Kells?"

"Sure. It's in the old library. You'll want to take the tour. You can purchase a ticket right through that gate."

"Thanks." She smiled. "You must love being a student here."

In her eyes, at least, I belonged.

I smiled back. "It *is* pretty great."

Because you know what? It was. For once in my life, in spite of all my doubts, I was happy exactly where I was.

And Toni was not. The reversal in our usual roles struck at my heart.

T he school courtyard swarmed with blue-plaid uniforms. Lily stood with a cluster of girls near the steps.

"You're late," she said as I approached.

She sounded so much like Toni that I smiled. "And how was your day?"

"It sucked. Can I go home now?"

"You know Sophie has football practice."

"I'm old enough to stay by myself."

I waved to Sophie. "Not according to your mother."

Sophie ran over and thrust her book bag at me. I slung it over my shoulder and herded the girls toward the bus stop.

"I bet when you were my age you were allowed to be home alone," Lily said.

"I was never alone. I had to stay with my little sister."

"Well, I don't. That's your job."

"I'm supposed to stay with both of you. Come on." I smiled. "I'll let you use my phone to watch TikTok videos during practice."

"Does Mummy know you bribe us?"

"Only if you tell her," I said cheerfully.

We were not, after all, late.

Sophie ran off to join her team at practice. Lily eyed her usual perch on the Ping-Pong table and pulled a face. "It's wet."

"This is Ireland," I said mildly. "It's always wet and raining. Or just finished raining. Or about to rain."

She almost smiled, I swear. "Can you dry it off?"

She was twelve, more than old enough to dry her own seat. It wouldn't kill her to get her uniform wet. On the other hand, she was *twelve*. Her body was changing, her emotions were all over the place, and soon she would learn—if she hadn't learned already—that no one was as good and nothing was as simple as she'd once believed. Being a tween basically sucked.

I swiped the table with the sleeve of my sweater and handed her my phone.

The older boys—Tim's team—were back on the other side of the pitch. Tim was on the sidelines. I raised a hand in tentative greeting, but his eyes were on the boys, sidling down the field in awkward squares of four.

"Keep your distance," he called. "That's it. Now, pass, *pass*."

Under his windbreaker, he wore shorts. His calves were thick and muscled, his knees reddened from the cold. There was a thick purple scar along one of them. An athletic surgery, I assumed. I looked away.

Sam's sister Grace sat on a park bench, her book neglected in her lap as she watched the boys drill.

And there was Sam, his tall figure slouched next to a rack of bicycles. My pulse picked up pleasantly. Hey, just because my heart was broken and my faith in men and my own judgment was destroyed didn't mean I was immune to the lean-and-brooding look.

He sauntered over, hands in his pockets. "All right there?"

"Hi. Yeah. Great," I babbled. "How are you?"

His eyes, the blue green of the Irish sea, crinkled at the corners. The air smelled like wet pavement and, faintly, of car exhaust. His poet's hair, waving around his lean face, was misted with silver droplets.

"Can't complain. I brought you this." He pulled something from his pocket.

A paperback, worn and well-read. "Brendan Behan. Plays?"

He nodded. "Consider it part of your introduction to Dublin."

I wanted to get to know Dublin, sure. But I wanted to know Sam more. Talking to him sometimes felt like being in class where everyone had done the reading assignment but me. "What's it about?"

"Death. And waiting. With funny bits."

"That sounds . . ." *Intimidating.* "Great. Thank you. But I don't have anything for you."

His gaze drifted over me, touching, lingering, sparking tiny fires in its wake. "We'll think of something." His eyes focused over my shoulder. Narrowed. "Fuck."

I was jolted. "What?"

"That little shit is chatting up our Grace."

I turned. A red-haired boy from Tim's team was talking to Sam's sister. She was laughing up at him, her book closed on her lap. Something about his face . . . I'd seen that face before.

I frowned. "Is that . . . ?"

"Doyle!" Tim shouted.

One of the boys who'd followed me.

"Trouble," Sam said grimly.

Grace watched the boy jog back to his position on the field.

"Is he . . . Would he hurt her?"

"Danny Doyle's harmless enough. But he's a shit-for-brains. He'll always be a shit-for-brains. He's no good for our Grace."

Her cheeks were pink. She looked so hopeful. Happy.

"Maybe he'll change," I offered tentatively.

"Not in our world. Not in the real world. It's all about opportunity, isn't it? Even if he wanted to be something better, he'll never have the chance."

"Are we still talking about Danny Doyle?"

"Who else would we be talking about?"

He'd gone to Trinity, I remembered. An English major. "When did you graduate?"

"I didn't, did I? Dropped out."

"Why?"

"It doesn't matter now."

"Then why not tell me?"

He shrugged. "Why does anybody leave school?"

Short of being lampooned by your lover and disgraced by your department . . . "Bad breakup?" I guessed. "Bad grades?"

He raised an eyebrow. "Maybe I had better things to do."

"How long have you been working at Clery's?"

"All my life."

"But how long have you been . . ."

"In charge?"

I nodded.

"Since our da died. Must be nine years now."

"And that's why you quit school."

It was his turn to nod.

Out on the field, the girls' coach called them in for a huddle. The boys were still running, kicking the ball back and forth.

"Look at your target!" Tim shouted. "You have to communicate."

"Do you ever think of going back?" I asked Sam.

He slanted a look down at me. "Why?"

"Well . . . It's just . . ." I floundered. "You seem to love reading so much."

"Books don't pay the bills."

"But if you got your degree . . ."

His lips twisted. "You Americans and your eternal optimism. Not every man can grow up to be president, you know."

"But you could do anything. Go into teaching or publishing or communications or something."

"Life's not a fucking fairy tale, Boots. Sooner or later, you have to accept there are no happy endings."

Sophie ran up as her team dispersed. "It's time to go."

I glanced over her head. Sam's sister Aoife was still on the pitch, bouncing a ball from knee to knee. "Is practice over already?"

Lily slid off the Ping-Pong table and came over. "Thank God. I'm so bored."

Sam's gaze met mine. His mouth crooked. "Better go back to your tower, princess."

I wanted to protest. But I'd never been any good at saying what I wanted. Besides, the girls were waiting. "Thanks again for the book."

"Sure."

"I'll return it," I said, like a promise. *I want to see you again.*

"Anytime." His smile jabbed my heart like a fishhook. "All you have to do is cross the river."

M y room at the Nortons' didn't have a television.

When she showed me the room, Glenda had asked if I

minded. It had been an issue, apparently, with "*the last girl.*" I assured her the lack of a TV didn't bother me. Look at the cute slanted ceiling! The carved wooden headboard! The gilt-framed mirror over the dresser! It was like staying in a bed-and-breakfast, with the bath down the hall.

She was so nice to let me stay at all.

I knew the rules of make-believe. Generally, it paid to be an orphan. Cinderella, Rapunzel, Anne Shirley, Jane Eyre—they *had* to be motherless children. How else could they prove they were worthy of love? But sometimes I wondered what it would be like to be part of a different kind of story, to grow up under the protective wing of Marmee in *Little Women* or Ma in that little house on the prairie, to belong in a house like this.

The thought felt vaguely disloyal. Our mother wasn't like other mothers. Ordinary mothers. She was special.

My bedside lamp glowed against the early-evening dusk. Glenda and James were downstairs, Sophie and Lily in their rooms, doing homework. Or, I suspected, playing computer games. For all the perfection of Glenda's family, they didn't seem to spend a lot of time together. Not like, say, Sam and his sisters.

I traced the cover of his book with my fingers. Tonight, reading would have to wait. Maeve Ward's face loomed like a dark cloud on my horizon. She wanted "*something new,*" she'd said.

Maybe I'd call Toni first. Talking with my sister always made me feel better. Made her feel better. I reached for my phone, but after six rings, the call went to voice mail. She must be in class. Or maybe she was with friends? I hoped so. She needed to get out more.

And now I sounded like our aunt. *Go somewhere. Do something.*

I opened my laptop and started a new file.

Half an hour later, I was staring at my cursor blinking against a bright, mostly blank screen. When my phone pinged with an incoming message, I seized it with relief. *Toni!*

Not Toni.

GRAY: The semester started and you're not here.

A sound escaped me, a gulp of air like a laugh or a sob. *Gray.*

I pressed my fingers to my mouth, memories unspooling in my head.

I should have suspected something when Gray didn't share the details of his new book. He hadn't asked for help editing or proofreading, hadn't given me an advance copy to read. Maybe, in the most secret recesses of my brain, I'd known things weren't right. But I'd gone to his book release party, flush with pride and love, hugging our special relationship to myself. The bookseller introduced Gray. Our eyes caught as he approached the podium. He smiled.

And then he started to read. Out loud.

At first I didn't get it. People from the department—my friends, his colleagues—started to turn, to look at me. I stood there with my face burning and my heart on fire, convinced this was all some giant misunderstanding. A mistake. At the end of the reading, I waited to catch his eye, hoping for a look, a disclaimer, an acknowledgement. *Nothing.* I tried to approach him through the crowd of readers and hangers-on. He turned away, enveloped in a swarm of attention and praise.

I couldn't elbow my way past his publicist and fans. But that was okay. When I got home, I told myself, when I read *Destiny Gayle* for myself, the whole story—the story of our love—would be different.

It was worse.

"Despite her name, Destiny exists as a mere accessory in Kettering's

masterpiece of male egoism and literary desire," said the reviewer in the *Washington Post. Elle* put it more simply: *"Hungry and hollow. A body rather than a character."*

I felt exposed. Used. Violated. How could he do this to me? What had I done?

In the days that followed, Gray wouldn't answer his phone or the door. He hadn't replied to my texts.

In desperation, I went to see him during office hours, sitting in the chair on the other side of his desk as he closed his office door and explained with weary finality that it was over. We were through.

I cried. But I hadn't argued. I hadn't yelled or screamed or made a scene, too conscious of the department assistant at her desk outside and his colleagues in the adjoining offices. Too aware of my own humiliation.

He had shamed me. Ruined me. I could ruin him, or at least prompt a stern discussion with the dean or a #MeToo piece in the student newspaper.

But I shrank from anything that smacked of revenge. I hated myself, but I still loved him. Had loved him. And he loved me. I had proof. I had emails. Sooner or later, I'd thought, Gray would remember that.

Eventually, he would come back to me. Choose me. (Unlike, say, our mother.)

I imagined it over and over again, the words he would use, the assurances, the excuses. For months afterward, while Covid-weary readers distracted themselves with Gray's sexy pseudo-confessional, while his detractors and supporters debated on Twitter, I'd read and reread his old emails. Even when I moved back into the farmhouse, even as I applied to Trinity, I'd comforted myself by composing his apology in my head, assembling it like a quilt out of well-loved, well-worn phrases. We were soul mates, he'd told me at the start of our relationship. Partners for life.

I miss you, I dreamed of him writing. *I love you. I'm sorry.*

I would forgive him, of course.

Except . . . Standing in the Nortons' spare room four thousand miles away, I read his text over again carefully.

Nope. It didn't say any of those things.

My body tingled. My brain buzzed. I needed to reply, to answer him right now, to tell him . . . what, exactly? I couldn't think.

I stood, bumping awkwardly into the corner of my tiny desk, lurching like a wounded animal trying to escape. Reeti! I needed my bosom friend. Not fictional Anne of Green Gables. I needed Reeti.

I messaged her. Hey. Can I come see you?

"Pop over anytime," she'd told me more than once. But there was no answer. I checked the clock. Almost nine. She would be home soon, right? By the time she responded to my message, I could be there.

She had to be there.

But she wasn't.

I stood on the landing outside her apartment, my energy draining away. I felt deflated. Stupid. Obviously, Reeti had a life and friends of her own. She couldn't put them on hold to wait on my personal messes. I turned and blundered into the newel post, smacking my elbow.

"Ow! Crap. Ow ow ow."

A door opened—not Reeti's, one of the first-floor apartments— and there was Tim.

"Can I help you?" he asked, sounding like Darcy at Netherfield. *May I inquire after your sister, Miss Bennet?*

I jumped. "Tim. Hi. No, I'm fine."

"You pressed my buzzer."

I rubbed my elbow, heat scalding my face. "I may have. Sorry. I was in a hurry. I'm here to see Reeti."

"She's out."

"I know."

"Her parents are in town." A pause. "I believe they went to dinner."

I tried to imagine it, having the kind of parents who took you out to eat. Em and Henry came occasionally to campus—for Family Weekend my freshman year, and move-in day for two years after that, and for my graduation. But they never stayed for dinner. They had to get home to the farm.

I swallowed. My elbow throbbed, matching the ache in my heart. Animallike, all I wanted now was to get away. To hide. "Right. Thanks. I'll just . . ." *Wait? Come back?* The prospect of dragging myself on the bus—twice—suddenly seemed more than I could face.

He stood regarding me for a long moment. "Is there something I can do?"

My throat closed. Tears blurred my eyes. "No. I was just . . . We were just going to watch TV. Sometimes we do that. I don't have a television." *Shut up, shut up, shut up.*

"What program?"

My arm tingled. I wiggled my fingers. "Sorry?"

"Which program," he asked patiently, "were you going to watch?"

"Oh. Um." I sniffed. "It doesn't matter. Reeti likes cooking shows, mostly."

So did I. Comfort TV, where the greatest tragedy was an overcooked filet or a soggy bottom.

He opened his door wide. A large TV was mounted on the opposite wall, glowing with scenes from a kitchen.

"*Great British Menu*," Tim said. Another pause. "You should put ice on that."

"What?"

He nodded to my elbow. "Your arm. I have ice. If you'd like to wait inside."

He could have been asking if I took sugar in my tea. There was no pressure. Nothing to suggest he was a serial killer who lured his victims home with the promise of TV and ice packs and then cooked them into pies.

"If you don't mind," I said in a small voice.

He stood back from the door. Inside, his apartment was as neutral as a hotel suite. Somewhere to hide. Even the pictures on the walls looked like someone had purchased them by lot. No pizza boxes or game controllers, no plants or family photos. A grown man's home, functional and a little boring.

He disappeared into the kitchen. I heard a drawer open and close before he returned with a bag of frozen peas wrapped in a towel. "Twenty minutes on, twenty minutes off," he instructed. "Can I get you something else? Paracetamol? Water? Coffee?"

"No, thank you," I said, mimicking his good manners.

"I have bottled water, if you prefer. Or you can watch me open some wine."

I smiled. "So I can see if you slip something into my drink, you mean?"

He stared at me with his usual lack of expression. "If that's a concern."

"Well, it's not."

I sat on his stuffy-but-comfortable couch while he opened a bottle of white wine. He went back into the kitchen. I stirred myself to text Reeti, letting her know where I was.

Tim reappeared with wineglasses and a plate, which he set on the coffee table.

"Thanks." I adjusted the peas. "Yum. Are those . . . ?"

"Chelsea buns."

"I saw those on *Great British Bake Off*. Bread week." I reached for one, reacting on an animal level to shelter, food, comfort. "I love bread week."

"Yes." Another pause. "The recipe's online."

"Wait!" I licked icing sugar from my lip. "You made these?"

Faint color stained his cheekbones. "They're not difficult."

"They're delicious."

I ate the whole thing.

I was intruding. I knew I was intruding. But . . . I had been so miserable and confused, and now there were buns. And wine. *Twenty minutes on.* He could endure my company for twenty minutes. It was oddly reassuring to have a time limit on our relationship. I didn't have to make an effort to be smart or entertaining. I didn't need to worry about making him like me or be concerned that he was hitting on me.

After twenty minutes, I set my empty wineglass on the table, more relaxed than I'd felt in ages. My elbow felt . . . Not fine. But not bad. There was no reason for me to stay. I set the peas, still wrapped in the towel, on the coffee table. "I should go."

"You'll miss the next episode."

"But . . ."

"It's the dessert round."

I settled back on the couch. "Can't miss dessert."

He refilled my glass. "A good philosophy."

A joke. I smiled. "Plus, it's anyone's game now."

"Why?"

"Because they're baking, not cooking."

"I don't see the difference."

"You can't simply throw things into pans in baking. You need to measure."

"That's why I enjoy it. It's . . . precise."

"Exactly. You have to follow the recipe. Men don't follow instructions. It's too much like asking for directions."

His lips twitched. Practically a smile. "HR would call that gender-typing."

"No. Well, yes." I cleared my throat. "My aunt and uncle have a pretty traditional relationship, I guess."

"The chicken farmers."

"Wheat farmers. But we kept chickens, too. For the eggs."

"What about you?"

"That was my responsibility—getting the eggs."

"I was inquiring about your relationships."

"Oh." Flustered, I took another bun.

Gray used to call me his support, I remembered. His inspiration. And for two years, I *had* supported him, picking up milk and the occasional houseplant, providing him with healthy meals and clean sheets and his favorite Scotch so he was free to create.

What we had was rare, Gray assured me. A unique bond between soul mates. But now, months later, I thought that in some ways the role I'd played was very ordinary. Even traditional. Not like my mother at all.

Tim was watching me, waiting for me to go on.

"I'm not in a relationship," I said.

That stupid lump was back in my throat. Grief. Or swallowed rage? My eyes were wet.

Tim handed me a paper napkin. "Sorry. None of my business."

I blew my nose. "No, I'm sorry."

We turned our attention back to the TV. The competition was heating up, fucks and testosterone flying around the kitchen.

It felt warmer on the couch, too.

Tim got up to put the peas back in the freezer. Right. Mustn't leave drips on the coffee table.

"I heard from my ex-boyfriend today," I said when he came back.

Tim turned his head. "The one you're not in a relationship with."

I nodded, pretending to watch the chef from Scotland plate up for the judges.

"What did he want?"

His message flashed in my head. The semester started and you're not here.

My mouth opened. Shut. "I'm not sure."

"He must have said."

"Not really. I mean, I haven't spoken to him in nearly six months."

"Don't make this harder than it has to be," Gray had said to me. *"Why don't you get on with your own life?"*

"His loss."

I blinked. "Was that a compliment?"

A small dent appeared in his right cheek. "It was."

"Oh." Heat crept up my face. "Well . . . Thank you. But I didn't want to. Break up, I mean. He didn't leave me much choice."

"He cheated."

"Nope. I could have forgiven that." I was pretty sure.

"So, what was this unforgivable offense?"

"I don't want to talk about it."

"Then why bring it up?"

Because Reeti's not here. Because you've been nice to me. Because I'm lonely. "Because I wanted a man's perspective. Him contacting me, out of the blue like that. It made me wonder . . ." I hugged Tim's square, stiff pillow to my chest.

"Wonder what, exactly?"

"If . . . You know. Things were different now. If he were different. I mean, people can change, right?"

"Not their basic nature, no," Tim said coolly.

"But their feelings can change."

"Feelings are meaningless without action to support them. Did this person say anything to make you believe he had changed?"

"N-no."

"Or that he wanted to change?"

"No. But he . . ."

Tim waited.

"Reached out," I said.

"Called you, emailed, what?"

"He texted."

Tim didn't say anything.

Someone knocked on the door. He got up to open it.

"I got your text," Reeti said as she blew into the apartment. She grinned. "It sounded like a booty call."

Tim made a noise.

I couldn't look at him. "I should go."

"But I just got here." Reeti flung herself on the couch. "Is that wine?"

"You don't drink," Tim said.

"After dinner with my parents I do," Reeti said.

He went into the kitchen to get another glass.

"How was it?" I asked. "The dinner with your parents."

Had I gone out to dinner with our mother as a child? I must have. We'd lived in New York.

"Long." Reeti's gaze narrowed. "Everything okay? Do you want to go upstairs?"

Her kindness caught in my throat. "Now *that* sounds like a booty call," I said in a husky voice.

Tim returned. "You can't leave now."

Reeti's smile showed her teeth. "It's Girl Talk time, Woodman. Unless you've switched teams . . ."

"She asked for the male perspective," he said stiffly.

Reeti glanced at me. "Your call."

TEN

"You can't leave now."

Which was about the last thing Tim should have said. Or intended to say. Right up there with, "*I have ice if you'd like to wait inside*" and "*You'll miss the next episode.*"

Only she'd looked so sad, and then she'd looked so happy—her emotions close to the surface, as easy to read as a blush—that his deadened heart had stirred in response.

It wasn't as though Dee expected anything from him, Tim reassured himself.

Except now, of course, both Dee and Reeti were looking at him, waiting for him to offer his "male perspective." Well, Dee was waiting. Reeti was looking to pounce. The likelihood that he could give them what they wanted, that he could be what she needed, was very low. "Your call," Reeti said to Dee.

Dee's teeth sank into her lower lip. "You haven't had any wine yet."

A deflection. Tim frowned. But at least—*at last*—she was erecting some barriers. She should learn to protect herself better. The way she walked around, open as a wound, her heart exposed . . . It was dangerous. For her. And to him.

To buy himself time, he poured some wine.

"So, what happened?" Reeti asked after she'd taken a sip.

Good. Let her take the lead. She could be the supportive best friend. He was merely a . . . resource.

"Gray texted me," Dee said.

The ex. Tim filed the name for future reference.

"The fucker," Reeti said. "Did he grovel?"

Dee shook her head. "He just said . . . Well, that he was thinking of me. Not in those exact words, but . . ."

"What words did he use? Precisely," Tim said, and then clamped his jaw shut. He had no interest in keeping this conversation going.

"He *said*"—Dee swallowed—"'The semester started and you're not here.' That means he misses me. Doesn't it?"

"I guess it could," Reeti said doubtfully. "Or it could be like, 'You still up?' Sure, he's thinking about you. But he's not thinking about *you*."

"It's not an actual booty call," Dee said. "He's in Kansas."

Kansas. Another fact to store away. It unnerved Tim, how greedy his mind was for bits of her, absorbing the smallest details—her frank, open gaze, her friendly American smile.

"But does he know where you are?" Reeti asked.

Dee's mouth opened. Closed. "I'm not sure."

"Besides, emotionally, it's the same thing," Reeti said. "He's fishing for a response from you without any commitment from him."

Dee appealed to Tim. "What do you think?"

He thought her boyfriend was an arsehole. "I think if he wanted to tell you that he misses you, he would have said so. Or he could have called."

Reeti nodded. "He's just not that into you."

Dee's lips curved. "Are you really giving me relationship advice from a movie?"

"It was a book first."

Tim had no idea what they were talking about.

"I'm just saying, he's not going to a lot of effort," Reeti continued.

"Then why text me at all?"

Reeti shrugged. "Who cares about his reasons? Especially after what he did to you."

Dee flushed.

What *did* he do? Something unforgiveable, Tim thought. Not cheating. She could forgive cheating. Which made her a bigger person than Tim. "You deserve better," he said.

"That's it?" Reeti asked. "That's your male perspective? I could have told her that."

"But you wouldn't be as objective," Tim said. "Not being a man."

She sputtered.

The corners of Dee's mouth indented, as if she were trying not to laugh. "Thank you. Not just for the . . . For saying that. For the peas and the Chelsea buns and the wine and all."

"D'you want to spend the night?" Reeti asked.

Tim's mind blanked, flooded with fantasies of Dee spending the night. With him.

"I wish I could." Dee stood. Reluctantly, it seemed. "But I have to get the girls off to school in the morning."

Tim lurched to his feet like one of his mother's well-trained dogs. "I'll take you home."

"I can catch the bus."

"It's raining," Reeti said.

Tim waited, willing Dee to say yes. Hoping she would say no.

"Well . . ." Her smile hit him square in the chest. He almost rubbed his scar. "If it's not too much trouble . . ."

"No trouble at all," he said coolly.

He couldn't find and kill the arsehole ex. But he could deliver her home safe and dry.

The Rover's interior wrapped them in a bubble of leather and intimacy. The wipers beat against the comfortable silence.

"It's your turn," Dee announced.

He looked at her, fingers pleated together in her lap. Apparently, she did not find silence comfortable. Or perhaps she wasn't comfortable with him.

"My turn?" he repeated.

She nodded vigorously. "I've been going on about me all evening. Now's your chance to talk."

"About . . ."

"Anything. How was practice today? I was there," she explained. "With Sophie."

"I'm aware."

"I didn't think you noticed me."

He noticed everything about her, the slope of her nose outlined by the spangled window, the curve of her cheek in the glow of the dashboard. He realized he was staring and jerked his gaze back to the road.

Now's your chance . . .

The touch screen lit up. **Call from LAURA SMITH.**

Dee glanced at the display and then at him. "Should you get that?"

His jaw set. "No."

"Kind of late for a work call," she observed as it went to voice mail.

"Yes."

Dee slid him a shy, mischievous smile. "But not a booty call."

She was teasing. Even flirting a little. He should shut that down. But her smile had scrambled his brain. His tongue felt thick in his mouth. For the life of him, he couldn't think of what to say.

"I thought Laura would be back in the UK by now," Dee continued. Apparently that whole it's-your-turn-to-talk business couldn't silence her natural friendliness. Or else his silence made her nervous.

He cleared his throat. "We're moving more of our staff operations from London to Dublin to guarantee access to the EU single market." Christ, he sounded dull. "And the practice was fine," he added. "The boys did well."

She blinked at the abrupt change of subject. "You seemed very focused. Lots of kicking and stuff."

He bit down on a smile. "Passing drills."

"I never played soccer. Football. Any sports, really."

"Indeed."

"My sister did. After we went to live with Aunt Em and Uncle Henry, I enrolled her at the Y. But I was a klutz."

"Has it ever occurred to you that you weren't good at sports because you didn't have opportunities to play, rather than that you didn't play because you weren't any good?"

"Tim, you had to put peas on my elbow because I walked into a banister. I'm pretty sure I've always been a klutz." She said it quite cheerfully, an engaging mix of self-deprecation and acceptance. "I suppose you played sports in school."

Captain of his House team in football. Upper Boat eight for the school. "Yes."

"Football? Quidditch?"

He did smile then. Naturally, she was a Harry Potter fan. "Football and rowing."

"Your parents must have been proud." She sounded wistful.

"Enough. It was more that it was . . . expected. My father and grandfather were pleased when we won, of course. My mother used to worry I'd get hurt."

"She must have hated it when you went into the army."

His hands tightened on the steering wheel. "Yes."

She turned in her seat. He could *feel* her studying him, the weight of that soft brown gaze, but eventually she must have decided to let it go, because all she said was, "And now you coach."

"Yes."

"And are you pleased when your team wins?"

He sighed. "We're talking about fourteen-to-sixteen-year-old boys. Obviously, they want to win games. But they need to develop the right skill sets. Not just for the game. Coaching football—it's about teaching them communication. Team building. Conflict resolution. Giving them opportunities to be the best they can be."

Another of those inviting smiles. "Then you *do* think people can change."

Did he? The possibility prickled like a limb coming to life, heavy and painful.

His phone vibrated with an incoming text. He glanced at it.

LAURA: It's Charles.

His mouth compressed. "Excuse me. I have to . . ." He pulled to the side of the road. Switched off the Bluetooth to make the call from his cell.

"Tim. Thank God," Laura said without preamble.

"What is it?"

"Charles is here."

"'Here'?"

"Outside my flat."

So she was safe. "I fail to see the problem."

"He's been drinking. He won't leave."

It was still raining. Eventually, Charles would get wet enough—

or sober enough—to give up and go home. Tim hoped. "Give him time."

"He's bothering the neighbors. You have to come and get him, Tim. I don't want to call the police."

He ground his teeth together, hearing the implicit threat. "Fine. I'll be over as soon as I can."

He slid his phone back in his pocket.

"So . . . Not too late," Dee said softly from the other side of the car.

For a booty call, she meant.

He could correct her. But she was too warm and pretty. Too vulnerable. It would be dangerously easy for him to make a mistake with her.

He pulled away from the curb. "Just helping out a friend," he said to the darkness beyond the windshield. True enough.

They drove the rest of the way in silence.

She exited the car before he could get around to open her door. He walked her to her front steps, the streetlights reflected in the puddles.

There was a moment on the stoop, with the porch light spilling on her hair and shining in her big dark eyes, when, if things were different—if *he* were different—he would have kissed her good night. But there was no question of that. No chance she would invite him up to her single room with her charges sleeping down the hall.

He tried to be glad. He was glad.

"Thanks again," she said, fumbling in her bag for her key.

He nodded, hands clasped behind his back like he was standing on parade, watching her down-bent head as she unlocked the door. He was still braced, legs shoulder-width apart, when she got the damn thing open, turned, and . . . hugged him. Quick. Friendly.

Shit. He hadn't seen *that* coming. His body reacted before his brain. Her breasts squashed briefly against his chest. Her hair smelled great. "You're a good friend," she said, not quite looking him in the eye.

And before he could respond, she was gone.

S he doesn't love me," Charles sobbed.

He was sodden and shit-faced. Exactly what Tim didn't want to deal with right now. He put a hand on his former buddy's shoulder. His jacket was soaked, his face streaked with water. Hard to distinguish the tears from the rain.

A worm of sympathy wriggled under the careful layers of non-feeling. "Let it go, mate," Tim said.

"I just want to talk to her."

He'd probably shown up hoping for more than that, but Tim wasn't in the frame of mind to argue. Not with the man who had once saved his life and was currently drunk off his ass.

"You've got to leave it," he said. "Let her go."

Charles knocked his hand away. "Take your fucking hands off me. Laura!" He howled at her window like she was the moon. "Laura, you bitch! I love you!"

Christ. He'd have the neighbors out in a minute. Or the police. "Easy, man. Leave it."

"If she'd just talk to me . . ."

Tim glanced up at the window where a shadow hovered behind the blind. "In the morning. You'll both feel better." Or not. Charles would have a hell of a hangover. "You can call her in the morning."

"She won't . . . She won't fucking see me." Charles's voice was sad. His breath reeked of gin.

"Because it's late." *Not too late for a booty call*. Tim shook the thought away. "Time to go home. Let's get in the car."

Charles jerked away. "Laura!"

"Come on, now." Another hand on Charles's shoulder, guiding, reassuring. "You don't want to scare her."

"Never. I wouldn't . . . Never do anything to hurt her."

"Sure, mate." Tim steered him to the car.

"I never touched her."

Which Tim knew for a fact was a lie. He'd seen them together. "Here we go," he said, cool and emotionless. A machine.

"She doesn't love me," Charles confided as Tim tried to load him into his Range Rover. Into the back seat, where he couldn't puke all over Tim's console.

"Watch your head."

"She doesn't love me because she. Still. Loves. You." Every word punctuated by a blast of gin and a finger poke.

The pokes were hard enough to hurt. But otherwise Tim felt . . . nothing. Except something he identified dimly as anger, old and unproductive. Nothing changed.

"And you don't love her," Charles said. "She told me. You can't love anybody."

"Get in the fucking car." Not so neutral now.

"Robot Man," Charles slurred. "Should have let you die."

Leave no man behind, the Americans liked to boast. But the British Army did not surrender its wounded, its weapons, or its honor without a fight. Which was the only reason Tim didn't toss Charles into the gutter now.

Instead, he buckled his former best friend into the back seat and drove him home.

ELEVEN

He didn't kiss me good night.

Not that I wanted him to. It's just there was this moment on the front porch when Tim stood there, looking at me, where I'd thought . . . You know. That he might. Instead, I'd hugged him, stiff and upright as a tin soldier, and then—before I could embarrass him or myself anymore—run away.

I turned to bolt the front door behind me, my face hot. It was only a hug. Friends hugged each other all the time, right? He'd been so nice all evening, letting me into his space, fetching ice for my elbow, feeding me Chelsea buns and wine. He made me feel comfortable. Safe. Probably because he felt sorry for me, but still. He'd acted like a friend. A real friend, not the with-benefits kind. Nope, that position in his life was clearly reserved for Laura Formerly from London.

A single lamp shone from the living room. Glenda left a light on, I thought, smiling at her thoughtfulness. I went in to turn it off before going up to bed.

"You're out late."

I jumped.

James sprawled in a leather chair, nursing a crystal glass of whiskey.

I pressed a hand to my rapidly beating heart. "Sorry. I thought I was the only one here."

"Almost. I'm quite, quite alone. Come in."

I froze, my mind spinning with stupid comparisons. "*'Will you walk into my parlour?' said the Spider to the Fly.*" Or Rochester to Jane: "*'Draw your chair still a little farther forward . . .'*"

Except James Norton wasn't going to eat me. And Glenda Norton was no mad wife, conveniently disposed of in the attic.

I needed to get a grip.

"Care for a nightcap?" James asked.

An alarm chimed distantly in the back of my head. "Oh. No, thank you. I was just going up."

"I suppose you were out with the boyfriend. I assume there is a boyfriend?" he inquired with fatherly interest.

Or not so fatherly. "*I heard there was a problem with the last au pair,*" Reeti had warned. "*I'd watch out if I were you.*"

But how did I tell my employer/mentor's husband that my personal life was none of his business?

"Glenda said it would be all right if I went out sometimes. After the girls were finished for the night."

"Of course, of course. I simply meant a pretty young girl like you has better ways to spend her time than entertaining an old man like me."

"You're not that old," I assured him.

He smiled, raising his glass in a silent toast. I flushed, annoyed at how easily I'd been drawn into playing his game. Why did I *do* that? Pandering to his male ego, taking care of his feelings instead of listening to my own.

"*You deserve better,*" said a voice like Tim's.

"You're right, though," I said. "I *do* have things to do."

I turned and went upstairs, gripping the banister, forcing myself to take the steps slow and steady. *Not* running away. A strategic retreat.

I locked my bedroom door, feeling foolish at the precaution. I hadn't done that for a long time. Not since Toni and I went to stay with our mother's friend Cindy, the one whose boyfriend wanted Toni to sit on his lap. *Better safe than sorry*, I told myself then. I'd always had to protect my little sister.

Maybe I could learn to protect myself better, too.

I picked up my phone. Reread Gray's text. The semester started and you're not here.

How did I reply to that? Should I reply to that? He'd ghosted me for months. His silence had been a kind of death, a fall into a dark chasm—like the silence after my mom had died, a void without an echo.

I hesitated. Typed, I read you're casting on Destiny. Congratulations. Hit SEND. There, I thought with a flash of satisfaction. That was adult. Neutral. Noncommittal. Done.

Almost immediately, three dots appeared. Gray, typing his reply. I held my breath. None of them will be you.

My breath whooshed out. Which was . . . What did that *mean*? He used to tell me I was special. "*I can't imagine my life without you in it,*" he'd said. Did he miss me now?

"*If he wanted to tell you that he misses you, he would have said so.*"

God, I was stupid. As easily as that, I'd let Gray knock me off-balance. Again. He wanted me to get on with my life. So why wouldn't he let me?

His words were a phantom soundtrack that followed me through the week, a constant loop of *never was*es and *might have been*s that drowned out everything else. It played me into sleep, streaming in the background while I packed the girls' lunches and met them after school, when I sat in class or tried to study.

But I didn't text him back.

H ello? Earth to Dee," Reeti said on Sunday as we poked along the flea market stalls.

"Sorry." I picked up a sweater—mohair, I thought, stroking the front—and put it down again. Gray said I looked sallow in green. "I'm kind of out of it."

"I can tell. Everything all right? How's your sister?"

"She's fine, I think. I hope." I sighed. "She's mad at me because I won't let her quit school."

Reeti cocked her head. "Not really your decision, is it?"

"No, but she only went to KU because I was there. And now I'm not." I tried to imagine what our mother might have said, what wise advice she might have given me. Given us. As usual, I had difficulty summoning her voice. She'd been absent, after all, for large parts of my childhood, for almost all of Toni's. Following her art.

Which was no help at all.

"You should focus on your own self, *didi*," Reeti said.

"Yeah, but . . . What did you call me?"

"*Didi*. It means 'big sister.' Because you're acting like one."

"Because I *am* one."

"Yes, but Toni is your sister. Not your child."

"She's only eighteen. She still depends on me."

"And who did you depend on when you were her age?"

"That was different," I protested. "I'm used to taking care of myself."

"Yourself? Or everybody else?"

I stared at her, mute.

"Maybe a little separation would be good for both of you," Reeti said gently. "How are your classes?"

"My teachers are brilliant."

Even Maeve, who only tolerated me. They were all practicing writers, encouraging and often kind. They urged us, in various ways, to pay attention, not only to the world around us, but to our thoughts, feelings, memories.

The problem came when I actually sat down to write.

Gray had stripped me naked. I cringed now from exposing bits of myself on the page for others to gawk at and criticize—the softness of my belly, the mole on my scalp, the awareness that my own mother had never found anything in me worth staying for.

Every time I sat down at my laptop, Gray's face, Gray's words, filled the screen. *Don't be trite. Don't be sentimental. Don't be a sellout. Don't,* full stop. *You could be special if you tried.*

So I tried.

But it had been so long since anyone besides Gray had read my stories. The prospect of sharing too much at the weekly writing workshop—of being told that I sucked—terrified me. In the end it seemed safer to use something he had critiqued, a scene from my Dust Bowl novel he once praised for its raw intimacy, where Rose, the farmer's daughter, seeks out the traveling magician, sleeping over in her parents' barn.

At first, the other students talked about things Gray had liked: the spare description of the barn at night, the menace evoked by the unforgiving landscape. I breathed a sigh of relief, my shoulders creeping down from around my ears.

Alan cleared his throat. "I didn't get why she would meet him—the magician fellow. He's a bit of a tool."

Claire, thin and cool, shot him a pitying look. "Women go out with tools all the time. Her choices are rather limited."

"Especially in rural Kansas," another girl said. "Good use of setting, I thought. Wasn't the Dust Bowl the result of poor agricultural practices?"

"It's all about scarcity, isn't it? Isolation."

"Man's rape of the environment."

"It wasn't rape," someone objected. "The magician represents an escape for her. Something outside her gray, boring existence."

Ryan—who wrote storyboard scripts for video games—shrugged. "Or she just wants sex."

"Not sex. Connection," Erinma said.

I opened my mouth. Shut it.

"Which is why she goes for it. She feels like life is passing her by," someone else said, trying to be sensitive.

"So she gets drunk on magic elixir and takes off her clothes for a traveling carny," Claire said, not trying to be sensitive at all. "Fabulous idea."

"Are you victim blaming?" Erinma demanded.

"I'm only saying she's not a child. She's what, eighteen? Nineteen?" Claire looked at me for corroboration.

This was almost as bad as reading the reviews for *Destiny*. Worse, because it was my words, my story, they were talking about. I nodded dumbly.

"So, old enough to know better," Claire said.

My stomach churned.

"Can we try to be more sex positive here?"

"The magic is a metaphor," someone said. "The magician, he's the one with all the power. He totally takes advantage of her."

"I don't see that," Ryan said. "He never touches her."

"He gets her to unbutton her blouse."

"Yeah, but she wants to," Shauna, who wrote flash fiction, said.

"Where does it say that?" Alan asked.

"It's implied, isn't it? All that description." She read from my manuscript. "'She touched his hand to her breast . . . Her diaphragm expanded with her breath.'" Shauna managed, barely, not to roll her eyes.

I knew the rules for receiving feedback. *Listen. Take notes. Don't take it personally.* But it felt personal. As though they weren't critiquing my story or characters but attacking me. I looked at Maeve, hoping for rescue. She seemed to be listening, her expression slightly bored, an executioner waiting for the verdict in a trial.

"The problem is, it's not clear how much agency Rose has," another student piped up. "She's obviously an unreliable narrator."

"Maybe the ambiguity is the point."

"So which is it? Is she a victim? Or is she a slut?"

They all looked at me.

"We can only judge what's on the page," Maeve said.

But it didn't feel that way.

It felt like they were judging me.

"*The girl always gets blamed,*" Reeti had said.

I stared down at my notebook, my face flaming, pretending to write while they said the requisite nice things to end the critique. "*Strong imagery.*" "*Varied sentence structure.*" The workshop rule about not responding was suddenly a blessing. My throat was too tight to speak.

"The thing is, you made us care about her choices. So, good job," Erinma said.

I mumbled thanks as they collected laptops and book bags. They headed off, in twos and threes, until only Maeve Ward and I were left.

My insides felt hollowed out. I needed to go. It was Thursday. Sophie had football practice. But I couldn't find the energy to stand.

"They didn't understand it at all," I blurted to the nearly empty room. I wanted desperately for her to approve of me, to reassure me, to tell me I belonged.

"Maybe they understood more than you think," Maeve said.

Denial burned inside me. But I'd never been good at confrontation.

"Don't dismiss their comments because your feelings are hurt. What they're saying tells you where you need to improve, that's all."

The lines in my notebook blurred.

"I encouraged you to try something new," Maeve continued relentlessly. "Why are you still working on this project?"

Because Gray thought it was good. Because he said it showed promise.

I looked up, near despair. "I've been working on this story for *three years.*" Closer to four. "I know the setting. I know the characters. I can't just throw it all away."

"Dorothy, you're not in Kansas anymore. What you know encompasses an incredibly limited view of the world. You're only twenty-six, for Christ's sake. Anything you know is bound to be derivative. You should be writing what you don't know. Write from what you feel or want to explore or need to work out. What is it? What do you have to say for yourself?"

Her words hammered me like stones.

"I *don't* know, okay?" I snapped. "I don't *know.*"

"Well." Maeve regarded me, a look almost of satisfaction on her face. "That's a start."

told you she was a witch," Reeti said. "What will you do now?"

I tucked the phone between my ear and shoulder. "Now? I'm at soccer with Sophie."

I watched my ten-year-old charge line up to kick the ball with the other girls, oblivious to my presence. That was good, I thought, remembering long-ago practices with Toni. I didn't want Sophie to think she had to perform for me.

"I meant about The Ward," Reeti said.

"Oh." I felt stress rising, a hot lump in my throat, and swallowed. "Find some way to give her what she wants, I guess."

"You're good at that."

"Apparently not."

"I'm not talking about your writing. I'm talking about *you*. You're so *nice*."

I smiled. "That's a compliment, right?"

"Of course. You need cheering up," Reeti declared. "I'm going to a party tonight. Do you want to come?"

"I can't," I said with some relief. I'd gone with Reeti to a party last week. It was loud and noisy, and everybody there seemed to have read the same books and gone to the same schools and shopped at the same stores. Like high school, only with better shoes and accents. "I've got the girls for dinner tonight. But thanks for asking."

"Anytime. At least you can hang out with Hot Chai Guy."

"He's not here."

It was embarrassing, how much I'd hoped to see Sam at practice. How disappointed I was when he wasn't there. His sister, Grace, was sitting with her book on the sidelines, along with a younger boy who looked enough like them to be the other brother. *Jack?*

"Anyway, I'm not looking for another relationship," I said. I was still . . . in love? In mourning, maybe, for Gray. Or mourning the girl I used to be, the one who imagined a man like that could love me.

"What about sex?"

I flushed, glancing reflexively at Lily, standing right in front of me, waiting to use my phone. "What about it?"

"Have you slept with anybody since the fucker?"

"Er, no."

"It might be what you need to get over him. You have the boots. Get back on that horse and ride, cowgirl!"

I laughed. "It's been so long I'd probably fall off. Tim's here," I said, hoping to change the subject.

On the far side of the pitch. I'd waved to him when I first arrived and gotten a short nod in return. It was as if I'd dreamed that buzzy moment at the Nortons' door, when I'd thought he was going to kiss me. Was I really so desperate for approval, for affection, that I'd make up an attraction where none existed?

Probably.

Crap.

"Tell him I said hello," Reeti said.

"I will."

"Can I have your phone now?" Lily asked.

"I have to go," I told Reeti, and ended the call.

Not many parents stuck around to watch practice. A few mothers, holding jackets or snacks. A father, attempting to coach from the sidelines, screaming at a miserable-faced kid on Tim's team.

The girls finished first. Sophie ran over, her cheeks pink with exercise or excitement. "Dee, can I go to Aoife's house for dinner?"

I looked over her shoulder at Sam's little sister, hopping from foot to foot. "Honey, you're having dinner with Lily and me tonight."

"Please?"

"You'll have to ask your parents." I smiled into their disappointed faces. "Another time, girls. I'm sorry."

Sophie scowled. "No!"

Aoife appealed to her older sister, approaching from the bench. "Gracie, make her say yes."

Grace gave me a friendly look. "You're Sam's friend, aren't you? The American at university."

Sam's friend. I smiled. "Dee. Yeah. Hi."

On the other side of the field, practice had ended. Tim was on the sidelines, talking quietly to Screaming Dad.

". . . welcome to eat with us," Grace was saying.

"Thanks. It's just . . . Sophie's parents are out tonight." A dinner at the college. "I'm not sure what time I'd be able to pick her up."

"Come with her, then," Sam said.

My face was suddenly hot, as if I had sunburn, even though the day was cool and gray. He was here! Slouching beside Jack, wearing black jeans and a black T-shirt promoting some Irish band I'd never heard of.

"I don't want to impose," I said. "And Lily . . . I still have Lily."

His mouth quirked. "Bring her, too. We can feed the lot of you. Janette always cooks enough for an army."

I expected Lily to object or at least roll her eyes. But she was staring at Jack, her mouth slightly open. The same way I looked at Sam, probably.

"*Please*," Sophie said again.

Why not? A night out could be exactly what they needed. What I needed. So much better than obsessing over Maeve Ward all night.

"I'll have to text your mom," I said to Sophie.

Sam smiled.

Somehow, between messaging Glenda and collecting book bags and water bottles, we left without me saying hello to Tim.

The Clerys lived above their shop, up a narrow flight of stairs. "Mam! We're home!" The younger Clerys crowded through the door.

"This is nice," I said to Sam. "Cozy."

Lace curtains at the windows. Overstuffed, comfortable furniture. A scattering of photographs. I felt immediately at home, in spite of the crucifix and the picture of Pope Francis on the wall.

"Bit too cozy, if you ask me."

I smiled. "Right. Sharing a bathroom. I remember."

"I'm a big boy. I have my own place now." Those sea-colored eyes met mine.

My breath suspended. I wasn't imagining the attraction this time. Was I?

"You must be Sophie. And Dee, is it? Sam texted me you were coming." A brisk blond woman with her hair in a clip bustled into the room with a stack of plates. "Welcome."

I tugged self-consciously on my sweater. This wasn't a date. Sam hadn't invited me home to meet his mother. (No guy had ever invited me home to meet his parents. Certainly not Gray.) Still, I wished I had brought flowers or baked cookies. Something. "Dee, yes. And this is Lily." I put on my best visitor smile. "Thank you for having us, Mrs. Clery."

"Call me Janette. Wipe your feet," she said to Sam's brother. "Set the table, and use place mats."

"Why?" Jack asked.

"Do as you're told."

"We have company," Grace said.

"It's just Aoife's friends."

"She means Sam's girl, you dope." Fiadh stood in the door of the kitchen.

Sam's girl. My heart bumped. "Can I do anything?"

"All taken care of," Janette said.

"How are you at peeling potatoes?" asked Fiadh.

"Don't listen to her. Potatoes are done, meat will be out in ten minutes," Janette said. "Go wash your hands."

"Yes, ma'am," I said.

Sam grinned. "She's talking to Aoife."

"Talking to all of you. Jack, those rolls are for dinner. Sam, get the girl a drink."

I washed my hands, helped set the table, poured water and milk for the kids, and accepted a glass of wine. Meals at the farmhouse had always been serious affairs. Food was fuel, methodically consumed for the energy needed to get the fields planted and the animals fed. Uncle Henry ate silently, sometimes grunting his appreciation. Aunt Em occasionally reminded us girls to clean our plates.

At the Clerys', everyone talked and ate at once, constantly interrupting, leaping from complaints about the school uniform (Aoife) to the Bohemians' prospects against Drogheda United (Jack). I listened wistfully as the noise swirled and soared around the table. I was good at keeping quiet. At fitting in. But somehow I was drawn into a conversation with Grace about an English essay, an argument between Sam and Fiadh about selling artisan foods to their very mixed clientele.

I complimented her baking. "I've never made bread."

"I'll give you a recipe. It's easy," she said, apparently registering the doubt on my face. "You don't have to knead or any of that."

I was sure I could bake bread. Less certain how Glenda felt about me baking in her kitchen. But she hadn't objected when I made cookies with the girls. "Thanks. That would be great."

An orange cat wound under the table. Aunt Em would have had something to say about *that*. Sophie and Aoife whispered with their heads together. Jack and Lily were talking about teachers they disliked.

Janette never once told them not to talk with their mouths full. But when Jack threw a roll at Aoife, she caught it neatly before it reached its target. "Enough of that, now."

"Showing off for company," Fiadh said.

The tips of Jack's ears turned red. "Feck off."

"Language," Janette said mildly. "And what is it you're studying at university, Dee?"

"I'm a writer. Well. Trying to be." ("*You write*," Tim's voice said in my head. "*I believe that qualifies you as a writer.*")

Grace nodded. "Like our Sam."

"Leave it," Sam said in the same voice his mother used to stop Jack from throwing the roll, and the conversation skipped on to other things. Football. *Fortnite.* Through it all, I was aware of him beside me, those blue-green eyes, his poet's hair.

Something brushed my leg under the table. His knee? I blushed.

Janette's eyes narrowed. "Aoife, don't feed my food to that cat at this table."

The cat. Of course.

After dinner, Aoife and Sophie went to the room she shared with Grace. Jack grabbed two game controllers and offered one to Lily. I got up to clear.

Janette took a plate from my hands. "Grace can help wash up. You spend time with Sam."

She and Grace went into the kitchen, leaving us alone.

I smiled. "I feel like we're being sent off to play."

"No one ever accused Janette of being subtle."

The TV roared to life.

Sam turned in irritation. "Jesus, Jack, turn it down."

"We should probably go," I said.

"They're all right," Sam said. "Come outside a minute."

Outside was a cobblestoned alley littered with cigarette butts. Two chairs sheltered beneath the fire escape, screened from a pair of dumpsters by a few yellowing plants and some bicycles chained to a NO PARKING sign. I took a chair, careful not to kick over the black plastic ashtray by one leg. Sam lounged against the wall.

"Thank you for inviting us," I said. "Your family is amazing."

"They can be a bit much."

"Better than not enough." I loved the way they talked. Teased. Argued. "My aunt Em and uncle Henry never said more than three sentences at dinner. It must be nice, being part of a large family."

"You have a sister."

"Toni. She's eighteen. A freshman at KU—that's where I went to school. She's having trouble adjusting without me. It's always been the two of us before." I made myself as comfortable as I could in the hard plastic chair. "Our mother traveled a lot."

"For her job?"

"For her art."

"*It's not that I* want *to be away from you, darling*," she always said before she jetted off on some new adventure. Leaving us waiting, princesses in the tower, for our mother the queen to ride to our rescue.

"She did these big installations all over the world. Larger than life." I smiled a little, remembering her exuberant hair, her expressive face, the way she blew into a room like the wind. "Well, that was Mom."

"Where is she now?"

"She died when I was twelve." Her friend Leslie didn't go into details, but I'd looked up the news accounts online. *Artist Dies in Tragic Fall in Joshua Tree, Halting Installation.* "Toni barely remembers her. I always felt I had to make that up to her somehow."

Sam nodded. "It was like that for me when our da died."

When he left Trinity to take over the shop. My heart squeezed. "At least you had your mother."

He lifted an eyebrow. "Mad about that, are you?"

"No." *Maybe.* "It's not like our mother chose to leave us."

"Sounds like she did."

"I mean . . . She didn't choose to die. It was an accident." Equipment malfunction, the witnesses said. No one's fault. "It's only . . . We never got to say good-bye."

"Our dad, it was lung cancer. Plenty of time for good-bye. Didn't change anything. He left us behind, all the same."

"I'm sorry."

He raised one shoulder in a shrug. "Sure, look, life goes on. 'Some things are more precious because they don't last long.'"

"Tennessee Williams again?" I guessed.

He smiled crookedly. "Oscar Wilde."

I didn't know what to say. He was so smart. It wasn't fair. He deserved the chance to go to school. To graduate. To live his best life. Isn't that what he wanted? Isn't that what his father would have wanted for him?

"Would you like to go to a lecture with me?" I blurted. "Oscar Diggs—you know, the children's author?—he's coming to Trinity in a couple weeks, and his talk is open to the public."

Sam shook his head.

"It's free."

"Not my thing."

"You don't like children's books?"

"It's too late for me."

I stood. "You should stop saying that. If you tell a story often enough, it comes true. You need another story, one with a happy ending. The princess gets rescued. The witch is defeated. The orphan children find a home." I stopped, embarrassed by my own vehemence. "Anyway, that's what I always told Toni."

"Trying to make her feel better, were you?"

"Well, yeah."

"Or deluding yourself." He smiled, but his eyes were sad. I wanted to hug him. Or shake him. I wanted . . .

I kissed him, surprising us both.

After a moment of stillness, he kissed me back.

He smelled like rain. He tasted like tea and, faintly, of cigarettes, and his kiss was as far beyond my experience as the moon. I closed my eyes, fitting myself to his angular, unfamiliar body, the sound of my heart rushing in my ears like the sea.

TWELVE

S am stood outside the lecture hall, a thin sweat under his arms and in the small of his back.

He didn't want to be here. He'd left nine years ago. It didn't help that Fiadh had teased and Janette had urged him to come.

But Dee had kissed him. He'd kissed her. In Sam's mind, he owed her. When their lips had parted, her eyes, which had been so soft and dreamy, sharpened.

"Well?" she'd asked.

For a second, he'd been confused. "Well, what?"

"Are you coming to the lecture?"

He didn't know what to tell her. It sounded suspiciously like a date, and he didn't do dates. It was at the university, and he was done with university. Common sense and experience—that had been Dad. Sam didn't pretend to be a better man than his father.

But she was such a nice girl, and the kiss . . . Well, that was better than nice. After that kiss, Sam's brain couldn't come up with a convincing reason to say no fast enough. Hurting the girl's feelings without good reason was a dick move. So he'd made some vague statement like, *If I can get away*, and she'd smiled at him as if he'd promised her the moon.

For the next two weeks, every time she came into the shop or he saw her on the sidelines of Aoife's games, she'd worn the same damn smile. Happy. Hopeful.

He should have found a way to tell her he wasn't what she thought. Not boyfriend potential, any of his usual hookups could have told her. Not university material, his old guidance counselor would have said. But Dee never asked. Anyway, she was headed back to America when her year was up. So there was this temptation, right? To pretend, for a little while, that this could be something else. That he could be something else.

He wanted a fag. He thrust his hands into his hoodie, surveying the square.

"*Fancy yourself too smart for us,*" his da used to say, joking, back when Sam thought he had a future here.

At least this wasn't the regular lecture crowd. Fewer gray-haired alums and book club mums, more families with kids. He could have brought Aoife and fit right in. But he wasn't using his little sister as camouflage. He didn't need a chaperone.

"Sam!"

He turned in relief toward the sound of Dee's voice. She was hurrying across the cobblestones, bright smile in place. He smiled back before he noticed the two with her, her pal Reeti and that Tim fellow, clean-shaven and self-assured and wearing a fecking jacket like a proper grown-up. So she'd brought her own chaperones. Or support.

Dee kissed his cheek—she smelled like lemons—and then Reeti did, too. Tim held out his hand.

Sam shook it. "What's with the fancy dress?"

"Oh, the kids' costumes." Dee beamed. "Aren't they cute?"

Now that she mentioned it, Sam noticed a bunch of tweens wandering around with dark clothes and rainbow hair.

"Those are the Shivery Tales fans," Tim said.

"The what?"

"Shivery Tales. The series?"

"Never heard of them."

"I read them all." Tim opened his blazer, displaying a graphic book cover T-shirt. "That's why I'm here."

"Your reading taste stopped in middle school, did it?" Sam asked.

Tim smiled, either unoffended or too well-mannered to let it show. Frustrating, that. "Gross-out humor and cheap thrills, that was me."

"I never read them, either," Dee confessed.

"His earlier stuff is better. I'll loan you one," Tim said.

Point to him, Sam thought. If anyone was keeping score.

They went inside and found four seats together. Sam sat on the aisle. Dee was next to him, Reeti on her other side. Not Tim, Sam noticed with satisfaction.

There were the usual droning introductions before Oscar Diggs bounded to the lectern, a gnomish little man with wispy hair and sharp eyes.

"Snakes. Spiders. Monsters. Death." He twinkled around at the audience. "These are human fears. Universal fears. My Irish granny used to tell me bedtime stories about banshees and hobgoblins." Diggs chuckled. "No wonder I had nightmares as a child."

The audience laughed politely.

He was a bit of a humbug, Sam thought. Like every tourist who had a great-grandmother from the old country and thought that made them Irish. He saw them in the shop all the time.

"As adults, we know that what we really fear is extinction," Diggs continued. "Not simply loss of life, but loss of self, loss of control, loss of connection, all the things that make life worth living. And this, my dear friends, is the stuff of fiction, from Shakespeare and Orwell to horror greats like Stephen King. Even little stories such as mine can reveal not just the boogeyman hiding in the closet but our own monstrous insecurities."

Sam slouched in his seat, watching Dee's profile. Better that than listening to some stranger talk about primal fears and man's evolutionary instincts.

Diggs knew how to play to his audience, though. He skipped nimbly from haunted houses to *The Walking Dead*, from campfire tales about ghosts and serial killers to modern anxieties about climate change and system collapse.

"Fear is cathartic. To be scared from the safety of the couch or reading under the covers at night . . ." He waved his hands, winding up for the big finish. "What could be more fun? But the story is not the fear. The story is about surviving the danger. About facing your fears. About defeating your monsters!"

Lots of clapping for that.

The audience rose like a flock of pigeons, flapping, cooing, and puffing their chests. The tweens surged forward. Diggs perched on the edge of the stage, signing books and posing for selfies.

The four of them left the hall together. Somehow, without much discussion or decision, they found their way to a pub near campus, Sam swept up and pulled along like a leaf in the gutter.

He went out sometimes. He didn't spend every night working, reading behind the register, or alone in his room. But this felt different from grabbing a drink with his mates or scouting for a spot of sex.

The pub was all right, eighteenth-century exposed beams and flat-screens over the bar. A few creatures of the night on the prowl, a girl group celebrating a birthday, posh lads with beards or beanies throwing darts. Tim bought a round of overpriced drinks. Sam nursed his Guinness, listening to the others talk.

They were all so bloody secure in their privilege, confident in their opinions and their right to be heard. Even Dee.

She sat with her drink—white wine, terrible choice—her face shining in the golden glow of the bar. "Wasn't he paraphrasing Neil Gaiman at the end? That stuff about facing your fears?"

"From *Coraline*," Tim said. Trying to impress, the sod. "'Fairy tales are more than true: not because they tell us that dragons exist, but because they tell us that dragons can be beaten.'"

Sam absolutely did not need to show off. He had nothing to prove to anybody. "It was Chesterton," he said. "Originally."

"What?" Reeti asked.

"The quote. 'The baby has known the dragon intimately ever since he had an imagination. What the fairy tale provides for him is a St. George to kill the dragon.'" He took a sip of Guinness. "G. K. Chesterton."

Dee grinned at him. She was a nice person. Too good for him. He pushed the thought away.

Tim inclined his head, acknowledging the point. "Another case of great artists steal, lesser artists copy."

"Who said that?" Reeti demanded.

"Steve Jobs," Tim said at the same time Sam replied, "Picasso."

It wasn't a contest, Sam reminded himself. But it felt like one. How much sprang from his egalitarian desire to puncture Tim's privilege and how much was due to Dee he hadn't figured out.

The dart players moved on, probably to do heavier drinking at a livelier club.

"Fancy a game?" Sam asked Tim.

Tim held his gaze. Challenge met. "All right." And then he turned to the girls. "You in?"

Dee smiled and started to get up.

"Unlike the male of the species, we do not need to whip out our shafts to have a good time." Reeti waggled her fingers, dismissing them. "Go play your game. I want to talk to Dee."

"You've been avoiding me," Sam heard Reeti say as he got up to play. "How are things going with Dr. Ward?"

Dr. Ward. Maeve Ward. The name conjured memories of a broomstick of a woman at his father's funeral, the only one of his instructors to attend, wearing black and carrying a black umbrella. They'd all worn black, except for Aoife, who was only a year old, and Grace, in her First Communion dress. Even Jack wore a little black tie. Janette made Sam put on one of his father's two suits, the one he wasn't being buried in. It was too big on Sam everywhere but the shoulders. He kept tugging on the jacket, conscious of everyone staring.

Dr. Ward came up to him after Mass. "I'm sorry for your loss," she said.

Which is what everyone said. Sam hadn't cared. His da was dead, and his mother looked like death, and Fiadh was red-faced with crying. Sam had wanted to cry, too.

She'd written him a letter that summer, he remembered. Ward. After he'd rejected the fellowship and notified the college he wasn't coming back. He'd never responded. She would have forgotten him by now, one more faceless undergrad who had taken a single class with her nine years ago.

Tim gestured to Sam to go first.

He threw, just missing the double ring.

"Bad luck," Tim said.

Condescending bastard. Or maybe he was genuinely a good sport. A decent guy. He doubled in on the first throw, hitting a five and a twenty with his next two darts.

Fuck. Sam went up to the line again, focusing this time. Double twenty. Double fifteen. Outer bull's-eye.

Tim gave him a nod as he stepped back. He scored two decent shots and then a triple nineteen on the last throw.

Sam lifted an eyebrow. "Play a lot?"

"I did. Years ago."

"A man of leisure."

Tim gave him a straight look. "Not much else to do on deployment."

"Lisburn?" In Northern Ireland.

"Kabul."

Which made Sam feel like a right arsehole. The score went back and forth. At some point, the girls stopped talking to watch. Sam won, checking out with a double eighteen. Gratifying, that.

"Good game," Tim said, as if they were schoolboys on the pitch.

Dee was smiling. "Very Ted Lasso," she said, which made Reeti snort. Sam didn't know what she was talking about.

Tim looked pained or maybe amused. He was so damn British it was hard to tell.

"Another?" Sam asked, signaling their server.

Tim pulled out his wallet. "I've got it."

Sam didn't want his charity. "You bought the last round."

"Loser pays."

"Actually, I should go," Dee said. "I have to get the girls off to school tomorrow."

"Poor Cinderella," Reeti said.

"I'll take you," Tim said.

Sam finished his beer in one smooth swallow. "I'll do it. Have to get up myself in the morning."

Dee and Reeti exchanged glances, messaging each other in that mysterious way girls did.

"You can take me home," Reeti said to Tim. "Since we live in the same building and all."

So Sam left with Dee. It felt like another win.

Rain spangled the pavement. Dee walked like a tourist, looking about her, not checking her phone or her reflection in the shop windows as they passed. They did not hold hands.

"I hope you had a good time tonight," she said finally. A sideways look. "Especially since you're not a Shivery Tales fan."

"Maybe you've converted me. I might even pick up one of his books now. For Aoife," he added.

Dee laughed. "Sophie loves them."

"You should have brought her, then."

"I'd already asked you." Hard to tell in the light of the streetlamps, but he thought she blushed. "Besides, it's my night off."

He didn't get why she was working at all. She must have money. She couldn't afford to be here otherwise. Trinity didn't lavish financial aid on foreign graduate students.

"You said you were just helping out your professor."

"I was. At first. But I needed a place to stay and Glenda—Glenda Norton—needed someone to take care of the girls after school, so this seemed like a good solution for everyone."

"I hope the pay is good."

"It's fine."

Which meant it was shit. "So, it's really only a good deal for her."

"No, I like the girls. Her home is lovely. And working for Glenda . . . It's sort of a protection in the program."

"You make it sound like the Mafia. Lots of criminal violence in academic circles, is there?"

"You'd be surprised," Dee said ruefully. "I got pretty roughed up on my last critique. That quote we were talking about? That's my workshop instructor."

"Dr. Ward."

"You know her?"

He shook off the memory of his father's funeral. "I had a class with her once. She's your dragon that needs defeating?"

"I don't . . . Maybe? I meant the quote about how bad artists copy. She thinks I'm copying another writer."

He couldn't imagine why she was telling him this. Unless she wasn't worried about trying to impress him. "Plagiarism."

That was serious. Academic misconduct. You could be disciplined for that, although hardly anyone was. But Sam wrote—notebooks full of entries that no one ever saw, fragments of ideas, snatches of dialogue, observations about his family, descriptions of characters who came into the shop. The thought of someone using them as their own made him slightly sick.

Dee winced. "Not plagiarism. More like a depressing lack of originality. She thinks I'm copying his style."

That was better. "Easy enough to take on the style of someone you admire," Sam said. He'd done it himself, when he was younger. "Who is it?"

She marched along the sidewalk, her boots fragmenting the puddles into rainbow shards of light. "Grayson Kettering. He . . . He was at KU when I was in the program there."

"But you left."

She averted her face. "To get away from him."

Him. Grayson Kettering.

"Wait." Sam lengthened his stride to catch up. He owned a newsagents. He read the papers he stocked, including the books and entertainment sections. "Dee Gale. You're never . . . ?"

She stopped then, in front of one of the fancy houses lining the street, her eyes dark in her pale face. "Destiny Gayle."

"Fuck."

"Yeah. We did." Her gaze dropped to her boots. "So . . ."

He had to say something. "Good for you. Leaving, I mean.

You don't want to be in Kansas anyway. Not when you could be in Ireland." She didn't look at him. "All the great writers are Irish," he added.

That dragged her head up. "I'm not great." Her smile was wan. "According to Dr. Ward, I'm barely competent."

"At least you're writing," Sam pointed out. "You didn't let that bastard stop you from doing what you want. Going after what you want." It was more than Sam had ever done. But he didn't say that.

Dee frowned, as if she'd heard him anyway. "You could, too," she said. "If you reapplied now, you could—"

He kissed her, which at least shut her up.

There was a desperation to this kiss that hadn't been there before. Clutching hands, open mouths. As if they both needed to get something right and for one moment it was this. His heart pounded in his ears. She inhaled, quick and sharp, as she broke away.

Sam watched as she ran up the stairs, Cinderella in reverse.

He had never felt less like a prince in his life.

THIRTEEN

S o, cowgirl," Reeti said. "Are you back in the saddle again?"
I almost spurted chai through my nose. "Nope. There was no riding last night. Sam walked me home."

"I thought maybe you would go to his place. Did he kiss you good night, at least?"

I hid my hot face in my mug. Thank God we were in Reeti's condo and not Sam's shop, where anyone—his sister, his mother, *Sam*—might hear us.

"He did!" Reeti crowed. "Was it any good? He looks like he'd be a good kisser."

The memory of Sam's kiss surged, hard and fast and low. His tongue in my mouth. My hands in his hair. My lips still tingled, and not from Reeti's liberal use of ginger in the tea. "It was. He is."

"I sense a 'but' coming."

"No 'but.' I feel like I'm in a rom-com. *Eat, Pray, Love. Under the Tuscan Sun.* Sad Girl goes to Europe and finds her mojo with Hot Irish Poet."

"Soon to be a major motion picture," Reeti joked.

Like *Destiny Gayle.*

My lungs emptied. I stared at her, stricken.

"Oh shit," Reeti said. "I wasn't thinking. Sorry."

I forced myself to breathe. "It's fine. I'm fine. It's just . . . I know I have this tendency to see what I want to see." Gray used to mock my rose-colored glasses. And he was right. Because I'd looked at him and seen my soul mate. "I imagine things. Even if what I'm looking for isn't really there. I don't want to make another mistake. I'm not ready to jump into another serious relationship."

"It doesn't have to be serious," Reeti said. "If Sam makes you feel better, if he boosts your confidence, that's a good thing."

A good thing. I took another sip of chai, relieved. "What about you? I don't see you with anyone."

"I date. Dated," Reeti amended. "I got tired of the bullshit. All these guys saying I'm so exotic. Or asking me where I'm from. The last boy I went out with waited until we were naked before he told me he'd always wanted to be with 'a foreign girl.'" She hooked air quotes around the words. "So I tell him my family is British. Like, is that foreign enough for you, you Irish arsehole?"

"Ugh. I'm so sorry."

"It is what it is." Her nails, perfect pale-blue ovals, tapped her mug. "My parents want to introduce me to a boy while I'm home over the break. He's Sikh."

"How do you feel about that?"

She raised one shoulder in a delicate shrug. "It's just a meeting. If I don't like him, that's fine. My parents are progressive. They would be happy if I found someone suitable on my own. But I'm twenty-three. When my sister was my age, she was already married and expecting a baby."

I was twenty-six. "And you're in grad school."

"Sheena was taking her Legal Practice Course when she married Aaraav. And now she is a solicitor with two children."

"Did your sister have an arranged marriage?"

"Arranged, not forced. First the boy and the girl have a meeting, to see if they like each other."

"Did you call him a boy? How old is he?"

Reeti grinned. "In a *rishta*, the men are always boys, and the women are always girls. He's twenty-seven. An architect. A good son, a good match. He just moved to London. Close to my father's restaurant. My parents love that, of course." She rolled her eyes.

"Isn't that where you want to teach? In London."

"Southall, yes. Not that it matters. My mother is hardly going to say, 'Good, Reeti, be a teacher, at least you're not an old maid.'"

I laughed. "I think it's great that they care. I'm just trying to imagine having my romantic partners vetted by Uncle Henry and Aunt Em."

"They never met Gray?"

I shook my head. "Aunt Em invited him once. But . . ."

I'd told myself Gray would be bored at the farm. I couldn't picture him discussing grain prices with Uncle Henry or recipes with Aunt Em. Maybe I'd worried he would judge my family home, with its fading wallpaper and scarred linoleum. Maybe I wasn't sure what my aunt and uncle would think of him.

Maybe my reluctance to find out should have told me something.

"*All hat and no cattle*," Henry had remarked after one of my mother's flying visits. I'd never forgotten.

"When we were growing up, it was like two worlds," I said. "Our mother's world"—full of glamor and color and terrifying independence—"and Kansas." Flat, predictable, safe, and gray. "Even when she'd bring us there—Toni and me—she never stayed." I swallowed. "After she died, I guess I did the same thing. Two separate worlds, school and the farm. I made myself into one person when I was with my aunt and uncle and another person with Gray. I didn't know how to be both at once."

"When worlds collide," Reeti said.

I nodded. "*Boom*."

"You like Sam's family, though," Reeti said.

"I *love* Sam's family," I gushed.

"More than Sam?"

I opened my mouth and closed it. Several times, like a fish.

"Look, I get it. Family is important," Reeti said. "I love my parents. And when I get married, I want to get along with my husband's family, too."

"I'm not looking to get married," I said automatically.

"What are you looking for, *didi*?" Reeti asked gently.

The question opened up a void inside me. Like standing on the edge of a cliff and staring into the abyss. Once you took away what other people thought of me, was there anything even there?

"You keep calling me that."

"Because it is your name, yeah? Almost your name. And I think of you as a sister." She narrowed her eyes. "Stop avoiding the question."

Right. "I want to find where I belong, I guess. A world of my own."

"It's a good thing you're a writer then, isn't it?"

"Why's that?"

She smiled. "You can make your own world."

A rush of affection filled me. "I love you, Reeti."

"I love you, too." Her smile widened. "But I am still going to let my parents set me up with this boy."

The smell of baking drifted up the stairs as I left Reeti's, butter and . . . I took a deep, appreciative sniff. Vanilla, maybe?

Tim popped out of his apartment as I passed. Like the troll under the bridge in "Three Billy Goats Gruff," lying in wait for the sound of my footsteps.

The image made me smile. "Hey, Tim."

"I have something for you." His tie was off, collar unbuttoned, shirtsleeves rolled back. I wasn't going to pretend there was some imaginary attraction there. But he did have very nice forearms.

"Chelsea buns?" I asked.

He looked blank.

"I thought I smelled baking," I explained.

"Scones. In the oven." He frowned. "Did you want Chelsea buns?"

I sighed. "It was a joke, Tim."

"Ah. Yes. No, I wanted to give you this." He wiped his hands on the towel tossed over his shoulder. Reached inside his apartment.

A book, I saw as he offered it to me. "Oscar Diggs?"

"His Guardians series. One of the early ones."

I glanced at the lurid cover, a hedge of thorns pierced by a sword. "What's it about?"

He held it out. "Read it."

"Really, I . . ."

"The heroine reminded me of you."

"That's very nice of you. But I don't have time. I already have so much reading to do for class." And there was the book of plays from Sam I hadn't even started.

"Then this will be an escape."

Which is what reading was. Or used to be. How did he know? All those times I'd hidden in the library or curled on the floor between the wall and my bed, lost within the covers of a book. All those stories I'd told Toni or myself.

"I don't need to escape my life anymore."

He took a step back. "Of course."

"It's just this one class is giving me a little trouble."

"Right."

"It's Dr. Ward. The instructor. She thinks I should start something new."

Tim regarded me steadily, not speaking.

"She said my writing is derivative," I said to fill the silence. "That I don't have anything to say for myself."

"Clearly untrue."

"Ha." I swallowed. "The thing is, I can see . . . You know. Similarities. Between my work and"—*Gray*—"other writers. It's possible I've been influenced. Inadvertently."

"Perhaps you should try reading different writers."

"It's hard to read anything anymore. For pleasure, I mean. If it's a bad book, then I spend all this time fixing it in my head. And if it's a good book . . ." My throat swelled. I swallowed, my doubts rushing in like a pack of flying monkeys. "If it's a good book . . ." I inhaled through my nose. "I think, *I'll never be that good.* Ever. And when I pick it apart to see what's working, when I try to be better, to be like that, then I'm not really writing, I'm not creating, I'm just copying someone else's style."

He handed me the dish towel. Apparently I was crying. Again.

I blotted my eyes. "Say something."

"I have to go now."

I sniffed. "Oh. Okay."

"The scones are burning."

"*Oh.*"

He retreated to his apartment, leaving the door open behind him. In invitation? I was still clutching the dish towel. I had to give it back eventually. So I followed.

Tim's apartment was laid out like Reeti's, with an open counter providing a view of the kitchen. I watched as he slid a baking sheet from the oven.

"When I was in rehab, I needed to learn to walk with crutches," he remarked out of nowhere.

Wait. What? Oh my God. "When?"

"Five years ago."

He became a consultant five years ago, he'd said. Before that, he was in the army. "Were you hurt? Wounded? What happened?"

He set the pan on top of the stove. The scones were a beautiful golden brown, I saw with the part of my brain that wasn't picturing him lying in some hospital. Not burned at all.

"Suicide bomber," he said briefly. He cleared his throat. "Anyway, afterward, I couldn't . . . My legs wouldn't do what I wanted them to do. I was pretty frustrated for a while."

"Of course you were," I said. "Tim, I'm so sorry."

One by one, he removed the scones from the baking sheet to a cooling rack, focusing on his task. "My point is, the therapist told me I had to keep moving, get the fluid in the joints flowing so I didn't stiffen up. The crutches were a tool, he said, to strengthen the muscles until I could walk on my own."

The scar on his knee, I remembered. "Are you okay now?"

"Yes."

We were back to one-word answers, I noticed. "Thank you for telling me."

"I only mentioned it because it seemed relevant to your situation," he said stiffly.

"My situation." I didn't follow him at all. "I'm not wounded."

"I'm referring to your writing. What you said about copying other writers you admire."

"So?" I hated the defensive note in my voice.

"Using someone else's style . . . It struck me as the same thing.

A crutch. Something you can lean on while you work out your own. And then, when you're strong enough, when you don't need it anymore"—he looked up, finally, his eyes opaque as silver—"you can let it go."

I melted. "Tim . . ."

He moved around the counter, lifting his hand toward me. "You have a, ah . . ." He leaned in closer. I held my breath. "Flour. Right there." His fingers brushed my cheek before he shifted back. "From the towel."

My face flamed.

He put two scones in a bag for me to take home. I couldn't blurt out *I love you* the way I had to Reeti. We weren't that kind of friends.

But when I left, clutching the scones, I took his book with me, too.

When I was in eleventh grade, I went to see the guidance counselor. I already knew I was going to KU, because of Toni. But after I took the SATs, the postcards started coming from other colleges: Columbia in New York, Northwestern in Chicago, little glimpses of my mother's world arriving in the mail. Maybe I thought Mrs. Bradford would encourage me to apply.

But all the counselor wanted to talk about was our dead mother. "*Mourning a loved one isn't a linear process, Dorothy,*" Mrs. Bradford had said, fixing me with a professionally sympathetic smile. "*We say that grief has five stages, but you can experience any of those feelings at any time.*"

I'd pretended not to know what she was talking about.

But now, working on my writing assignments, I remembered Mrs. Bradford and her five stupid stages of grief. Week after week,

I went through them all. Denial. Anger. Bargaining. Depression. My Dust Bowl story was dead, and I was in mourning.

Acceptance, unfortunately, was still a long way off.

I didn't give up on my protagonist as Maeve suggested. But as the term went on, I grew increasingly impatient with Rose. She was not a victim, I thought. Or a slut. But was she the hero of her own story? I made her older. No, younger. Maybe her real adventure began after she left the farm. Maybe she was abducted. Trafficked. *No, too dark*. Maybe she ran away. *Too close*.

"What happened to her parents? Her mother?" Claire asked in the workshop, and my mind froze.

"It doesn't matter," I said. Except a part of me knew that it did.

We brainstormed ideas. How could Rose set off on her own, a twelve-year-old in 1930s Kansas? Not on her own. Not with the traveling magician. Rose needed to defeat her own dragons, I decided, or at least to fight them. It would take some magical event, a portal to another world. Caught up in a dust storm, maybe? A cyclone? It was no voyage to Narnia, but it was a start.

Maeve raised her eyebrows over the morphing of my bleak literary novel into middle-grade fantasy. It wasn't *serious* fiction. Not like the other students were writing. I had no deep insights on the human condition, no clever exploration of social or political themes. But my classmates accepted the transformation without a blink. They threw around words like *commercial* and *mainstream*. Most of us were taking Oscar Diggs's seminar next term. "Quests are big," Ryan, the game writer, assured me. "I like that she is too young for a love interest," Erinma said with satisfaction.

When Reeti declared we should celebrate a real American Thanksgiving at her flat the following Sunday, I invited the whole group over for dinner.

We asked Tim, too, since the bird barely fit into Reeti's oven and we needed his kitchen to cook the stuffing. And Sam, because . . . Well. *Sam*. My heart skipped at the thought of seeing him again, away from the shop, where he always had one eye on his customers, or the sidelines, where his sisters and Sophie and Lily were always watching us.

He came, bringing a loaf of Fiadh's bread and a package of crisps. I was half-afraid he would spend the evening holding a beer and propping up a corner of Reeti's fireplace like the angry Irish revolutionary in a period drama. But Sam was in shopkeeper mode, quick and affable.

"He's very charming," Claire said after she'd spent half an hour in close conversation with him, alternately touching his arm and her hair. "Where did you say you met again?"

"Clery's Newsagents. He's Sam Clery," I said.

Shauna grinned. "Well done, you."

"Vegetables do not belong in pudding," Alan declared, sampling my pumpkin pie. But he had two helpings of Erinma's Nigerian yam dish, I noticed, and someone ate up all Reeti's saag paneer, and everyone drank too much.

"Happy Thanksgiving, *didi*," Reeti said after the last guest left.

Tim, who had spent the evening quietly refilling glasses, went downstairs, taking the chairs we had borrowed with him.

I beamed at her. I was happy. And thankful. Could I finally be finding my place?

How can you not be coming home for Christmas?" Toni asked. "You promised."

I winced at the phone. "I said I'd try." Which wasn't good enough, I knew. Our mother used to try, too. "But Glenda asked me to help out over the holidays. I can't say no."

"You could if you wanted to."

Guilt stabbed my chest. I really couldn't.

For one thing, plane tickets at the holidays were ridiculously expensive. Plus, the Nortons were leaving on their annual ski vacation and wanted me to come along.

"Consider it an early Christmas present," Glenda had said. "You can room with Lily and Sophie. The girls will be on the slopes most of the day, so you'll hardly be working at all. You need to purchase your own lift ticket, of course."

"But I don't ski."

"Even better." She'd smiled. "You can go shopping. Get a massage. I want you to enjoy yourself. As long as you're with the girls in the evening, you can do whatever you want. It's a wonderful opportunity for you."

I imagined myself reading a book by the fire, sipping on hot buttered rum. But telling Toni I was ditching her to go to a resort in the Alps would only make things worse. "How about I come home over spring break?"

"It's not the same," Toni said.

No, it wasn't. We'd never spent Christmas apart. "Or you could come see me. After New Year's," I suggested. When I got back from the Nortons' vacation. "I'll buy your ticket." Fares went down after January 3rd. I'd checked online already.

"If I haven't dropped out by then," Toni muttered.

I rubbed my forehead. "Sweetie, you can't run away from your problems."

"You did."

Another stab, deeper than the first. "You're right. I'm sorry. What can I do?"

"Don't worry about it."

"Toni . . ."

"I'll take care of it," Toni said.

Which only made me worry more.

But my life didn't allow for too many distractions. My assessments loomed—a structural outline and short story due in January and a five-thousand-word essay on something (I was still figuring that part out) after that. Plus, I had to help the girls pack for their trip. I browsed the bookstalls to find graphic novels for Lily and took Sophie to football. Her last game was on Saturday. I didn't have to go, since Glenda had decided to attend the final game of the season. But I wanted to cheer Sophie on. Besides, I was eager to see Sam before we left for Switzerland.

He was not, apparently, equally excited to see me.

"So." I inched closer on the sidelines, breathing in his unique Sam smell, tea and newsprint. "Any special plans for Christmas?"

He stuck his hands into his pockets. "Not really."

"Claire mentioned she'd seen you around."

"She's been into the shop a few times," Sam said, his eyes still on the game.

"I thought you were maybe, um, seeing each other or something."

"I'm not exactly her type."

"She said you were charming." *Very* charming. And Claire was pretty and confident and far cooler than I would ever be.

"Yeah. Bit like dating the help for her, though, isn't it?"

"That's ridiculous and snobby and classist."

"Realistic." He glanced down at me, a smile tugging his crooked mouth. "What about you?"

My heart thumped. "*What* about me?"

Sam's grin broadened. "Any special . . . plans?"

"Are you asking me out?"

"Janette is cooking Christmas dinner for half the neighborhood. You're welcome, if you've nowhere else to be."

Which didn't really answer my question. Or maybe it did.

"Thanks. I wish I could. But I'm going away with the Nortons."

I didn't want to be Sam's pity date. I'd had enough of existing on emotional crumbs.

I watched Glenda hug Sophie after the game. Trailing after them on the way home from the bus stop, with buskers on every corner and Christmas shoppers all around, I was swamped by a wave of homesickness. It was probably snowing in Kansas this time of year. I wondered how Toni was doing. I regretted how we had left things. Hated disappointing her. Maybe we would have time for a nice long video chat tonight.

A thin figure huddled on the town house steps, shoulders hunched against the cold, a backpack at his feet. Her feet? My heart tugged in sympathy. It must be awful to be homeless at any time of year, but especially at the holidays.

At our approach, the figure stirred. Stood.

"Who is that?" Glenda asked.

Even before she looked our way, I knew.

"Toni!" I cried.

FOURTEEN

"What are you doing here?" I couldn't believe my sister was in my arms again. I hugged her skinny little body before pulling back to look at her, her dancing black eyes, her got-to-love-me grin. "Oh, I'm so glad to see you! Is everything all right?"

"Everything's great." She tugged off her knit cap, releasing her silky dark hair. "I wanted to surprise you."

"Well, you did." We were in the library, snatching a moment of privacy while Glenda and the girls were in the kitchen. I should be in there making lunch. But for now . . . "When did you get in?"

"This morning. It took me a while to find a ride from the airport."

"There are taxis. You should have called."

"I met some guys from University College. I grabbed a ride with them."

I swallowed the usual scolding about getting into a car with strangers. It never worked with my sister anyway. I hugged her again. "How long can you stay?"

"I'm not going back."

"What?"

Her gaze met mine, bright and defiant. "I dropped out."

Oof. The air left my lungs. "Toni . . . Why?"

A shrug.

"What did Aunt Em say?" No point in asking Uncle Henry's opinion. We were his sister's children, but he left all decisions about our raising to his wife.

"I didn't tell them."

"But they know you're here," I ventured.

Toni shook her head. "They think I'm coming home for Christmas."

Our aunt was not a sentimental woman. She never sat down with us to watch a Christmas movie all the way through. She gave practical gifts: winter coats and underwear. But every December she set out the china bell collection that had belonged to her grandmother and the pottery nativity figures our mother brought back one year from Mexico. Toni and I used to arrange them together on the sideboard. What would Em do, how would she feel, if neither of us were there?

"Toni. You have to call her. You have to tell her."

"I thought maybe you could do it."

Of course she did. Didn't I always?

"Dee, dear, could I speak with you a moment," Glenda said from the doorway. Not a question.

"I'll just take my things to your room," Toni said. She shouldered her backpack. "Where is it?"

"Up two flights. Third door on the right."

"Great. Nice to meet you," she said to Glenda as she passed.

"Welcome to Dublin!" Toni's footsteps faded up the stairs.

"Of course she can't stay," Glenda said to me.

Of course, I echoed silently. Because housing a live-in au pair was totally different from hosting a random American teenager over the holidays.

I sucked in my breath, remembering Mom dropping us off with Aunt Leslie. Or was it Cecily?

"*This apartment isn't really set up for children,*" Leslie/Cecily said.

I stood in the center of her living room, holding tight to Toni's hand, our suitcase at my feet. "*We don't take up a lot of room.*"

Our mother's friend sighed. "*I thought you girls were older. You're fine. But some of the supplies I work with are pretty toxic. If the baby gets into things . . .*"

"*She won't,*" I assured her. "*We won't be any trouble. I'll take care of her.*"

That's what I did.

I met Glenda's gaze. "I didn't expect . . . That is . . . Would it be okay if Toni slept in my room tonight?"

She nodded. "You want to visit before we leave for Gstaad on Monday."

The day after tomorrow. I winced. "Yeah. Thank you. The thing is . . . My sister just got here."

"I'm aware."

"I can't leave her alone on Christmas."

Glenda's perfect brow creased. "Naturally, you'll *miss* her. But you're sharing a room with Lily and Sophie. There's simply no way your sister can come, too."

"I wasn't suggesting . . . I mean I can't go."

Glenda blinked her pale-blue eyes. "I'm not sure I understand. I thought you were looking forward to our trip."

"I am. I was. But Toni's only eighteen," I said.

"Old enough to get on a plane. Old enough to make her own decisions. She needs to learn that actions have consequences."

"She applied to KU because of me. She's here in Ireland because of me." *Because I ran away.*

"My dear girl, you mustn't let a misplaced sense of responsibility deprive you of a wonderful opportunity. Not every girl gets to go to Gstaad."

"I know. I'm sorry."

"We had an understanding," Glenda said. "The girls will be so disappointed. I'm disappointed."

I swallowed. "I'm really sorry. I'll make it up to you," I promised. "To all of you. Somehow. When Sophie and Lily get back, we can—"

"I'm afraid that won't be possible," Glenda said.

"Excuse me?"

"If I can't trust you to honor your obligations, I can't possibly leave the girls in your care. Unless . . ." Her gaze met mine. "You were to reconsider . . . ?"

I recognized the invitation. And the threat. Gray used the same tactic all the time—nothing stated, everything implied. *Do what I want and all is forgiven. Be what I need or else.* I had made myself who he wanted—what I thought he wanted—me to be. I wouldn't make myself what Glenda wanted.

Even if it meant I could stay.

I shook my head silently.

"In that case, I expect you to be gone when we get back. Both of you," Glenda said, as if that wasn't clear.

"This won't affect . . . I mean, we'll still see each other. At the writing center," I said.

"I told you when I hired you that your job performance and your academic evaluation have nothing to do with one another. Fortunately." She smiled thinly. "I only hope Maeve was wrong."

My stomach swooped. "Dr. Ward? Wrong about what?"

"When we considered your application, she questioned your ability to commit to the program. After your experience at Kansas . . . Well. Do be sure to say good-bye to the girls before you go," Glenda added.

For tonight? I wondered. For the week? Or for good?

Not that it mattered.

I was dismissed.

B efore Toni and I went out for the night, I gave the girls hugs and their Christmas presents. Sophie ripped hers open, popped the training jersey over her head, and galumphed down the stairs to model it for her mother.

Lily sat on her bed, staring down at the exquisitely drawn cover of the first issue of *Monstress* that I'd found in a shop near the Ha'penny Bridge.

"The heroine is a teenage girl. It's kind of dark," I said. "But I love Marjorie Liu's writing. And the artist—Takeda—is a woman." (*"She'll love it,"* Toni had said.)

Lily's face scrunched. "I hate you for leaving."

The misery in her eyes made my heart squeeze. But I wasn't going to make things better by throwing her mother under the bus.

"I'll miss you, too," I said gently. "But you have your mom. And your sister. They're all you really need."

All I'd needed.

I swallowed the lump in my throat. At least I still had Toni.

T his is great," my sister said brightly, looking around the pub. Lights gleamed on burgundy wood and whiskey bottles. A guitarist and fiddle player, jammed into a corner, belted out a song about bells on Christmas Day. The revelers at the bar joined in the chorus.

Reeti had met us for dinner. "So . . . Surprise?" she asked when Toni went to the bathroom.

"Big surprise," I admitted. "I knew Toni wasn't happy, but I didn't think she'd drop out."

"How long is she staying?"

I made a face into my wineglass. "I'm not sure."

Toni's allowance from our mother's trust was almost enough to live on, but she couldn't touch the principal—except for school expenses—until she turned twenty-one. Which meant she needed a plan. I needed a plan. Toni was too young to know what she was doing. I had to fix things somehow.

"I'm going to find us a nice hotel for the holidays," I said.

I could afford to treat us both for a few days. Unlike Toni, I could draw on my portion of the trust. Although now that I no longer had a job or a place to live, I needed to budget.

"Good luck with that," Reeti said. "It's Christmas. The hotels will all be full. Why not stay at the Nortons'?"

"Not an option."

"Why not?"

I told her.

"Shit," Reeti said. "What a witch."

"That's what you said about Maeve."

"So maybe they're more alike than they seem."

"Wise and powerful?" I suggested.

"Selfish and practical." Reeti's eyes were sympathetic. "I'm so sorry. But that settles it. Now you have to stay with me."

She was *such* a good friend. "I don't want to put you out."

"I won't even be there. I'm going to London to visit my family over the holidays."

I could do it, I thought. For Toni. "Does your family celebrate Christmas?" I asked, buying time.

"In our own way. My family likes all holidays. Any excuse to eat, get together, and gossip."

I smiled. "And fix up their daughter with a nice Sikh boy."

Reeti blushed. "That, too. Anyway, I have a big empty guest room. You'd have a kitchen. And your own bath."

A kitchen! If the restaurants were closed on Christmas Day, I could cook. "Well . . . If you're sure we won't be in the way . . . Maybe for a few days?"

"As long as you like," Reeti said firmly.

I smiled mistily across the table. "Thank you."

Toni returned to the table by way of the bar. "What?" she said when I eyed the whiskey glass in her hand. "I'm totally legal here."

"You're not used to drinking."

"How do you know?"

I didn't, of course. I hadn't been there to help her navigate freshman year. Underage drinking was a problem on campus. Maybe . . .

My sister sighed. "Don't worry." She slid into the booth, bumping her shoulder affectionately against mine. "I was very good while you were gone. She's such a mother hen," she said to Reeti.

"You're lucky to have her as your *didi*," Reeti said.

Toni grinned, suddenly looking about seven years old. "I know."

A rowdy pack of students in Christmas sweaters and Santa hats swarmed through the door in a swirl of noise and cold.

"Uh-oh," Reeti said. "Time to go."

The group ordered pints and started taking off their shoes, hopping and shuffling around.

"What are they doing?" Toni asked.

"They're Twelve Pubbers. They're swapping shoes."

"They're what?"

The ugly sweater set roared and giggled, clutching one another and the bar, jostling stools and other patrons.

"The Twelve Pubs of Christmas. They hit twelve pubs in one night, with a different rule at every pub."

"Looks like fun," Toni said.

Someone stumbled into the microphone, which crashed to the floor. Reeti and I exchanged glances.

"Maybe another pub?"

"They'll be everywhere this time of year," Reeti said. "It's a Dublin tradition."

"I don't want to leave," Toni said.

I didn't want to go home—that is, back to Glenda's—yet, either. "Clery's?" I suggested.

"I need to pack," Reeti said. "I'll text you the code for my door. My house is yours. Anytime."

We parted on the sidewalk with hugs and thanks. Outside, the evening was alive with fairy lights and music. Toni and I wandered through a changing soundtrack spilling from pubs and playing on street corners, pop and carols, choirs and acoustic guitars. Roaming packs of Twelve Pubbers, their sweaters flashing red and green, crowded the streets. Couples bundled against the cold, their breath streaming in the air. We crossed the bridge. The river flowed under our feet, shimmering in the dark. Toni's eyes shone like stars. Somewhere overhead, obscured by the glow of the city, real stars twinkled and throbbed. It was Christmas, after all, the season of joy and new beginnings.

The newsagents windows were bright with advertising flyers and strings of lights. Sam was behind the counter, a scarf around his neck against the draft from the door, head bent over a book. Bob Cratchit, working late on Christmas Eve.

He smiled when he saw us, and fairy lights sparkled to life inside me. "Who's your friend?"

"My sister, Toni. She's visiting me for Christmas." *Possibly longer.* I pushed the thought away. "Toni, this is Sam."

Fiadh came out of the back, a pair of reindeer antlers atop her blue hair. "And Sam's sister Fiadh."

"Fee."

"I love your hair," Toni said.

Fiadh smiled. "Ta."

"You're working late," I said. To her? To Sam?

"It's the holidays, isn't it? Everybody wants a Christmas cake and no one wants to make it."

"What kind of cake?" Toni asked.

"Come see, if you like."

"I thought you were off skiing," Sam said after they left.

"Change of plans," I said.

He handed me a mug of spiced chai. "I get it."

"Get what?"

"Putting aside what you want because of family."

"It's not like that."

He lifted one fluid, beautiful brow, a trick I couldn't pull off even when I practiced in a mirror. "Tell me you didn't give up your trip to be with your sister."

"Okay, yeah, I did. But only because I wanted to."

"How does your boss feel about that?"

"She's not my boss anymore."

"She fired you? Fuck."

"It's all right," I said, wanting to believe it. "It doesn't affect my standing in the program at all. But . . . Well. Obviously, she was disappointed. This trip was supposed to be my Christmas present."

"So she'll get a refund."

"I was rooming with the girls."

"Then it wasn't a present. It was a transaction. She was using you."

"She was paying me. Helping me. I thought she liked me."

"You're a lousy judge of character, then."

I opened my mouth. Shut it.

"The way I see it, she's done you a favor," Sam said. "Now you know what she is."

"She was very professional."

"I didn't say she was evil, just ordinary. I see it in the shop all the time. Most people are just doing what they can to get by, to make their own lives easier."

I thought back to the man in the cap, reading the paper without paying for it. The woman bargaining for a loaf of bread. Sam was right. Of course he was right. I had, as Maeve said, an incredibly limited view of the world. I saw things—people—*Gray*—the way I wanted them to be, overlooking clues that would be obvious to anyone else. But . . .

"You didn't," I pointed out. "Do the easy thing, I mean."

Sam had given up his chance at college to provide for his family. I might be naive, but at least I wasn't wrong about that.

He shifted, folding his arms. Apparently I could make him as uncomfortable as he made me. "Once upon a time, maybe. But don't fool yourself, Boots. I can be as selfish as the next bastard."

I grinned, suddenly more confident. "You can tell yourself that, if you want. But I don't believe you."

Toni and Fiadh returned from the back.

"Fee invited us for Christmas!" Toni said. "I told her yes. We can go, can't we?"

Sam looked at me, the devil dancing in his deep-sea eyes. I'd already turned down his invitation to Christmas dinner.

But Toni was almost bouncing with excitement. I recognized the signs of an incipient crush.

"We aren't doing anything else," Toni said.

"Not anymore," Sam murmured.

A memory surfaced of the last—second to last?—Christmas with our mother, in the brownstone apartment that had been her home base for a couple of years. For some reason, we weren't at one of her usual parties, Mom in the front room with her friends, Toni and I in someone's back bedroom, put down to sleep with the coats. That Christmas, it was just the three of us, eating take-out from little white boxes on a blanket on the floor. "*A Christmas picnic*," Mom had said gaily. I remembered how strange everything had tasted, garlic and . . . eggplant, maybe? And Mom laughing as she taught me to use chopsticks.

She had set fat candles all around the blanket, red and yellow, indigo and violet. I'd worried Toni would burn herself, but the warm rainbow of lights was so beautiful, a private art installation on the hardwood floor. I'd been so happy to have our mother's attention all to ourselves. To myself. Toni was too young to remember.

In the back of my mind, I'd thought I might re-create it with her, for her, this year, a picnic for the two of us.

Or, if Toni felt homesick, I would cook. I'd cooked for Gray all the time. I was becoming familiar with Reeti's kitchen. I could make Aunt Em's cola-glazed ham and tater tot casserole. Assuming I could find tater tots in Ireland.

But Toni was beaming, clearly delighted at the prospect of spending Christmas with the Clerys. There had been too few large family gatherings with noisy children around the table in her life.

In my life.

Fiadh was regarding my sister with the tolerant amusement

she might have shown a puppy. "Mam always makes more than enough," she told me. "You're more than welcome."

"Thank you." I smiled at her. At Sam. "We'd love to."

Tonight was so much fun," Toni said on our way home. "I love it here."

I wanted her to be happy. I wanted her to be stable and secure. Not like our mother, abandoning her commitments. Toni needed to find her direction. Make connections. Go back to college.

"You seemed to get along with Fiadh," I said cautiously.

"She's so cool." Toni slid me a grin. "And her brother's hot. Are you guys doing it?"

I flushed. "Sam and I are friends."

"Whatever you say."

"I am totally focused on school right now," I said, determined to be a good role model. "Plus, I recently got out of a relationship, remember?"

"Thank God for that."

I blinked. Toni and Gray had never spent much time together. It was true, what I'd told Reeti. I'd kept my worlds, my two selves, separate, Dee-at-college and Dorothy-at-the-farm. But Toni had visited me often. Inevitably, she and Gray had met.

"You never said anything negative about Gray before."

Toni strode over the bridge as if she knew where she was going. "Because you wouldn't listen."

"You said you liked him."

She shrugged. "Because that's what you wanted to hear."

Maybe I'd been a better role model than I'd thought. Or else a horrible example. I didn't want my little sister to feel she needed to please other people to get by.

"I want you to be honest," I said.

"Okay," Toni said agreeably. "I hate him. He trashed you in his stupid book. He deserves to die."

I smiled, warmed by her loyalty. Ridiculously reassured by her rage. Maybe I hadn't screwed her up by my example after all. "Thanks, Toto."

She flung herself at me, wrapping me in her thin, strong arms. "I *love* you, Dodo."

I hugged her back. "Love you, too."

That night we shared a bed for the first time since our mother died and we moved into the farmhouse. Toni had offered to take the floor. But this was better, squeezing together on the full mattress the way we'd once curled on the pullout couches of our mother's friends.

My brain was fogged with anxious thoughts about tomorrow and the day after that and the semester to come. But gradually my body relaxed, lulled by the warmth of Toni's body and the sweet, familiar smell of her hair.

"Tell me a story," my sister murmured drowsily.

I smiled, recalling years of whispers in the dark. "I don't have any stories."

"You always have stories," Toni said.

I did. Or I used to.

"Once upon a time, there was a girl named Rose," I began obediently. I had no idea how my story ended. But it didn't matter. Toni would be asleep long before then. "Who lived with her aunt and uncle in Kansas."

That was how it began.

"Does she have a sister?" Toni asked.

I smiled. That was our story, after all. Two children on a trip into the magical unknown.

Maybe that was my problem. I'd been writing Rose's story, but I'd forgotten to give her a companion on her journey. Someone she needed to protect, to force her to be braver, kinder, wiser. It wasn't enough to defeat the dragon. Fairy tales—the ones I loved—weren't only about survival. They were about hope and love and joy.

"She has a pet," I decided. "A chicken." I knew chickens. And a chicken would be funny.

"I don't want to be a chicken," Toni protested sleepily.

"What, then?"

"A dog."

She had always wanted a puppy. Not a working dog, like Uncle Henry's, or one of the feral strays along the highway. So, yes, okay, a dog. I could see it in my mind, small and dark and bright-eyed.

"A dog named Toto," I said, and my sister made a sound like a hen on its nest, low and contented.

I spun my story, Rose and her dog Toto on Christmas Eve, and Santa gliding in on a rainbow to take them up in his sleigh as the sky darkened to twilight and the stars came out. My sister's breathing deepened and slowed.

"And when they woke up," I said softly, "they were in a country of marvelous beauty."

But Toni was asleep by then.

I stayed awake a long time after that, the plot meandering along, winding up and down in my head like a road leading . . . somewhere.

And wondered what story I was going to tell Aunt Em in the morning.

FIFTEEN

When Tim was deployed in Afghanistan, he communicated only sporadically with his parents. He couldn't make calls in a combat zone, not when he was out on a mission, and the Internet at the duty station was frequently unreliable. So he emailed and managed occasionally to Skype, grateful his parents never pressed him for more. "*No news is good news,*" his grandfather the brigadier said gruffly.

All that changed when a suicide bomber plowed through Tim's checkpoint in Helmand Province and blew him up. The casualty notification officer had visited the family pile in Gloucestershire to give his parents the news. Tim hadn't spoken to them until he was aeromedded out to the hospital in Birmingham.

Now, though Tim's mother would never say so, any silence was cause for concern. Which meant Tim now called dutifully every Sunday and listened without complaint while his mother chatted lightly on neutral topics—the altar guild's Advent decorations or last night's roast—the mundane details a substitute for the things they did not say. *I love you. I worry about you. I'm fine.*

Naturally, he was going home for Christmas.

His parents' house would be permeated with the smells of woodsmoke, his father's Scotch, and his mother's dogs. His eighty-nine-year-old grandfather would come for dinner on Christmas Day. After his mother served the pudding, they would pull crackers—she was big on observing traditions—and the four of them would sit around the eighteenth-century dining table, paper crowns perched incongruously on their heads while they painstakingly read the jokes out loud. Tim had been looking forward to it.

But it seemed his mother, Caroline, had other plans this year.

"A little party on Boxing Day," she was saying with bright holiday cheer. "Everyone is dying to see you. You haven't been home in ages."

"I'll pack my dinner jacket," he said, teasing her gently.

She laughed, a high, false note in her voice that made him frown. "Don't be silly. It's just a few friends coming around. Although I've seen Laura's dress, and she looks smashing."

Something inside him froze. "Laura?"

"I know you two aren't engaged anymore," his mother said in that light, brittle voice. "But you did say there were no hard feelings."

No hard feelings. He rubbed the ridge of scar tissue on his chest. No feelings at all.

That was how he functioned. He had to work with her, after all. Laura. She wasn't his direct report. Since her transfer to Dublin, he'd been largely able to avoid her, treating her with distant, professional courtesy in meetings and on the elevator and in the halls. *Robot Man,* she called him, adopting Charles's old nickname.

He wondered what she had done to prompt his mother's transparent attempt to get them back together.

"Our families have always been so close. The Smiths are our neighbors," Caroline was saying. "You don't mind, do you, darling?"

Feelings stirred under the ice, an oily trickle. He shut them down, shut them off, before they spilled, corrosive as acid, over the phone.

Appalling to realize he did mind. Quite a bit, actually.

But since he had never told his mother why he had broken his engagement, he lied. "Not at all."

"So, that's all good, then." Caroline's relief was instant, palpable, and genuine. "We'll see you in a few days."

They ended the call. Tim stared out the window at the gray rainy street, absently rubbing the center of his chest.

A cab pulled to the curb outside, discharging its passenger, a young—very young—dark-haired woman in a striped knit cap. The driver came around to pop the boot.

The other door opened, and Dee got out.

The sight of her struck him, sharpening his awareness to patrol focus, making him sensitive to every movement and sound. She joined the driver and the dark-haired girl unloading things onto the sidewalk. A suitcase. Two suitcases. A duffel. A couple of cartons.

He frowned. If Dee needed a ride, if she needed help, he had a car. She should have called him. Asked him.

Or not. She didn't really know him. He didn't know the other girl at all.

He stood there, watching her, her loose braid slipping over one shoulder. Her round hips as she bent to grab another box.

He was turning into a stalker. Like Charles, howling up at Laura's flat.

He moved away from the window.

He heard the heavy entrance door open, the sound echoing up

the stairs. A thump. Some of those boxes had looked heavy. He went out.

It was the girl in the knit cap, the one who wasn't Dee. He fought an unjustified disappointment. She was lugging the larger of the two suitcases up the short flight to his landing.

"Can I help you?" he asked politely.

The girl stuck her nose in the air. Or maybe that was just the angle of the stairs. "I'm perfectly capable of carrying my own bag, thanks."

Apparently he had offended her. "Quite."

Dee backed through the front door, her arms around a box with a plant poking out the top, like an office worker ordered to clear out her desk and vacate the building by five o'clock. She tipped up her face, smiling, and his focus whirled and settled on her, a vibration in his chest, in his bones. "Hi, Tim. This is my sister, Toni."

"Nice to meet you," he said to the girl.

She gave him a look. He moved out of her way as she dragged the suitcase along the landing and up to Reeti's apartment. *Thump, thump, thump.*

"Moving in?" he asked. Not that it was any of his business.

"No. Maybe. Temporarily. Toni's visiting for Christmas," Dee said, and there was a note in her voice, not like his mother's, but not . . . right.

"That must be nice," he said.

"Well, it *is*. Only I wasn't expecting her, and Glenda was upset, because I was supposed to go with them on vacation tomorrow— the Nortons. So now I'm not working for them anymore, and Reeti offered to let us stay here for a while."

She paused to draw breath, her arms around the carton, her gaze on his, her face open. Expectant.

I'm not working for them anymore.

So he was right about the plant. She'd been fired.

How did she do it, blurt everything out like that? Walking around with her feelings exposed, her heart naked . . . It made him uncomfortable. Like he should offer her his jacket or a blanket or a drink or something.

He gestured to the box in her arms. "Is that everything?"

"There's more on the sidewalk."

He frowned again. "You shouldn't leave your things out on the street."

"Reeti says this is a very safe neighborhood."

Whatever he said next would sound like mansplaining. He waited until she passed him and then went down the steps, propping open the security door with a box while he moved the second suitcase and the duffel inside. Then he hefted the carton—books, by the weight—and carried it upstairs.

The door to Reeti's flat was open. Dee was standing motionless in the middle of the living room, a flush in her cheeks, her lips tight. Her sister was nowhere to be seen.

"Where do you want this?" he asked.

He watched as she pulled herself together. "Oh. Thank you! Um. Over there?"

He set it down against the wall, where she wouldn't trip over it. Her smile flickered. "Thanks. You really don't have to . . ."

But he was already moving, going down for the rest of her stuff, driven by a desire to help, to ease that look off her face. When he returned, Dee was setting the plant by a window.

"That's a cactus," he said.

"A Christmas cactus." She angled it to get the light. "It blooms at Christmas."

He eyed the green drooping—stalks? branches?—dubiously. "That's rather optimistic of you."

She touched a fat pink bud. He felt it, that single, delicate finger, like an electric shock. "Rather." She slid him a small smile. Mimicking him, he realized with another spark. "I thought it would make it feel more like home."

Her attempt to make a home, to make a holiday, out of so little, wrenched something inside him. He didn't have any plants in his flat.

He cleared his throat. "Where's your sister?"

Dee glanced at the closed bedroom door. "Toni's not very happy with me right now. I want her to call home. She didn't tell our aunt she was coming here."

"It's Christmas. She's your sister," Tim said. "Your aunt will understand."

Or not.

No-surprises management worked well enough at the office. Tim expected his team to communicate clearly, to inform him of what was going on, good and bad. But that was business. This was family. Her family.

"It's not just Christmas. Toni wants to drop out of KU." Dee sighed. "She didn't tell Aunt Em that, either."

"The gap year."

"You remember that?"

I remember every word you've ever said to me. Tim stuffed the thought away. "You mentioned it," he said stiffly. He glanced at the carton of books. "How did you like the Diggs book?"

"I haven't read it yet. Sorry. Did you want it back?"

"No. Keep it."

He should go.

"I'm worried she's following in my footsteps. Running away," Dee said.

She was talking about her sister, he reminded himself. "Running away? Or running toward something?"

Those wide brown eyes met his. "Running toward what?"

"I don't know. Perhaps that's what"—*you*—"she had to leave home to find out."

"Maybe." She bit her lip. "I just keep thinking if I hadn't left, she'd still be in school."

Hm. "How old was she when your mother died?"

"Four. But even before that . . . Our mother was Judy Gale." She said it like he should know the name. "The artist? She's famous," Dee said earnestly. "She exhibited all over the *world*. But she was gone a lot."

"Where was your father?"

"California? Colorado? Someplace like that. He was married. Is married, I think. Not to my mother. To someone else. And Mom met Toni's father when she was doing an installation in Elba. I'm not sure she knew his name. She was kind of casual about things like that. Even when she was there . . . She wasn't really there, you know? I was the one Toni could count on."

Which explained her reluctance to turn to others, he thought. When you were always expected to take care of things, it became hard to ask for help.

"But you had your aunt and uncle."

"Sure. We were lucky they were willing to take us in. Uncle Henry was Mom's brother. Aunt Em never had any kids of her own. Maybe that's why I always felt I had to look out for Toni."

"Or your aunt didn't want to interfere. Your mother had just died. Perhaps she saw that you needed each other."

Dee nodded. "To feel useful."

"Valued."

"Loved," she said softly.

"Er . . . Yes."

"What about you?"

He stiffened. "Me?"

"Any brothers or sisters?" she clarified.

"No." The word felt stingy in the face of her warm interest. "Only child to elderly parents," he added.

"That must have been lonely for you."

"Not lonely." You didn't miss what you never had. "Quiet, perhaps."

"I was quiet, too. I didn't want to be in the way."

"I never felt in the way." Growing up without other children around, he had simply followed his parents' schedule, adopted their habits. But he'd never doubted that they wanted him. Loved him. "I read a lot," he offered.

She smiled at him shyly. "Me too."

The moment stretched between them, sticky as caramel.

"You should call your aunt," he said abruptly.

"I will. I want to. I just don't know what to say."

"Happy Christmas," he suggested.

She laughed, a little ruefully. "That would be a start, at least. Will you see your family this Christmas?"

"Yes." And half the neighborhood on Boxing Day. Including Laura.

She tilted her head. "And are you looking forward to it?"

"It will be nice to spend time with my grandfather." A good nonanswer.

Her gaze rested on him, soft and warm and far too perceptive. "But . . . ?"

Feelings churned inside him. This was what came of talking. The ice broke, and suddenly you were wading through a hot, messy, emotional slush. What should he say? What could he say?

All of it.

No.

"Holidays are meant to be endured, not enjoyed," he said.

Mischief lit her smile. "That's very Mr. Darcy of you."

"Pardon?"

"Standing around brooding at a party," she explained. "It's so two centuries ago."

"You clearly haven't been to one of my parents' parties."

Dee laughed.

He grinned back, rewarded and relieved. "And you? Do you and your sister have plans for the holiday?"

"We're going to Sam's. Sam Clery?"

"Ah." *Sam.* The long-haired Irishman with the lorry-sized chip on his shoulder. Tim took a step back, into the friend zone where she so clearly intended him to be. "Have fun."

SIXTEEN

"Dorothy? Is that you?" Em asked.

As if my name didn't show on caller ID. And maybe it didn't. I'd called the landline at the farmhouse, not the old Android phone that went with Uncle Henry into the fields.

"Hi, Aunt Em. Merry Christmas," I said, following Tim's script.

"It's not Christmas yet," Em said. "Have you heard from your sister?"

I took a deep breath. Let it out slowly. "That's why I'm calling. Toni—"

"Is she all right?"

Guilt jabbed me. "She's fine. We're both fine. She's here."

Silence. Our aunt was never what you'd call chatty. But I'd never struck her speechless before.

"Aunt Em?"

"She could have called to let me know."

I winced. "Yeah. I'm sorry. The thing is . . ." Another deep breath. "Toni's going to stay awhile."

"In Ireland."

"For now." Unless/until I could convince her to go back to school.

"And do what?"

"I'm not quite sure. She's staying with me."

"You can't afford that," Em said in the voice she'd used when I told her I wanted to buy my lunch from the school cafeteria instead of packing a sandwich.

Money was tight on a farm. Even if the weather and the markets cooperated, the cost of planting crops or an unexpected equipment failure could throw everything into the red. But Aunt Em had never touched a penny of our trust, except to pay our college tuition.

"We'll be fine," I assured her. "How are you?"

"Well, now, Dorothy, I've been out of my mind with worry, I've got a pile of your sister's Christmas presents I don't know what to do with, and a ham that's too big for two people sitting in the fridge. Other than that, I'm dandy." Another silence. "Does the school know Toni's not coming back?"

"She finished the semester. She doesn't need to withdraw officially. Not unless she registers for classes in the spring."

Though if she skipped the whole semester, she would have to apply for readmission. I'd looked up the requirements online.

"What about housing?" Em asked. "Who's going to pick up her things?"

Our aunt was always practical. Maybe I hadn't appreciated that enough when I was growing up. Or maybe I was more like her than I realized.

"I don't know. The residence halls are already closed for Christmas break." I'd looked that up, too.

"She's just like your mother. Taking off and leaving someone else to pick up the pieces."

"Aunt Em . . ."

"Never mind." A short, exasperated breath. "Guess I'm driving to Lawrence come January. You tell Toni her stuff will be here waiting for her when she makes up her mind to come home."

There. Waiting. All those times our mother couldn't find a friend or a nanny to look after us, and in the days and months after she died, Em was always there, the second choice, the backup plan. I hadn't appreciated that enough, either. I was suddenly ashamed.

"Thanks, Aunt Em. We'll call you on Christmas. On the cell phone. We can WhatsApp. Or Skype." We'd done it with our mother often enough.

"What for?"

"Well. It would be nice to see your face. You and Uncle Henry."

She made a sound that might have been assent. "Do what you want. Henry and I aren't going anywhere."

"I'm sorry about Christmas," I said. "I didn't know Toni was coming here."

"Bound to take off sooner or later. At least she came to you."

"Thanks, Aunt Em." A pause. "I love you," I added as if we were the kind of family that said that sort of thing to one another.

Another grunt, for *Get off the phone*. Or possibly, *I love you, too*.

How did it go?" Toni asked when I returned to Reeti's guest room.

She was sprawled on one of the two twin beds, scrolling on her phone, her duffel open but still packed on the floor.

"Okay. She's going to pick up your things from the dorm."

"Good."

"*Just like your mother*," Em said in my head. "*Leaving someone else to pick up the pieces*."

"Toni."

She looked up, eyes glistening. "Thanks for calling, Dodo."

"Oh, honey, of course. But are you really sure you want to give up your housing? If you decide to go back—"

"I'm not going back."

I sat on the foot of her bed. KU was pretty inclusive. "*GayU*," Todd Nelson at the feed store said dismissively the last time I was home. Which just went to prove that the administration's support for diversity on campus wouldn't always protect Toni from narrow-minded assholes.

"Did something happen at school that upset you?" I asked gently.

"I'm good," Toni said. "Not everybody leaves Kansas because of a broken heart, you know."

"So, no more roommate issues?" I persisted.

Toni hunched one shoulder. "Madison was fine. Her boyfriend was a jerk."

"We could get you a single," I suggested. "If you gave it some time . . ."

"I'm not like you. I can't wait forever to go after what I want." Toni flushed. "Sorry. I know you only stuck around so long because of me."

"Oh, Toni, no, I—"

"You're so smart," Toni said. "You could have gone anywhere. You got all those postcards and stuff."

I was surprised she'd noticed. She was only nine when I started looking at colleges, poring over the glossy brochures of campuses I would never visit. Columbia. Emory. Northwestern.

"I never applied," I said.

"Because you wouldn't leave me. Like Mom did."

That was true. But also . . .

"I was afraid to put myself out there," I confessed. "As long I didn't actually apply, they couldn't reject me."

"You applied here," Toni said.

"Only because I couldn't face Gray again. I had to go somewhere."

Toni grinned. "Me too."

And maybe, after all, Tim was right, I thought hopefully later that week. Maybe I wasn't only running away from a broken heart and public humiliation. Maybe I was searching for something. Finding my voice. Making a space where I could belong.

It was Christmas Day. The Christmas cactus had not bloomed. It was still too early to call Em and Henry, and I was trying to fill the hours before we went to the Clerys' for dinner. Toni and I were walking back to Reeti's apartment. The streets were almost empty, but we'd found an open convenience store that sold coffee (for Toni) and strong black tea. We had pitched our to-go cups into a corner bin when I spotted a family going into a church around the corner—a little girl, a lanky boy, a mother in a puffer coat. The square bell tower rose against the sky.

I tugged Toni's arm. "Let's go in."

"Seriously?"

"You know Aunt Em would want us to go to church on Christmas."

Our mother had described herself as spiritual, not religious. Her brother, Henry, wasn't interested in anything he couldn't touch, see, or smell. Em had never pushed her own regular church attendance on us girls. But once a year, she took us all with her to the white clapboard church by the highway where her friend played the piano, Toni and I in our best school sneakers, Henry in his one good suit, the one he'd been married and probably would be buried in.

"We're not Catholic," Toni said.

I glanced at the entrance, the tall double doors with green wreaths and bows, the stone arch crowned by a woman with her arms open wide. "I don't think they'll card us," I teased.

So we went into the half-filled church. I sat next to Toni on the hard wooden pew. It felt strange: the unfamiliar rituals, the smell of wax and incense, the lilting accents—Irish, African, and French—all around. The stained glass windows, the statues around the altar, were nothing like the church back home. But it was familiar, too—the gray-haired women in Christmas sweaters, the scrubbed, fidgety children, the solemn-faced men. The story they read, the one from Luke, I recognized that and the carols rolling from the organ. Toni sang beside me, loudly and out of tune. Her knee bumped mine. Our shoulders pressed together. Warm. Connected.

A surge of joy came over me, like the rush of angels' wings.

*C*hristmas *dinner for half the neighborhood,*" Sam had said.

They crowded the Clerys' modest apartment, a couple with two toddlers, an elderly nun, a man with dreadlocks who worked at the shop. I counted three aunts, four uncles including Gerry-the-cabbie, two handfuls of cousins (*Or the children of cousins?* Below a certain age, I couldn't tell the generations apart), and a baby. There was lots of chatting and drinking and passing plates of food. The TV crackled with pop carols and a streaming yule log, adding to the noise. The smells—turkey and Brussel sprouts, beer and bodies—pervaded the close, warm space.

Anything less like Christmas in Kansas was hard to imagine.

Toni was laughing, throwing herself into a competitive card game with Sam's brother and sisters. I wasn't sure of the rules, but exploding kittens were involved. Under the table, the orange cat groomed itself, apparently unconcerned.

Gerry, the cab driver, knocked a cigarette from the pack in his pocket.

"No smoking in the house," Janette said. "You know the rules."

"Your husband smoked."

"Right. And now he's dead."

My gaze flew to Sam. His crooked mouth lifted on one side.

"Rest his soul," Gerry said. He raised his glass. "To Martin."

The chorus ran around the table. "To Martin." "My brother." *"Ar dheis Dé go raibh a anam."*

They all drank. The baby knocked over a water glass, prompting a flurry of napkins and exclamations.

"Sorry, Aunt Jan," the young mother said, blotting the tablecloth.

"No problem, darling."

Grace peeled off an orange section for the baby, who promptly flung it to the cat under the table.

"And when is one of you lot going to give my sister a grandchild?" an older woman asked, with a look around at the Clerys.

"I'm going to uni, Aunt Nora," Grace said.

Fiadh crossed her arms. "Don't look at me. I'm not wanting crotch fruit yet."

"Sam?"

"Sorry, love." He winked. "I always use protection."

"Gerry, you light up that fag in this house, and I'll put it out on your forehead," Janette said.

The doorbell rang.

"Come in! It's open!"

"One of you get that," Janette said.

With a put-upon sigh, Jack left the card game and slouched into the hall. "It's for Grace," he said, returning a moment later.

"Well, don't leave whoever it is standing there. Invite them in."

A figure materialized behind him. A lanky, red-haired boy. My mouth soured as I recognized him.

"Well, look at that," Fiadh drawled. "It's Danny Doyle."

I reached for my wineglass, rinsing the flat taste from my mouth.

"What the fuck are you doing here?" Sam asked.

Janette's eyes narrowed. "Language."

Danny's Adam's apple bobbed as he swallowed. I almost felt sorry for him. Almost. "Happy Christmas, Mrs. Clery. From my mother." He handed her a box of chocolates. "And this is for you." He offered a smaller box to Grace.

She took it, turning a pretty pink.

Danny's gaze met mine. His blush rivaled Grace's before he jerked his head in acknowledgment and looked away.

"Get the boy some pudding," one of the aunts—Ruby? Eileen?—said.

"We're out of forks," Fiadh said.

Grace took a step toward the kitchen. "I'll wash some up."

"I can help," Danny said eagerly.

"You stay where I can see you," Sam said.

Janette rolled her eyes and rose from her chair. The baby started to cry.

"I'll do it," I said.

I could hear Reeti scolding in my head. *"Dee, you don't have to be useful to be liked."* But I could use a minute of quiet to clear my head. I loved Sam's family, but they were—just a bit—overwhelming. Also, Sam's mom had spent all day cooking dinner. She shouldn't have to do dishes, too.

I pushed up my sleeves. The kitchen was a disaster, half-empty glasses and dirty plates abandoned on the counters, containers of food everywhere. No dishwasher. I dunked a handful of flatware in the sink.

"Mam said to give you a hand."

My heart skittered pleasantly. I smiled over my shoulder at Sam, leaning against the doorjamb, his hair tied back like an eighteenth-century poet's. "It's not necessary."

"You don't know my mother." He uncurled from the doorway, coming up behind me.

Another skitter, indefinably less pleasant, like the brush of an insect on the back of my neck.

"She wouldn't want me to leave you alone," Sam murmured close to my ear.

I tensed. *Gray's hand on my hip as I stood at the sink. His thumb, exploring under my sweater.*

My throat was suddenly tight. I cleared it. "Fine. You can dry."

One heartbeat, two, before Sam moved away, reaching for a dish towel.

My shoulders lowered from around my ears. What was the matter with me? I *missed* having warmth at my back. I wanted the connection I'd felt the other night.

Sam picked up some forks and started to dry.

I was ruining everything.

There was a burst of laughter from the other room. A cry of "Boom!" from the card players, followed by groans and cheers.

I squirted more soap into the sink. "Toni's having the best time. I think she has a little crush on your sister."

Sam looked amused. "Noticed that, did you."

I was good at not seeing things I didn't want to see. Or not acknowledging them to myself. But I could be a hawk where Toni was concerned. "Toni tends to charge into things. Especially new things."

"Like you."

"Um. Not like me at all. I'm terrible at letting things go."

"Beat a dead horse, do you?"

I rinsed a glass under the tap. Only a hundred more to go. "Maybe. I was with Gray for two years." *Stop talking*, said my brain. My mouth didn't listen. "Even when he used me in his book and dumped me, I begged him to explain. I thought he'd take me back. I *wanted* him to take me back."

My face was hot.

"For Christ's sake, why?"

"I thought he was special." I concentrated on scrubbing lipstick from a glass. "I guess I thought, if he cared for me, I must be special, too."

That's what he'd said. "*You could be special if you tried.*" Shame on me, for believing him.

"You are special, Boots."

I wanted to latch on to his words and wrap them around me like a security blanket. But this time I wasn't going to let myself imagine what he felt. Or ignore how I felt. Or yearn for things he was unable or unwilling to give.

I swallowed. "Sam. Do you like me?"

"Sure, I like you fine," he answered easily.

"But do you . . ." *Like me, like me?* My cheeks burned hotter. This was too humiliatingly like middle school. "Want to be with me?"

"Sex, do you mean?"

My mouth dropped open. "Yes. No. Maybe?"

"I'm willing. But I'm for fun, not for keeps. And you're leaving at the end of the year."

For fun.

My insides contracted. That didn't sound very safe. Unless . . . What if going into a relationship knowing it would end was the best way to protect your heart?

"Maybe that makes us compatible?" I suggested. "Sharing an actual end date, I mean."

"Might be. But I hate to lose a good customer over sex." His gaze was steady on mine. "Or a friend, either."

"We are friends."

Sam's eyes were warm. "Good friends. I'm not looking for anything beyond that."

"You're right." I smiled. "Or . . . you're honest, at least."

He wasn't leading me on, the way Gray had, saying what I wanted to hear, letting me imply the rest. I didn't want to make this into something it was not. And maybe friendship would be enough.

Maybe friendship was better.

"So, if you want to be friends who have sex," Sam said. "I'm here for that."

Confusion churned my stomach. "I don't know what I want. I don't trust myself to make the right decisions." I swished another glass under the tap and handed it to him to dry.

His fingers brushed mine as he took it, sparking a tingle up my arm. "You don't have to decide. You could just let it happen."

I raised my chin. "If it happens."

"If you want it to happen."

I took a deep breath. Released it. "What are you doing New Year's Eve?"

SEVENTEEN

Sam had to work on New Year's Eve.

"Can't ask anyone else to do it," he'd explained with a note of regret.

Which . . . okay. New Year's had never been my favorite holiday, anyway. All that pressure to have an amazing night, and then what? Standing around at a party in an uncomfortable bra and impractical shoes, drinking Cook's champagne until midnight, when some random drunk would catch me by the restroom and stick his tongue in my mouth.

Covid, and Gray, had spared me that, at least. Last New Year's Eve he had gone off to a "faculty only" dinner party while I stayed home alone with a book. Until his inevitable two A.M. text (Am I bothering you?) followed by his equally inevitable appearance at my apartment twenty minutes later. "*God, what a boring evening,*" he'd murmured, nuzzling closer in my bed. "*You don't know how much I envy you, getting to stay home.*"

I pretended to believe him.

So. Sam was working. Reeti was in London. Toni was out with Fiadh and her friends. (Fiadh had invited me along, but a pleading look from Toni persuaded me not to play chaperone.) And I was home with a book. Again. No bra, no shoes, no pressure.

Honestly, it was fine.

Maybe I didn't have anyone to kiss, but I had Anne Lamott for company. Our class was reading *Bird by Bird*. *"If there is one door in the castle you have been told not to go through, you must. Otherwise, you'll just be rearranging furniture in rooms you've already been in."*

I reread the passage, feeling it settle into my brain. This was what I'd originally loved about school, even more than the stability of the routine or the chance to be good at something. I felt the words take up residence in my head, pushing out walls to make room.

And I thought about my story, about my protagonist, Rose, stranded in the magic kingdom, and I wondered what was behind the doors of her castle and if she'd ever find her way home.

Just before midnight, my phone pinged. *Reeti*.

I smiled. She'd sent a video from her parents' house, a party, with high-energy music and dancing in the background, and Reeti, glowing and gorgeous in a chrysanthemum sari with twists of gold embroidery. I tapped the screen to take a closer look at the young man next to her. Her *rishta*? Slim, with liquid dark eyes and a neatly trimmed beard.

His name's Vir, she'd told me over Christmas without offering any supporting details. I'd worried she didn't like him. I hoped she wasn't being pressured into anything.

Happy New Year! I texted. Is that him?

My screen lit. A smiling, blushing emoji. Not bad, right?

He's cute! I typed, and waited for a reply.

But there were no more dots. No answer. Which was . . . good, right? It meant she was having a good time.

I turned on the television, picking up the BBC countdown to midnight. Big Ben chimed. Fireworks exploded over the Thames as London rang in the New Year in the aftermath of the pandemic.

"Happy New Year," I whispered.

I didn't want to be there in that crowd. But maybe, after all, I wished Sam were free tonight.

My phone chirped. Reeti, again. **Happy New Year, didi!**

And a selfie from Toni, accompanied by a burst of emojis, with her arms around Fiadh and some other girl, all of them grinning under sparkly party hats.

See? I was loved. I wasn't lonely. I typed replies, hearts and fireworks and kisses.

All the world was celebrating. Almost all the world. I messaged Aunt Em, too, even though it was only dinnertime in Kansas. The ball drop in Times Square was still hours away, but there was always the cooking channel. I left it on for company, for comfort, and picked up Anne Lamott again.

But reading couldn't hold my attention any longer.

Restless, I opened my laptop, resisting the urge to check my email, to search for Gray or check the bestsellers rank of his stupid book. That was over. We were over. I was finally over him. I had better things to do. Like working on the assignment for my Structure in Fiction and Poetry class. At least it was something new.

I clicked on the file. I'd managed about three hundred words, waiting up for Toni, when a noise from downstairs penetrated the apartment. Raised voices. A scuffle. A grunt.

"Get your fucking hands off me!"

My heart quickened in alarm. I shoved my feet hastily into boots. Leaving the chain on, I inched open the door to Reeti's apartment.

"Easy, mate." That was Tim's voice.

I slid open the chain. Ventured into the hall. Peered over the railing in time to see the man with Tim shove him away and take a swing at his head. I squeaked. They grappled, crashing into a wall.

"Hey!" I yelled. They glanced up. "Um. Hi."

"It's all right," Tim said.

The guy with Tim scowled. "Who are you?"

I eased down a step. "I'm Dee."

He squinted. "Oh, the new bird."

"Dee, Charles Lynch," Tim said stiffly. "Charles, my upstairs neighbor."

"Nice boots," Charles said. "Big bum."

"Shut up." Tim steered him into the apartment. "Sorry," he said over his shoulder.

I followed him cautiously through the open door. "I've heard worse." He supported Charles toward the couch. "Can I do anything?"

Charles swiveled his head. "You're American."

"Um. Yes?"

"Thash not . . . You're not his usual type. Big change from Laura." His hands curved in front of his chest, sculpting the air. "Big, *big* change."

"Put a sock in it, Charles."

"Sorry." He smiled and then lurched in my direction. "Whoops."

I steadied him. "It's all right," I said, the way Tim had, even though I was pretty sure it wasn't.

He breathed gin fumes in my face. "I think I'm gonna be sick," he confided.

"Right," Tim said, tight, controlled. "This way, then."

He manhandled him down the hall. I listened as a door opened and closed.

I wasn't helping. I should go.

I went into the kitchen and put the kettle on.

orry for ruining your New Year's." Tim, emerging from the shadows of the hall.

I popped up from his couch. "You're not. You didn't. It's not like I had plans." Which made me sound like a total loser.

"I thought you'd be out with your friend Sam."

Was that code for, *Why are you still here?* "He had to work," I explained.

"Ah." A pause. "I'm sorry."

All this politeness was getting awkward. "No, it's fine. My aunt always says that whatever you do on New Year's, you'll do all year long."

"Let's hope not," he said, very dry.

I grinned. "Well, I think my aunt was making a case for finishing your chores and going to bed early. But I was actually up writing. Or trying to write."

"Assessments?"

I'd forgotten he was taking classes, too. Executive management something. I nodded. "A short story. Due at the end of the month."

"What is your story about?"

"Two little girls. On an orphan train."

"Sorry?"

"Back in the late 1800s, early 1900s, they shipped orphans from New York City out west. They were supposed to find families, but a lot of them were used as free labor on farms."

"That sounds . . ."

"Very literary, right?"

"I was going to say depressing."

"Well, it was sad. Sad and hard. They used to separate siblings.

But that's what I love about writing. I can fix things. I can give them a happy ending."

His mouth relaxed. Almost a smile. I felt the pull of it in my chest. "Did you ever read that Diggs book?" he asked.

"Not yet." I searched for another subject. "I made tea."

"Tea sounds wonderful. Or I should have a bottle of bubbly around."

"I'll have tea, too." I hurried to the kitchen to get it. "Unless you want something stronger."

"I think there's been enough alcohol tonight," he said, following me.

"Will your . . ." Friend? Were they friends? "Will he be all right?" *Are you all right?*

"Right enough." He got out milk. "He'll sleep it off now. Sugar?"

"Thanks." I busied myself with the mugs. "Why do you put up with him?"

"We served together in Afghanistan. I owe Charles my life." A pause, while he stirred his tea. "Quite literally."

We carried our tea back to his boring square couch. "Does he do this kind of thing often?"

A glint from steel-rimmed glasses. "Get drunk and pick fights, do you mean?"

"Need you to take care of him."

"Infrequently. Poor sod."

"That poor sod tried to punch you."

"Er, yes. But, in his defense, he was provoked tonight."

Something wasn't right. I studied his down-bent head as he blew on his tea. I couldn't imagine Tim—careful, kind, polite—provoking anybody. "Who provoked him?"

His face was carved from oak. "It doesn't matter."

"Then why not tell me?"

"I'd prefer not to have this discussion with you."

From another man, at another time, that would have been enough to shut me up. But I wasn't Old Dee anymore. And Tim wasn't Gray.

"You can tell me," I said. "I can give you a woman's perspective."

Our eyes met. Did he remember? We were sitting on this exact same couch when he'd fed me buns and I'd cried and asked for his male perspective. That kind of thing created a bond. At least, I hoped it did.

"How did you know there's a woman involved?"

I blinked. "I didn't, actually. But now that you've said it, you can't stop there."

"We were at a party. Charles misunderstood something someone said. I attempted to explain, but he'd already had a bit too much to drink, and Laura suggested I bring him home before the situation . . . escalated."

"Laura, from-the-London-office Laura?"

"Yes."

We were back to one-word answers, I noticed. "So, do you all, like, work together?"

"No." I thought that was it, and then he added, "They met when I was in hospital."

"When you were in the army."

"Laura and I knew each other from before."

"Oh." Apparently this one-word thing was catching.

"Our families are neighbors."

I nodded.

He ran a hand through his hair, making a dark cowlick stand up in front. "Also . . . We were engaged at the time."

Oh. I waited. "So, what happened?"

He frowned at his tea. "It didn't work out, obviously."

My heart tugged. I wondered if he were haunted by her memory, the way I (still) sometimes thought of Gray. That feeling you had lost the one person who claimed to love you the way that no one ever had. The ache for what might have been. "I'm so sorry."

"Don't be. She never . . . That is, we didn't suit."

"But you were engaged."

"Yes. Well. As it happened, I didn't meet her criteria for a partner after all."

"That's stupid. You're good-looking, kind, principled, educated. You have a job. You don't live in your parents' basement. Unless you wrote her into your novel or keep a pet snake next to your bed . . . You don't, do you?"

He smiled faintly. "No."

Encouraged, I continued. "Maybe your communication skills could use a little work, but what does she want?"

"A whole man."

"Oh God." *The scars.* I grasped his hand. "When you were hurt, were you . . . Can't you . . . ?"

He looked at me, a gleam of amusement in his eyes. Or maybe that was a reflection on his glasses. "I'm quite capable, thank you. But I was in hospital for three months. Rehab for six months after that. At the time, Laura felt—based on the doctors' reports—she hadn't signed on to take care of an invalid for the rest of her life."

"So she broke up with you." I squeezed his hand again.

"Actually . . ." Another pause, as if he were debating how much to tell me.

"You broke up with her," I said. "To set her free."

Unexpectedly, he laughed. "Nothing so noble, I'm afraid. Laura expected me to work for my father after uni. She was willing enough to wait while I did my military service. But when things went south, she was afraid she'd made a mistake. She didn't believe in me. She didn't believe in us."

"And Charles?" I asked.

"He came to see me in hospital. Rather frequently. They both did. I believe they comforted each other."

"Cheated on you, you mean."

"Yes."

"Ouch. And now she wants you back."

He tilted his head. "I didn't say that."

But I'd seen them together. How she touched him. The way she'd warned me. *"Be careful with this one. He has no heart."*

I waved my hand toward the hall, where, presumably, Charles was sleeping it off. "He was provoked, you said. So there must still be a chance for you and Laura to get back together."

"None at all. I don't have your forgiving nature."

"Me?"

"You said you could have forgiven cheating. When we were talking about that Kettering fellow. Who's an arse, by the way."

"He's actually considered brilliant. A new lion of American letters." It was in his bio.

"Full of himself, I thought."

"Wait." I thought back desperately, trying to sort out what I'd said to whom. "You know who he is?"

"Gray from Kansas. It was obvious once I'd read the book."

"Shit. You read it?" I cringed, recalling Gray's descriptions of Destiny Gayle's *"long, udder-shaped nipples"* (page 73) and *"lusty barnyard sexuality"* (page 219). Her parrot-like intelligence. That horrible horned-mask scene. I covered my face with my hands. "Oh my God. You must think I'm—"

"Nothing like the character in the novel," Tim said firmly.

I lowered my hands.

"I may not be an English major," he continued. "But I recognize a complete fiction when I see it. That girl isn't you."

"Thanks." I hadn't realized how much I'd needed to hear

someone say it like that. Flat out. "You're the only one who thinks so."

He frowned. "Surely your family . . . Your friends . . ."

"Haven't read the book. Or they pretend they haven't, because they don't want to hurt my feelings."

"You want me to pretend."

"Um. No? Honestly, it's kind of a relief. Being able to talk about it with someone who doesn't confuse me with Destiny."

"No one who knows you could do that."

"They did." I swallowed. "Everyone in the department assumed Gray must know me better. We were together for two years."

"You could sue him. For defamation. He damaged your reputation."

I shook my head. "There's just enough difference in the names—Dorothy, Destiny. And there's that bit the publisher always puts in the front, about it all being fiction or used fictitiously. 'Any resemblance to actual persons, living or dead, is entirely coincidental.'"

"Bollocks," Tim said.

"Anyway, the damage is done." I winced, remembering the reviews. "All I'd get from suing would be more publicity. I just want the whole thing to go away."

He was silent.

"I know that sounds cowardly," I said.

"It sounds very normal. Most women are reluctant to report sexual harassment because they're afraid it will affect their advancement at work."

He sounded so cool. So factual. Like he didn't care.

Or . . . I snuck a look at his carefully blank face. Like he was giving me space to feel my feelings without worrying about his reaction.

Gratitude loosened my chest.

"The thing is, I was complicit. That's the part I can't get over. I trusted him, and he dismissed me as someone unworthy of love or trust or respect. Publicly. In print. And now they're making a movie about it."

"He abused your trust. That's on him, not on you."

"No, it's me." My throat was suddenly tight. "That's what I do. Yeah, Gray wrote a book that made me out to be something I wasn't. But even before he wrote it, I made myself into somebody else to be with him. Nobody forced me to put my thesis on hold so I could cook his dinner or grade his papers." Or have sex when he wanted it. "I made myself less when I should have made myself more."

"We all want to meet the expectations of the people we care about," Tim said.

"Your family?"

He cleared his throat. "Yes."

I waited, but apparently that was all he was going to say. "I do it with everybody," I confided. "When I was younger, I was always trying to fit in. To make people like me."

"Why wouldn't they like you? You're very likable."

Another compliment, I thought. A good one. "I have a big butt."

"Yes." A near smile. "And a large heart. Quite attractive, that."

I grinned at him. "My butt or my heart?"

"Both."

He set down his tea and leaned forward, giving me plenty of time to pull back or move away. Giving me space. His lashes dropped, veiling his eyes.

Mine were wide open. His face blurred as I closed the distance between us and pressed my mouth to his.

His lips were slightly parted. I could taste the tea we'd been drinking, warm and sweet. One second, two seconds, three . . .

Something inside me stirred. Fluttered. Hitched. I drew back, inhaling shakily.

Tim watched me from behind his glasses, a small half smile on his face. "Happy New Year, Dee."

I gulped. "Yeah. Absolutely. Happy New Year."

It was New Year's. I had to kiss somebody.

But I thought it would be Sam.

"I should go," I said. "It's getting late. Toni will be home soon." *Maybe.* "And I still have lots to do. Writing. I have to write."

"Tell me about it."

"My writing?"

"Yes."

"Well . . ." I wanted to, I realized. It was the space he made for me, around me, a kind of No Judgment Zone. As if I could say anything, and it would be okay. I opened my mouth.

My phone pinged in my pocket.

"Sorry." I fumbled for it. "That must be Toni now."

It wasn't Toni.

SAM: Just finished closing up. Happy New Year, Boots.

As messages go, it was certainly better than the usual, U up? Better than Gray's, Am I bothering you?

But a text at two in the morning could only mean one thing. *"If you want to be friends who have sex, I'm here for that,"* Sam had said.

Was that what I wanted? How I was going to spend my New Year?

I looked up at Tim. "It's Sam."

His face rearranged itself to its usual blank politeness. "You'll want to get that."

EIGHTEEN

"Y ou watched the cooking channel," Reeti said in disbelief. "You and Tim. On New Year's Eve."

"His friend was sleeping it off down the hall. Besides, I love the cooking channel," I said.

We were seated at our usual table at Clery's, refueling after the library. Me, swaddled in a Trinity hoodie, my hair a messy lump above my makeup-less face, like a writer on deadline. Reeti, shiny and perfect—bright glossy lips, dark glossy hair, touches of gold at her ears and throat. Like she'd just stepped away from the makeup counter at Brown Thomas instead of spending the past four hours studying for her accounting exams.

"Still." She wrinkled her nose. "Disappointing."

I smiled. "Two weeks ago, you wanted me to ride Sam like a pony. Now you want me to hook up with Tim?"

"I suppose not," she conceded. "I adore Tim. But he is a bit of a Pinocchio."

"Stiff?" I guessed.

"Solid. Wooden. Not a real boy."

"He's reserved."

She grinned. "He has no pulse. Although I suppose stiff could be a good thing. If you got together."

I choked on my chai, aware of Sam, stocking shelves at the back of the shop. The spices burned my nose. Or maybe that was embarrassment.

"Actually," Reeti said thoughtfully, "if you were looking for nonrecreational sex, Tim would be a good match. Not exciting, but he'd always take care of you."

"I don't need someone to take care of me," I protested (pushing away the image of Tim bringing me buns). "I can take care of myself." And Toni. I always had. "Anyway, we're friends. Not every relationship between a man and a woman has to end in sex or marriage."

"Not according to my aunties."

The bell over the door jangled. Sam appeared from the back, giving us a nod as he moved smoothly behind the counter to take care of a customer.

I seized on the change of subject. "How are things going with Vir?"

"It's hard to say." She studied her mug, as if the answer were hiding in the tea leaves. "I like him. His mother likes me. But there's so much pressure. Am I really attracted to him, or do I want to please my parents? Is he into me, or do I simply check all the boxes?"

"Tim said he got engaged once because he met all this girl's criteria for a partner."

"Our Tim? What happened?"

I wanted to tell her. But it wasn't my story to share. "They weren't right for each other after all." Because he was honorable and responsible, and she was a heartless cheat. "So he broke it off."

"That's what I'm worried about," Reeti said. "Vir's parents are

more traditional than mine. They say they're okay with me doing whatever I want to do. But what they really expect is for me
to work for my papa and then have six kids and stay home like a
good wife. And I am not that girl. I want to teach, to make a difference in girls' lives. What if Vir doesn't support me?"

"At least you know who you are. You know what you want.
That's the important thing."

"Except I don't own it."

Behind the counter, Sam finished with the customer and
started restocking displays.

"Have you talked to Vir about what you want?" I asked Reeti.

"How can I? I've never even told my parents."

"I get it. I do. I've been trying to win other people's approval
all my life. But your parents love you, Reeti."

"People love you, too, Dee."

Gratitude made my eyes misty. "Maybe in Dublin. Not in
Kansas."

"Because you didn't let them know the real you."

My mouth fell open. I closed it. Because yes, okay, I'd always
been afraid to share my true thoughts and feelings. Afraid of being judged as too weird, too opinionated, too much, or not
enough. Shamed when I didn't speak up, embarrassed when I did.
And now I had friends who listened.

What if the difference wasn't in them, but in me?

"I don't know who I am yet." I smiled ruefully. "Maybe I
should find someone to tell me."

"No. As in, hell, no, girlfriend. Your ex, the fucker, did that.
What you need is someone to adore you while you figure it out."

Toni burst out of the kitchen, her face shining. "Dee, Fee's
taking me to the beach!"

Sam looked up.

"When?" I asked.

"In January?" Reeti said.

Fiadh appeared. "It's less than an hour on the DART to Howth," she said. "We can see the sights and be back before ten. Walk the cliffs, maybe, if the wind's not bad."

"I thought we were looking at apartments this afternoon," I said to Toni.

Sam raised an eyebrow. "Feeling optimistic, are you?"

My sister's face fell dramatically. "Do we have to?"

"We can't stay with Reeti forever," I said.

"But I like having you stay with me," Reeti said. "I have the room. The place is too big for me by myself."

"You don't mind?"

"I do not. And my parents are thrilled. My mother thinks I'm safer with you there."

"Well, if you're sure . . . But only if I start paying rent."

"I can pay, too," Toni said.

"Honey, you can only use the trust to pay for your education."

"Travel is educational." I regarded her steadily. She flushed. "Fine. I'll get a job. I can help Fee in the bakery."

"Not without a work permit," Sam said.

"That's not fair. Dee had a job. For that professor."

"The rules are a little different for students," I said gently.

Toni rolled her eyes. "I should have known you'd make this all about school."

"You have something against school?" Reeti asked.

"I just don't think it's necessary for everybody, that's all. Look at Banksy."

"Who is Banksy?"

"An artist," I said slowly. *Like our mother.* Troubled, I looked at Toni.

She wouldn't meet my gaze. "Not only artists. You didn't go to school," she said to Fiadh.

"Not to uni. But I got my certificate in baking and pastry."

Sam rubbed his jaw with the back of his hand, his usual three-day beard edging on five. "Experience is the best teacher, Da said."

"Yeah, but school gives you training, doesn't it?"

"And credentials," Reeti said.

"And faith in yourself," I added.

"Fine, if you have the opportunity," Sam said.

Fiadh snorted. "What's stopping you now, then?"

"Besides you swanning off to Howth whenever you feel like it?"

She folded her arms. "I wouldn't, would I, if you'd let me and Mam take more responsibility in the shop."

"The shop's on me," Sam said. "It's been all on me since Da died."

"Because I was twelve, you stupid git, and Mam had her hands full with Jack and Aoife and the rest of us. But it's been nine years, Sammy boy. We've moved on. Why the hell can't you?"

"Because you lot won't let me," he flashed back. "You need me."

"Not as much as you think."

The air crackled between them. Poor Sam. He'd given up so much for his family. Of course he felt responsible. And unappreciated. It sucked. But was Fiadh . . . right?

"Toni could still help out," I said.

Four heads swiveled toward me.

"What?"

I swallowed. "Toni could still help Fiadh in the bakery. It would be like an internship. Toni would get training, and Fiadh would have more time for . . . Well, to do other stuff. If she wanted. If that works for everyone."

"Works for me!" Toni said cheerfully. I wanted to hug her.

"It's all right by me." Fiadh looked at her brother. "Sam?"

"An unpaid internship," he said. "I'm not hiring cash-in-hand and having the garda coming around."

"You can pay me in bread," Toni said.

I smiled, relieved. Maybe she would learn something, working here for Fiadh.

And maybe Sam would, too.

I applied for a job shelving books at the library.

"Man does not live by bread alone," I told Toni and Reeti.

"Or pay rent, either," Toni said, and Reeti rolled her eyes.

Joking aside, I didn't have much hope I would actually get called for an interview. Most positions were filled in September. But Alan said there was always some turnover at the beginning of a new term.

We were hanging out in the common room—Alan and me, Erinma and Claire—writing or pretending to write and angsting about the status of our portfolios, when Maeve walked in.

We reacted to her entrance like dogs at an animal shelter. *Look at me! Pet me! I'm scared.* Even Erinma, who just had a poem accepted in the *Southword Literary Journal*, and Claire, who pretended not to care.

Our little workshop tribe switched instructors this semester. None of them would face her judgment again, at least not in seminar. But the slick confidence I'd admired in my classmates turned out to be mostly an act. That wasn't the reason I liked them so much now, but it did make me feel less alone. After four months together, we were gentler with one another, more aware of bruises and scars.

Maeve's gaze fell on me. "You used my name as a job reference."

"Um. Yeah?"

I mean, yes. Obviously. Unless or until I could convince another member of the faculty to be my supervisor, Maeve was the one who knew me best. And I couldn't count on Glenda for a recommendation. Not after leaving her in the lurch over the holidays.

Maeve's gaze swept the room, cataloging, dismissing. "Come into my office."

Alan gave me a sympathetic look. I hitched my bag on my shoulder and grabbed my sweater. Erinma flashed me a thumbs-up as we walked by.

"So," Maeve said, seating herself at her desk. "Do you think it's wise to start a new job when you should be working on your portfolio?"

I swallowed. Work on our dissertations formally began this semester, and everyone but me had a supervisor who adored them, or at least thought their proposals had potential. "It's only ten hours a week," I said. "Less than I was doing for Glenda."

"I'm aware of what you did for Glenda."

That sounded ominously ambiguous. I straightened my spine. "I need the money. And I thought the job experience would look good on my CV."

"So would completing your degree," Maeve said.

According to Glenda, Maeve had questioned my commitment to the program from the start.

"You're always saying in class that we shouldn't base our characters on books. That we need to get out in the world and observe people in real life. That's what I'm doing."

"I can't imagine working in the stacks will give you many opportunities to interact with other people."

I crossed my fingers in my lap, where she couldn't see. "Does this mean you won't be a reference?"

"I informed library services that I've found you to be hard-working and reliable."

Not talented. Not creative. Still . . . a recommendation! I beamed at her. "Thank you."

"Make sure your academic work doesn't suffer."

"It won't," I promised.

"It's more difficult to balance job obligations and writing than you might imagine," she said dryly.

She was a working writer. She would know. I thought of Sam, who had given up his chance at college to take over his father's shop.

"Dr. Ward." Unlike most of the faculty, she had never invited me to call her by her first name. "If a student didn't finish their degree at Trinity, how would they, like, reregister? Asking for a friend," I added hastily.

Her heavy eyebrows rose.

"No, really," I insisted. "An undergraduate. Say they had to withdraw for financial reasons."

She pursed her lips. "Assuming they took an official leave of absence . . . How long has it been?"

"Nine years."

"They'd have to start over. Reapply."

I gnawed the inside of my cheek. "But they could still get in, right? I mean, if they made good grades before . . ."

"It's not that simple. Even applying as a mature student, they'd have to prove they kept up somehow. That they're still reading and writing."

"I think he is. I'm sure he is. Sam always has a book behind the register."

"Sam?"

"Sam Clery. He used to be a student here. His family owns a newsagents on Abbey Street."

"Yes, I know."

"You do?"

"I didn't ask you in here to gossip about former students. I'd like to talk with you about your assessment for the Structure in Fiction and Poetry class."

The orphan train story. "I turned it in," I assured her. On time. A week ago.

"Yes. Noel sent it to me."

Noel Dalton, novelist and poet, the instructor for the course. He was tall, thin, and kindly, all bones and angles, like a crane with a comb-over.

"Was there . . . Is there a problem?" I asked.

"Why do you assume there's a problem?"

"Well." *Because you hate me* did not seem like a good response. I struggled. "It's different."

"Indeed."

I'd ended the story with the little girls on the train platform, waiting to be claimed. Maybe the sisters didn't find the loving family they longed for. Maybe they didn't get to stay together. But I'd left it as a possibility, okay? *Rose-colored glasses,* Gray mocked in my head.

But that was me. Deep inside my corny Kansas heart, I believed in happy endings or at least in hopeful ones. Because if you told yourself a story often enough, it could come true.

"You said I should try something new," I reminded her.

"Yes. Noel was quite impressed. Not only by the technical aspects of the story, but by the maturity of the writing."

A smile bloomed inside me. Spread to my lips. "Really?"

"We'll be meeting next month to formally allocate supervisors. He's expressed an interest in working with you on your dissertation."

My grin threatened to take over my face. "Wow." She was almost certainly as relieved as I was. I started to collect myself, my bag, my thoughts, my sweater. Preparing to leave. "That's . . ."

"Or . . ." Maeve continued as if I hadn't spoken. Her black gaze pinned me to my seat. "You could work with me."

NINETEEN

Mornings at the shop had a rhythm, set by the beat of the foot traffic outside and punctuated by the in-and-out ringing of the bell over the door. First the staccato demands for coffee, tea, and cigarettes, then the steady shuffle of pensioners looking to fill the hours until noon. The stop-and-go of mums pushing strollers, picking up a can of beans or a loaf of bread after dropping off the older kids at school. A rush of office workers, squeezing errands and a sandwich made on Fiadh's fancy bread into their lunch hour.

Some days after lunch, Dee and her friend Reeti came by. Sam would hear them talking about how hard this class was or how tired they were after grinding at the library. And Sam, who had been on his feet since five that morning, would smile and bring them tea.

Sometimes his impatience swelled and grew, ripping him up from the inside. Life was happening out there, outside the shop, on the sidewalk, across the river, passing him by.

It hadn't always been that way. In the first months after his da died, Sam had been too numb, and too busy, to feel much of anything, overwhelmed by worries for the shop and his family, focused on learning what he needed to survive. What they needed to survive.

In the beginning, the mindless routine was a comfort. Old pals dropped in to share stories of his da. Neighbors offered condolences. Then the stories and condolences stopped, replaced by the awkward unsaid, the judgment of strangers. *What's a young guy like you doing behind the counter?*

Whatever. Dreams didn't pay the bills. So his life hadn't turned out the way he'd planned. It was still a good life, his father's life in his father's shop. What was good enough for Martin Clery was good enough for Sam.

Or it had been until Dee came along.

Sometimes he almost resented her for stirring up old dreams, for making him twitch with unspoken restlessness.

But that wasn't fair. She never wanted anything but the best for him. Never saw less than the best in everybody.

This wistful jealousy . . . That was on him.

The lull came after lunch—he could tell time by the way the traffic died. He picked up his book. He was reading *A Goat's Song* again, drawn in as always by the stark poetry of Healy's language and the destructive love of his playwright protagonist. And maybe Sam read to make himself feel better, too. Because he might be a moody, whingeing shopkeeper, but at least he wasn't an alcoholic on a fishing boat like the guy in the book.

The bell jangled. Sam glanced up, the smile for Dee already forming on his face. But the woman standing there was older, flat-chested, with brilliant dark eyes and lips the color of dried blood.

"Dr. Ward," he said in surprise, and then wanted to kick himself. She wouldn't remember him.

He recognized her, though. She could have come straight

from his father's funeral: same mannish black shoes, same pointy black umbrella. What was she doing this side of the river?

"What can I get you?" he asked, keeping the smile in place.

"I hear you're thinking of reapplying," she said without preamble.

"No," Sam said.

She glanced at his book. He resisted the urge to hide the cover. "You could be doing that."

He attempted a joke. "Getting shit-faced on a trawler?"

She didn't crack a smile. "The deadline for mature students is February first. You still have time."

Longing leaped like flame, using up all the air in his lungs. He shook his head, unable to find breath to answer.

Her dark lips twisted slightly. "You used to be more articulate."

"I used to be a lot of things," he said, desperate to get her out of his shop before he . . . What would he do? She was a customer. "Look, I have to . . ." He cast about the nearly empty shop. "Do inventory," he said. "Did you want something?"

She gave him a look like Janette's, only meaner. An *I see what you're doing and don't think you can get away with it* look. "Are you still writing?"

Like she could see the thought of those notebooks branded on his forehead. "What would be the point of that?" he asked.

They stared at each other across the counter. *Standoff.*

"I'll take a package of the chocolate digestives," she said. Not a retreat, but a concession.

He rang her up and made change, focusing on each small action as if it could ground him permanently in this shop. In his reality. "Will that be all?"

Of course it wasn't.

The woman was a witch.

"Writers graduate all the time who don't have half your tal
ent." Maeve put the biscuits in her purse. "You know what they
have that you don't have?"

"A piece of paper?" Sam suggested.

She snapped her purse shut. "Don't be facetious."

"Brains."

"Commitment," she said. "You'll never get anywhere without
commitment. I can write you a recommendation. But whether
you're willing to take the help, take the chance . . . That's up to
you, isn't it?"

His heart burned.

The bell over the door chimed and Dee walked in. Thank Jesus, Mary, and Joseph. Sam turned to her in relief.

"Dr. Ward!" She sounded as taken aback as he felt.

"And here's another one," Maeve said in apparent disgust, and
stomped off, trailing black clouds of smoke.

Sam watched her go, his soul on fire.

TWENTY

W hat was that about, then?" Sam asked.

I watched Maeve progress down the sidewalk, clearing the way with her umbrella. "I think she's pissed at me."

"Dr. Ward?"

I looked back at Sam. "You took a class with her, you said."

"Donkey's years ago."

"She still remembers you."

He winked. "So many women do." He reached for a mug. "Why is she pissed at you?"

"She offered to work with me. To supervise my thesis."

"She can't be that mad, then. Not if she wants to help you."

"Yeah, well . . . I haven't given her an answer yet," I confessed.

"Why not?"

"I was foisted on her at the beginning of the year. I thought she didn't like me."

Sam lifted an eyebrow. "Not the sort who pretends, I would have said."

"No, you're right." But how did he know? I watched him brew my tea, my mind niggling over the scene I'd interrupted. "What was she doing here?"

He foamed milk, the sound of the steam wand drowning out whatever he might have said. "She bought biscuits."

"And . . . ?"

He tipped the hot milk into the mug, releasing the warm scent of spices. "Will that be all?"

It was *not* all. Frustration churned my stomach. He'd shared his family with me. Why wouldn't he share more than bits of himself?

"Sam . . ."

"Boots." His eyes met mine, dancing with secrets, bright and impenetrable as the sun on the sea.

"Talk to me," I begged.

"Nothing to say." He set my tea on the counter. "You were telling me why you don't want to work with Ward."

Right. "Well, for starters, she only asked me after someone else offered."

His mouth twisted. "Must be nice to have choices."

"But I don't know if she really wants me or if she's just protecting her turf."

"Why does that matter?"

"What if she actually thinks my writing sucks?" That I suck. *An emotional and creative vampire.*

"You're giving her too much power. You don't need her approval. She's not your mam."

"Obviously." I attempted a joke. "My mother loved me."

"If you say so."

My breath caught. "What does that mean?" His gaze slid away. It didn't mean anything, I told myself. He was just being . . . "Sam?"

"Your mother left you. Traveled for her—art, was it?—with two growing girls at home. Nothing you could do about it then. Nothing you can do to fix it now."

I'd wanted him to talk to me. Now I wished with all my heart I'd never started this conversation.

"And nothing to do with Maeve Ward," I said.

"Unless you're trying to get from her what you couldn't get from your mam."

My mind went bright and blank. "That's a terrible thing to say. I thought we were friends."

"Friends tell each other the truth. You go on doing the same things over and over again, as if the ending will ever be any different. Believing if you're nice enough or smart enough or brave enough, everybody will love you and all your wishes will come true." His voice was light and relentless. "Well, life isn't like that, Boots. Ward is who she is. Take her help or tell her to go to hell, that's up to you. Just don't expect her to care one way or the other."

His words struck me like a harpoon, straight through the chest. For a second I couldn't breathe. "Then why was she here today?"

He shook his head. "Don't make this about me."

But it was. Even dazed and hurt, I knew this anger, this resentment, was about something more than Dr. Ward. Someone other than me. This was not my fault. I drew in a painful breath. "You think I'm hung up on my mother? What about you and your dad?"

"What about him?"

"Aren't you still trying to impress him? You want his approval, the same way I want my mom's. Only it's too late. For both of us."

"The difference is you can pretend. Easy enough to make be-

lieve your mother loves you when she's never around. I lived with
my father's disapproval every day."

Oh, Sam. My chest ached for him, for the boy he had been, for
the man he'd made himself. I wanted to go back in time and hug
him. But I wanted to hurt him, too. Because he hurt me.

"I never knew your dad. But I've met your family. They love
you. They're proud of you. I'm not making that up."

Up went the eyebrow. "Aren't you full of giggles and rainbows
today."

"And you're full of shit. You go on doing the same thing, too.
Day after day, year after year. You *know* things won't ever be any
different, and you don't even try to change."

He scowled. "I think we're done here."

I dug frantically in my bag for my wallet. "Oh, we're done."

Shaking, I pulled out money for my tea. Slapped the bills on
the counter and walked away.

don't remember much of the trip back to Reeti's. Back home.
Only that it rained, and every other passenger on the bus was
coughing or sneezing, gray puffs of germs that mingled with the
diesel in the air.

I tramped the wet sidewalk, head down, shoulders hunched,
wounded and confused. I'd always tried to be positive. To see the
best in people, including Sam. I'd never imagined he was capable
of cruelty.

I glanced up at the glowing windows of our apartment. I
couldn't face Toni or Reeti right now. Toni was thriving at the
bakery, surrounded by Clerys and buoyed by Fiadh's example of
fearless self-acceptance. Reeti was beginning to explore a relationship with Vir, even if at this point it consisted of texts and

long phone calls alone in her room. I didn't want to be a drag on their happiness. Also maybe I was jealous.

I went around back, where a wrought iron bench occupied a patch of slate and gravel between the dust bins on one side and Tim's car on the other. The seat was wet. A miserable wind slid between the houses, plastering a plastic bag against the railings.

Tim came out with the garbage. I took a step back, balling my icy hands in my pockets. Too late.

"Everything all right?" he called.

"Fine." I huddled deeper into my jacket. "Go back inside."

"You should come in, too. Out of the rain."

I clenched my chattering jaw. "I won't rust."

I watched the almost imperceptible calculations flit over his face. Good manners dictated he go away, as instructed. I could see his reluctance to intrude warring with his desire to help and felt a tug of sympathy.

I stayed stubbornly put.

He deposited his bag in the bin. Dragging his keys from his pocket, he depressed the fob. The car beeped. He opened the passenger door. "Get in. Please," he added, the manners asserting themselves.

I shook my head. "I'll get your upholstery wet."

He stood there patiently, without speaking, holding the door. The rain spangled his hair, darkening the shoulders of his sweater.

I let out an annoyed huff and got into the car. Tim walked around the hood, sliding in behind the leather-wrapped steering wheel. I refused to look at him.

He handed me a handkerchief, like a white flag in the corner of my vision.

"I'm not crying," I said as I dried the rain from my face and hands.

He didn't say anything.

This was becoming a habit. Him, a mostly silent witness. Me, a hot mess. I hated it.

"I'm just confused," I said.

"And angry."

"I don't get angry," I protested automatically.

Did I?

I took a swift physical inventory—the tension in my face and neck, the dryness in my mouth and throat, my grinding teeth, my shaking hands. *Angry.* Yes. The word settled inside me, hard and sure. I was angry at my mother for leaving. Angry at Sam for pointing out her choice. Angry with myself, for all the times I'd given up or gone along or failed to speak out because I was afraid of being abandoned. Rejected. I was angry at Aunt Em for not loving me enough, at Gray for using me, at Toni for needing me and dropping out, at Dr. Eastwick for dying, and Maeve Ward for being alive.

Oh God. *I was angry all the time.*

There was a certain relief in naming the emotion, as if giving it a label gave me power over it.

"Maybe I am a little angry. I guess I didn't . . ." I swallowed. "How did you know?"

"Anger's always difficult to admit." He fiddled with the car's controls. Heat rushed from the vents. "Or express."

"Not for men," I said, my tone truculent. "When men get mad, they get to punch things."

"Shall I punch someone for you?"

"Haha. No." The windows were steaming up. My knees were thawing, the tension easing from my shoulders. I stretched my fingers toward the hair-dryer blast from the dashboard. "Have you?" I asked, curious. "Ever punched anybody?"

"I was a soldier," he said mildly.

"I mean, in anger."

"Not recently."

"Not even . . ." He was leaning against the driver's-side door, leaving me space. Making me say it. "Not even Charles?" I asked.

"No."

We were back to monosyllables, I noticed. But at least we were talking. This conversation couldn't be pleasant for him, but he hadn't shut me up. He hadn't shut me out. "Did you ever say anything to him? Or to Laura?"

"There wasn't much point," he said stiffly. "Rehashing the situation doesn't change what's done."

"The point is, he betrayed your friendship. Your trust. They both did." Poor Tim. I knew how that felt. Although now that I thought about it, being humiliated in your ex-lover's novel was a degree less horrible than having your fiancée sleep with the man who saved your life while you were recovering from a suicide-bomb attack. Several degrees less horrible, in fact.

"They'd made their choice. I made mine."

He'd broken off the engagement, I remembered. "A man of action."

"Yes."

"And few words." His cheekbones colored. I resisted the urge to pat his hand. "Did you ever talk to anyone?"

His glasses gleamed in the gray light from the windows. "You think I need counseling to get over my hurt feelings."

"I think everybody can use a little support sometimes."

"Thank you, but I managed. One has one's pride. I wasn't going to be a burden."

"It's not a burden to tell someone how you feel." It occurred to me that this was a pretty hypocritical thing for me to say, given my reluctance to talk to Gray. Or about Gray. But maybe I was getting better. Now that I had friends who listened.

"Especially if they get paid to listen," Tim said dryly.

"Okay, well . . . What about your friends? Your parents?"

"Definitely not my parents. It would have been . . . awkward."

"Not as awkward as your dick best friend and your cheating fiancée getting it on while you were in the hospital, I bet."

"Ah. No."

The rush of the blower eased to a quiet, warm flow. The car smelled of wet wool and some woodsy aftershave. My nose dripped.

I blew it on his handkerchief. *Blergh.* "Sorry."

"No need to apologize." The silence stretched between us. "When I was in hospital," he said, and stopped, his hand smoothing his shirtfront.

I opened and closed my mouth. *Give him space. Let him talk. Channel your inner Tim.*

"My mother came every day," he said at last. "While I was laid up. It was . . . hard for her. Being apart from my father. I wasn't responsive—conscious—for a long time. And Laura was there, you see. Bringing my mother tea, bringing her magazines, making sure she got out occasionally for a meal or a walk. Like a daughter would."

"She was your fiancée."

"Yes. But more than that, we practically grew up together. Neighbors. It was a great comfort to my mother, having her there."

"That doesn't excuse what she did. Or Charles."

"Not everything, perhaps. But in the beginning . . . My parents knew Charles was my corporal. My friend. He'd saved my life. He bought my mother flowers. Naturally, they were grateful.

I was grateful. And when I realized . . . Well. I'd already put the family through so much. I wanted to shield them from . . . the ugly truth, I suppose. Better to go on as we were. Keep calm and carry on. Stiff upper lip and so forth."

"That was very kind of you."

He glanced away, out the window, as if I'd embarrassed him.

"Very British," I amended.

A shadow of a smile crossed his lips, causing a funny flutter in the region of my chest. Not that I had feelings for Tim Woodman. There had been no repeat of that New Year's kiss. But it was a nice smile. "Indeed."

"We have a saying in Kansas, too. No use crying over spilled milk."

"What are you supposed to do? With spilled milk." The smile was in his voice now.

"Clean it up and feed it to the hogs, according to Aunt Em."

"You must take after her, then." I looked at him in surprise. "Making the best of a bad deal," he explained.

"Oh. Thanks. The thing is, I don't really." "*Nothing you could do about it then*," Sam said in my head. "*Nothing you can do to fix it now.*" "I mean, I tell myself things aren't that bad. Or that they'll get better. But it's all fake. Pretending. Sam says I'm afraid to face reality."

"Sometimes pretending isn't an act of cowardice. Sometimes it's a matter of survival."

I stared at the drops of rain streaking the window, remembering the suitcases and the Cecilys. The stories I told myself to survive. *Our mother loved us. She was coming back for us soon. Maybe next time she would take us with her. Maybe this time she would stay.* "But I don't do anything," I said. "I can't change anything."

"You moved to Dublin. That was a big change."

"That's location. It's not me. Inside, I'm the same."

"You seem fine to me."

Another compliment, I thought. Understated—this was Tim, after all—but real. "But what am I doing here?"

"Staying warm, I would have said. Out of the rain."

"You made a joke."

His mouth curved in another of those slight, surprisingly effective smiles. "Maybe you needed to come to Ireland," he suggested. "Maybe this is part of your journey."

We sat awhile longer in the car, in the quiet, listening to the rain on the metal roof. Our breath fogged the glass. I was sweating.

"Did you ever read that book by Oscar Diggs?" he asked.

"Not yet. I will. I have to read one of his Shivery Tales first. For his seminar this term."

I found myself glancing sideways, noticing little details. The cowlick in his short, thick hair. A prickle of rash on his throat from shaving. He had very fair, fine skin. Sensitive.

I cleared my throat. "This is a nice car."

"Thank you."

"It's awfully big for the city," I said brightly. "It looks like you should be tootling around the countryside, delivering baskets to the peasantry on your estate." I was babbling, I realized with a fresh wave of humiliation. But he didn't seem to mind. "Possibly with a footman," I added. "Or, I don't know, maybe a Labrador."

"My mother has Labs."

It was another detail, a piece of himself, offered like a gift.

Or maybe I was projecting again, seeing what I wanted to see, making a big deal out of small talk.

I gestured vaguely toward the house. "I should probably go in now."

"All right, then?"

"Yeah. Better." I smiled. "Drier, anyway. Thanks."

He nodded shortly—the lord of the manor accepting the curtsies of his tenants. Or maybe . . . like a kind, shy, decent man, uncomfortable with being thanked.

And so . . ." I took a deep breath, pleating my fingers together. "I'd like you to supervise my dissertation."

Maeve Ward regarded me across her desk without any perceptible change of expression.

My heart beat furiously. Maybe Sam was right. Probably he was right. *"Don't expect her to care one way or the other."*

"If you still want to," I added.

She may have rolled her eyes. Or possibly that was a twitch. "Very well. Let's see how you get on. It takes time to develop a portfolio topic."

"I want to finish my Kansas story."

Yep. Definite twitch that time. "You're still shaping yourself as a writer. Concentrate this term on your required modules. You have all summer to work on your final dissertation."

"You asked me what I had to say for myself. Well, this is it. This is my story."

"Are we speaking autobiographically?"

As if I could simply rewrite the story of my childhood. And maybe that's what I'd done, what I kept doing, re-creating a pattern I knew too well—the girl who loved someone who didn't love her back. Who convinced herself each time that if only she could make it work, if she could convince this one to love her, it would be enough.

Maybe that's why I'd fallen for Gray. He was exactly my type. Charming, exciting, emotionally unavailable. This was love, as I knew it. The kind where you felt anxious and untethered and blamed yourself when the person you loved inevitably walked away.

These were not the sort of thoughts I should be having in my supervisor's office.

But the thing was, I didn't need Maeve to like me. She'd never pretended to like me. No surprises. No sabotage. I wasn't at the mercy of her feelings. Or my own.

I could trust Maeve to tell the truth.

"Maybe a little," I said. "I'm changing things."

"I thought we had moved beyond that."

Was she regretting her offer already? What I was writing . . . Well. It wasn't literary fiction. But it was authentically mine.

"Focus on what I feel, you said. What I need to work out."

Her dark gaze fixed on me. Assessing. Judging. "Write it, then."

Classes started. Rows of student desks crammed Oscar Wilde's former parlor between a black-and-white poster of the writer in the back of the room and the lecturer—the other Oscar, Oscar Diggs—in front. With his flyaway hair and the light reflecting from his shiny scalp, he looked a bit like Yoda. He sounded like him, too.

"You are not *trying* to write a book," he said. "You are *going* to write a book. Will it be any good? Maybe. It could be great. It could be terrible. But you will *finish*. And once you have finished your book, you can . . . What?" He rocked on the balls of his feet, surveying the class for a response.

We looked up, fingers poised, our laptops and notebooks open to capture his words of wisdom.

"Sell it?" Ryan suggested.

"Probably not," Oscar Diggs said quite cheerfully. "Rejection is the name of the game. But you will know that you can *do* it. You will have proven to yourself that you can write a story. And once you know that, all you need is . . ." Another expectant pause.

"An agent," Claire said.

"Practice," Oscar said. "Eventually, you'll want an agent, too. But practice first."

Several students looked uncomfortable. Uncertain, as if he'd farted or something. But I was inspired. Finishing a book was all I wanted.

Almost all I wanted.

The library called to offer me a job. For ten hours a week, I sorted through books and returned them to the shelves, trundling my metal cart through the open, endless stacks in Ussher, breathing in the smell of print and paper. I ran my fingers along the multicolored book spines with an almost sexual pleasure, imagining my name on one of the covers. I attended lectures and did my reading and waved to Tim when I ran into him taking out the garbage or picking up the mail.

I did not go back to Clery's.

"Fee misses you," Toni said when she came in one evening after her stint at the bakery. I was making pasta for dinner, filling and cheap. She slid me a sly look. "Sam misses you, too."

I was aware of Reeti pulling out her earbuds to listen. "Did he say so?"

"No, but he's been really grumpy." Toni grinned. "Course, it could just be that I annoy him."

"You annoy everybody, darling," Reeti said. "By the way, your shit's all over the bathroom counter again."

"I'll take care of it," I said automatically.

"Not your responsibility," Reeti said. She looked at Toni.

"The bathroom or Sam's feelings?" Toni asked.

Reeti narrowed her eyes.

Toni heaved a dramatic sigh. "Fine. I'll clean up after dinner."

I stirred the pasta sauce, to have something to do with my hands. Reeti was right. The mess in the bathroom was not my responsibility.

And Sam's feelings . . . Well. Maybe I wasn't responsible for those, either.

TWENTY-ONE

S am sat at the small table that served as his desk in the poky
storeroom/closet/office at the back of the shop. Through the
open doorway he could hear Fiadh faffing about, the clang of trays
being loaded onto the bakery cart, but for the moment he was
alone.

Janette came in. "Cleanup," his mother said, reaching for a
mop. "Sarah Murphy—you remember Sarah—came in with her
twins. Hot chocolate and crumbs all over the floor."

"Sarah, yeah."

She was never his girlfriend or anything. They'd done the usual,
though, back in the day, making out by her locker and under the
bleachers after some dance. Married and mother of three now,
working part-time in an insurance office on weekends. Everyone
getting on with their lives but him.

Sam shut down the window on the computer screen. "Who's
watching the register?"

"Toni."

"Jesus." He pushed back from the desk.

"Tom's out there." One of the regulars. "It's fine, Sam."

"Unless he walks out with the newspaper and half the till," Sam said. Which was ridiculous, and they both knew it.

He watched Janette fill the bucket at the utility sink. "I'll get that," he said.

"I'm not so old I can't push a mop. I did it often enough for you lot," his mother said. "What's that you were looking at? When I came in."

"Nothing."

"It's all right, you know. It's natural to be curious. Nothing to be ashamed of."

The back of his neck got hot.

"As long as you know it's not real life," Janette added. "Real girls don't look like that."

She thought he'd been looking at porn. *Jesus.* He'd been taking care of her, of all of them, for years. It infuriated him she could reduce him to a fourteen-year-old rubbing one off in his room. "It's not what you're thinking."

She raised an eyebrow. Like a dog on a scent, his mother. She wouldn't let it go until she'd sniffed out what she was after. "Speaking of real girls, I haven't seen Dee around lately. What happened with that?"

He didn't want to talk about Dee. He wasn't proud of himself there, what he'd said about her mother. "It's an application, all right?" he said to change the subject. "Nothing important."

"Loan or job?"

He didn't answer.

"Sure look, it's none of my business." Janette stood in the doorway, unmoving. Waiting.

"It's for school. Mature student enrollment, they call it. But don't worry, I'm just curious." He winked. "I know it's not real life."

She didn't laugh, as he'd hoped. "Why would you say that?"

"That's what he said. Da. You don't need a fancy degree to make good. Common sense and hard work, that's the stuff."

For a few seconds, she didn't answer. "Sam, when your da died . . . You did what you had to do. Jack and Aoife were so young, and I missed your father so much. Most mornings, it was all I could do to get out of bed and get us all dressed. You gave up a lot to be there for us, and I'm grateful."

He closed the laptop. "It's what he would've wanted."

"It's more than he ever would have asked. He'd be proud of you, son."

To his horror, he felt his throat close. He cleared it. "Ta."

She set the bucket on the floor. "He was proud of you, you know."

He looked down at the worn silver Apple logo on the laptop lid. The MacBook had been a graduation gift from his parents. It wouldn't run the latest operating system, but it worked well enough for the shop. For now. His mouth twisted. "Uni Boy."

That's what his da had called him, always with a smile or a clap on the shoulder. *C'mere, Uni Boy. Give us a hand stocking these shelves.* Or, *"Ask Uni Boy. He's the smart one in the family."*

"That was just his way. He'd never say it to your face, but he was always talking about you."

"About me putting on airs."

"Martin wasn't perfect, God knows. But I don't recognize this straw man you've made of him. Your father never wanted you to be like him, tied to this place all your life."

"What are you talking about? This shop was his life."

"No, *we* were his life. Me, you, your brother and sisters. The shop was how he provided for us."

That jerked his head up.

Janette looked back steadily. "He wanted you to be happy," she said. "And you're not. Apply to school, if that's what you want. We'll manage."

His heart pounded in his ears. "I might not get in."

"That's what you said the first go-round."

"There's no money, anyway."

"There must be aid, right? Loans, Scholarships. Bright boy like you, you'll figure it out." She smiled. "I'll be in front. You take your time."

TWENTY-TWO

B ut you're missing game night!" Toni protested. "Fee's coming over to play Monopoly."

I loved that we had a routine—Reeti, Toni, and me—developed over the months we'd lived together. Friday pub nights, Tuesday board games, Sunday cooking shows with Tim. Secure and predictable but fun, like the imaginary family I'd yearned to be part of when we were growing up. Sometimes Fiadh joined us, or someone from my writing group dropped in. Tonight, though, I was going to a reading at the college. Attendance wasn't required, exactly. But any absence would be noticed.

"Yeah, well, adulting means sometimes you have to do things you're not really excited about." I tugged on my puffer jacket, an Oxfam find that made me look like a turquoise version of the Stay Puft Marshmallow Man.

"If this is about school again . . ."

"It's not. Although if you want to talk about your plans . . ."

Toni wrinkled her nose.

I suppressed a sigh. As much as I'd enjoy a little more room for my stuff, a little more quiet to study, there was something reassuring about having my baby sister so close I could almost reach her across the space between our beds. In two weeks she was leaving, her ninety-day tourist stay almost up. I would miss her. And I couldn't shake the feeling that I was still responsible for her. I'd bought her plane ticket back to Kansas, but despite my best efforts, Toni was alarmingly evasive about what she was going to do after she got home.

"Right. Not the time. No serious talk on game night." I kissed the top of her head. "Back by nine."

Reeti's phone jangled with a high-pitched drumbeat. Bhangra, Reeti told me when I'd asked.

I smiled. "Vir?"

She blushed and nodded. "Let me just . . ." She texted a quick reply.

"But who's going to be the banker?" Toni asked.

"Reeti can do it. She's good with numbers."

She glanced up from her phone. "I do enough accounting in my classes. I'll call Tim."

Which was great. I got the sense that Tim was lonely. It made me happy that my sister was hanging out with my two good friends. My best friends, since Sam and I still weren't speaking.

"That will be fun," I said. "Sorry I won't be here."

"You just want him for his muffins," Reeti said.

"If that's a euphemism, I'm going to throw up," Toni said.

"Stop." I flushed. "It's not like that." Tim and I were *friends*.

He arrived as I was leaving, plate in hand.

"Wow." I took a deep, appreciative sniff. "Are those scones?"

He nodded. "Earl Grey with lavender icing." A tiny V appeared between his eyebrows as he took in my jacket and the purse over my shoulder. "You're not staying?"

I shook my head regretfully. "I can't. I have this reading thing to go to."

His mouth curved. "The full Trinity experience."

A memory surfaced. Tim, his dorky graphic T-shirt half concealed by his navy blazer, when we all went out together the evening of the Oscar Diggs reading. The night that Sam kissed me.

"Um. Yes." We stood on the landing, arm's-length apart, the plate between us. I swallowed. "Well . . ."

"Have fun," Tim said at the same time.

"You, too."

Our eyes met. For a minute, I thought he was going to say something. Do something. I held my breath in anticipation. But all he said was, "Take a scone with you."

"Thanks."

It was still hot from the oven. I ate it on my way to the bus, savoring the warmth on my hands, the faint, floral sweetness lingering on my lips.

The reading was followed by a reception in the Arts Building. Glenda Norton shepherded the visiting speaker—a debut writer who had graduated from Trinity some years ago—from group to group. I recognized the creative writing students and staff, some English faculty, a deputation of administrators. They'd all read his book. Anyway, they pretended they had.

I missed the rainbow-haired tweens queuing for selfies, the friendly onsite bookseller with colorful stacks of Shivery Tales books.

Maybe Oscar Diggs did, too. He was standing on his own, blocked from the refreshments table by a knot of postgraduates drinking tepid wine and eating cubed cheese like it was their first solid food in days. I felt a tug of sympathy.

I wished Reeti were here. Tim. Sam.

"Can I get you anything, Mr. Diggs?" I offered. "Some wine?"

"Oscar, please. Thanks," he said when I handed him a plastic cup of red. "Dee, isn't it?"

I had been in his class for almost two months. I shouldn't be gratified he remembered my name. "Yeah, hi. Um. Did you enjoy the reading?"

His eyes twinkled. "Bit long, I thought. But then, I have the attention span of a five-year-old. After twenty minutes, I'm ready for a drink."

I smiled. "Should I have offered you apple juice?"

"Might be better than what they're serving. How did you like it?"

He wasn't asking my opinion of the wine.

"Well." I paused, embarrassed to appear to criticize another writer. A published writer. I'd read his novel, strung with small, significant observations, polished hard and bright as diamonds. "It was very detailed."

"Long on description, short on story." Oscar sniffed at his glass. Grimaced comically. "That was a nice job you did with the character sketch. The little girl. What was her name?"

I glowed. "Rose. Thanks." The last writing prompt for his seminar had been to write from the point of view of a child. "You don't think she's too ordinary?"

He cocked his head. "You want her to have superpowers?"

"Ha. No. But some of the students in my workshop found her sort of . . ." *Bland,* Claire had said. "*Too much Cinderella, not enough Snow Queen,*" Erinma said. "Nice," I finished weakly.

"Hm. What do you think?"

"I think she's *real,*" I burst out. "She's swept off to this magic country where she isn't in control and she doesn't know the rules and she's still finding her way. Fitting in. She's doing what she's been told to do all her life. Be quiet. Be good. Be kind. Smile."

"How's that going for her?"

"I . . . She's surviving."

"I'd work on that," Oscar said. "Throw her out of her comfort zone, threaten her life, and see what happens."

My protective instincts surged. Or maybe that was panic. *But she's just a little girl*, I wanted to protest. "That sounds pretty scary."

"But interesting, am I right? Scary never hurt Stephen King." He chuckled. "Or me, for that matter. Try it. See what your girl does. She might surprise you."

I swallowed. "Okay."

"I'd be interested in reading it. When you're ready."

"I don't feel like it will ever be ready," I confessed. *That I'll ever be ready.*

"Occupational hazard. Send me a proposal, when you have it. Say, the first three chapters and an outline."

"Wow. That would be . . ." *Almost the length of the entire dissertation.* "Amazing. Thank you so much."

"There's a group headed to The Duke when all this is over, I hear," he said. "Are you going?"

I wasn't dressed for networking. "I would *love* to," I said honestly, flattered by his invitation. "But . . ."

"Oscar, here you are." It was the dean, Richard, resplendent in tweed and an unironic scarf, doing the rounds. "We have another American with us tonight. I believe you know Grayson Kettering."

I froze like a possum in the headlights as the man beside him stepped forward with a ready smile and handshake.

Gray? Here?

"Oscar, good to see you again. I didn't know you were into literary fiction." The gibe slid in, slick as a stiletto, before he turned to me. "And Dee, darling, how are you? I hoped I'd run into you tonight."

"Always happy to support a fellow writer's debut," Oscar said.

Gray smiled, his eyes crinkling, broadcasting charm. "Ah yes, the appeal of young talent." Smoothly, he moved in. His scent enveloped me, Dior Homme and starch and the faint, intimate smell of his neck. At the last second, I managed to turn my head, so his kiss only brushed my cheek. It flamed like a brand.

I felt ambushed. Sick. Flattened, as if I'd been hit by an eighteen-wheeler on the highway.

They were all looking at me. At least, I thought they might be. They must be. Ryan and Claire shooting glances from the shelter of the refreshment table, Maeve's dark eyes boring from across the room, Dr. Dalton with a distracted frown.

The conversation rolled around me as I stood there in my vintage sweater and stretchy pants, my face fixed in a rictus possum grin, like roadkill.

"Quite inspiring, isn't it?" Gray said. "Being surrounded by all these fresh young minds."

"Trolling for ideas, Mr. Kettering?" Maeve Ward inquired truculently from behind him. "Or graduate students?"

Gray stiffened. "I don't believe I've had the pleasure."

"Maeve Ward," she announced.

"Maeve is Miss Gale's supervisor," the dean said.

Around the lobby, conversations slowed. People turned to stare. Like drivers passing a car wreck, helpless to assist. Curious. Horrified.

"Ah yes, Dee." Gray smiled at me, all warmth and teeth. "I had her first. When she was at Kansas. We worked together quite closely for a while. I've missed her."

Oscar choked into his glass. Maeve scowled. The dean cleared his throat.

Glenda floated into my vision, wearing pink cashmere and a hard, cool expression. "Excuse me, Richard. We seem to be running low on wine. Dee, would you mind giving Shauna a hand . . . ?"

I seized on the excuse, desperate to leave the pull of Gray's orbit. "Yes. I mean, no. I don't mind. I . . . I'll be right back."

"Bring me something, will you, darling," Gray called after my retreating back. "You know what I like."

Looks from around the lobby licked at me like flames. My throat, my face, my whole body burned.

"Holy shit," Shauna breathed as we made our way to the half kitchen. "Are you okay?"

Tears welled at the sympathy in her voice. I couldn't make eye contact. How much did she know? Or guess?

"Actually, I feel kind of sick," I said, not looking at her. "Would it be all right if I went home?"

"God, yes. Do you know what he wants?"

I jerked as if she'd jabbed me. "What?"

"Kettering's drink. What does he want?"

"Oh." The years I'd spent keeping track of his preferences, catering to his needs, rose up. "Vodka martini. Grey Goose."

She rolled her eyes. "So, red or white?"

"Red," I said, and fled.

let myself quietly into the apartment, hoping I could say my good nights and escape to the room I shared with Toni.

Reeti looked up from the Monopoly board. "You're home early."

"Good. Let's start over." Toni waved a game token in the air. "I saved you the boot."

I managed a smile. "Thanks, but I . . . I don't want to interrupt your game. You guys carry on. I think I'll go to bed."

"I can't. I'm out. Tim and his stupid hotels," Toni said.

Rows of property cards and pastel play money were neatly

stacked in front of Tim. He ignored them, his gaze focusing on my face. "What's wrong?"

I opened my mouth. Closed it.

Reeti's eyes narrowed. "Sit," she commanded. "I'll get you some chai."

"Something stronger," Fiadh said. "From the look of her."

"No, really," I protested weakly. "I just . . ." The effort of pretending that everything was all right stuck in my throat.

They weren't falling for my act anyway.

"Dodo?" Toni's voice was higher, like a child's.

"You might as well talk to us," Reeti said. "We won't leave you alone until you do."

I was hemmed in, pinned, by the pressure of their attention.

My friends. I was so lucky, so grateful, that they were there for me, emotionally and every other way. Only as long as they had my back, I had to show up for them, too. No hiding. No lying. I needed to be honest. Even if it felt like peeling off my skin.

I took a deep breath. "Gray was there. At the reading."

"What?"

"The fucker."

"Who's Gray?" Fiadh asked.

"Her douchey ex," Toni said. "He's, like, this famous writer. He used her for his book and then dumped her."

I winced. But at least her explanation meant I was spared going into details.

"Dick move," Fiadh observed. "Showing up at her school like that."

"So, what happened?" Reeti asked.

Tim pushed out an empty chair with his foot, silently inviting me to sit.

I sank down, sneaking a glance at him. He was wearing his

Mr. Darcy face, cool and aloof. Once I might have been duped into thinking he didn't feel anything. I knew better now. "Nothing."

"What do you mean, nothing?"

"What did he do? What did you say?"

"Nothing," I repeated. The memory burned.

My phone buzzed in my pocket. I fumbled for it.

"Forget the phone," Reeti said. "Talk to us."

I stared at the little screen, the blood draining from my head. "It's Gray."

Reeti scowled. "What does he want?"

"Let me see." Toni grabbed the phone from my numb fingers, turning it so they all could read the message.

GRAY: You ran away. Again.

"Bit of an arsehole," Fiadh said.

"He's right." They all looked at me. I swallowed, hard. "I didn't confront him. I didn't defend myself. He said things and I . . . stood there. Like an idiot. Smiling." *Letting him bring me down in front of everybody. Just like I let him tear me apart in his book.*

Three pulsing dots appeared on the screen. Gray, typing.

Toni handed back my phone, her dark eyes wide and questioning.

I need to see you.

Fiadh snorted. "He needs to go fuck himself."

More dots. More typing. Dinner. Tomorrow night. Not a question.

"I have to answer," I said.

"No, you don't," Reeti said. "You don't owe him anything."

Tim was noticeably silent.

I twisted my fingers together in my lap. "Maybe I owe it to me."

"Owe yourself what, for God's sake?" Reeti asked.

I stared at Gray's message, a tiny spark kindling inside me. *Anger.* I had a name for it now. "Closure."

"He's not worth your time," Tim said.

I studied the game board as if the answer were there some-where, between the Jail and Chance. "You don't understand. I thought . . . I hoped I'd never have to deal with him again. But I can't run away from what he did to me."

"Wherever you go, there you are," Toni said.

I nodded. "When I saw him . . . I thought if I ever saw him again, it would be different. I would be different. And instead, I froze. I need to fight."

"Defeat your dragons," Tim murmured.

I flashed him a look of gratitude. "Face them, anyway. I have to meet him."

"Then I'm going with you."

Fiadh glanced sharply from him to me.

"No," I said more firmly than I felt. "I need to do this myself."

"Every knight needs a squire." His right cheek indented. "Be-sides, it's only fair. You came to my rescue."

"When?"

"The first time I saw you." Behind his steel-rimmed glasses, his gaze was clear and direct.

I smiled a little. "So I did."

He gave a nod, as if everything were decided. "Right, then. I'll be happy to buy him dinner while you tell him to piss off."

"Not dinner," I said. "Drinks only. Me and Gray. You can wait for me at the bar."

Because it was time to throw myself out of my comfort zone.

And maybe I'd surprise myself.

TWENTY-THREE

"S hould you be going to his hotel?" Tim asked the following night.

We were in his car, driving to my meeting with Gray. Tim had offered, and I . . . Well, honestly, I was not dressed for the bus. No puffer jacket, no faded sweater, no stretchy pants tonight, no, sir. I was armored down to my underwear in a charcoal gray sweater dress with a deep V-neck and crocheted hem, dangly silver earrings, and my cowboy boots. My hair was down and styled in loose waves, which had taken twenty minutes and the use of Reeti's curling iron to achieve. I wanted Gray to look at me and see New Dee, unflappable, poised, shit pulled together. I wanted him to be consumed with remorse and regret and also possibly swallow his tongue.

"His hotel is fine. This won't take long," I said with more confidence than I felt. "Quick in, quick out."

"Indeed." A trace of a question, a hint of a joke.

I laughed. "I'm not going to his room."

"He doesn't know that."

"He should. I told him we'd meet in the bar. Drinks only, I said." A sidelong look. "Besides, you'll be there."

"I won't be sitting with you. Unless you've changed your mind."

I shook my head. "I appreciate the support. I do. But I've got this."

At least, I hoped I did. I wanted to show Gray he couldn't awe, charm, or shame me into letting him set the terms of whatever this twisted thing was between us anymore. Or maybe I needed to prove it to myself.

I stared at my knees, pleating the scalloped hem of my dress between my fingers. Anyway, that was the plan.

We drew up to the hotel, which had a discreet sign and three doormen out front. Not the sort of place you stayed on an adjunct professor's salary. *Destiny Gayle* had obviously been very good to Gray.

My stomach clenched. In anger, I told myself.

Tim gave the keys to the valet, and we walked into the lobby.

"Right." I slipped off my wrap. Took a deep breath. "Let's do this."

Tim's gaze dropped briefly before he looked me in the eyes. "Nice dress."

I grinned, reassured. "Reeti calls it cleavage, cuppage, and the Underwear of Death."

"Because you look . . . lethal?"

"Because it's killing me," I confided. "I can't breathe."

An actual smile. "Ah."

He put his hand at the small of my back, a polite touch to guide me across the lobby. Something inside me tensed and then relaxed. "I'm going in alone," I blurted.

His hand dropped away. "As you wish."

"It's not that I don't trust you. I just need . . ." *To trust myself.*

"Space," he supplied.

I nodded gratefully.

"I'll be at the bar," he said.

I walked away, already missing that light, reassuring pressure at my back.

The hotel bar was decorated like a library with dark wood and red leather, old books and portraits of dead white men. Gray was already seated at a table.

He got up as I approached. "Dee, darling."

This time he didn't make the mistake of aiming for my mouth. He kissed me on both cheeks, lingering long enough to make my stomach swoop in remembered desire and revulsion.

I inhaled, more shaken than I wanted to admit. "Hi." That double kiss . . . It was pretentious, right? What was he, French all of a sudden?

"Menus, please," he said to the server.

"I told you I don't want dinner."

"But here you are." He smiled. "You ran away before we had the chance to celebrate my success. Let me treat you."

The familiar pull of his gravity sucked at me. I set my feet, standing my ground. "Can I have some water, please?" I asked the server.

"Don't be a martyr, darling. A glass of pinot grigio for the lady," Gray said, waving me to a chair. "And I'll have another Hennessy."

He owed me, I thought. A drink, at least. And he'd managed my order without sneering about my taste in wine. I sat.

The server looked at me. I nodded. "Thank you."

He handed Gray a menu and went off to fetch our drinks.

Gray gave me a droll look. "I hope you don't mind if *I* order. I'm hungry," he said with little-boy plaintiveness.

"Do what you want," I said. "You always do."

He leaned forward. The pink light in the bar was kind to him. He looked like he hadn't changed at all, like the man I'd fallen in love with, like his author photo—that lock of hair falling onto his forehead, the top three buttons of his shirt undone beneath his blazer. "Thank you for coming."

I blinked. I couldn't remember him thanking me before. Maybe he had changed. A little. And maybe I was falling under his spell, into his lies. Giving him the benefit of the doubt, the way I always did. "What are you doing here?"

"Didn't I say?"

"No."

The server returned with our drinks. I was dimly aware of Tim coming in behind him, taking a seat at the bar.

"I came to see you." Gray aimed the full focus of his dark gaze on me, the look that made me feel like the center of his world. "I missed you."

The words pinged inside me. I would have given almost anything to hear them once. "It took you seven months."

Longer, if you counted the confused, painful, lonely months after his book release, before Dublin.

I was totally counting them.

"I wish you knew how much I regret that," Gray said with apparent sincerity. "I texted. But you never really responded."

That's what I'd come for, wasn't it? His regrets. But he was still acting as if our breakup was somehow my fault. "You said it was over," I reminded him. "You said we were through."

"Because it wasn't until you were gone that I realized how much I needed you."

He'd always been good at that, I remembered. Using things I said as a springboard for his own arguments, turning my words around.

I gulped wine. "You were stifled by my domesticity, you said."

He smiled ruefully. "That was before you deserted me. I've missed coming home to you and your little dinners. Eating in restaurants isn't the same." He signaled the server. "I'll start with the oysters. And then the salmon."

The man looked at me. "And for miss?"

I smiled and shook my head. "Nothing, thank you."

He glided away again, like a butler in a movie.

"It was easy to forget who you really are when it was only words on the page," Gray said. "But now that the movie is in production, I can actually see you, all that you are, all that you did, everything you meant to me. I don't think I truly appreciated your funny, caring ways before."

My blood pounded in my ears. I took another sip of wine. "I didn't desert you."

"Let's not argue. Isn't it enough that I came all this way to see you? You look amazing, by the way."

I looked down at my wineglass, tracing the sweating rings on the table with my finger. All my life, I'd waited for someone to come back to me. To choose me. "Thanks."

"Ireland must suit you."

"It does."

"Quite a change for you, working with that scary-looking woman. Maude, is it?"

"Maeve Ward. She was longlisted for the Booker Prize. And what does it matter what she looks like? You wouldn't comment on her appearance if she were a man."

He lifted his hands in fake surrender. "You're right, of course." He sat back against the leather banquette, assessing me. I resisted the urge to touch my hair. To squirm. "But enough about her. I want to hear about you. Tell me what you're working on."

Something dormant bloomed in me, responding helplessly to his interest, unfurling for his approval. "I'm reimagining the Kansas story."

He smiled. "Ah, the seductive farm girl."

I stiffened. "She's changed." *I've changed.*

"I'm sure you'll do her justice," Gray said. He might as well have patted me on the head.

I reached for my wine. "Oscar Diggs says I did a good job with her."

"Of course he did." Gray mirrored my action, his eyes bright over the rim of his glass. "You two seemed very friendly the other night."

"I'm in his seminar."

"Smart of you to find someone to take you under his wing, so to speak."

Warmth swept up my neck to my ears. "It's not like that."

"Darling, I wasn't suggesting you're sleeping with him. He's a bit old, even for you."

My hand tightened on my glass.

"I'd simply hate to see you lose your voice," Gray continued as the server set his appetizer on the table. "You don't want to find yourself writing children's books."

I was furious. With him. With myself. "Better than trolling reader events to pick up fresh . . . ideas."

His eyes laughed. "Oh, brava. I suppose the genre could be a good match for you, after all. It doesn't require the same, shall we say, sophistication? Go ahead and bring the salmon," he instructed the server. "I have to be somewhere at seven."

"Where are you going?" I asked after the server left.

Gray's long fingers squeezed lemon over the oysters nestled in ice. "You're not jealous?"

"No."

"I have a little reading at Chapters. There's been so much pub-licity around the movie . . . Well, you know how these things go. My publisher insisted."

He hadn't come to Dublin to see *me*. He was on tour to pro-mote his fucking book.

"You should come," Gray said.

Heat moved through my veins like alcohol. "You're kidding, right?"

He gave me a half grin. "It will be like old times."

That's what I was afraid of. "You mean, when you blindsided and humiliated me in front of your fans and the entire English department?"

"I hope you know I never meant to embarrass you like that."

"Is that an apology?"

His eyes flickered. "Darling, you can't expect flowers and prom-ises. I thought you'd be flattered. After all, you were my muse."

"I was your girlfriend. And you . . ." I choked. "You betrayed me. You lied to me. You lied about me."

Other diners glanced our way.

"Lower your voice, for God's sake. You're making a scene."

Fight your dragons. "Go to hell."

Gray sighed. "I can see you're upset. If the signing makes you uncomfortable, then of course you should stay here." He slid his wallet from his pocket.

"What do you mean, stay here?"

He removed a credit card—no, a key card, a room key—from the wallet and laid it on the table between us. "Until I get back. It's a very nice room."

"I'm not staying in your room."

"Darling, I don't want to fight."

"I don't have to care what you want anymore." My heart hammered. This was my moment to find my voice and use it. "I trusted you and you used me. It won't happen again."

"Could we have a little less drama, please? You're acting as though I held you captive in my basement. You're hardly the innocent victim here. I took an interest in you. Ill-advised, perhaps. But I'm not responsible for your romantic disappointment."

"You abused your position to take advantage of me."

"You got what you wanted. You were begging for it."

"I wanted to be a writer."

"Then be a writer." He sipped his whiskey. "Or be the derivative second-rate talent you were shaping up to be. It's not my fault you can't produce an authentic thought without me."

"You stole from me to write your book. You self-absorbed, narcissist hack."

"I gave you your fifteen minutes of fame. I had no idea you'd be so bitter about it. Have another drink. It will put you in a better mood."

"You're not listening to me." He had never listened. He never really cared. He took two years from me I could never get back. I wasn't giving him another minute. "I'm done. We're through."

"You won't get better from Diggs."

I threw my wine in his face.

At the bar, Tim stood. There were audible gasps around us. "Oh, I say." "Here, now." The server hurried toward us, threading between tables.

"Cliché until the end." Gray wiped his face with a napkin. "I suppose it was too much to hope for some originality from you."

I grabbed the oyster plate and upended it in his lap.

The melting slush spattered and spilled, soaking his pants. Empty shells scattered and slid, bouncing on the carpet at my feet.

"You vicious little bitch!" Gray started up from the banquette, dripping. Furious.

But Tim was in the way, calm and solid. "All done here?"

"Yes," I said, and swept out.

was on fire.

"Well done," Tim said as we drove home.

I glowed. "I fought the dragon."

"I couldn't hear what you said. But you crushed him."

"I doubt it. He's kind of uncrushable."

"Like a cockroach."

I snort-laughed at the image of Gray. Not a dragon. A bug. "Exactly. But it was epic. I was awesome. I didn't freeze. I finally told him off. Plus, he won't have time to eat. He'll have to change clothes before the signing." Gray hated missing meals, I remembered with satisfaction.

"I wasn't referring to the inconvenience." Tim slowed to cross Baggot Street Bridge. The rush of water over the locks penetrated the car windows. "He knows he's lost you now. That has to hurt."

I shook my head. "Only his pride. Not his feelings." The dark ribbon of the Grand Canal gleamed through the trees. "When we were first together . . . I couldn't believe someone like Gray could love me. And then, when everything went wrong, it sort of confirmed what I secretly believed all along. That I didn't . . . You know. Deserve him. That I wasn't good enough."

"For an intelligent woman, you can be remarkably obtuse sometimes."

A compliment. I wouldn't let it go to my head. "The thing is . . . I tried so hard to be worthy of him. And I guess I've realized that he was never going to love me. No matter what I did. I couldn't change him. I can't make him give me what I want. All I can change is my own response."

"By dumping oysters in his lap."

I smiled. "Well . . ."

"Excellent job, by the way."

"Thanks. Anyway, it's good to finally have . . ."

"Victory?"

He had been a soldier. Of course he thought in terms of fighting, of winning and losing. "I was going to say, closure."

"Indeed." One word.

I studied his profile, illuminated by the streetlights—the cowlick in his thick, dark hair; his hands, quiet and controlled on the steering wheel; his well-defined jaw. When his fiancée cheated on him, he'd managed a kind of victory by breaking up with her. Salvaged his pride. Kept his integrity. But he was still working with her, right? Putting his drunken buddy to bed, protecting them both by hiding their betrayal from his family. He'd never had *closure*. It wasn't fair.

"Tim . . ."

"Here we are," he said, pulling in behind our building.

I didn't move. I was still buzzing from the confrontation with Gray, my mind churning, my body seething with energy. I wanted to ring bells or fire cannons, not go up tamely to my quiet apartment. Toni was out with Fiadh tonight, and Reeti was at the temple for some celebration. I couldn't even replay my triumph for them until they got home.

"Will you be all right?" Tim asked as I sat there like a lump.

"I'm fine. I'm great." Impulsively, I touched his forearm. The expensive wool of his jacket prickled my fingertips. "Thank you. For everything."

He glanced down at my hand. Back at my face. He was wearing his contacts tonight, his eyes lambent in the dashboard's glow. "It was nothing. You did it all. I was merely there."

"My squire."

He smiled, just a little. "Yes."

The moment crackled between us. I slid my hand from his arm, reluctant to lose that small connection. My skin tingled with static. "Do you want—"

"I suppose—" he said at the same time. He broke off. "Sorry."

"No." I waved my hand. "You go on."

"You haven't eaten. As your squire, I believe it's my duty to, er, provision you."

"Have dinner together, you mean?"

"If you'd like."

I beamed, suffused with relief that I didn't need to leave him, that I didn't have to come down from this high. "I'd love to."

I perched on a barstool in Tim's kitchen, watching him make grilled cheese as carefully and methodically as he did everything else, slathering even slices of homemade bread with butter, grating a mixture of Gruyère and cheddar, heating it slowly in a cast iron pan until the edges were brown and crispy.

He cut the sandwich on the diagonal, the way I did for Toni, and set both halves on a plate in front of me.

"Where did you learn to cook?" I asked.

"My grandmother's." He plated a second sandwich. "I used to go there after school to have tea with her and my grandfather. You should eat that while it's hot."

I took an obedient bite. "Mm. This is fantastic."

Color tinged his cheekbones. "It's just a sandwich. Wine?"

"Please. I promise not to fling it at you."

Which won me another near smile.

We sat side by side at the open counter to eat, our knees angled together, our shoulders almost touching. "Did your grandmother teach you to bake, too?" I asked.

His laugh was deep and unexpected. "Hardly. She bought her biscuits from Fortnum and Mason. But when she died . . ." He chewed. Swallowed. "I'd pop round and fix tea for my grandfather. Not up to Nana's standards, obviously. But I could do beans on toast. Cucumber sandwiches. That sort of thing."

"At least he didn't starve," I said without thinking.

"That was the goal," Tim said dryly.

"Sorry. That's something my aunt Em used to say."

An early memory surfaced. Me, standing on a chair in the farmhouse kitchen, swaddled in one of Em's aprons as she taught me to scramble eggs. I must have been very young, five or six. Toni wasn't in the picture yet. Everything warm and golden, the sunlight streaming from the window over the sink, the butter in the pan, her hand over mine on the fork. *"At least now you won't starve,"* she'd said.

"She was big on teaching me the basics. How to heat soup in the microwave. Cut up fruit. Make peanut butter sandwiches." I'd done my best to learn, trying not to be a burden.

"Survival skills," Tim said.

I blinked. "I never thought of it like that. Cooking as a love language." As my aunt's way of making sure I was fed, even after my mother took me away from her and the farm. A lump formed in my throat.

"And now you cook for your sister."

I nodded. "And Reeti." A pause. "I used to cook for Gray, too." Putting it out there, almost daring him to judge.

Tim didn't say anything.

"I didn't mind," I added. "I like to cook. I liked taking care of him, doing little stuff. Looking up recipes. Buying his favorite cereal. Cutting up pineapple and veggies so he would eat healthier snacks."

Tim looked at me as if I were speaking a foreign language. "And what did he do for you?"

"He didn't have to do anything. He just . . . was. I'd never really been in a serious relationship before. I liked that he needed me. Or he said he did. I miss that," I confided. "Feeling necessary to someone, like I was part of something, half of a couple. Well, you know."

"Not really."

I opened my mouth. Shut it. Maybe over the weeks and months, I was absorbing some of his ability to listen without interruption. Without blame. I took a big sip of wine, giving him space.

"Laura and I didn't have that kind of relationship," he said at last. "She never needed me."

"But you were engaged." The words slipped out.

"Yes." Tim took his time refilling my wineglass. "She wanted . . . what I represented, I suppose."

His voice was even. Unbothered. But I knew him now, recognized the furrow he got between his brows, the slight tension in his shoulders. I knew how it felt, not to be wanted for yourself.

My heart tugged. "I'm sorry. That's really shitty."

"She cared for me," Tim said. "It's just . . . She was ready to get married, and I checked all the appropriate boxes—the right schools, the right background. She worked for my father. Our families approved."

"I get it," I said. *She belonged.*

"She was looking at houses," Tim said. "We both wanted children. Marriage seemed like the logical next step."

Children.

I was suddenly, excruciatingly aware of him, of his body, the quick rise of his chest, the dense muscles of his back. Of how he would be in bed, solid and methodical. My face got hot.

"What about sex?" I blurted.

His mouth twitched. "I'm in favor of it, generally."

A joke, not an answer. Obviously, Tim Woodman was not the type to kiss and tell.

"Did you love her?" I persisted. "Do you love her?"

"Now? No." Chopped short. An obvious signal to let it go.

I didn't, of course. The possibility that Tim might be heartbroken—or worse, pining—was like probing a wound or picking at a scab, painful and irresistible. "It's all right," I said. "It would be natural if you still had feelings."

"I assume you're speaking from experience."

He meant Gray. Flustered, I took my plate to the sink. "I'm just saying, when somebody hurts you like that, it leaves a scar. You can heal, but you're never quite the same."

He shot me an unreadable look.

I flushed. Probably I shouldn't have mentioned the scar thing. There was his knee. And who knew what other injuries, hidden under his clothes. Not that I was picturing him naked . . .

Tim sighed. "I assure you, I have no attachment to Laura. I've moved on."

"Really? Has there been anyone since?"

"There could be."

Oh. I busied myself putting our plates in the dishwasher, regretting I'd ever brought the subject up. I didn't want to know if Tim was interested in someone. Did I?

I waited. Nothing.

I turned, propping my hips against the sink. "You know, you can take this whole buttoned-up Brit act too far. It wouldn't hurt you to open up once in a while. Especially if you're involved with somebody."

"I've actually been quite open," he said steadily.

"Ha."

"If she doesn't know how I feel at this point, it's because she doesn't want to see."

My heart slammed into my ribs. "Meaning, you haven't told her."

He met my eyes. "I've always thought actions speak louder than words."

My pulse stuttered. "And you are a man of action," I teased.

A corner of his mouth tipped up. "Yes."

The energy surged back, a thousand pins and needles under my skin. The air was charged, thick with anticipation and doubt.

This was a risk, this was always a risk . . . I had a stubborn tendency to imagine things that weren't there, to ignore facts that were staring me in the face. Tim might not mean what I thought he meant. He might not feel what I hoped he felt. He might say no.

I swallowed. His gaze dropped briefly to my throat.

If she doesn't know how I feel at this point, it's because she doesn't want to see.

I didn't need to pretend with Tim. I didn't have to project into the future. Now could be enough. This could be enough. Tonight, I was brave with victory. I'd said no to a man I didn't want. I could say yes to one I did.

Actions speak louder than words.

I grinned. "Prove it."

Tim went still. For a second I thought he wouldn't move. And then he smiled, full on, and . . . Wow. That was a great smile.

He held out his hand. Like we were saying hello, like we were making a pact. I looked down at his wide, square palm, his blunt-nailed fingers, and up at his face. Without his glasses, his face looked oddly naked. Vulnerable.

Something inside me relaxed. I slid my hand into his, feeling the current leap between us. Our fingers interlocked. He tugged me toward him, bringing our bodies together, breast to chest, hips to thighs, every contact sparking along my nerves, a full-on connection like his smile. My heart jolted.

He cupped my face with his free hand, his gaze intent and seeking. The kitchen was so quiet, nothing but the sound of his breath and mine and the hum of the refrigerator. I closed my eyes. His lips brushed my forehead and my eyelids, drifted down my cheek and found my mouth. I returned the soft, exploratory pressure, learning him.

His kiss was . . . nice. Normal. No slobber, no stabbing, no fancy technique.

He nipped at my mouth and I opened to him, meeting him, matching him stroke for stroke. His free hand slid down, pulling me closer. He smelled unexpectedly familiar, like wilted cotton and woodsy aftershave and clean male sweat. I was suddenly hungry, craving more, more taste, more Tim. I ran my hands up his back, molding myself to his solid torso, his muscled abdomen. He was hard in all the right places. My thoughts scattered. I was lost in kissing, drunk on the feel of him, the subtle urging of his hands, the exciting friction of his body. He palmed my butt. I gripped his shirt, tugging it free of his belt.

"Dee." He broke our kiss, resting his forehead against mine. His skin was faintly damp. I wanted to lick him.

I sought his mouth again.

He kissed me back before pulling away. "You've had a busy night."

"I'm about to get busier."

"And you've been drinking." His breathing was ragged, his voice strained. "I don't want to take advantage."

My heart melted. Such a gentleman. I twined my arms around his neck, filled with new certainty.

"Okay," I said agreeably. "I'll take advantage of you."

He gave a choked laugh. We staggered to his bedroom, bumping against walls, trading licks and bites and kisses, feeling for each other as we went. His room was dark, illuminated only by a beam of light from the hall. He backed me toward the bed, dragging his mouth along my collarbone, dropping a kiss under my ear, while his hands ranged over me, warm and gentle, hips, waist, ribs. He paused at my breast, as if asking permission, and I covered his hand with mine, increasing the pressure, arching into his touch.

"Oh God, Dee." He reached for my hem, rucked up my skirt.

"Wait," I whispered.

He stopped instantly. "Do you want . . . ?" He sucked in his breath. "We can stop."

"*No.*" I was shaking, ravenous. Embarrassed. "I just have to change."

He looked blank.

"It's my, um . . ." I flapped my hands over my body. "I have to take it off."

His face lit with comprehension. He smiled. "The Underwear of Death."

I nodded, my face flaming.

"Let me help."

"Ha. No."

"Let me see."

His hands were coaxing, soothing, smoothing, lifting my dress carefully over my head until I stood before him in cowboy boots and bodysuit.

"You're beautiful," he said.

"Until I take it off," I joked.

He shook his head. "Even more beautiful."

His voice was warm, and his eyes were warm, and his hands were warm and clumsy with eagerness as we tugged and yanked my stupid shapewear down to my ankles. He steadied me as I stumbled out of my boots. *Free.* Being with Tim felt real, the awkward bits and the laughter and the box of condoms he pulled from the nightstand drawer.

I looked at them, assailed by a second of doubt. I hadn't done this recently or with anyone but Gray in a long, long time.

"They're not expired yet," Tim said, understanding my need for reassurance, even if he didn't know the cause.

I smiled. He wasn't carving notches in his bedpost. There was no bedpost. This was Tim, careful and caring. Of course he had birth control handy.

He gathered me against him, my bare body against his clothed one, the contrast stunning. Erotic. I couldn't keep from touching him. I ran my hands everywhere I could reach: the short, bristling hair at the back of his neck, his broad shoulders, his back, his abdomen. Lower. He made a sound deep in his throat. Encouraged, I fumbled with his buckle. He helped me, shucking his briefs with his pants.

I tugged at his buttons, but he distracted me, taking my mouth, pushing me down on the mattress, focused and not so polite now. I slid my fingers into his hair, matching his urgency, urging him on as he covered me. His square, scarred knee pushed between mine, his hair-roughened thigh teasing my nerve endings to life, and then he was there—*there yes please yes there*—his weight solid and focused right where I needed him most. He felt so good I gasped. I stroked him, discovering him in the dark—blunt, thick, and silken.

It wasn't enough. I wanted all of him. Naked. Now. I wrestled with his buttons. He stiffened, capturing my hands. I tugged free, desperate for the feel of his flesh, struggling to get his shirt off.

"Dee . . ." Half plea, half protest.

My fingers grazed his chest. He froze. My touch slowed. Gentled. The texture there was different, soft hair and smooth skin sundered by ridges of raised tissue.

"Let me help," I whispered. *Let me see.*

His jaw knotted. He levered his weight, holding still as I opened his shirt. His fists clenched and unclenched as I pushed the fabric from his shoulders and down his arms.

Whatever I'd been picturing, it was not this. His chest was a road map of scars: a constellation of stars high on his shoulder, an oval divot to the right of his sternum, a brutal patchwork on his left pectoral bisected by a darker pink line. As if someone had cut out his heart.

Tenderness welled. I blinked back tears. "Does it hurt?"

"No." He cleared his throat. "The opposite, actually. I can't feel it at all."

I touched the divot. "Here?"

"It's fine."

"How about here?" The burst of stars.

"Also fine." A thread of amusement in his voice.

I scraped his nipple gently with my thumbnail. "And this?"

"That's . . ." His voice roughened. "That's good."

I kissed his chest. He shuddered under my lips. I raised on my elbows, tracing his hurts with hands and mouth, feeling him unravel under my touch, his control fraying. He grabbed for a condom and pushed me down. I lifted to him as he entered me in a slow, thick slide, as he held me tightly, real and solid and there in the darkness.

In bed, Tim was perfectly himself. Careful. Thorough. Steady. It worked. It worked very well. Both times.

TWENTY-FOUR

He'd only wanted to help.

But here they were, in his bed, Dee curled against his side, facing him. Flushed. Sated. Asleep.

He'd done that. Tim grinned like a fool in the dark.

Her hair tickled his jaw. Very carefully, so he didn't disturb her, he pulled a strand from her lips, smoothing it back against his pillow. She made a soft, protesting sound, and nestled her head against his shoulder.

The trusting gesture bored into his chest.

He'd wanted to be there for her. As support, as backup, if that's all she would accept. As a friend, if that's what she wanted. She shouldn't have to face that prick alone.

But at some point—when she'd slipped off her wrap, maybe, or dumped the plate of oysters onto that tosser's lap—Tim's brain had detonated, right along with his best intentions. She'd looked so beautiful. She always did. But tonight . . . The images burned his retinas like the aftermath of an explosion. Dee in that dress, with her hair down. Dee, marching into the dragon's lair, flushed and shining with courage. Dee, wearing only her body armor and boots, or naked and under him.

He hadn't been able to breathe, let alone think.

She'd wanted it, he reassured himself, relieved and grateful. Wanted him. But he couldn't help feeling he'd taken advantage, whatever she said.

Mildly alarming, that, since he'd spent his entire life trying to do the right thing. What if she decided this had all been some horrible mistake?

She shifted, her round knees pressing his thigh, and he wanted her again. Over him, under him, any way she wanted. He ran his hand gently up her bare arm, unable to resist touching her. Her lips curved against his shoulder. Something expanded in his chest, his blasted lung or his shrapnel-pierced heart.

His phone vibrated on the nightstand.

Dee stirred. "What time is it?" she murmured drowsily.

He glanced at the screen. **Charles.** *Not now*, he thought. He cleared his throat. "Almost midnight. Go back to sleep."

He didn't *have* to answer. It was probably nothing.

Notifications lit up his phone screen. **Missed Call. Voice Mail.** He tapped. The download circle spun, transcribing the message to text.

Dee raised on her elbow, her soft parts shifting under the sheet. "Is everything all right?"

"Everything's fine." *Probably*. He watched the circle go round and round and round . . . He put down the phone and looked at her. The light of the screen burnished her profile to a silver glow. The curve of her cheek, the tip of her nose, her parted lips . . . "How are you feeling?"

"Glorious."

"Dragon slayer," he said.

Mischief crept into her smile. "Debaucher of squires."

A laugh broke from his chest at her unexpected boldness. He thought she was brave before, facing down her old lover, defying public embarrassment in the hotel bar. But this, the way she found the courage to put herself out there, over and over again, to risk her body and her heart—with him—was taking bravery to a whole different level.

He was jealous, frankly. And determined to make sure she didn't regret it.

"I did some debauching myself. Dee . . ." His phone buzzed with an incoming text. His mouth tightened. "Sorry, I should . . ."

Dee flapped her fingers. "Go ahead."

Charles's message was short and to the point. **Pick up, you bastard.** Heaviness invaded Tim's body.

"Do you need to get that?" Dee asked.

No. *Yes.* "It's fine."

Another buzz. Another call. From Laura, this time. *Hell.*

"I don't mind," Dee said.

"Thanks. I just . . . I'll be right back." He swung his feet out of bed and stood, taking the phone with him into the bathroom, shutting the door behind him before he returned Laura's call.

"What is it?" he asked without preamble when she answered.

"Are you busy?"

"I had a call from Charles. What's he done?"

"He's here. Tim, I'm afraid."

Cold steel ran through Tim's veins. "Call the police."

"Not for myself." Impatience edged Laura's voice. "I'm afraid for Charles. I honestly think he might hurt himself."

"I'll talk to him."

"Not on the phone. How soon can you get here?"

"I don't . . ." Tim rubbed his face with his hand, pushing his fingers through his hair as if that would restore some order to his thoughts. "Twenty minutes."

"If that's the best you can do."

He had to go, Tim thought as he disconnected. Dee had to leave. *Fuck.*

"It's Charles," he said, emerging from the bathroom. Better to leave the other woman's name out of it. "He's having a bit of a crisis."

Dee nodded. "I should go."

Thank God. Except . . . "There's no rush." *Twenty minutes.*

Dee regarded him thoughtfully. "Are you going to see him?"

"Yes."

She leaned over the edge of the mattress, flashing him as she fished the Panties of Death from the floor. "Will it make any difference?"

He dragged his mind off her nice round bum and back in the game. "It doesn't matter. I owe him."

She stepped into her shapewear and tugged it up her thighs, making her breasts jiggle pleasantly. "What about what you owe yourself?"

Focus on her face, you wanker. "You're talking about closure again."

Her brown eyes were warm, wise, and too perceptive. "There does seem to be a pattern here." She fastened her bra, hiding her lush breasts from view. "Maybe your buddy Charles needs more help than you can give him."

"I do my best," Tim said. On the defensive. Clearly, his best wasn't good enough.

"Because you're a good friend. A good guy. But Charles needs to be the hero of his own story."

"He is a hero," Tim said. "He saved my life. I can't turn my back on him now."

Dee sighed. "Do what you want." She plucked her dress from the floor. "You will anyway."

The words sounded rehearsed, as if she'd heard or said them someplace else to someone else before. The slightly false note— after he'd had her, warm and real and glowing in his arms—set his teeth on edge. He still had the taste of her on his tongue, her scent on his skin.

He wished her dress zipped up the back. He was desperate for any excuse to touch her. Any way to explain.

Laura and Charles were part of his life. They were woven into the fabric of his childhood, the fiber of his military service. He didn't know how to rip out those threads without tearing the whole thing apart, without destroying the person he'd always tried to be. Even if he changed, his circumstances wouldn't.

Dee . . . She was amazing. But this thing between them was so new. She was on her own journey, only passing through his life. In May—or September—or next spring, at the very latest—she would be gone.

He had no reason to expect more. No right to ask her for anything. He didn't have the words or the time to justify himself. *Twenty minutes.* But he tried anyway, reluctant to let it go. To let Dee go.

"It's not about what I want," he said stiffly. "I have a duty. You can understand that." She was so loyal to her sister. Surely she could sympathize with his need to do the right thing?

"I understand you think so," Dee said. Her tone of gentle pity somehow made everything worse. She smoothed her dress over her thighs. "I'll see you."

He seized on that. Of course they would see each other. She lived upstairs, at least for now. He should be grateful she was leaving on her own initiative, rather than making him kick her out. "I'll call you."

She gave him a look he couldn't quite read—Dee, who wore her heart on her sleeve, whose face was an open book. "Sure."

He followed her to the door, battling regret, resisting the urge to catch her hand, to call her back. Should he say something? Should he kiss her?

But then she left, taking all the warmth and life in the apartment with her, and it was too late.

Tim rubbed his chest. *I can't feel anything*, he'd told her.

And now he felt too much.

TWENTY-FIVE

I floated into the apartment on an oxytocin high.

"Your face is all red," Reeti said from the couch.

"Is it?" I asked vaguely.

Her eyes narrowed. "And your neck."

My hand covered the tender abrasion on my throat.

"Oh God." She bolted upright. "Tell me you didn't sleep with him."

"I . . ."

"Dee. The guy is an arsehole. You went there to tell him to fuck off. What were you thinking?"

I gaped at her, equally horrified, my brain abruptly reengaged. "I didn't have sex with Gray!"

"Thank God." Reeti collapsed against the couch cushions. "I knew you had more sense than . . . Wait." She sat up again. "You were with Tim. You didn't . . . You never had sex with *Tim*?"

The warmth surged everywhere, my chest, my face.

"You *did*!" Reeti crowed. "I told you he was relationship material."

"We're not in a relationship," I said automatically. Were we? Didn't a relationship include dating? We'd never been on a date.

"Okay," Reeti said. "So it was recreational sex. That's okay."

That didn't feel right, either. But I wasn't making the mistake I had with Gray, making assumptions simply because we'd slept together. At least, that's what I told myself.

So I nodded. "We were celebrating."

"Celebrating is good," Reeti said encouragingly.

The apartment door opened.

"Hey. You guys are up late," Toni said, heading for the kitchen.

"You're home early," Reeti said.

"Some of us have to work in the morning," Toni said virtuously. She grabbed the carton of milk and chugged it standing in front of the open refrigerator.

Reeti made an *Oh no you didn't* sound low in her throat.

"Glass," I said.

Toni wrinkled her nose, but she pulled a glass from the cupboard. "How did your thing with Voldemort go?"

"I called him a hack."

"That's good," Toni said. "Use your words, you always tell me."

"It *was* good. It felt great, actually. I finally got to say my piece. And then . . ." My smile spread. "I threw wine in his face and dumped food in his lap."

Toni whooped.

"My warrior princess," Reeti said.

"Very badass," Toni said.

"Thanks."

"I thought maybe Tim was going to challenge him to pistols at dawn or something."

"No. But he was . . ." *There.* Trusting me to do the right thing.

"Waiting in the bar the whole time," I said lamely. "And then he brought me home."

"Proving chivalry is not dead," Reeti murmured.

My face flamed.

Toni glanced from her to me. "What? What am I missing?"

Reeti studied her perfect manicure. "It's not for me to say."

"He . . . I . . . Um . . ." I said.

It's not as though I'd never talked to Toni about sex before. Aunt Em's idea of preparing me for puberty was to buy a box of maxi pads and another of junior tampons and stand outside the bathroom door while I read the instructions. Our school's health class was a series of PSAs about the dangers of smoking, drinking, drugs, or sex of any kind. I didn't want that for my little sister. I was determined that Toni grow up able to make informed decisions about her body and her choices.

But answering her questions was different from sharing the details of my own life.

I cleared my throat. "You know Tim and I have been friends for a while."

My sister's eyes danced. "Is this the *when two people like each other very much* speech? Because we've already done that."

Reeti laughed.

"I just want you to know you can always talk to me," I said earnestly. "About anything."

"So you've said. No fear. No judgment." She cocked her head. "You also told me I shouldn't be with anyone who wasn't respectful, responsible, and kind."

"I said that?"

"You did. Good advice, right?" She got up from the couch and kissed the top of my head. "I'm going to bed now. Good night."

I sat, stunned, as the door to our room closed behind her.

"Your little sister is growing up," Reeti observed.

"I guess she is."

"And Tim." Reeti flashed a wicked smile. "Was he respectful?"

I pressed my hands to my hot cheeks, remembering him kneeling above me in the dark. His hands. His mouth. His eyes. "He was . . ." *Everything.* "Really, really great."

"Good for him. And good for you."

"You don't think it's too soon?"

"Honey, you've known him for months."

I twisted my fingers together. "I meant, after Gray."

She patted the cushion beside her. "You think it's like a rebound thing?"

"I wasn't really thinking at all," I confessed, sinking obediently onto the couch. "I'm trying not to project." (*"Darling, you can't expect flowers and promises,"* Gray repeated in my head.)

"Me too. But it's hard not to think about the future. Everybody judges you by whether or not you're in a relationship. There's all this pressure. Like if you don't have a boyfriend, if you're not getting married, if you're not ready to start a family, there must be something wrong with you."

"And you're not ready."

"I might be. That's the problem. I always thought when I found someone it would be like fate. True love at first sight. Like Romeo and Juliet."

"Or Cinderella," I offered. *A fairy tale.*

Reeti nodded. "And instead my parents introduced us. It's so unromantic."

"At least you know they like him. And you like him. Why can't that be enough for now?"

"Because it feels like cheating. I thought falling in love would be harder."

"Love is hard. I mean, living with someone takes work. But maybe it's easier if you share the same kind of background." Like Tim and Laura. Okay, horrible example. "Like you and Vir."

"That's what my parents say. But you need the feelings, too. The butterflies, my mother says. It's more than being compatible. You have to feel something."

"And do you have . . . feelings for Vir?"

"So many feelings. It's scary."

I squeezed her hand in sympathy.

"My mother says you need to have faith," Reeti continued. "If a couple has good intentions, if they respect each other and try to please each other, then everything will work out."

Have faith. Tim had certainly never given me any reason to doubt him. But . . .

"He had to leave," I said.

"Who? When?"

"Tim. After we . . ." I waved my hand.

"Had a shag? Banged the headboard? Slytherined the Hufflepuff?"

I blushed and laughed. "Stop. Anyway, he had to go help a friend."

"Male or female?"

"Male. An army buddy. His corporal, Tim said." I didn't want to say too much. It was his story to tell.

Reeti nodded. "Charles."

"You know him?"

"I've bumped into him a few times. Quite literally, as he was drunk." Reeti wrinkled her nose. "Bit of an arsehole, honestly."

"He saved Tim's life. I understand that he feels an obligation. I do." I knew how he felt—the tug of loyalty, the desire to be needed, the impulse to do the right thing.

"But your feelings are hurt."

"Maybe. A little." Hard to overcome all my insecurities in one night. "Also, I think Tim needs better boundaries."

Reeti raised her brows. "You think?"

I smiled. "Pot calling the kettle black?" I had trouble saying no, too. Or asking for support. Or expressing how I felt or what I wanted. "But that's why I recognize it in Tim. If he didn't always rush to Charles's rescue, it might be better for both of them."

"For Tim, maybe. Charles is getting exactly what he wants out of their relationship."

I sighed. "I guess they have to work it out for themselves."

Reeti nudged my leg gently. "Look at you, setting boundaries. I'm proud of you."

I rested my head against her shoulder, love flooding through me. I'd never had a girlfriend wait up for me before, to compare notes and confide in. For all her prying and teasing, Reeti was sensitive and caring. "Thanks, pal."

"So, where did you leave things?"

"He said he'd call."

"Which is what guys always say."

Unfortunately true.

But maybe I should listen to Reeti's mother, since I didn't have one of my own. Have faith, trust in Tim's good intentions, and maybe everything would work out.

"Vir calls you," I pointed out.

"He does. He says we are at the point where our relationship needs to be about him and me and not about our families."

"That's awesome. When are you going to tell him?'

"Tell him what?"

I blinked. "That you want to be a teacher."

"His family is so conservative." She picked at a couch cushion.

"What if he takes their side? What if he thinks I should work for my father?"

"If he wants you, if he loves you, he'll support you. No matter what."

"What if he doesn't?"

"Wouldn't you rather know?" I asked gently. Her elegant shoulders moved in a shrug. I covered her hand with mine. "It *is* scary. I get it. But maybe you should trust him. Trust yourself. Don't blind yourself to what could be because you're afraid."

Her eyes met mine. "Are you giving advice to me? Or to yourself?"

I laughed in acknowledgment. "Maybe . . . both?"

Just because I'd been wrong to trust Gray didn't mean I was wrong about Tim.

He didn't call.

He sent a text. My phone pinged as I was hopping the bus to class. Thank you for last night. Very stiff, very polite, very Tim. He'd signed with two small *x*'s, the way the British do, virtual kisses as punctuation.

At least there were two. Not that I was trying to decode his feelings by counting *x*'s. Okay, maybe I was trying. I was totally trying.

I texted back. Thank YOU.

He could decide for himself whether I was thanking him for his support with Gray or the wonderful sex. (Both.) I signed with three kisses—sue me, I was an enthusiastic American—and then deleted one, because *xxx* looked porny.

I shut off my notifications, stuffed my phone away, and walked into my writing workshop.

Conversations stopped. Every head turned. Like I had Gray's book cover taped to my forehead. Or a Scarlet Letter pinned to my chest. Every person in the room had attended the reading two nights ago. Half of them had witnessed my freeze-and-flight response to Gray at the reception afterward.

Of course they were talking about it.

Then Erinma caught my eye and smiled, and Alan waved. Even Claire broke off chatting with Ryan to nod. Shauna shifted her book bag to the floor, clearing the seat next to hers. I sank into the empty chair, relieved. Grateful. One of them.

Our instructor for the term—"*Call me Brian,*" he'd invited us on the first day of class—started critique with the skill of a kindergarten teacher or a marriage counselor, inviting us to share our feelings, to use *I* statements, to be kind. After the past semester with Maeve, we all knew how it felt to be judged. We pulled up or pulled out our marked-up pages, offering comments and encouragement on one another's work, pointing out places we thought there could be room for improvement, noting a slow opening here, questioning a character's motivation there.

Ryan had written a short story set in the violent dystopian future of his game world, a kaleidoscopic scene of a city's sacking written mostly from the point of view of a brutal, unnamed warlord. We did our best with it, struggling—I struggled—to find things we liked, to be honest and constructive.

"The details are very raw."

"Real."

"Risky."

"Lots of visceral emotion."

"But it's shit," Erinma said.

We drew in our collective breath, looking instinctively to Brian for guidance.

"Respect the oeuvre," our instructor said. "There is no right or wrong in writing, only what works and does not work."

"You can quote Yoda all day long," Shauna said. "That doesn't make it right."

Erinma nodded. "I can't respect a pile of misogynistic crap that glorifies violence against women."

"In all fairness, video games are historically masculine narratives. Objectifying or sexualizing female characters is pretty common," Alan said.

"So it's not only wrong," Claire said, "it's derivative."

Ryan flinched, staring into his laptop screen as if he could disappear inside, like Alice through the Looking Glass.

"Maybe we're supposed to see how wrong it is," I suggested. "Like in *The Handmaid's Tale*."

Heads swiveled to Ryan.

"Yeah, I guess," he mumbled.

"You could work on that," I said. "Make it clearer."

"Instead of feeding the stereotypes," Erinma said.

"And I think that's all we have time for today," Brian said. "Dee, do you have anything for us?"

"I'd like another week," I said. "Mr. Diggs suggested I push my protagonist out of her comfort zone, and I want to take more time with it."

"Certainly."

I sailed out of class on a little cloud of self-confidence that lasted through my library shift and all the way home. When I reached Tim's landing, my hand rose to knock on his door. But I didn't have *that* much courage. Or maybe I didn't want to take the shift in our relationship status for granted. Just because we'd seen each other naked didn't mean he'd be glad to see me first thing after work. He might not even be home yet.

I should trust him. Trust myself, the way I'd told Reeti. He wasn't going to ghost me. But it had been eighteen hours, and he still hadn't called.

Reeti and Toni were eating on the couch when I walked in the door.

"Good, you're home," Reeti said. "We're going to The Old Spot and get pissed."

"It's Thursday." Friday was our regular pub night.

Toni made puppy eyes. "But it's my last week. You have to come."

I messed up her choppy black hair. "Sure." It's not like I had other plans. "What are you eating?"

"Cookies," she said through a mouthful of crumbs. "Chocolate chip. Tim brought them."

"Tim was here?"

"He left them at the door," Reeti said.

"Oh, and there's a note for you," Toni added.

I snatched it from the coffee table, a crisp white square, neatly folded. *For Dee*, it said on the outside in a firm, square script. Eagerly, I opened it. *Tim*.

I turned the paper over, searching for . . . Something. "That's it?"

"What do you mean? The man brought you cookies," Reeti said.

"Which you are eating."

"They're really good cookies."

I rolled my eyes. "I'll be right back."

"Take your time," Toni said, and grabbed another cookie.

I ran downstairs.

Tim answered my knock promptly. "Dee." He was wearing his Mr. Darcy face, polite and a little stiff.

I grinned. "You were expecting someone else?"

"No." One word.

I should have kissed him when he opened the door. Too late now. "Thanks for the cookies."

"You're very welcome." He started to say something else. But nope.

"How's Charles?" I asked.

His jaw squared. "As well as can be expected."

"Meaning, still a pain in your ass?"

He sighed. "Things are difficult for Charles right now."

It was really none of my business. I should shut up. But I'd done that before, with Gray, shutting down my feelings, stifling my opinions. I wasn't going to do that again, not with Tim or any other guy.

"Right now?" I asked. "Or all the time?"

"Charles had a rough go of it before he joined the army. And since he left, he's lost his way."

"I'm sorry. Really. But he won't get anywhere trying to relive the past. He needs to move on." *You need to move on.*

"It's not that easy. Charles was a warrior. A hero. He saved the life of his commanding officer and won the hand of the fair princess, and when he quit the service, he figured he had it made. Except he didn't. Because he doesn't live in a fucking family castle, and the princess dumped him at the curb. He's angry, and he drinks, and the drinking makes him angrier. That's a deep hole for him to climb out of." Tim ran his hand through his hair, making it stick up in front. "The least I can do is give him a hand up from time to time."

"That's a very masculine narrative."

"I beg your pardon."

My fingers itched to reach out and smooth that errant cowlick.

"I'm just saying, Laura isn't to blame for Charles's poor decisions. Neither are you."

He stared back at me without speaking.

"Also, you never called," I said.

His lips twitched. "I beg your pardon." Same words. Different voice, warm, deep, and amused. "I baked you cookies."

"Thank you. My roommates ate them."

His smile spread, the slightest bit. "I'll have to take you to dinner, then. Feed you properly."

My heart soared. But . . . "I can't."

"Ah."

"I mean, I really can't. I promised Toni we'd go to The Old Spot. It's her last week."

He nodded politely. "Of course."

"We're having a going-away party for her next Saturday," I blurted. "Will you come?"

His gaze met mine. "Yes."

"Great." I beamed at him breathlessly, foolishly. "Well."

"Text me when you get home," he said.

"You want a booty call?" I asked, half teasing.

"I'd like to know you're home safely." That smile tugged the corner of his mouth. "Although of course I am always happy to see you. If you wanted to come by."

"There's no 'of course' about it. I could have been a pity shag."

His eyes glinted. "Not both times."

I gaped. "Did you just make an actual sex joke?"

He reddened, that small, endearing smile still lurking. "Dee." He cleared his throat. Took my hands. "I like you. I want to see you. I want to sleep with you again. Tonight and as often as you want."

I melted like a chocolate chip cookie in the oven, warm and gooey inside. I'd never been with someone who was so straightforward about their intentions, who didn't keep me guessing about their feelings. "I want."

He smiled. "Very good." He leaned forward and kissed me. "Have a nice time with your sister. I'll see you when you get back."

TWENTY-SIX

S o are you and Tim, like, official now?" Toni asked.

I blushed. *Official?* What did that even mean? I didn't keep a toothbrush at his place. He hadn't left a razor in the tiny bathroom I shared with Toni. But for the past week, I'd been slipping in at dawn to shower and change clothes before going to class or to the library. Tim and I were together. For game night. For pub night. For cooking shows on his couch. (*"You'll miss the judging,"* I said on Sunday as he slid off my panties. He glanced up from between my legs, smiling. *"You can tell me who won later."* But by then I didn't care.)

"We're not in kindergarten," I told Toni. "He didn't pass me a note with little boxes marked, *Will you be my girlfriend? Check yes or no."*

"Because that would be too easy," Reeti said. She'd been grumpy all day. Ever since her phone call with Vir, in fact.

I frowned, concerned. "Did you and Vir have a . . . ?"

"You should look online," she said, interrupting me.

My flush deepened. Because of course I'd checked Tim's relationship status. *Single.* "That doesn't mean anything. He hasn't posted on Facebook since before the pandemic."

Reeti tapped her nails. "Did you search for a dating profile? Tinder? Bumble?"

"No!" Tim had made it clear he liked me. I trusted him. I wasn't trawling the Internet for bits of him, the way I had with Gray. "If I want to know something, I can ask," I said with dignity. "Like a normal person in a healthy relationship."

"Good luck with that," Reeti said.

My sister smirked. "Go ahead. I dare you."

So of course then I had to.

"Are you seeing anyone?" I asked that night over dinner.

We were at a restaurant. In public. Tim had called to ask if I were free, as if we hadn't spent every one of the last six nights together, and afterward—being Tim—he'd probably insist on picking up the check. That was some serious boyfriend stuff right there. If I'd needed evidence. Which I didn't.

Two parallel lines appeared between his brows. "Dating someone else, you mean?"

"Yes, Tim. Dating, sleeping with, in a relationship."

"No." A pause. "Are you?"

I shook my head.

He continued looking at me, his expression unreadable in the flickering tea light. "So we're exclusive."

"I . . . Yes?"

"Very good." The warmth in his eyes, that smile tugging his lips, almost knocked me off my chair. My heart hammered.

So . . . Yeah. Unofficially, I was feeling all the feelings. Officially, we were . . . Exclusive. Committed, without the label.

But I wasn't going to throw myself into another relationship only to crash and burn. I didn't need to grasp at every sign of attention or affection. I wasn't about to ruin the moment by projecting too far into the future. What we had right now was good. Very good. Great, in fact.

Over dinner, we talked about my story. Or rather, I talked and Tim listened.

I broke off after I'd gone on for a bit about Oscar Diggs's suggestion that I throw poor Rose under the bus. I'd upped the role of the antagonist—an evil witch—and I was still figuring out her motivation. "Am I boring you?"

"No."

"You're not saying anything."

"Because I'm interested." He refilled my wineglass. "Go back to the little girl. Rose. What's her motivation? What does she want?"

"To defeat the witch."

"Why?"

"Well, because she needs to get home."

"But why wouldn't she stay in the magic world? She's happy there."

"Because if she doesn't go back to the real world, she'll never see her mother again."

"Why not?"

Because her mother is dying. A flash, like an opening door. I slammed it shut. "She's twelve. She needs her mother."

"I think she's stronger than you give her credit for. Look how far she's come already."

"Not alone," I pointed out. "She has companions now."

"Every hero needs allies."

"And she has her dog." Loving, irrepressible Toto.

Tim studied me, his glasses reflecting back the candlelight. "You'll miss your sister when she leaves," he said out of the blue.

I blinked. "Well, sure. She's grown up so much. It's been really nice spending time with her." I sighed. "I just wish she had some kind of plan when she gets home."

"She'll figure it out."

"I hope so. She can't sit around the farmhouse in her pajamas forever." I pulled a face. "And now I sound like Aunt Em."

"A woman of good sense," Tim said, and I smiled.

We walked home along tree-lined streets in the dark, past red-brick houses fronted with iron railings and crumbling stone walls protecting sleek glass entrances. The night air was cool and damp, the streetlamps ringed with light like an Impressionist painting. I went up the stairs first, hoping my butt looked good from behind. Tim stopped me outside his door to kiss, tasting lightly until my lips parted and I wrapped my arms around his neck, pulling him closer, reveling in the feel of his strong, solid torso. He kissed me, long, hot, deep kisses, pressing me back against the wood until my blood hummed and my thoughts scattered.

"Come inside."

I thrilled at the husky invitation. "I . . . Wait. No. I have to . . ." I twisted my neck, resting my forehead against his chest, rising and falling under his starched shirtfront. I was drugged on the smell of him, clean cotton and warm male. "I promised Reeti we'd talk when I got home."

He was silent, his hand moving idly over my back, stroking and soothing.

I was so new at setting boundaries, I wasn't sure how they worked. If they worked. I held my breath.

"Sure," he said at last, and let me go.

I was filled with relief and disappointment, already missing the imprint of his body, the touch of his hand. "Good. I mean, not good, obviously. I'd like to . . . You know. Come in. But Reeti needs me." I sounded so lame. "Sorry," I added.

"Is she all right?"

I loved that he cared enough to ask. "I think so. I hope so. She says she is. But she's been sort of grumpy since her"—*rishta? boyfriend? match?*—"since this guy called yesterday, and I told her I was there for her if she wants to talk or vent or whatever. Sisters before misters." Oh God, had I actually said that bit out loud? I bumbled on. "Anyway. I promised we'd hang out."

The smile was back in his eyes. "And you always keep your promises."

The air charged between us. "I try." I swallowed. "Thank you for dinner."

"My pleasure," he said in that deep, delicious Darcy voice.

Little electrons danced over my skin. "Maybe I could come down later. If it's not too late."

"I'm here. If you want to talk. Or . . ." Another of those almost smiles, amused, affectionate, as if we shared a joke or a secret. "Whatever."

I glowed from the possibilities in that pause. From the prospect of seeing him again, soon, tonight. From the suggestion that I might, in fact, be someone Tim Woodman considered worth waiting for.

He leaned forward and kissed me on the forehead. "See you," he said, like a promise, and I ran upstairs with my heart dancing in my chest.

"Something smells wonderful," I said as I let myself into the apartment.

Reeti turned from the cutting board, where she was smashing garlic with a large knife. "I'm marinating kebabs. For Toni's party."

I was touched. "You didn't have to do that."

"Yeah, she did," Toni piped up. "They're my favorite."

Reeti thwacked another clove of garlic as if it had personally offended her.

"What can I do?" I asked.

"Nothing." *Thwap.*

Toni and I exchanged glances. I gestured with my head toward the door of our room.

"What?" my sister asked.

"Don't you have to go, um . . ."

"Wash my hair?" Toni suggested brightly. "Organize my socks?"

"Leave us in peace for five minutes?" Reeti asked.

Toni heaved a dramatic sigh. "Fine. Thanks for the chicken tikka."

Reeti's face softened. "You're welcome, *choti.*"

Toni went into the living room and flung herself on the couch.

"I want to help. What can I do?" I repeated.

"Nothing. Really," Reeti said.

"There must be something. You look ready to stab someone."

"Only stupid Vir," she growled.

"Oh no. What happened? What did he do?"

She ripped the plastic from a package of chicken breasts. "He said he never thought his parents would make such a wonderful choice for him, but now we had met he couldn't imagine being with another woman. He said he doesn't believe in this Punjabi patriarchy bullshit. He wants a partner who is strong and independent."

"But that sounds . . ."

"Good, right?" She attacked the chicken with the knife. "So I tell him my dream. I say, I want to be a teacher. I don't want to go to work for my father after graduation. And he says—he asks me—how do I feel about disappointing my parents?"

"Fair question." I knew how close she was to her family. How much she wanted their approval.

"You don't get it." Her knife sliced into the chicken breast, chopping it into chunks. "Vir made this big point about how the gurus teach that women's rights are a matter of social justice. He says he supports the equality of women. But it's all lip service. He doesn't support *me*."

"Is that what he said?"

"He didn't have to." Her tone was fierce. Her eyes glittered with tears. "It's obvious he's as conservative as his parents. He'll never go against them."

"I'm so sorry," I said. "This is all my fault. I told you to talk to him."

"No, you were right. Better to know, like you said." She swiped her eyes with the back of her wrist.

"Well, then, I'm proud of you for having the conversation. You don't need him."

Her face crumpled briefly. "I don't *want* to need him. I don't want to feel this way. It hurts."

"Oh, honey." I rubbed her arm. "Maybe he'll come to his senses and apologize."

Reeti sniffed. "As if I would have him back." Her knife flashed and slashed. She stopped and looked at me. "Do you really think he might?"

"Of course I do," I said staunchly. "He said himself he'll never find anyone as awesome as you. And he's right. You are amazing."

"Darling *didi*. You can't have it both ways. Either I am awesome and Vir is an arsehole, or he truly respects me and I am a jerk."

"You're not a jerk. But it takes time to really get to know someone. To build trust."

"Except for you. You see the best in everybody all the time."

"Whether they deserve it or not," Toni called from the living room.

Reeti laughed.

I forced myself to smile, ignoring the funny clenching of my stomach. I was beginning to have faith in my own perceptions and judgment, learning to feel safe inside the boundaries I'd set myself. *It takes time to build trust.*

But inside me was a little girl waiting for her mother, the child who knew that sometimes it didn't matter how much you longed to trust the people you loved. It didn't matter what excuses you made for them or what stories you told yourself. You could still always be disappointed.

It hurts.

The couch was pushed against the wall, the table loaded with food. Reeti had rolled back the rug and was teaching Bollywood dance moves to a line of Fiadh's friends.

"Fingers together, thumb out," Reeti shouted over the beat of the music. "Good. Now, hands side to side."

Toni waved her skinny arms, laughing and tripping along.

I grabbed a stack of dirty cups to carry to the kitchen. Across the room, Tim offered a plate of chicken tikka and Aunt Em's mac and cheese to ninety-one-year-old Mrs. Kinsella, chatting with Janette Clery in a corner. Our elderly neighbor tapped Tim's arm, flirting like the pretty girl she must have been. He bent to listen, courteous interest in every angle of his body, and I fell the tiniest bit more in love with him.

He was such a good guy. Unerringly polite. Thoughtful. The very opposite of heartless.

"Nice party," said a man behind me.

"Sam." I turned with a rush of nerves and pleasure. "Thanks for coming."

We hadn't seen each other since our fight a month ago. I'd missed him. I didn't have so many friends that I wanted to lose one.

He tipped his beer in salute. "Thanks for having me." His eyes, deep and changeable as the sea, studied me over the neck of the bottle. "You look well."

"You too," I said honestly. Like a poster for Irish tourism, with his lean poet's face and his curly poet's hair and that five-day scruff on his jaw.

"Dip, dip," Reeti called. "Like this. Keep your hands going. Five, six, seven, eight . . ."

"How have you been?" I asked.

"Grand."

"I'm glad. So, everything's . . . okay?" I asked. *With the shop. With you. With us.*

He nodded. "Heard from Trinity."

I blinked. "What?"

"The admissions office." His smile flashed like the curl of a wave in the sun. "I've been shortlisted in English. Got an interview next week."

I felt suddenly stupid standing there, holding my plastic cups in front of me like a shield. I set them down and hugged him. "That's great! I didn't even know you'd applied. Why didn't you tell me?"

"We haven't been speaking much, have we? And I haven't been admitted yet."

"But you will be."

"Maybe. Dr. Ward said she'd put in a word. Still have to get through the essay, though. Part of the assessment for mature students." Another glint of a smile. "That's me. Mature now."

"You were hardly Peter Pan before." If anything, his father's death had forced him to grow up too soon. We were alike that way.

He shrugged. "Bit of a lost boy, though."

The dance line dissolved in giggles. Toni flung an arm around

Fiadh. Reeti hurried over to refill the kebab platter, throwing me a significant look as she passed.

I ignored her, focused on Sam. He'd been so sure that school was not for him. *What changed your mind?* I wanted to ask. But I didn't want to go there. Not yet. Not so soon after our fight. "What's your essay about?" I asked instead.

"They tell you at the interview." He sipped his beer, watching me.

"I'd be happy to proofread it for you," I blurted. "Not that you need . . . Well. But if you wanted . . ."

"That'd be grand," he said, mercifully interrupting me. "Ta."

I beamed. "I'm just so happy for you." I hugged him again.

His arms went around me, pulling me into his hard, lean body. My nose mashed against his chest. I raised my head to breathe, and he kissed me. A long kiss, sweet and bitter and complex as the Guinness he'd been drinking. A kiss between equals. Not between friends. I pulled back, confused.

And saw Tim, standing in the corner watching us, his face impassive, his hand clenched hard on his glass. *Crap.*

Before I could think, before I could react, the dancers swarmed the table, raiding for drinks and food.

"So, what's next for you, then?" one of the girls asked Toni. "Back to the cows, is it?"

Toni shook her head vigorously. "Nope," she said through a mouthful of pakora.

"She's going to New York," Fiadh said.

I looked at Toni in shock.

"I've been in touch with some of my mom's friends. Artists," my sister said, avoiding my eyes. "They offered to work with me. Like an internship."

A chill chased along my bones. This was the first I'd heard of it. "I thought you were going back to school."

"Maybe. Eventually. Mom went to Bard, didn't she? In New York. I want to be an artist. But I need to build a portfolio first. Explore different places, different styles."

My mind whirled. "But where will you live?"

"With Aunt Leslie, to start. She has a great studio in Crown Heights."

"Where?"

"Brooklyn. And her couch pulls out!"

I swallowed bile. "I remember. But, Toni—"

"And then," she rushed on, "Jeff and Brad invited me to stay with them in Connecticut. They have a gallery. It's not the city, but Uncle Jeff promised me the train is really convenient." Her eyes met mine with a mixture of pleading and defiance. "I've thought it all through."

Without once saying a word to me.

My stomach knotted. She didn't know these people. Didn't she understand how dangerous it was? How risky? This wasn't like going away to college in our hometown or even running away to Ireland. I wouldn't be there to move her in, to make her bed or buy her toiletries or protect her.

I bit back my words, mindful of our audience. I couldn't argue with her now. "We'll talk about it later."

Across the room, Tim downed his whiskey in one swallow and set the glass carefully on a table.

"It won't make any difference." Toni raised her chin, holding my gaze. "This is my dream, Dodo."

It was my worst nightmare. Sleeping on couches, no stability, no security. "Toni, you can't possibly—"

"Your sister's right," Fiadh said, patting Toni's arm. I turned to her in relief, grateful for an ally. "You can talk it out later."

And she led my sister away.

I stared after them, my head reeling, my face stiff and my lips numb. I'd spent years trying to shield Toni from our mother's life. And now, after everything I'd done to keep her safe, she was blindly throwing herself back into it.

Sam offered me his beer. "Here. You look like you could use this."

"No, I . . ." My vision swam. I couldn't cry. Not in the middle of Toni's going-away party. I took a deep breath. "Give me . . . I just need a minute."

I stumbled away. The kitchen was bright and full of people, the bedrooms full of coats. The music started pounding again in the living room. Opening the front door, I slipped out onto the landing, shivering with cold and reaction. Hoping I wouldn't be seen. Praying I wouldn't have to talk to anyone.

My baby sister was going to New York. Alone. To be an artist, like our mother.

I wrapped my arms around my waist, trying to stop trembling. The door opened behind me.

"Is everything all right?" Tim asked.

I sagged against the railing, almost weak with relief. I should have known he would come after me. This was Tim, after all: patient, thoughtful, perceptive.

I swiped my fingers hastily under my eyes. "Fine."

His jaw tightened. "Did he bother you?"

I blinked. "Who?"

"Clery."

"Sam? No."

"He kissed you," Tim said without expression.

I winced. "Oh, that. That wasn't anything."

"Indeed."

I was still vibrating with worry and . . . anger? "Tim." I set my hands on my hips, the churn of feelings finding an outlet—a target—in the man in front of me. "He didn't do anything. It didn't mean anything. He was *holding* a *beer* the *whole time*."

His iron jaw relaxed a fraction. "Poor planning on his part."

"There was no planning on anybody's part."

"Just a spontaneous moment, then."

"Pretty much." I cast my mind back to the time before Toni dropped her bombshell, ten minutes and a lifetime ago. "Sam told me he applied to Trinity."

"And you congratulated him."

"Of course I did." I was not going to be flustered into apologies because Tim's former fiancée was a cheating slut. "And I would appreciate it if you wouldn't make a big deal out of it. I don't freak out when you jump every time Laura calls."

"That's different."

"How?"

"I don't happen to be attracted to Laura," he said stiffly.

I was suddenly, absurdly comforted. "Well, I'm not attracted to Sam." *Much.*

He held my gaze a long moment. "I apologize for overreacting."

"That's okay."

"So . . . Not Clery. But something happened to upset you."

I sighed. "Yeah. Sorry. I'll handle it." That's what I did. I handled things.

He took a measured step closer. "Tell me."

I wasn't used to sharing my worries about my sister with anyone. But, really, why not? I'd told him about Gray. We'd discussed my writing and my childhood (parts of it, anyway). He had seen me crying and angry and flushed with victory. Hell, he'd seen me naked. I could talk to him about my sister's idiot plan. Or lack of plan.

So I told him everything, spilling my fears and frustration

over my sister's crazy scheme to couch surf in New York, expecting him to offer his support. Maybe a handkerchief.

He listened, that familiar pleat digging in between his brows. "How well do you know these friends of your mother's?" he asked when I was done.

I gaped. Not what I was expecting him to say. "Not well. I mean, we stayed with them. For weeks, sometimes." Leslie, with her studio full of toxic art supplies. Gentle Jeff and his husband, Brad, who had been completely clueless about what two-year-old Toni would eat or when she needed a nap. "I used to worry the whole time."

"Serial killers?"

"Ha. No. I never found any bodies in the basement or anything." But that wasn't fair. "They were nice, mostly. Brad used to buy us ice cream. They just had no idea what to do with us."

"Your mother trusted them."

"Because I was there," I said sharply. "But Toni doesn't know them. I'm surprised she even remembers them. She hasn't seen them since she was a baby."

"She's not a baby anymore."

"You think I'm being overprotective."

"It's understandable," Tim said carefully. "You're used to taking care of her. You've done a great job. Which is why she's probably capable of taking care of herself now."

"You don't know that."

"I know she's never going to grow up if she doesn't figure out for herself what makes her happy. If she doesn't learn to solve her own problems."

He had a point. I hated that. "Look, if she wants to go to New York in a couple of years . . . But right now she has no degree, no work experience, and no idea what she's doing. She's setting herself up to fail."

"You can't always protect her from the consequences of her own actions."

"The way you do with Charles?"

"The circumstances are rather different," Tim said stiffly.

"Yeah, Toni is my sister. And she's only eighteen."

"Not to mention that the more you focus on her needs, the less you have to think about yourself."

I sucked in my breath, hurt ricocheting around my insides. "I don't have to stand here and be judged by you. I think I understand what my sister needs more than you do. This is about our family. And you're not part of it."

He was silent so long I thought he wouldn't answer. Silent and . . . disappointed? Angry?

I swallowed the golf ball–sized lump in my throat. "Are you mad at me?"

"No." One word. His expression softened slightly. "I'm sussing things out. Same as you."

Which should have made me feel better. But somehow it did not.

I touched his arm. "Come back inside?" I invited hopefully.

He gave me a polite twist of the lips that was not a smile at all. "I'm not really in a party mood at the moment." He gave a shake of his head, as if to rid it of some thought. "Will you come down tonight?"

"I can't," I said with genuine regret. "Sorry. Maybe later? I have to . . ."

"Talk to your sister. Of course. I'll say good night now, then."

A kiss that was not a kiss, like the brief punctuation to an argument.

I listened to his footsteps echo down the stairs, leaving me alone.

TWENTY-SEVEN

The party didn't break up until midnight, when Toni went out with her friends. Avoiding me, as if she were two years old again, hiding behind the corner of the couch to poop, leaving me to clean up her crap.

"Go to bed. You must be exhausted," I said to Reeti as I bagged the trash.

"At least let me put the food away."

"You busted your ass cooking. It's not fair to stick you with the dishes, too."

"I can't leave you alone in the kitchen like Cinderella."

I smiled wryly. "I feel more like the evil stepsister."

Reeti sniffed and dumped the few skewers of leftover tikka. "You shouldn't worry about Toni."

"I can't help it."

"You cannot save her from all her poor choices," Reeti said as she scraped the veggie tray into Tupperware. "How will she learn, if not from her own mistakes?"

She sounded uncomfortably like Tim. I ducked my head defensively. "This isn't like letting her go to school without a coat. Or fail a quiz because she didn't study. This is her life."

Reeti's eyes met mine. "Exactly. *Her* life, *didi*. Her dream."

My throat constricted. I couldn't argue with Reeti about my sister's choices. Not with all the pressure Reeti felt to conform to her parents' expectations. Not after the fight she'd had with Vir.

But this was different, I told myself. Toni was only eighteen.

The dishwasher was loaded, the counters wiped down. There was nothing to do but go to bed.

I lay staring at the ceiling, trying not to think about Tim sleeping in his king-sized bed one floor down. Or not sleeping. Waiting or not waiting? This was the first night we'd spent apart. It felt awkward. Wrong. Especially after he'd seen me kissing another man.

The memory rushed back—the shock of Sam's hard, lean, angled body, the bitter sweetness of the beer he'd been drinking.

I flopped back against my pillow in a welter of guilt and confusion. Fretting over Tim or Sam or Tim-and-Sam didn't help anything. I had to think about Toni.

"*The more you focus on her needs the less you have to think about yourself,*" Tim said in my head.

Eventually, I fell into a restless doze, the messy tide of emotion dragging me into a churn of dreams.

I was awakened by a crack of light from the open door.

Toni shuffled forward, bumping into the dresser. Her jewelry tree rattled and fell. Earrings tinkled and spilled to the floor.

I rolled over, groping for my phone. "It's three in the morning."

"I thought you'd be asleep," Toni whispered.

"Not really." I struggled to sit up. "I was worried about you."

"I'm fine." A giggle. "Fee called me a cab."

I turned on the bedside lamp. "Did you have a nice time?"

Toni blinked in the sudden light. Her eyes were bloodshot, her cheeks flushed. I didn't have to sniff her breath to know she'd been drinking. Appletinis. The smell of gin and Jolly Ranchers wafted across the room.

"Are you going to yell at me?" she asked.

I suppressed a sigh. "It's your last night out with your friends. I'm not actually trying to ruin all your fun." Whether she believed me or not. Whatever Tim and Reeti said.

"Good." She pulled her top over her head, exposing the delicate bumps of her spine and the new tattoo on her shoulder blade—three spirals radiating from a center point. A triskelion, she'd informed me a week ago, displaying the fresh ink proudly. A sign of the triple goddess. A souvenir of Ireland.

I felt a surge of protective tenderness. "You don't know what it was like," I said. "Before we moved to Kansas."

"That's the point." She peeled her jeans down her thighs, stumbling into the bed. "*You* know. *You* remember. But we never talk about it."

"We're talking now."

"It's not enough. You tell me stuff. But I don't remember. Even Mom. I look at pictures, but I can't remember her voice or her laugh or even if she hugged us."

"She did. She loved us, Toni. She loved you." The words tumbled out. "She used to dance with you in the living room to Jackson Browne." I could see them, our mother with her wild hair and flowing clothes, bouncing my baby sister in her arms while I hopped and twirled beside them. I hummed a few bars of "Somebody's Baby."

"Don't sing."

I was stung. "Sorry."

"I don't even know what are real memories and what you've made up. Or what I made up from listening to your stories." Toni's eyes glistened with tears and rebellion. "That's why I want to go to New York. All my life, I've missed somebody I never knew. This is my chance to *know* her."

I was shaken to the core. I wanted to hug her and never let go. "All I'm asking is for you to take some time to think about it. I'll be home in the fall. Six months," I begged. "We can talk about it then."

Toni tossed her head. "So you can wear me down?"

Yes. No. "I just want you to consider your options."

"No, you want me to consider *your* options."

"Toni . . ."

"I don't have to listen to you," she flung at me. "You're not my mother."

Her words struck like stones. I reeled from the impact.

Her face slackened suddenly. "I'm going to puke."

I leaped from bed, galvanized into action. "Bathroom," I said. "Now."

We made it. Barely. I held her hair as she heaved and shuddered over the toilet, purging her body of gin, of too much food and emotion.

She coughed, wiping her mouth on her arm, her wet, raccoon eyes streaked with tears and mascara. "Sorry."

Love clogged my throat.

"It's okay, baby." I wrung out a warm washcloth for her face and a cool one for the back of her neck, the way Aunt Em used to do for us when we had a tummy bug. "Better?"

Her head wobbled. *Yes.*

"Let's brush your teeth, okay?"

I helped her into a clean T-shirt, tucking her into bed as if she were five again.

She sighed once and snuggled into her pillow. "Love you."

I stroked her choppy hair, my chest heavy. "Love you, too."

I sat there on the side of her bed a long, long time, until her soft snores almost drowned out the bruising memory of her words. "*You're not my mother.*"

My breath hitched. Because they were true. Our mother was dead. Nothing I said or did could ever make up for that one, deep, terrible loss.

"*I can't remember her voice.*" I tried to recall things Mom used to say, little phrases or advice. What were the stories passed from my mother to me? The lessons written in my heart, the things that made me her daughter? I was not like her. Was I?

Was Toni?

"*I want to be an artist.*"

I'd been proud that our mother wasn't like the ordinary mothers I saw, withering away on the Kansas prairie or stuck in some suburban rut. Our mother was always on the move, making larger-than-life installations in far-flung exotic locations. The celebrated Judy Gale: ambitious, brilliant, dedicated. *Irresponsible.* The word snuck in and stuck.

She loved us. She did. But never enough to stay.

"*All my life, I've missed somebody I never knew. This is my chance to know her.*" I swallowed hard. What would it be like, to follow in Mom's footsteps? To see her from the perspective of her friends and peers? To be seen as Judy Gale's daughter. A talent, a genius, an artist like our mother.

Maybe, I reflected, it was better not to know. But I understood Toni's choices better now.

I smoothed the covers over Toni and crept out of our shared

room. I felt itchy and empty and wired with a weird energy, unable to keep from moving, as if there were someplace I needed to be. I thought again of Tim, alone in his big bed downstairs. I missed his solid strength, his reassuring warmth. I reached for my phone and then pleated my fingers together to stop from texting. This hollow space inside me . . . Even Tim couldn't fill that.

Besides, it was really late. What would I say? Am I bothering you? like Gray? Or whatever it was Charles messaged at three thirty in the morning. Help me. Save me.

I winced. I didn't want Tim to feel I was using him, for sex or anything else.

It was only nine thirty in Kansas. Late for farmers, but maybe not too late to call.

Em answered on the third ring. "Dorothy."

"Hi, Aunt Em. Were you in bed?"

"Your uncle's sleeping. What's the matter?"

"Does something have to be wrong for me to call?"

"Usually. How's Toni?"

I cleared my throat. "Fine."

"She's not sick? They haven't canceled her flight?"

"No." I waited for her to ask about me.

"Right, then," Em said. "Tell her I'll be at baggage claim."

"Aunt Em . . . She's talking about going to New York. To stay with Mom's friends."

"Better than going off on her own. Leslie's not a bad sort."

I gripped the phone tighter. "You knew?"

"Toni asked me for her number."

I ignored for the moment the realization that Em had kept contact with our mother's life and friends in New York. "Aren't you worried?"

"Of course I'm worried, Dorothy. But I learned my lesson with you."

"What are you talking about?"

"I was scared to death when you were that age. All those colleges, sending you things. What if something went wrong? You'd be halfway across the country, all on your own. Naturally I was afraid. But I made you afraid, and I'm sorry for that. I never meant to hold you back."

"I thought you wanted me to go to Kansas because it was cheaper."

"No point in throwing money away, trust fund or no trust fund. But mostly I figured you'd be better off close to home. You didn't have a lot of confidence in those days."

As if I had a lot of confidence now. "Toni isn't afraid. Of anything. She's more like Mom."

Em made a noncommittal sound. "Toni's her own person. Same as you."

"But braver."

Another of those noises. Not agreement, not complete disagreement. "Because of you. Toni's always known she had you in her corner."

I thought it was a compliment. A nice one. But it left me even more confused. "So you're just going to let her go to New York?"

"Don't see how I can stop her. Girl's not stupid. She knows where she comes from. She knows who to come to if she needs help. She'll be all right."

Of all the women in my life, I had known Em the longest. I trusted her the most. Em—no-nonsense, undemonstrative, unsentimental—wouldn't tell you something simply because it was what you wanted to hear.

She was, I realized, the person I went to when things fell apart. When my mother died. When the pandemic struck. When Gray broke my heart and ruined my reputation and derailed my academic career, Em had given me refuge. And then pushed me off the couch and into the world again.

"Thanks, Aunt Em."

"It's late," she said. "You should be sleeping." Which might be as close to *I love you* as she could get.

I'd take it. "I love you, too," I said.

TWENTY-EIGHT

Y ou've checked your phone three times in the last two minutes," Charles said. "And you still haven't answered my
question."

Tim glanced up from his phone screen. Charles was silhou-
etted against Tim's office window, the view of the docks—steel
and glass, water and sky—shrouded in a veil of rain. "What's your
question?"

"That's my fucking point. Lunch, mate. Lunch."

Tim dragged his hand across his face. "Sorry. I'm waiting on
a text. From Dee."

"A nooner. Nice."

"I'm supposed to take her sister to the airport," Tim answered
repressively.

If she responded to his text. If she said yes. He didn't even
know the time of Toni's flight yet.

"Fallen for your fancy car, has she? You can at least buy me
lunch first. Or after. I'm not choosy."

The frustration pulsing behind Tim's eyes pounded at the back of his skull. Lack of sleep, probably. The past two nights without Dee had been . . . difficult. "I can't commit to anything right now."

"You sound like Laura."

"Very funny." Tim looked at the screen again.

Charles reached across the desk and plucked the phone from his hand.

"Give it over," Tim said.

"Nope. I want to see what's so fascinating." Charles turned back to the windows, scrolling up the message thread. "'It's eight o'clock. Coming downstairs?'" he read out loud. He glanced over his shoulder at Tim. "You do it on a schedule?"

"We watch cooking shows together on Sunday nights," he said stiffly.

"Is that your sad, posh version of Netflix and chill?"

Tim felt heat move up his face. "She likes *Great British Bake Off.*"

"You're pathetic. No wonder she blew you off." Charles looked at the screen. "With a fucking crying emoji."

Tim considered wresting the phone away. But the hallway windows provided a clear view of his office. He couldn't risk his team seeing him grappling with Charles. There had been enough speculation about him and Laura already. "It was her sister's last day."

"So she says. Poor sod," Charles said. "Stuck in the friend zone."

A memory flashed. Dee on his couch—soft, pink, warm, wet. Tim didn't say anything.

Charles raised his brows. "Or not. Good for you, mate. I wouldn't have said she was your type."

Tim hated this discussion.

He and Dee were friends. Exclusive friends. More than friends, on his part. It panicked him slightly to realize he had no idea if she felt the same way. She'd only recently gotten out of a relationship with that tosser from Kansas. And then there was Sam—one more unknown variable Tim didn't control.

"It's really none of your business," he said.

Charles's eyes widened. "Well, fuck me. You're really stuck on her."

"Give me the phone."

"It's okay, mate." Charles's genuine sympathy somehow made everything worse. "Well. Not okay. Sucks, right?"

Tim closed his eyes for a few seconds. Opened them again. "Dinner," he said abruptly. "We'll do dinner. Seven o'clock."

The phone buzzed in Charles's hand. He glanced down. "It's your bird."

Tim practically leaped around the desk to grab the phone.

Sorry. Just saw your message. Thnx! Would love ride. Flight at 4. 1 okay? Followed by another bubble with wavering dots. His breath stopped. **If not, don't worry,** Dee added. With two pink hearts.

Tim exhaled in relief. **See you at 1,** he typed. xx

"I'm guessing dinner's off now." Charles smiled wryly. "Enjoy the ride."

"Don't be stupid," Tim said firmly. "We made plans. I'll pick you up at seven."

He did not flake on a pal. Besides, Dee's message had made no mention of dinner. Or after dinner. She didn't owe him her time in return for a ride to the airport. They hadn't been together that long, really. He wasn't going to make assumptions simply because they'd had sex a few times. More than a few times. A week. Ten days, if he didn't count this last miserable weekend.

But Charles . . . He'd known Charles for nine years. The man had saved his life. Even if Dee were free, Tim couldn't blow Charles off.

Tim tucked his phone carefully away in his breast pocket.

Dee sat in the back, next to her sister.

Tim could see them in the rearview mirror, knees touching, fingers interlaced. Frankly, he was jealous. Not so much about the hand-holding but of their unthinking closeness, their ability to connect in such a direct and human way.

In the meantime, he'd been demoted from squire to chauffeur. Not part of the family. Useful but irrelevant. He parked in the drop-off zone, unloading Toni's duffel and a new suitcase out of the back while the sisters said their good-byes at the curb.

They hugged for a long time. He had a lump in his own throat when they let go.

Growing up, he'd rather enjoyed being the sole focus of his parents' attention. But as they aged, he wondered what it would be like to have a sibling to rely on, to share the burden of love and worry.

Toni disappeared behind the sliding doors, walking briskly. Tim opened the passenger door for Dee.

"Unless you'd rather sit in back," he said, only half joking.

Dee managed a wan smile. "Don't be silly. You're not my taxi driver."

When he slid behind the wheel, she was blotting her eyes with her fingertips. "All right?" he asked.

She nodded, averting her face.

His chest felt oddly tight. He didn't know what to do for her.

"I need to apologize," he said formally. "For the other night. It's not my place to tell you how to manage your relationship with your sister."

"No, you were right." Her throat moved as she swallowed. "Toni needs to find her own way. And I need to let her go. To give her the confidence to be on her own."

Generally, Tim liked being right. But her admission in this case didn't make him feel any better.

At least the rain had stopped.

When he merged north on M50, Dee turned her head. "Where are we going?"

Tim cleared his throat. "I thought you could use . . ." *Cheering up. A distraction.* "A field trip."

She leaned forward to read a road sign. "'Malahide Castle'?"

"There's a tour. Or we can walk around the grounds if you like. Or down to the beach." Anything she wanted. Whatever she needed.

"It's such a pretty day," she said. "Let's walk outside."

It was, in fact, quite overcast. But trust Dee to see things in the best possible light.

They strolled up from the lot toward the castle, the round, crenelated towers rising from the green lawn and dense vines.

She turned to him, her face shining. "It's like a fairy tale. Like 'Sleeping Beauty.'"

He gestured toward her feet. "'Puss in Boots.'"

She laughed, and his chest eased, loosening, lightening. For now, at least, he could make her feel better. She was with him now. Did it really matter why?

He bought tickets to the garden. They walked the landscaped paths, Dee smiling and exclaiming, pausing occasionally to take pictures with her phone: the drifts of daffodils under the gray-brown trunks of trees; the silvery lichen on the old stone walls; the frame of the glass conservatory, white against the bruised sky.

Children scampered past, shrieking, pursued by parents carrying coats. Couples wandered connected, arm in arm or hand in hand. Dee was still holding her phone. She bent to read an informational sign, her sweater tightening across her round bottom, and he wanted to touch her. Pat her. Right there, on the curve of her hip.

He stuffed his hands in his pockets.

George and Caroline Woodman were not given to public displays of affection. But once, at the holidays, Tim had walked in on his father in the library patting his mother's bum, the gesture somehow more intimate than a kiss: familiar, natural, unthinking. Embarrassing.

"Imagine if your family lived in the same place for the past eight hundred years," Dee said dreamily as he approached.

She wore her hair in a sort of a bun, with bits falling down. One dark strand blew across her lips. His hands clenched. "Imagine."

She turned her head, her smile like the sun edging the clouds. "Shit. They do, don't they?"

"Not eight hundred, no," he said uncomfortably. "The house was built in the seventeenth century."

"That's so cool."

"Drafty, at least." He attempted a joke. "Impossible to heat, my mother says. And the chimneys smoke."

She laughed. "But it must be nice to know where you're from. To have that kind of family. History. Traditions."

"It doesn't matter." Except it did. Or it had, to Laura. "Anyway, I'm in Ireland now."

"Do you like it? Living here?"

"It's not a matter of liking or not liking. After Brexit, a lot of our American clients moved their EU operations to Dublin. The firm needs me here. And it's convenient for now. For school." He sounded stuffy, even to himself. "I don't think much about it, to be honest."

Dee stopped to take a picture, a woman's face carved from a stump and crowned with flowers. "I wondered if you missed it, that's all."

"England?"

"Your family. The army."

He'd never put the two together in his mind. Not like that. But he supposed it made sense. The sense of commitment, of belonging, of being part of something larger than himself. "I don't regret serving my country," he said carefully. "But I was never going to make it a career like my grandfather. I was simply doing my part." Doing what was expected.

She nodded as if satisfied.

"What about your family? Did they always live in Kansas?" he asked, turning the subject.

"Since the turn of the century, at least. They were homesteaders—four generations of farmers. My mother couldn't wait to leave." Dee made a little face. "Mom was not a pioneer girl."

"On the contrary."

Her brow pleated as she puzzled it out. "I guess . . . maybe? She was considered pretty avant-garde as an artist." Her smile flitted across her face. "Not so advanced on the farm."

"I meant, leaving her old life behind to seek her fortune. That's your family tradition."

"Like Toni."

"And you." She blinked. "Making a fresh start in search of a better life," he explained.

"I am not like my mother."

He was quiet.

"I'm not," Dee insisted. "I hated moving around as a kid. All I ever wanted was to find a place to call home."

"Will you go back, then? To Kansas."

Her breath huffed. "I don't know. If Toni isn't there . . . I don't know where I belong."

With me, said an unregulated corner of his brain.

He shut it down. It was ridiculous. She was leaving in six months. She wasn't a part of his life. He wasn't a part of her family.

But he couldn't be silent. "Maybe it's not anyplace you've been," he offered. "Maybe it's somewhere you're going."

She looked at him then, her eyes wide, her lips parted.

And he kissed her.

They wandered without speaking until the grounds closed at four thirty.

Dee stopped him on the path as they walked out. "We need a selfie."

He took it because, she said, his arms were longer. He turned her phone so she could see. "All right?"

She smiled.

It made him happy to see them like that, their heads close together with the castle behind them. "Send it to me."

Her cheeks were pink. "Yeah. Sure."

He took her hand on the way back to the car. The sky was still light as they drove home.

"You're not coming in?" she asked when they got to their building. She sounded surprised. Maybe even disappointed.

"I'm having dinner with Charles."

"Oh. Well, that's okay." She looked up at him through her lashes. "I have plans anyway."

He was not going to ask if she was meeting Sam. The bastard.

"I have to turn in something to my writing group," she said.

His jaw relaxed. "Good luck with that."

"Thanks. Text me when you get in?" she asked, a hint of mischief in her voice. "So I know you're home safely."

He heard the echo of his own words and something in his

chest expanded, his lungs or his heart. "Are you offering me a pity shag?"

She lifted her chin at an angle, not giving ground. He liked that so much. "I could be."

"No dessert with Charles, then." A smile, wide and unfamiliar, stretched his face. "I'll save it for you."

TWENTY-NINE

knew Sam was smart. But reading his application was a glimpse into the workings of his brain, its contents as sharp and shiny as the inside of Em's pin box. His writing was pointed and graceful, bitterly cynical and yet deeply feeling. Like Sam himself.

I looked up from the laptop screen. He was watching me, his leg jiggling under the table, the only sign of tension in his lean, relaxed body.

"It's brilliant," I said.

"But it could be better."

"I don't see how. I'm intimidated, honestly."

"I told him it was good," Janette said from behind the counter. "Not that he listens to me."

I had stopped in Clery's before I did my hours at the library. Janette was working the register. Fiadh was training the new hire, an intense young woman with braids and eyeliner, on the espresso machine.

Sam winked at his mother. "Because you don't read anything but true crime."

"So she can help me dispose of your body," Fiadh said.

"Ha bloody ha."

"Have you heard from your sister lately?" Janette asked me.

"Not so much since her move." I mustered a smile. Toni had stayed with Em for barely a week, long enough to do her laundry and buy a one-way ticket to New York. "According to her Instagram feed, she's Queen of Crown Heights."

"She has a lot going on. Plus, it's not easy keeping in touch," Fiadh said. "With the time change and all."

"I'm sure she misses you," I said.

"I miss her, too." Fiadh grinned. "Like having a puppy that follows you around and chews on your shoes."

I laughed. "It was good for her, working here with you."

"While it lasted. She sounds happy, living with your mother's friend."

"Yeah. I've been replaced."

"Don't you believe it. Your children always need you." Janette came from around the counter and ruffled Sam's hair. "But sometimes what they need most is a good push out of the nest."

He ducked away from her hand. "Don't get too excited, Ma. I haven't been accepted yet."

"You will be," I said. "You belong at Trinity. More than I do."

Sam raised an eyebrow. "Feeling insecure, are we? You shouldn't."

I shook my head.

But Toni's departure had disturbed my routine, as if my reason for being had walked out the door. I didn't need to live my life for my sister anymore. I didn't even need to set a good example. Consequently, I was struggling to set priorities, to balance the demands competing for my attention. It was hard to spend time on required reading when Reeti's real-life romantic drama was playing out before my eyes. At the library, I had to force myself to shelve the books in my cart instead of dipping inside the covers.

I drifted between the stacks, stealing glances out the wall of windows at the emerald-green playing fields and the Pav outside, dotted with chatting students and lovers enjoying the weak spring sunshine.

And then there was Tim. We weren't like those couples on the green, holding hands and kissing in public. Tim was reserved (shy, I thought), and I didn't want to flaunt our relationship in front of Reeti. But when we were alone in his apartment, he made it clear he wanted me. Every time our eyes met or our hands brushed, I felt a strong, hot squeeze of lust. It was hard to immerse myself in my fictional world when all I wanted was to run downstairs to be with him. I was infatuated with his body, happiest in his company. But was it true love? Or was I losing myself—my purpose for being here—to another fairy tale? He didn't say. And I was too happy (or afraid) to ask.

"I'm just feeling . . ." *Overwhelmed.* "Busy," I said. "I have a five-thousand-word essay due next Thursday, and I'm supposed to turn in a big chunk of my portfolio for critique."

"Things to look forward to," Sam said.

Our eyes met. He smiled lopsidedly.

"Better get to it, then," Janette said. She poured my tea into a to-go cup. "You can take this with you."

That night after dinner, Reeti got out the game board.

"Not Monopoly," I said.

Tim looked at me, his brow puckering. "I have Catan. The *Game of Thrones* version."

Reeti rolled her eyes. "Of course you do."

"I *can't*," I said. "I have to write tonight. I've wasted too much time this semester."

There was a short, awkward pause as I realized how that

sounded. "Not that time with you is wasted. But if I don't finish this essay, I won't get my chapters done for critique before I have to give them to Dr. Ward."

"I thought that was a different class," Reeti said.

"It is. But I want the feedback."

Tim's face was smooth and expressionless. "Don't let me get in your way."

"How many players do you need for Catan?" Reeti asked him.

"At least three."

Reeti tapped her lavender nails against her glass. "I can call Fiadh."

I could feel my new boundaries disintegrating under pressure. I was frustrated—with them, sure, but mostly with myself. "Don't you guys have work to do? Studying for midterms or something?"

"No," Tim said. "I have an independent project this semester. Basically, getting academic credit for doing my job."

"And I don't really care. Maybe if I fail spectacularly Daddy-ji won't want me as his financial manager."

"You're kidding, right?" I asked. Failure was not an option for me. Not unless I wanted to prove Gray right all along.

"Of course I'm kidding. I couldn't let my parents down that way."

If I failed, I wouldn't be letting down anyone but myself. The responsibility—and the consequences—were all on me.

"You do realize you don't have to work in the family business," Tim said.

Reeti showed her teeth in a little cat smile. "Says the man who works for his father."

Ouch.

"By choice," Tim said. "There's always a choice."

The door buzzer sounded.

I looked at Reeti, confused. "Did you call Fiadh already?"

"No." She pressed the intercom. "Who is it?"

"It's Vir. Let me up."

"Vir? Here?" I asked. "I thought he was in London."

Reeti pressed a hand to her heart. "No," she said. To him? To me?

"We need to talk," said Vir's disembodied voice.

"I don't have anything to say to you," Reeti declared.

"Will you at least listen?"

She mashed the button to admit him, marched to the door, and flung it open before retreating across the room.

"Who's Vir?" Tim asked.

"Her match," I explained.

We listened to his footsteps on the stairs.

"Hello?" He appeared in the doorway: cute, slim, with curly dark hair and a short, neat beard. "Reeti, I—" He stopped when he saw us. "Hello," he said again.

"Hi," I said.

Tim nodded in acknowledgment.

"I'm Vir Singh Batra."

"They know who you are." Reeti gestured toward us. "My friends, Dee and Tim."

He smiled politely before turning to Reeti. "Can we talk?"

"I can't stop you."

He glanced at us. "Somewhere we can be alone."

"I'll go," Tim said.

I hugged Reeti. "I'll be in my room if you need me."

She gripped my arm. "Anything you have to say to me you can say in front of my friends."

Vir shifted his weight. Cleared his throat. "I know you're angry with me. But I don't know why. I want to make this better."

"How can I believe anything you say? You said you wanted to

move our relationship to the next level. To make it about us. And then you put our families right in the middle."

"How did I do that?"

"You asked me how I felt about disappointing my parents."

"Because I want to know."

"Because you disapprove," she shot back.

"Because your parents are important to you!"

Reeti tossed her head. "And *your* parents want you to marry a nice traditional girl who works for her father, not a teacher who wants to empower women to think for themselves."

"I don't care what my parents want." He took a step forward. "I care what you want. I am sorry I expressed myself so badly."

Reeti sniffed, but her hand on my arm trembled.

"Also, my mother thinks it is a wonderful idea to have a teacher as a daughter-in-law." Vir smiled, taking another step toward her. He really was cute. "She thinks it will be good for our children."

"I'm not having children with you. I'm not even speaking to you. Wait." Reeti stiffened. "You told your mother?"

Vir stopped, looking suddenly less certain. "Why not? I tell her . . ."

Reeti threw up her hands. "Everything."

"Not everything."

"I haven't even told *my* parents yet."

"But . . . I don't understand," he said. "You are Dilreet."

Reeti's lips parted.

"Did he just insult her?" I whispered to Tim.

Reeti shook her head. "No. It's my name. My full name, Dilreet."

"It means 'lion.' 'Lioness,'" Vir corrected himself. "The woman who is brave enough to change the world." He was close enough now to take both Reeti's hands in his. "I do not want anyone else," he said softly to her alone. "I do not want you to be anything less than yourself. All I ask is that you let me be with you."

A lump rose in my throat. The way he looked at her, with obvious adoration in his dark eyes . . . The way he *saw* her . . . It was everything.

Tim was watching them, too. I studied his face in profile, the fair skin, the square jaw, the fine scrollwork of his ear, the dark hair that never would lie flat in front. All familiar to me now and yet somehow unknown. He looked like what he was, a decent Englishman of a certain class, firm in his ideals, secure in his privilege. But . . . Maybe it was my imagination, but I thought I saw more to him—a subtle entreaty in his eyes, a slight diffidence in his smile.

My heart ached. Yearned. How did he see me?

He turned his head and I flushed as if he'd caught me staring. Probably because I was.

"Downstairs?" he asked.

I nodded. I could hardly wait. "Reeti, I'll see you in the morning. Or you can call me. Text. Whatever."

"Nice to meet you," Tim said politely to Vir.

But they were too wrapped up in each other to notice. Vir bent his head to murmur to Reeti, and she blushed and smiled.

"I don't think they heard us," I said as we went downstairs.

Tim closed the door to his apartment behind us. "Or they didn't care."

I set my laptop on his coffee table and turned, my body thrumming in anticipation.

He took one deep breath, like a swimmer surfacing for air, and asked, "Can I get you something while you're working? Tea? Wine?"

I blinked, unaccountably disappointed. "Oh. I, uh . . . Nope, I'm good. Thanks."

He tucked his hands into his pockets. "I'll let you get to it, then."

I'd *told* him I needed to write, I rationalized, making myself comfortable against the square, hard pillows of his couch. I couldn't blame him for listening to me.

He went into the kitchen.

I pulled up my five-thousand-word essay, "No Place Like Home: Setting and the Writer's Journey." I read it over, noting things I hadn't seen before, dissatisfied with a labored phrase here, a forced analogy there. My style was so different from Sam's. I wondered what he would think of it.

Tim made some noise in the kitchen. My mind drifted to what Reeti and Vir were doing (or not doing) one floor up. I shifted on the couch cushions. I was turning into a sex addict, that was my problem.

"That was pretty nice of Vir," I said. "Coming to Dublin to see Reeti."

"Perhaps."

Right. Because Gray came to Dublin to see me. Or said he did. I focused on the words on the screen. *The otherworldly fairy realm is rooted in the landscape of everyday life, with familiar obstacles and tests for the protagonist hero . . .*

It was no use. I couldn't concentrate.

"I liked what he said about Reeti being a lion," I said.

Tim opened a cabinet. "Some blokes will say anything to get what they want."

"But not you," I said, testing.

"Words are overrated."

I stared down at my blinking cursor, my eyes dry and hot.

Black lines squiggled across the display. My mind flitted to Gray, the way he'd used his words to seduce and shame me. I thought of the fairy tales I whispered to Toni in the space between our beds and the stories I was learning to tell. Words had power, to wound or to heal, to define and create.

"Words are important," I insisted. "Nothing tells you more about someone than what they say."

"Except what they do," Tim said, banging bowls together.

He was so annoying. "What are you doing?"

"Making muffins." His head appeared in the pass to the kitchen. "I thought when you were done with your essay you might be in the mood for a snack."

My irritation melted. So Tim hadn't traveled across the Irish Sea to feed me pretty words of love. But he was making muffins.

"Tim Woodman, man of action."

His eyes met mine. "Yes." One word. It was enough.

I smiled. "What if—when I'm finished—I'm in the mood for something else?"

An almost imperceptible tension eased from his shoulders. "Then I hope you'll tell me."

"That's it?" I teased. "That's all you have to say?"

"That, and . . ." His mouth curved in that heart-stopping almost smile. "Write faster."

THIRTY

In May, I sent the first three chapters and an outline of my Kansas story—everything I had written so far—to the students in my writing workshop. The instructor followed this with a group email reminding us that while we were here to provide feedback and encouragement, we were supposed to be working individually with our supervisors to develop our portfolios and that "larger projects were best considered in small groups outside of class."

I took this to mean I had screwed up by sending it out. Also that he probably secretly hated me. I spent the week before class feeling alternately depressed no one was going to read my story and relieved I wouldn't have to face their critiques after all.

"Can't you ask someone else to read it?" Reeti asked.

We were all studying together after dinner. At least, Reeti was studying. Tim and I had our laptops open. I was marking up another student's essay, and he was doing whatever he did.

"Not really. Everyone I know is in my workshop group. I can't go up to random strangers and ask if they'd like to read the opening chapters of my unpublished novel."

Tim glanced up, his glasses gleaming silver in the glow of his computer screen. "I could read it."

My whole self flushed. He might as well have asked me to take off all my clothes and stand naked in the middle of Great Court. I trusted Tim. I wanted to know what he thought. I knew he would be honest and even gentle in his critique. But letting him read my story was worse than letting him see me in the Underwear of Death. This wasn't my body he'd be judging. It was me, my heart, my soul, my most private self, revealed on the page. What if he hated my writing? Or he didn't hate it, but was kind in a way that suggested I should really consider doing something else with my life, like becoming a dog walker or a parking lot attendant.

I couldn't bear it.

I shook my head. "Thanks, but I need another writer, I think."

"What about Sam?" Reeti asked.

"I don't know." Expose myself to Sam's needle-sharp intelligence? No. "Middle-grade fantasy isn't exactly his thing."

"Oscar Diggs," Tim said. I looked at him, surprised. "You told us he offered to read it."

"When it's ready, he said."

"It won't ever be ready without feedback," Tim pointed out.

"He does know the genre," I admitted.

"Did you ever read that book of his?"

I dropped my gaze to my laptop. "I'm going to." As soon as I found the copy Tim had loaned me. "I haven't had much time to read."

"Too busy having sex," Reeti said.

Tim turned red.

I wanted to pat his arm. But maybe that would only embarrass him more. "I'll send it to Diggs after Dr. Ward has read it."

"Who are you more afraid of?" Reeti asked. "Oscar Diggs? Or The Ward?"

THE FAIRYTALE LIFE OF DOROTHY GALE   321

Put that way . . . Oscar Diggs was a kindly gnome. The Ward was a witch with the power to advance or destroy my academic career.

I sent the proposal to Diggs.

And spent the next four days on edge, waiting for a response. Maybe, I reasoned, he didn't have time to read it. Maybe he read it and was taking time to write helpful suggestions to make the story better. Maybe he and my workshop instructor were upstairs at The Duke, drinking whiskey and laughing together over my incoherent style, my dependence on stereotypes, my failure to grasp the most fundamental requirements of grammar and punctuation.

By Thursday, when the writing workshop met, I was a bundle of nerves. Thank God the instructor had basically told my classmates to ignore my story. But sitting in the conference room, listening to them read aloud, offering affirmation and advice, was surprisingly grounding. Even reassuring. Most of them were at least a little freaked at the prospect of writing their dissertations. I wasn't alone.

At the end of the three hours, we smiled around the table at one another like shipwreck survivors who have managed to make it into the same lifeboat.

"Right, then," our instructor, Brian, said. "If that's all . . ."

"I think we should talk about Dee's story," Shauna said.

For a moment, no one spoke. My heart, which had settled into a more or less regular rhythm, jolted into high speed. "Oh, that's okay."

"I'm afraid we're out of time today," Brian said.

Chairs scraped. A few students closed laptops or notebooks.

Erinma looked down the table at me. "I just want to say I like the witches. All the female characters are very strong now."

"I . . ." *Was so relieved.* "Thanks."

Shauna nodded. "Women of power."

"Not Rose," Ryan said.

"But Rose has an almost magical ability to make people like her," Claire said.

"That doesn't make her a witch," Alan objected.

"She does have the magic boots," Ryan said.

Claire flicked him a dismissive look. "The boots are a prop, not a character trait."

"I kind of thought the boots were, like, a metaphor for female empowerment," someone said.

I listened, frozen. Stunned. They were arguing about my story as if they'd read it. As if they were into it. As if they cared.

"Why must power be about waving swords and working spells?" Erinma demanded. "That's a reductively masculine concept. She gathers the other characters together, the scarecrow and the lion and that . . . mechanical man, is it?"

"Tin man."

"Whatever. She unites them. She brings them along on her journey. She's a catalyst. That's her power."

"I don't buy it. The other witches represent the female dichotomy, good and evil, Madonna-whore. If Rose is one of them, it's not clear where she fits in. Is she a good witch or a bad witch?"

The old question, reframed—*Is she a slut or a victim?*—beat in my brain.

"She's both," I blurted. They all looked at me. "Or neither. I mean, she's an ordinary girl in extraordinary circumstances. She tries to be kind and brave and wise, but obviously she fails sometimes. Like everybody. I wanted readers to identify with her."

"Not a lot of boys are going to identify with a character named Rose," Ryan said. "No offense."

Shauna rolled her eyes. "I suppose you hate Mulan, too."

"It's the name, okay? It's too old-fashioned. Like some character in a fairy tale."

"She *is* a character in a fairy tale," Claire said.

"You could call her Dorothy," Shauna suggested.

Ryan snorted. "Oh yeah, like that's an improvement."

"I believe we're getting a little off topic," Brian said.

"Not Dorothy," I said. "That's my name."

"Exactly." Claire met my eyes. "Own it."

"Yes," Erinma said. "Take it back from him."

My heart lurched. There was no question which *him* they were talking about. *Gray.* Most of them had been at the wine reception when he'd ambushed me, watching us with nearly identical expressions of excitement and concern. But this was the first time there had been an open acknowledgment of Gray's book. Of what he had done to me and my name.

My name, I thought suddenly. *My* story.

Take it back from him.

"Fine," I said. I started to smile. "Dorothy it is. Why not?"

It wasn't as though anyone outside of class would ever read it. Except for Maeve. And she already thought most writers in their twenties were hopelessly autobiographical.

Around the room, the after-class exodus resumed, a swell of shuffling feet, pushed-back chairs, and individual conversations.

"Nice job," someone murmured as they left.

I ducked my head, pleased. "Thanks."

The glow stuck with me, buoying me through the next week of lectures, workshops, readings, and meetings.

I walked into Oscar Diggs's seminar the next week feeling surprisingly positive. He hadn't read my story. Okay. That didn't mean it wasn't any good. That I wasn't any good.

"The thing to remember about kids this age is they're not

introspective," he said from the front of the room. "That goes for your characters and your readers. I'm not saying they don't have doubts and hopes and fears. I'm telling you that when something bad happens—and something bad better happen, or you don't have a story—nobody wants to see them sitting around talking about how they feel and bemoaning how helpless they are. They have to wade in there and do their best." He twinkled at the class. "Or their worst."

"I'm not writing for tweens," someone said.

"You think adults are that different? Humbug. Readers want to be entertained. No matter how old they are."

There was more. I took notes. I didn't need a personal critique to learn from him.

But when he asked if I would stay after class, I couldn't stop my heart from rising to my throat.

The classroom emptied. I stood, one hand worrying the strap of my bag.

"I read your chapters. They're very good," Oscar said.

Relief flooded my entire body. "Really?" I squeaked.

"Your voice—very sparky. And your kid—she's plucky now."

"Wow." My knees were shaking. "Thank you."

"They're so good, in fact . . . Do you mind if I close the door?" Oscar asked.

Oh no. Misgiving trickled down my spine like ice water. *Oh God. Not again.* If he touched me, if he made any suggestion that his help was contingent on special favors, I was going to spit in his eye and report him to the dean. "Is that necessary?" My voice was only a little shaky.

"I suppose not." He pulled a funny face. "At this point, my reliance on my coauthors is something of an open secret."

"Wait. Sorry. What?"

"Only for the Shivery Tales series. There's too much demand for me to keep up with it all on my own. Of course, I curate my team very carefully."

My mind whirled. "Are you saying you don't write your own books?"

"I *create* them," he said. "The ideas, the outlines, the editing . . . They're all mine. But the execution is in the hands of some other very fine writers. That's what I wanted to talk to you about."

"I thought you wanted to talk about my story."

"In a general way. Although if you give it another three to six months, I think you could really have something there. I'd be happy to take another look when you're done."

"You're not offering me a critique?"

"I was thinking I should offer you a job. At least, an opportunity. How would you like a chance to be part of the Shivery Tales family?"

"You want me to write for you."

"I do. I think you'd be good at it."

"Me." I needed to sit down. "Why?"

"You're a bit of a misfit here, genre-wise." He smiled. "Like me. And I could use more girl power on my team. I'd like to give you an outline, kick around some thoughts, and see what you do with it."

I sank onto a chair. "I . . . Would I get credit?"

"Your name wouldn't be on the book cover. But it *would* be on the check." He cocked his head. "Let me ask you, have you enjoyed taking my class?"

That one was easy. "Very much."

He beamed. "There you go, then. This would be more of the same. An intensive mentorship. A sustainable career, if that's what you choose. And you'd be paid."

I was dizzy with the possibilities. "Can I have some time to think about it?"

"Of course, of course. I'm not going anywhere. Except back to New York. Something else to think about, right? The Big Apple. Heart of the publishing world. It would be a great place for you to get your chops." He winked. "Just let me know before I go."

Did you know Oscar Diggs uses ghostwriters?" I asked.

"In the same way I know there is no Santa Claus." Tim's mouth curved. "You can accept something factually and still not want to believe it."

"Why does it matter?" Reeti asked. She was a little drunk. Her exams were over, and we had gone out to celebrate.

"He wants me to write for him. For Shivery Tales. It's his best-selling line."

Tim frowned. "Not really your sort of thing, I would have said."

"He wants more girl power."

"He liked your story, then."

"He did." I gulped wine, the alcohol adding to my general buzz. "I was so surprised. And flattered. He asked if I'd ever considered moving to New York."

Like my mother. Like Toni.

"You'd be closer to your sister," Reeti said.

"I know, right? She could live with me. Or at least use me as her permanent address, if she decides she wants to apply to school in New York next year."

"You're serious," Tim said.

"I don't . . . Maybe?" I took another sip of wine. "I mean, I was planning on staying in Dublin, at least through the summer. But now . . ."

"Yeah." Reeti looked guilty. "I've been meaning to talk to you about that."

"About what?"

"It's the condo. After I get my degree, I'm moving to London." She reached across the table for my hand. "You know you can stay in the flat as long as you want. And I'm not asking for a penny more in rent. But my parents bought it as an investment, so if you could give them a move-out date, it would really help them lease the place for next year."

"Oh." *Oh*. "Sure. Of course."

"I'm sorry. I should have said something to you earlier. I kept chickening out."

"No, it's okay." I squeezed her fingers, trying to disguise my shock. "So. London. Are you . . . ?"

Her pretty face set. "I'm going to teach. I've applied to a gurdwara school."

"Reeti, that's wonderful!"

"I still haven't told my parents."

"But you will."

"When they come for graduation." She smiled. "Vir said he wanted to be there when I tell them."

"I'm so glad you have his support. And I'm proud of you, for being brave and following your dream."

"Thank you. What about you? Have you talked to The Ward yet about the offer from Diggs?"

"I wanted to tell you first." I smiled at Tim. "Both of you."

He returned my look steadily, his expression hard to read in the dim light.

"You're very quiet," I said to him as we left.

"What do you want me to say?"

"'Nice work'?" I quipped.

"Right. Very nice. Congratulations to both of you."

"That's it?"

He held the door open. "Good luck getting what you want."

I stopped, stung. "You don't think I can do it."

"You can do anything." His deep voice sounded almost irritated. "Your problem is you don't know what you want."

THIRTY-ONE

was wondering about the possibility of my working remotely this summer," I said at my next meeting with Maeve.

Her heavy brows rose. "I don't advise it. Most students find they benefit from the support network here."

The sun slanted through the dirty office window, illuminating the dust on the filing cabinets. The thought of leaving Dublin—the campus, the library, my fellow students, *Tim*—made my heart ache. How could I even think of going now, when the college green buzzed with life and color and the sky was shot with rainbows? But Toni was gone. Reeti was going. I needed to move out of our flat sooner rather than later. I'd be stupid to turn down Oscar Diggs's offer because of the weather. Or the timing. Or Tim.

"But under special circumstances . . ." I said. "I mean, during Covid . . ."

"Obviously, we all made adjustments during the pandemic," Maeve said.

"And there's always email, right? And Zoom."

"I'm aware of the technology. I'm more concerned about your motivation." She regarded me with sharp black eyes. "Are you sick?"

"Oh. No." I explained about the opportunity with Shivery Tales. "Mr. Diggs—Oscar—said he'd mentor me. It would be like an internship. Paid."

"I thought it was only Gray Kettering who was trolling for graduate students," Maeve said in a dry tone. I couldn't tell if she were joking or not. "Did you accept?"

"I'm considering it." "*You don't need her approval*," Sam said in my head. "*She's not your mam.*" But I wanted her guidance. "A steady job making up stories? It's a dream career." Why was I even hesitating?

Maeve made a noise like one of Aunt Em's, neither assent nor disagreement. "What about your own work?"

"I'm making progress on my portfolio. By July—"

She held up her hand. "I'm not talking about your ability to complete your dissertation. I'm talking about abandoning your story to write for Oscar Diggs."

"I can do both." I was pretty sure.

"Unlikely," Maeve said coolly. "Even if you have the discipline to allocate your time between two projects, it will be a struggle to develop your own voice if you're being paid to mimic someone else."

I'd come to her for answers. And now I had one. I knotted my fingers together. "You think I should say no."

She leaned back in her chair. "Let me ask you something. Why did you come to Trinity?"

"I wanted to complete my degree. To prove"—to Gray, to *myself*—"that I could. That I'm not some . . ."

"Creative parasite?" Maeve supplied.

I flinched. Nodded.

"The purpose of this program is to prepare you to write. What we can't teach you is what to say. Most of our graduates do other work in order to make a living. They write reviews or features for magazines. They get jobs in publishing or public relations. Some do technical writing." A smile flickered so briefly I might have imagined it. "Some of us teach. I simply want you to understand the trade-offs involved. Before you decide to accept Oscar's offer, think carefully about what you want."

"Tim—someone I know—told me I don't know what I want."

Maeve scowled. "Think harder. Why do you write?"

I drew a deep breath. I told stories to make myself feel better, to make sense of a world where mothers disappeared and the landscape changed and the people you encountered weren't always what they seemed. I wrote because stories were my escape and solace, and I wanted to believe in the happy endings they held out like hope. *Tell yourself a story often enough, and it will come true.*

But I wanted more. To be heard. To be seen. To belong.

"I want to tell my own stories," I blurted. "Under my own name."

Maeve smirked. "You have a lot of work to do, then."

I couldn't wait to see Tim to tell him I was staying for the summer after all. In my mind, this was a simple discussion. We were together every night. It was a short step to moving in with him.

I had never lived with Gray. No matter what I did to make myself a necessary part of his life, he had always kept me on the periphery. But Tim was different. I trusted Tim. Our schedules were compatible. We shared friends. (Well, at least one friend. Reeti.) We had common interests—board games, cooking shows, and sex. We both loved sex.

I hummed as I did the shopping for dinner. It wasn't until I slid the pork chops from the oven that I realized I had made Gray's favorite dinner—my default man-pleasing meal. But then Tim came up behind me, giving my bottom an absent pat, and the casual affection of the gesture, his complete lack of awareness, melted me.

"Can I toss the salad?" he offered. Which was more than Gray had ever done.

"Already made." I kissed his cheek, handing him the bowl from the refrigerator. This is what it would be like, I thought with a happy skip of heart. Sharing chores, meals, a bed, a life with him. "Can you carry this through to the table?"

We sat down to eat.

"This looks delicious." Tim's gaze traveled to the candles, the place mats, the cheery gerbera daisies I'd purchased at a flower stall on Grafton Street because they matched my mood. He smiled. "You must have had a good meeting with your supervisor today."

It was the perfect opening. "I did."

"What did she say?"

I fiddled with my napkin. It wasn't as easy to get the words out as I'd thought. "Well, I went in to ask her if I could finish my dissertation remotely."

His knife paused above his plate. "Because you're leaving."

"Actually, we decided I don't have to. At least, not right away." I smiled brightly. "I told Oscar no."

Tim sliced into his pork chop. "Good."

I blinked. "I thought you were a fan."

"I am." He cut his meat the British way, keeping his knife and fork in his hands, eating one bite at a time. "But it's time for you to live your own life."

"Why don't you get on with your own life?" Gray had said.

I choked.

"All right?" Tim asked, concerned.

"Great." I smiled harder. Took another glug of wine, a very nice rosé that tasted, I was sure, like whatever rosé was supposed to taste like. This was the part where, with only a little encouragement, he would ask me to move in with him.

He topped off my glass. "When do you go?"

I swallowed. "Well. Reeti wants to move out the middle of June. I don't want to be allowed to stay on as some kind of favor." The memories of the Couch Years loomed. "So that kind of depends on you."

He picked up his knife again. "The sooner, the better, I would think."

A little chill chased down my arms. This was not going at all the way I expected. "What do you mean?"

"We can't go on like this much longer." He met my eyes. With difficulty, I thought. "Frankly, I'm relieved."

There was a roaring in my ears. I couldn't have heard him correctly. "I thought . . . I hoped you might ask me to stay here. With you." Was that too presumptuous? "Just until the end of the summer," I added.

He went still for a moment before he set his knife and fork down, very carefully, on his plate. "That's not . . . a good idea. You're going through a lot of changes in your life right now. We shouldn't rush into moving in together simply because it's convenient."

"I'd pay you," I blurted. "Rent, I mean."

"It's not a question of money. We haven't actually known each other that long."

"Nine months." I flushed. "Since I met you. Which, okay, maybe isn't very long compared with Laura. But she cheated on you with your best friend, so time doesn't really matter, right?" I was babbling. I knew it, and I couldn't bring myself to stop. "Anyway, look at Reeti and Vir. They practically just met, and they're happy. They will be happy. Together."

"Because they know each other's families. They share the same background. They want and expect the same things from life." His gaze dropped to the congealing pork chop on his plate. "This isn't you," he said, which had to be the worst cliché ever. "You're wonderful. This is me. If we had more time . . ."

The chill coalesced into a lump of ice in my chest. Okay, this was bad. He was scarred, because of Laura. And I was scared, because of Gray. But I was not running away this time. I wasn't hiding how I felt. We could fix this, whatever it was. We would talk it out, and then . . . and then . . .

"We could have two whole months," I blurted. Two months was a lot—more than Toni and I had lived almost anywhere. Any longer than that and we'd almost certainly overstayed our welcome.

"And then what?"

My mind blanked. "Well, I . . . I can't stay in Ireland. Not on a student visa. The program is only for a year."

"Precisely."

My chest felt tight. I couldn't breathe. "But I can come back. To visit. And for graduation."

"You want a long-distance relationship."

"Not really," I admitted. "But we could make it work."

"Not in my experience," Tim said.

"I'm not Laura."

"No."

We were back to one-word answers again. That couldn't be good. "So, what do we do?" I asked.

The light reflected off his glasses. "What do you want to do?"

Move in with you, dummy. But I wouldn't beg.

I gulped. "The thing is . . . I can't really think beyond the summer right now. I put everything I wanted on hold for Gray. I don't want to spend my life as an unemployed English major who once slept with a famous author. I have to finish my dissertation. I want to write my book."

"I understand. I'm not standing in your way. But I can't spend two months living with you, knowing that you're going. It's too painful. Like bloody hospice. Sitting around waiting for something to die."

"But I love you," I said, and sat there, waiting for him to say it back. *Willing* him to say it back.

Or not. This was Tim, after all, who thought words were overrated. But surely, I thought, my heart beating wildly, he would say *something*.

He rubbed his breastbone. Another bad sign. "I care for you." A pause. "Very much."

"Then . . . Don't you want to be with me?" I whispered.

"Too much." He looked at me then, and all the heat and misery I felt was there in his eyes. The longing. The loss.

Oh God. My words jammed my chest. I could have argued against his logic. I would have battered myself against his tight-lipped, buttoned-up British reserve until he broke or I did. But I had no resistance against his pain.

He cleared his throat. "That's why it's better if you leave now. Before I . . . Before this gets any harder."

"Don't make this harder than it has to be," Gray had said.

My heart cracked.

Tim wasn't Gray. But the words were the same. The rejection was the same. The feelings churning inside me—denial, anger, grief, confusion—were the same. Which meant that maybe the fault wasn't them. Maybe it was me, had always been me. Maybe there was something missing in me, some essential quality that would make someone love me. Choose me.

That would make someone stay.

B ullshit," Reeti said after I'd cried on her couch for several hours. "Of course you are lovable. I love you. Your sister loves you."

"Tim doesn't." I swallowed a fresh swell of tears.

She handed me another tissue. The coffee table in front of us was littered with the evidence of her caring: crumpled piles of damp, discarded tissues, two half-finished mugs of tea, an open bag of Oreos in a scattering of crumbs. "Tim is a heartless bastard."

I appreciated her fierce loyalty. But even as I blew my nose, I knew that wasn't fair. "He's not heartless." The look in his eyes when he said, "*Too much* . . . " My chest ached. My eyes welled. "He's hurting, too. He's trying to protect himself."

"Fuck him," Reeti said. "He hurt you."

"Not intentionally." I wiped my swollen eyes. "He just . . . He figures our relationship is on life support anyway, so he . . . he pulled the plug."

"I'm still disappointed in him. He led you on."

"But he didn't." Another raw hurt. I hugged a pillow close. "The clues were there, if I'd wanted to see. He never promised me a fairy-tale ending. He never gave me his door code. Heck, he didn't even ask me to leave a toothbrush at his place."

"Because you live upstairs."

"That's what I told myself. My point is, Tim never deceived me. I deceived myself. Again."

Reeti squeezed my leg. "Don't you dare blame yourself. You deserve better, *didi*. You deserve to be with someone who makes you feel like you are more, not less. Someone like Vir."

"I *am* with someone like that."

Her eyes narrowed. "Not Sam."

I smiled mistily. "You."

She wrapped her arms around me while I cried.

I couldn't have gotten through the next two weeks without Reeti. She made me shower and wash my hair and go to my job at the library. She kept pressing cups of tea and bottles of water on me. ("*You must hydrate*," she said firmly. To replace all the tears I was crying, presumably.) She cooked all my favorite meals, butter chicken and *amritsari machhi*, a spicy battered fried fish, and when her parents came with Vir for her graduation, she insisted I join them for dinner the night before.

"Nope. Not tonight," I said firmly. "Tonight's about you."

"But my parents want to meet you."

"I'll see them at the party tomorrow. You don't need me moping and whining at your family celebration."

"You do not mope."

"Ha."

She laughed. "Okay, you mope a little. But your whining has gotten much better."

"Thanks, pal. But weren't you going to talk to your parents about the teaching job tonight?"

"That's the plan. Sure you don't want to come? You can be my emotional support if my mother decides to play the Indian guilt card."

"You know I'll come if you want me. But you've got this." I grinned. "You lion, you."

She rolled her eyes. But in the end, she decided that she and Vir could tackle her parents without me.

Which is how I found myself alone the night before graduation, walking in the dusk across the bridge to Clery's Newsagents.

S am's not here," Fiadh said.

"Oh." I shifted my feet on the black-and-white tile, wondering what I'd expected. Wondering why I'd come.

"I can give you his address, if you want."

"I don't want to be a bother."

"No bother at all." She scribbled on the pad beside the register.

I glanced down at the piece of paper she slid across the counter. Up at her sympathetic face. "Um. Do you think he'll be home?" *Alone?*

She shrugged. "It's early yet. If he goes out, it's usually later."

I walked past the iron railings and dustbins and trudged up the steps of his building. Sam and I didn't have the kind of relationship where we showed up at each other's apartments. Would he be pleased to see me? Surprised?

My palms were sweating. I wiped them on my jeans and mashed the buzzer.

"Boots." Sam answered the door. Definitely surprised. His crumpled shirt was unbuttoned over faded jeans, revealing some kind of medal on a silver chain.

"I came to say good-bye," I blurted.

He lifted an eyebrow. "Where's the rugger bugger, then?"

"Tim? We broke up."

He gave me a long look from his sea-colored eyes. "You better come in, then."

His apartment was small and dark, like a hermit's lair or your typical graduate student's housing. Lumps of furniture loomed between shelves constructed of planks and cement blocks. I stepped closer to read the spines on the shelf, picking out the authors I recognized—James Joyce and Kevin Barry, Oscar Wilde and Sally Rooney.

"You look like you could use a drink."

I turned. Sam stood in the doorway, barefoot. His toes were long and straight. I jerked my gaze back to his face. "Oh, I—"

"I could use a drink." He crossed to the tiny galley kitchen and unscrewed a bottle of whiskey. He poured two glasses and handed me one. Between the plackets of his shirt, his chest was narrow, shadowed with soft hair where Tim was puckered and scarred. "We should celebrate."

"Absolutely." I sniffed cautiously at the drink. "What are we celebrating?"

"My admission to Trinity."

The whiskey caught the back of my throat. I coughed and coughed.

Sam brought me a glass of water. "Shocked you, did I?" he asked, grinning.

I sputtered. "I . . . No! Sam, that's . . ." I gulped more water. "Wonderful. Congratulations! I knew you could do it."

"Thanks to you."

I flushed with pleasure. "I just gave you a little proofreading."

"And a good kick in the arse. What you said about my da . . . You were right. He would have wanted this for me."

"You were right, too. You had to be there for your family after he died. Even if it meant putting your own life on hold."

"Same as you. After you lost your ma." Our eyes met in mutual recognition. "Take off your coat."

"What?"

He cocked his head. "Unless you're cold."

I was quite warm, actually. I fumbled out of my jacket. Moved a pile of books and papers from a chair to the floor and sat.

Sam collapsed bonelessly onto the couch. "What will you do now that you don't have your little sister to take care of?"

"I'm going home to Kansas."

"Pity, that." He smiled crookedly. "I was looking forward to seeing you around campus."

The whiskey was honeyed and sharp, like the taste of what might have been. "I guess we're both starting over." I raised my glass. "Here's to new beginnings."

"To moving on."

This time the fiery spirit went down without choking. The warmth seeped into my stomach.

Sam sipped his whiskey, watching me. "So why did you and the Brit break up?"

Because Tim didn't want what I was willing—ready—to give him. Almost every relationship I'd formed in childhood came with a time limit. To believe otherwise was to be disappointed.

The lump was back in my throat. I swallowed. "I told you. I'm leaving. Back to the States."

"Not until the end of summer, surely."

"I don't have a real reason to stick around. Maeve says I can finish my dissertation remotely. And Reeti is moving to London. It's not fair for me to live in her parents' flat if she's not there."

"You could stay with me."

I looked around the cramped little room. There was one door, presumably leading to a single bedroom/bathroom. "Where?"

"Here."

"And do what?"

"Sleep. Live. Write. Have the occasional spot of sex."

I laughed. "That's a very attractive offer."

His mouth tipped. "So I've been told."

His head was tilted back against the couch cushions, his long fingers cradling the whiskey glass. There was no tension in his body anywhere, no indication that my answer mattered to him one way or the other.

I took another sip of whiskey, letting the burn slide down my throat. "Nine months ago, I would have said yes."

"And what's your answer now?"

"Thanks, but . . . No, thanks."

"Because of him. The Brit."

Because of Tim. Because I knew now what it felt like to be cherished, even if he'd never said the words. My chest ached. But mostly . . .

"Because of me," I said. "Because I don't have to stay here because it's convenient. I don't need to be with someone to feel good about myself, and I don't need sex to feel validated."

Our eyes held for a long moment.

Sam's mouth twisted in a smile. "Ah well, then, I'm no good to you, am I?"

I felt a wave of affection for him. "Don't believe that for a second. You've been so good to me. For me. You and your family."

"Back at you, Boots." He reached for the whiskey bottle. Poured us both another drink. "To friends, then."

"To friends."

We drank solemnly.

"I'd still sleep with you, mind." Sam winked. "If you need it to get over him."

THIRTY-TWO

Tim drove Dee to the airport and then went home and got quietly, thoroughly pissed.

"The sooner, the better," he'd said when she told him she was leaving, and the weeks since—her upstairs, him downstairs—had, in fact, been hell. Like walking around with a hole in the middle of his chest, an animated corpse.

"I don't want to impose," she'd said when he offered to drive her. Her brown eyes—seeking, uncertain—knotted him up inside. "Besides, the drop-off lane is a terrible place for good-byes."

"No imposition at all," Tim had replied stiffly. He was desperate for the chance to be of some use to her, dying for another fifteen minutes of her company.

But she was right about the drop-off lane. It wasn't how he'd pictured their farewell, with airport security looking on and Reeti crying and hugging her.

As if privacy would have made the situation any better. Nothing could make it better. Dee was gone now, leaving him alone in his sterile apartment and empty bed, and it was his own bloody fault. He'd secured another fifteen minutes with her, the length of the drive, when he could have had another two months.

"I fucked up."

"Not for the first time," Charles said.

He'd shown up at Tim's one hour and a half bottle of whiskey ago, and Tim was miserable enough that even drinking with Charles seemed better than spending another too-quiet evening alone.

He tried to remember the last time he'd felt this bad. In rehab, maybe. But even then, with his knee screaming from the second surgery and the fresh wound of Charles and Laura's betrayal, he hadn't felt this lonely. This frustrated. This confused.

The solution with Laura was not to feel at all. The solution with Dee was . . . He poured another whiskey. "Dee isn't Laura."

"Not even close," Charles said cheerfully. "Bet you pulled your Robot Man routine on her anyway."

"I don't know what you're talking about," Tim said.

Dee's face flashed across his mind. That hopeful, expectant look in her eyes when she'd told him she loved him and he'd said . . . he'd said, *I care for you.* His jaw clenched. Stingy bastard.

"Uh-huh," Charles said. "Why do you think you and Laura broke up?"

Tim stared. *Because you had sex with her, you wanker.* "You can't be serious."

"You two were over before I slept with her, mate. After you got blown up, you shut down. *I* couldn't get through to you, and I at least had some idea what you were going through. Laura couldn't reach you at all."

"So I wasn't chatty. I was barely conscious."

Charles waved away his justification. "She told me once that even before the war, there was always a piece of you you wouldn't share. Locked away in that cold tin heart."

"You're telling me she slept with you to get my attention."

"To get some reaction, yeah, mate. She wanted to feel something. But she wanted to see if you would feel something, too."

"Don't you want to be with me?" Dee had whispered, and he'd said . . . He couldn't remember what he'd said.

Tim rubbed his face with his hand. At least she hadn't gone off and slept with the coffee guy. Although . . . He couldn't blame her if she did. Not after what he'd said. Not after everything he'd failed to say.

"What's your excuse?" Tim asked. *"Mate."*

"Christ, man, you know Laura. You had her. I knew she was out of my league. But I thought she wanted me. Until she threw me out like day-old fish because I wasn't you. Ruined my fucking life, the pair of you."

"Laura isn't to blame for your poor decisions." Dee had said that. *And neither am I.* It wasn't until Charles glared at him that Tim realized he'd said the words out loud.

"Never got over it, did I?"

"Why would you?" Tim asked. "As long as you can make everything about Laura, you don't have to deal with the rest of it."

"I'm not cut out for civilian life."

"You shouldn't have left the army, then."

"No choice. I drank too much. I drink too much. Unfit for duty, they said."

"Everybody drinks."

"Not everybody runs a jeep into a guard post." He peered at Tim. "What?"

"Nothing." *Not nothing.* "Just . . . You never told me."

"Because you don't listen."

"No." To his shame. Easier to dismiss Charles as a drunk, a clown, a cheat, than to confront his own failures as a friend.

"I can make some calls. Get you an appointment. Drive you to meetings, if you want."

"Tim Woodman to the rescue. Again."

"I'm not that guy." Tim frowned. "Am I?"

"You can be." Charles drank. "My best pal. My fucking crutch. Makes it damn hard to play the hero."

"Charles needs to be the hero of his own story," Dee had said.

Christ. "You are the hero," Tim said. "You saved my life."

"That's why they let me off. I didn't tell you that, either. General discharge, as long as I went away quietly. Because I was a fucking hero. To them, to you, to Laura. On top of the world. I was happy, you know?"

"I know."

"And now I'm just a fuck-up," Charles said sadly.

"You need to let that go," Tim said. "Lean on me while you find your feet. But you're going to have to walk on your own."

"I just loved her so much."

Tim didn't say anything.

Charles sighed. "Right. I guess . . . I want to be the bloke I was when I was with her."

The man I was when I was with Dee . . .

Happy. Alive.

Tim rubbed the center of his chest, where his heart used to be. "You need to move on, mate."

Charles blinked at him owlishly. "You and me both, pal. You and me both."

THIRTY-THREE

've got that, Aunt Em," I said as she reached for the baggage carousel.

She grabbed my heavy wheeled suitcase from the conveyor belt. "I'm not feeble yet."

A little grayer, a little thinner than I remembered, but definitely not feeble. I lengthened my stride to keep up with her, my second bag banging against my thigh.

"You look tired," she said as we walked to the parking garage. Not *How are you?* or *I've missed you* or *Tell me about Dublin.*

"Long flight."

I hadn't been able to sleep or to focus on the in-flight movie. An hour over the Atlantic Ocean, I'd opened the book Tim loaned me, about a beekeeper's daughter who chases after a runaway swarm and is caught up in a battle of good and evil. The story was funny and scary, beautiful and sad. I'd turned my face from my oblivious seatmate and wept for what I was leaving behind. Not the offer from Oscar, though I understood now why he'd made it. I missed Tim. *"The heroine reminded me of you."*

Em grunted without replying. I was used to her silences. But for the first time I wondered if, like Tim, she was simply leaving holes in the conversation. White space on a page, waiting to be filled.

"Also, it's been a stressful couple of weeks," I said, testing my theory.

"What do you have to be stressed about, I'd like to know?"

"Oh." I flapped my free hand. "The usual. Climate change, worldwide pandemic, financial crisis, school . . . a broken heart."

She threw me a sharp look, loading my bags in the back of the truck. "Well, whatever it is, you're home now."

There was a sudden lump in my throat. *Home.* The place where, according to Aunt Em and Robert Frost, when you have to go there, they have to take you in.

The farmhouse seemed smaller than my memories. In the room I shared with Toni, the floor space had shrunk, taken up by cardboard boxes stacked along one wall, moving cartons from my old apartment and the contents of Toni's dorm room.

Em frowned as she lifted my suitcase onto the empty bed. "There wasn't time to put all this away."

"It's fine," I assured her.

"The sheets are clean, at least."

"Aunt Em . . ." I touched her arm, the closest we'd come to a hug. "Thanks."

Under her tan, she flushed. She patted my hand and then dropped it. "Dinner at five thirty. You can set the table if you want to make yourself useful."

A woman of action, my aunt Em. Too bad she'd never met— would never meet—Tim. My throat tightened.

I texted Reeti to let her know I was safely back in Kansas and then went out to set the table.

Uncle Henry came in from the fields for dinner, smelling of fertilizer, dirt, and sweat. His bristles scraped as he kissed my cheek.

"How long are you staying this time?" he asked.

"Well." I swallowed. "I thought . . . August? I want to focus on finishing my thesis before I start looking for a job."

Uncle Henry nodded and dug back into his plate.

"I'm happy to help out," I added. "While I'm here."

"You can clean up your room," Em said.

"Sure." I helped myself to more mashed potatoes. And corn. And biscuits. I was back in Kansas, after all.

I needed to clear space in my room anyway. I couldn't write my dissertation on the kitchen table where Em rolled out piecrust and paid the bills and my sister and I had done our homework. Though I could count on Em and Henry not to say much.

That night as I was getting ready for bed, my phone dinged. A reply from Reeti. And—my breath hiccupped—a message from Tim.

We didn't have a chance for a proper good-bye. Good luck with everything. Let me know how you get on with your story. xx

No abbreviations, no emojis. Like getting a text from Fitzwilliam Darcy. With kisses.

My heart cramped. I sank onto the single bed, my hand curled around my phone. Thnx. I paused. Added a kissy face and deleted it. A red heart, also deleted. Crap, this was hard.

And I heard Tim's deep, well-mannered voice: *"It's better if you leave now. Before this gets any harder."*

I drew a painful breath and typed. Maybe it's better if we don't message. At least not for a little while. x

Three dots appeared.

Please, please, please. The silly prayer wobbled like the dots on the screen. But what was I praying for?

Of course. I'm sorry. xx

I didn't realize I was crying until a fat drop plopped on the screen. Was he apologizing for texting? Or for sending me away?

I wiped my eyes. I deserved someone who chose me. Who wanted to be with me.

"*Too much*," Tim whispered in my head.

I didn't fall asleep for a long time.

Over the next month, I fell into a kind of routine, familiar but different, like my aunt, like the farmhouse. I collected eggs and weeded the vegetable patch, took lunch to Henry and the farmhands, went to the grocery store for Em, the hardware store for Henry, and the library to say hi to old friends (books and librarians).

In the mornings and late into the night I wrote, propped on my old twin mattress or sitting at the kitchen table after Em and Henry had gone to bed. I didn't have to finish an entire manuscript to meet my thesis requirements, but the story itself drew me. Compelled me. I checked in regularly with Reeti and Toni by text, less frequently with Sam and Maeve by email. And when my eyes bleared and the words wouldn't come, I tackled the piles of moving boxes in my room.

Cleaning was mindless, dirty, satisfying work. I swept the Kansas dust from every corner, scrubbed the baseboards and windowsills, took down my teenage posters of Pink and Middle Earth on the walls. Maybe, I thought, I'd paint. When the book was done.

"Not bad," Em said when she came to inspect my progress.

I stretched my aching back. "Cleaning therapy."

"Hm." Another of those assessing looks. "Out with the old, in with the new."

"Not much new," I said ruefully. I'd given away most of the furniture from my old apartment or returned it to the curb where I'd found it, recycling for a new generation of graduate students. But I'd picked up a desk and a lamp at the Methodist Thrift Store and replaced the limp ruffled curtains with crisp modern blinds.

"You always did travel light," Em said unexpectedly. "Because of Judy. Your mother."

I looked at her, startled.

Her worn hand smoothed the blue gingham comforter on my bed. "I wanted you to feel at home here. But you always acted like you weren't going to stay. Like you were afraid to make a space for yourself. To take up room."

My pulse beat in my throat. *Don't make a mess. Don't make a fuss. Don't leave so much as a toothbrush behind, and maybe you can stay.* Oh God. I closed my eyes. Was that what I'd done with Tim?

"Your sister, now . . ." Em said.

I opened my eyes. Summoned a smile. "I can go through her things for you."

"No," Em said. "There's room in the closet now for her boxes. Toni will sort out her own stuff. When she's ready."

I sighed, looking from the big gay pride flag over my sister's bed, her painted mirror and mixed-media collage, to my own blank walls. "My side looks so empty now."

"Plenty of stuff under the bed," Em said. "If you want to hang something."

I knelt on the braided rug to drag out the box that held my mother's obituary, her review clips, and gallery show brochures.

There were photographs, too: my mother as a child with an un-smiling Uncle Henry, one of her holding me in one hand and a drink in the other, a candid shot taken on some Mediterranean island with a young, dark-haired man I'd always suspected was Toni's father. I sifted through them, trying to winnow my memories of my mother from the artifacts of her life. To see her. To *know* her, the way Toni said.

"I don't remember all these." I touched a photo of our mother on the front porch swing with Toni in the crook of her arm.

"I took that one." Em cleared her throat. "It's important for you girls to have memories of your mom."

Even if Em had to create them.

The realization brought tears to my eyes. I picked up the Annie Leibovitz portrait that had appeared in *Vanity Fair*: Judy Gale posed in front of a pile of twisted rope titled *Family Ties*. Ha. Good one, Mom. My mother stared back unapologetically.

"You should get that one framed," Em said.

I traced the features of my famous mother's face, the dark, expressive eyes Toni had inherited, the widow's peak I saw in the mirror, the irrepressible hair.

"Did you ever resent her?" I asked suddenly.

"Judy?" Em snorted. "How could I? She gave me you."

Which . . . My eyes welled and overflowed. All my life, I'd figured there must be something wrong, something missing in me, some secret flaw even a mother couldn't love. But I had been loved, all along.

I just hadn't seen it.

I gripped her hand. "I love you, Aunt Em."

She squeezed my fingers back, hard. "I know."

I laughed shakily, tears leaking. We sat on the braided rug, laughing and crying, holding hands, the portrait of my mother on the floor between us.

———

I t was after midnight in London when Reeti called, bubbling from her *thaka*, her official blessing by the groom's parents before the engagement ceremony. She propped her phone against the bathroom mirror to model the red lehenga Vir's mother had given her to wear on her wedding day.

"What do you think?" she asked, twirling for the camera.

"You look amazing." Not only the dress. Her face shone.

"You're coming, right?" she demanded. "For the ceremony?"

"When is it?"

"Not for months. My mother's going nuts with planning."

"I wouldn't miss it for the world," I promised before we ended the call.

She was so happy. And I was happy for her, that she'd found the person who saw her, who would be there for her, who cared for her and made her care.

The lump was back in my throat. I scrolled through my camera roll until I found it—the selfie I'd taken with Tim at Malahide, with our heads close together and the castle behind. Like a scene from a fairy tale. One of the old ones, where the princess wanders in exile for a hundred years, and the prince is blinded falling into a thornbush. The picture blurred.

Don't message, I'd said. And he hadn't.

I need space to write my dissertation, I'd said, and he'd given it to me. Noble, stupid prince.

I tapped the photo. Typed: I promised to send this weeks ago. Sorry it's so late. x Tap and tap and wait, my heart knotting, for a reply.

Which didn't come.

Because it's the middle of the night in Dublin, stupid. He's not lying awake, waiting for your not-a-booty call. I hoped he had his notifications turned off. But when I got back from brushing my teeth, my screen was lit with a message.

TIM: How's the story coming along? xx

I snatched up the phone. It's coming. Everything but the happy ending.

I still wasn't sure how my protagonist's journey ended. I knew she had to return to the real world. But how could she leave her companions behind?

TIM: You can do it. You deserve the happy ending. xxx

I stared for a long time at that extra *x*, like an unknown value in an equation, like the mark on a treasure map.

I think I've finally figured that out, I typed at last. xxx

Every morning from July into August, I woke with the rooster and wrote until nine or ten. Broke to feed the chickens and rake the yard. Wrote again and then pegged laundry. Wrote and harvested or chopped vegetables for dinner. I wrote late into the night and crawled into bed exhausted, sleeping with the book Tim had given me, my hand on the cover, taking comfort in touching something he had touched. In my dreams, the farm world and my story world bled and blended together, spilling onto the page—the field mice and twisted apple trees, the old water bucket and Em's china cream pitcher shaped like a cow.

I finally understood Gray.

I would never forgive him. But the way he'd taken bits of our real life, pieces of me, and twisted them into a narrative that felt true to him . . . I got that now. Wasn't I doing the same? Pulling threads from New Dee and Old Dee, Farm Dee and Academic Dee, my mother's Dee and Em's, and knitting them together. I didn't have to let myself or my story be defined by other people's expectations. I could make something wholly my own.

At one thirty in the morning on a Wednesday, I finished. I stared blearily at the computer screen, my body shaking with fatigue, adrenaline, and caffeine.

In the end, Dorothy went home, lessons learned, magic elixir in hand. But I left open the possibility that she would return.

Not a sequel. Not yet. But a promise.

I saved it in two files—the chapters and outline that comprised my thesis and the actual completed manuscript, nearly twice as long—and emailed them both to Maeve.

And to Oscar Diggs.

And, finally, to Tim. To happy endings, I wrote, and hit SEND.

There was nothing in my inbox the next morning. Or the next day. Or the day after that. Not even from Tim. Not even a text. Over the weekend, I drove to the hardware store and bought a bunch of painting supplies.

"What do you think you're doing?" Em asked.

I carefully rolled paint on my bedroom walls. Blue, to match the bedspread and the sky. "Painting. If I don't keep busy, I'll explode."

"Seems like a waste of time. Since you're leaving." There was nothing Em abhorred more than waste. "Not that it doesn't look nice," she admitted grudgingly.

"You could use this room as your office. After I'm gone."

Her hand stroked the desk. "I don't need an office."

I thought of all the years I'd watched Em do the farm books at the kitchen table. Maybe I wasn't the only one reluctant to take up too much room. Or maybe Em had given all the room she had, in her home, in her heart, to us.

"Shame to waste the space," I said.

"Hm."

I grinned. "Of course, you'd have to keep at least one of the beds in here. For when we come to visit."

"I could do that," Em said gruffly. My phone chirped from the bureau. "What's that?"

"It's . . ." My heart tripped. "Oh God. It's my phone."

"I can see it's your phone, Dorothy, I—"

"Hello?" I nearly stepped in the paint tray in my eagerness to answer. "Dr. Ward? Hi! I finished my dissertation."

"I read it."

I swallowed hard. "Yeah?"

"You have until the end of the month to submit your portfolio to the committee. I don't see any point in waiting."

"But . . . I thought you'd have feedback for me. Suggestions."

"No. You know what you're doing. If you have any difficulty accessing the guidelines for submission online—"

"Wait. That's it?"

Maeve's heavy sigh came clearly through the phone. "I suppose you want me to say 'good job.'"

"Well . . ."

"Your work is stylistically fluent and technically proficient. You seem able to engage your audience and your characters are interesting." A pause. "Particularly the wicked witch."

I jerked, my face flushing. "If you want me to make any changes . . ."

"Why?"

I floundered. "It's . . . I know how it feels when . . ." The witch was based, at least physically, in part, on Maeve. But what had seemed like an academic exercise when I was writing alone in my room—an inside joke, even a homage—suddenly struck me as the most terrible insult. "I don't want to write anything you don't like," I said feebly.

"Get over it," Maeve said. "You'll never get to what you have to say if you're worried about offending people."

"Sorry. It's just . . . I owe you so much."

"Then pay me the courtesy of telling your story. I'm sure the committee will be entertained. Women who tell the truth have always been called witches."

"Thank you. I could never have done this without you."

"Don't be ridiculous," Maeve said. "You had the power inside you all along. You just had to find it."

THIRTY-FOUR

I don't suppose you've reconsidered writing for Shivery Tales," Oscar Diggs said when he called.

"Ha. I mean, thank you, but—"

"If it's moving to New York that's the problem, most of my team works remotely."

"Mr. Diggs . . . Oscar . . . I really appreciate the offer. I'm flattered, honestly. But a very wise woman told me recently I should tell my own story."

"Maeve Ward."

I laughed. "It was. And I actually don't have a problem with New York. I grew up there."

Another piece of myself I could own now: Dorothy Gale, the Couch Years. Sure, parts of my childhood had sucked. But without those years, I wouldn't be me. I'd be a different person with a different story. And there had been good times, too, I thought, remembering story hour at the Brooklyn Library, Chinese takeout, Central Park on a sunny day. Good people, friends who had taken us in. A big, exciting city I wanted to experience as an adult, the same way I'd explored Dublin.

"You should come for a visit," Oscar said.

"I will. That is, I'm planning to. My sister's there now."

"Great. We'll have lunch with my agent."

"Sorry, what?"

"You sent me your book."

"You said I could."

"Because I thought you had something there. I gave it to Susan. She thinks so, too."

I was stunned. Shaking. It was every writer's fantasy, the literary equivalent of being discovered at a soda fountain by a famous Hollywood director. "I . . . Thank you!"

"No obligation," Oscar assured me. "But it's a free lunch."

My mind whirled. "Maybe . . . Maybe I could ask you for a cover quote?"

"You should." He chuckled. "I may be a very lazy writer, but I must admit I'm a very popular brand."

Dee!" My former faculty advisor flinched behind his desk, like a dog running headlong into an electric fence. "What are you doing here?"

Good question. The last time I'd visited Barry's office, I'd been vacillating between shock and denial, barely able to function. The meeting had been unsatisfying and deeply uncomfortable for both of us. It was time to face what had been done to me, stop blaming myself, and move on. *Closure.* Finally.

I smiled brilliantly. "I came to thank you, actually."

He eyed the doorway, but I was blocking his escape. "For . . . ?"

"First, for not trying to convince me to stay in the program here." I sat, projecting warm friendliness. "And second, for writing a recommendation to Trinity."

His posture relaxed slightly. "Good. It's gone well, then?"

"Very well. I just finished my thesis. The Court of Examiners meets next month. My supervisor says I should have no trouble receiving my degree."

"Your supervisor. That would be . . . er, Dr. Eastwick?"

"Maeve Ward."

His eyebrows climbed toward his receding hairline. "Ah. Very good. I read her book, of course. Longlisted for the Booker Prize. Can I get you something? Coffee, water?"

"I'm good, thanks." I was excellent. "Also, Oscar Diggs thinks I have a very good chance of having my story published. I'm meeting his agent next week."

"That's wonderful news. I'm glad you came to tell me." His hangdog eyes met mine. "I've always . . . Well, I've regretted I didn't do more when you came to me last year."

"Me too."

He winced. "You did say the relationship was consensual. And since Gray wasn't in a supervisory capacity . . ."

I didn't speak. Silence, I'd learned from Tim, could say quite a lot.

"Still." Barry dropped his gaze to his desk. "To the extent that his behavior was indicative of a pattern . . ."

I sat up straight. "Wait. Was there something else? Someone else?"

Barry cleared his throat. "It's not . . . I have to respect the confidentiality of everyone involved."

My hands curled in my lap. *I have the power*, I reminded myself. I just had to use it. "Because," I said slowly, "if there were a complaint, I want to give a statement about my relationship with Gray. If that would help."

"If the investigator decided your information was relevant to the complaint, then yes," Barry said. "Your story would certainly have some weight, at least with the faculty committee. There's even a possibility Gray's contract would not be renewed for the coming school year."

"I'll do it," I said.

"Gray's still quite popular with some members of the department. You could get pushback. You'll be criticized."

"They can say whatever they want. I honestly don't care. Women who tell the truth have always been called witches."

Barry looked confused. But Maeve would understand. I'd have to thank her when I saw her again.

Oscar excused himself after dessert (cheesecake, and it was *delicious*), leaving me alone with his agent, the mildly terrifying Susan. She had curly red hair and a throaty laugh and reminded me—in a good way—of my mother's friends.

"I don't expect you to make a decision today," the agent assured me as we parted outside the restaurant. "But I love your story, and I'm a big fan of your voice. Think it over, my dear, and let me know."

I promised to get back to her soon. We both knew my answer would be yes.

The city still felt like summer, smells drifting from grates and gutters, heat breathing from concrete and asphalt. I decided to take the bus instead of descending into the bowels of the subway. Students with backpacks swayed casually in the aisles, absorbed in their cell phones.

I pulled out my phone, too, smiling over a picture of Reeti in a classroom full of girls with blue kerchiefs and bright faces. Sam had sent a selfie, too, smirking in front of a statue of Oscar Wilde. From Tim? Nothing.

A wave of longing swept over me and rolled away. I knew I had a tendency to see what I wanted to see. Maybe I *had* read too much significance into those three little *xxx*'s. But I'd come so far from the girl who left Kansas. I'd hoped sending Tim my story would be a signal that I was ready to take the next step with him.

I should have remembered he thought words were overrated.

But you know what? I was better for knowing him. For loving him. For being his friend. So, fine. We'd both be at Reeti's engagement party in a couple of months. Let him try ignoring me then.

It was a ten-minute walk from the bus stop to my rental apartment, a tiny Airbnb where I was spending the month, relearning the topography of my childhood, discovering half-familiar streets, pursuing half-forgotten landmarks. The neighborhood—Ditmas Park—still felt strange. But there was an elegance to the old Victorian homes that reminded me of Dublin, an energy to the city that felt like it could be mine one day.

I rounded the corner onto the tree-lined street of my building. And there, at the bottom of the steps . . . I recognized the familiar set of his shoulders, the shape of his head, and the feeling of coming home flooded me so fast I was dizzy with it.

"Tim." I couldn't think. What was he doing here?

His tie was loosened. His eyes were worried. His hair stuck up in front. "I missed you," he said.

Hope choked my throat. "I was at lunch. With my agent."

"You have an agent."

"Sort of. Oscar set us up. But she likes my story."

"It's a wonderful story. Congratulations."

"Thank you."

We stood there awkwardly.

"What I meant was . . ." Tim shook his head. "I *missed* you, Dee."

"You could have called."

"It didn't seem like enough to tell you. You deserved for me to show you. So . . ." His gaze met mine. "Here I am."

I was so, so glad to see him. My mouth curved. "A man of action."

"Yes. I want to apologize for the way I behaved before you left. I tend to shut down in moments of, ah . . ."

"High emotion?" I suggested.

He shot me a grateful look. "Yes."

"And I talk too much."

"You talk exactly the right amount," Tim said. "I admire the way you feel things. The way you express yourself. Your enthusiasm. Your optimism. I'm afraid to feel, let alone talk about my feelings."

I seemed to be crying. With one hand, he cupped my face. Wiped my tears with his thumb. "I'm working on that," he said. "The talking."

"You're doing really well," I blurted.

He smiled a little, making my ovaries melt. "I need to apologize, too," I said. "I was hurt because you set limits on our relationship. But I did it first, with that 'I'm only staying two months' business."

"Because your visa was up."

"Because I was afraid to ask for more."

"It doesn't matter now. I'm here."

"I'm glad." Our eyes met again and clung. "How did you find me?"

"Reeti told me."

"How long can you stay?"

"I promised them a year." I must have looked blank, because he added, "My degree is finished. I requested a transfer to our New York office. After that . . ." He shrugged. "I don't know."

Holy crap. He'd changed his job. For me? My heart thudded. "You'll figure it out."

"I hoped we would figure it out together. Dee." He took my hands in both of his. My palms were sweating. "I had to show you how I feel. But you deserve the words, too. Or maybe I simply need to say them. I don't know where I belong, except with you. When you left, my heart went with you, and now I'm walking around with my heart outside my chest. I love you. And so . . . And so I came from the airport to tell you."

He loved me. It was all the words I'd ever wanted. Everything I yearned to hear.

But he was right. Sometimes words were not enough.

"Where's your bag?" I asked.

"I dropped it at the hotel. I didn't want to assume . . ."

"You should go get it."

He looked at me, a question in his eyes. "All right."

I smiled. "Later. You should get it later."

He held me as we kissed, his body warm and firm and real and solid, tears sliding down my face and his smile against my lips.

We went up the steps to my apartment. It was not the certain happy ending I'd dreamed of. It was something better—a beginning, the start of an adventure into the magical unknown.

AUTHOR'S NOTE

When I was seven years old, I discovered my mother's or grand-mother's copy of *Dorothy and the Wizard in Oz*. A kindly librarian guided me to and through the rest of the original series (fourteen books! an entire shelf!), starting with the first book, *The Wonderful Wizard of Oz*.

I was hooked.

Like Dee, I've always loved stories about children on a journey into the magical unknown. When I started writing this book, I couldn't travel outside the United States because ... pandemic. So I pored over maps and catalogs instead, searching for images and newspaper articles about Dublin online.

Stuck at home on my computer, the Emerald Isle became my Emerald City, full of wonder and adventure. When I was finally able to visit Ireland last summer, I retraced Dee's footsteps, ducking into bookstores, poking into alleys, and wandering the Trinity College campus. I found my way around Dublin by a combination of memory and instinct, surprised by the thrill of discovery and the shock of coming home around every corner.

"Look, look!" I'd say, grabbing my husband's arm as we walked along the dark waters of the Grand Canal. "There's the church Dee and Toni went to on Christmas." And, "The bridge is that way." We drank whiskey at The Duke, hopped the DART, and re-created the selfie Dee took with Tim in front of Malahide Castle.

Whether you travel to Ireland like Dee or only visit from your favorite reading chair, that's the feeling I want to share with you—that joy, that escape, that sense of fun and adventure. I hope this story makes you fall a little in love with Ireland . . . and maybe even find the power that's been inside you all along.

ACKNOWLEDGMENTS

Every story needs help being born. This one would never have been conceived without L. Frank Baum, who provided the inspiration for Dorothy, my American heroine in a strange land.

I couldn't do what I do without the support of my amazing editor, Cindy Hwang, associate editor Angela Kim, Jennifer Myers, Randie Lipkin, brilliant cover artist Colleen Reinhart, and the entire talented team at Berkley. Thank you! You are the very best midwives any writer could wish for.

Thanks to my wise agent, Robin Rue, and Beth Miller at Writers House, for being such an important part of labor and delivery.

I am so grateful to Bernice M. Murphy, Associate Professor in Popular Literature at Trinity College Dublin, for responding patiently to my emails, questions, and requests for selfies in her office. I'm so glad we finally got to meet! Thanks, too, to Deirdre Madden at the Oscar Wilde Centre for Creative Writing for providing me with the handbook, without which Dee and I would be still be floundering. The real-life Trinity College Dublin is where the true magic happens. I couldn't have created my fictional TCD without you.

To my wonderful friends and companions (too many to name) on this writing journey, thank you! Special thanks to Sonali Dev, for helping bring Reeti to life and for all the "beats"; to Brenda

Harlen, for endless encouragement and sound critiques; and to my deadline pals, Jamie Beck, Tracy Brogan, Sally Kilpatrick, Priscilla Oliveras, Barbara O'Neal, and Liz Talley, for keeping me sane.

Thanks to my mom and kids, who mostly remember not to call in the morning and generally put up with me.

To Michael, all my love, always, for telling me I can do this and then making it possible. Also, for the literary pub crawl through Dublin.

Thank you to librarians everywhere, who introduced me to the magic kingdom and provided escape and refuge.

And finally, thank you, readers, for coming along on the journey. You are the best.

THE
FAIRYTALE LIFE
OF
DOROTHY GALE

VIRGINIA KANTRA

READERS GUIDE

QUESTIONS FOR
DISCUSSION

1. How do the characters in *The Fairytale Life of Dorothy Gale* feel the same or different from the familiar characters in *The Wizard of Oz*?

2. A big part of Dorothy's journey is the friends she makes along the way. Are there similar companions in your life?

3. Dee thinks of libraries as her magic kingdom, her refuge, her home. Do you have special memories of a library from your childhood?

4. Both Dee and Sam feel they need to take responsibility for their families after the death of a parent. How are their situations the same or different? Are they sometimes *too* responsible?

5. How does Dee's perception of Em change over the course of the story? How does Aunt Em compare with the other mother figures (Judy Gale, Glenda Norton, Janette Clery) in the story? Have your feelings toward a parent or other adult ever changed as you got older?

6. Sam and Tim are romantic possibilities for Dee. Do you think she made the right choice for her? Which one would you choose to be with? Why?

7. Dee, Reeti, Fiadh, even Glenda, deal with various forms of discrimination, from academic bias to being exoticized to catcalls on the street (Dee describes it as "the cost of being a woman—the crime of being female in public"). Have you ever been harassed or discriminated against? How did you deal with it?

8. Toni is very young when their mother dies. She has trouble separating real memories of their mother from the stories Dee tells. Are there memories/stories from your childhood that feel that way?

9. "Women who tell the truth are always called witches," Maeve says. Who are the influential women in your life? What truths did they tell you?

10. Tim and Dee speak different "love languages." How do they bridge the gap between them? How do you express and receive love? Which do you appreciate most in a partner: what they say or what they do?

11. Maeve tells Dee, "You had the power inside you all along. You just had to find it." What do you consider your power? When did you first realize it?

IN DUBLIN WITH OSCAR WILDE

New York Times bestselling author Virginia Kantra's lifelong love of stories led her to write over thirty award-winning novels about strong women, messy families, and the journey to find yourself. Her books, including *Meg & Jo* and *Beth & Amy*, contemporary retellings of *Little Women*, have received starred reviews from *Publishers Weekly* and *Booklist* and praise in *People* and *USA Today*.

Virginia is married to her college sweetheart, who keeps her supplied with ideas, caffeine, and cocktails. They make their home in North Carolina, where they raised three amazing children. Like the witches of Oz, Virginia believes firmly in finding the power that was inside you all along.